Daughters of Strathannan

Twi stared as if she was seeing Isobel for the first time. 'I never really understood about you before,' she whispered, at last.

'It's a curse,' Isobel said flatly. 'I would do anything to be rid of it. Anything. I wish I had never been born. Better it had died with Granny Guthrie.' And she turned away with such a depth of despair on her face that Twi was frightened for her.

But something bitter and unforgiving prevented her from trying to comfort her sister now.

Anne Vivis lives in Warrington, Cheshire. She was brought up in Fife, East Scotland, the setting for her books. *Daughters of Strathannan* is her first novel; her second, *The Lennox Women*, is published by Heinemann.

ANNE VIVIS

Daughters of Strathannan

Mandarin

For Bill
With Love

A Mandarin Paperback
DAUGHTERS OF STRATHANNAN

First published in Great Britain 1992
by William Heinemann Ltd
This edition published 1993
by Mandarin Paperbacks
an imprint of Reed Consumer Books Limited
Michelin House, 81 Fulham Road, London SW3 6RB
and Auckland, Melbourne, Singapore and Toronto

Copyright © Anne Vivis 1992
The author has asserted her moral rights

A CIP catalogue record for this title
is available from the British Library

Printed and bound in Great Britain
by Cox & Wyman Ltd, Reading, Berks

PART ONE

Isobel

ONE

*S*tinging salt water forced its way up his nose and down his throat. His hands were clenched so tightly on the wheel that the raw blisters bled. He held his breath and waited, his lungs bursting, until the pressure inside his head became unbearable. Only when he was starting to believe that, this time, he really was going to die, did the steam drifter surge wildly upwards, caught on the next wave. The water gushed away. Choking he sucked a deep, convulsive breath and coughed the sea from his mouth.

Time and again her bows dipped into bottomless troughs at the mercy of the living fury of the mountainous North Sea. Time and again her superstructure was engulfed. Time and again she emerged miraculously, spewing water, to perch precariously on the very crest of another titanic wave before plunging down again into the black, icy ocean.

Betrayed by the failure of her steam–driven engines, the old 'Pride of Fife' fought her impossible battle alone, long after the other boats in the fishing fleet had run for safety.

In the wheelhouse her skipper, Geordie McLean, stayed resolutely where duty placed him. Desperation locked his hands to the wheel, wrenching his shoulders in the massive effort required to hold her steady. Below, his three crewmen toiled hopelessly to pump the relentlessly rising water from the bowels of the small craft.

Geordie was deafened and blinded, his world shrouded by beckoning greyness and the unremitting roar of a vengeful ocean. Rain drew a curtain so dense that even the bucking bow of the boat was invisible.

She soared, hovered, then started another sickening, lurching drop. The old steam drifter protested, sending creaking tremors along the deck, through Geordie's booted feet and into his salted bones.

Once more water crashed through the wheelhouse. Once more Geordie waited for the boat to tear herself free, to begin the whole death-defying sequence again.

Water filled his nostrils, his ears, his mouth, forcing him to hold his breath. Hold . . . hold . . . hold. Red lights flickered dully in his brain; pressure thumped in his ears. Flecks of blood oozed from his flaring nostrils and merged in long filaments with the sea.

And still he held on, waiting for that sudden, jarring leap upwards, his hands locked in convulsive battle with the juddering wheel. He held on even after the boat rolled, crushed and shattered, and sank with slow, deathly grace into the eerily still waters of the deeper reaches of the ocean, falling with tired, silent beauty to settle in the black depths of the sea which had been its life.

The storm wreaked havoc and destruction wherever it touched. In the small communities dotted along the broad vale of Strathannan, tiles flew, chimneys crashed and folk crouched shivering round flickering fires. But it was the proud fishing villages nestling into the Strath's coastline which faced the full fury of the gale. They would long remember that terrible night of December 1926.

In Kilweem the wind drove in from the North Sea with vicious, ice-tipped fury, lashing mercilessly at the straggle of stone-built houses lining the quayside. The grey waters inside the protected harbour swelled into furious, crashing breakers, sending the sea swirling into puddles on the cobbled road and unleashing spume, like spittle, to splatter against boarded windows. Rain fell in impenetrable sheets, propelled by squalls strong enough to rip the pantiles from

4

roofs and tattooing against wooden shutters, as if demanding entrance, before falling to seep under ill-fitting doors.

Across the small harbour the sea wall was battered by waves so high that it seemed to have ceased to exist, temporarily overwhelmed by the terrible onslaught of the ocean. The shock of each watery assault reverberated through the stones of the quayside and on into the chill, damp houses like echoes of distantly rolling thunder.

Despite his powerful build, Malcolm McLean had to use both hands and the strength of his burly shoulders to force the heavy wooden door of his harbour-side house open against the storm. Outside the wind whipped his unruly crown of red hair into a fiery halo round his head. Fifteen yards in front of him, barely visible through the stinging rain, a lamp flickered yellowly, illuminating the shadowy forms of half a dozen people, huddled together on the bitter quayside, watching, waiting. He knew his sister-in-law was among them.

Malcolm shuddered. If it had not been for the back injury which regularly and conveniently kept him at his own hearthside through the worst of most winters, he too would have been with his brother on the missing 'Pride of Fife'.

As he watched a sound reached him, swelling above the keening, screeching wind, stopping the blood in his veins. A woman's scream, shrill with the agony of long-endured pain. It jolted him back to his purpose. Scowling he turned towards the untidy cluster of buildings which meandered up the steep brae from the harbour. As he screwed his eyes up against the bite of the wind the short and immensely fat, bundled figure of a woman emerged from the maze of wynds and struggled towards him.

Malcolm greeted her tersely and turned back to his front door, already resenting the money he was going to have to pay for her services. The door opened easily this time, thrown inward by the wind as soon as he released the catch. Jeannie Moys had her saturated, shabby, black coat off and was panting her way up the narrow stairs before he got it shut again.

Inside the bedroom a fire burned in an undersized grate. Despite its fierce orange glow and fitful crackling it offered little warmth against the wind which battered directly onto the window and found its way through stout shutters and glass in sharp, icy draughts.

The young woman on the bed was glad of the cooling air. Approaching the end of her labour she was beaded in the sweat of unflagging effort. Her face glowed red with strain and her breathing was the rapid panting of exertion.

'Oh Jeannie! Thank the Lord! I was starting to think I'd be having this bairn on my own.' The weak smile was lost in a grimace of pain. Her hands and jaw clenched as the contraction tightened. Every muscle in her slight body tensed as she fought the searing agony in determined silence.

Agnes McLean had allowed herself the release of that one scream only when she was quite certain that Malcolm was out looking for Jeannie, confident that the noise would be covered by the crescendo of the storm. She wouldn't give way again.

'Jeannie will look after you now.' Malcolm abdicated responsibility with gruff relief.

'Aye. Away you go and check on the wains. Then make yourself a cup of tea and try to get some sleep. There's nothing you can do here.' Agnes meant it kindly but it emerged as an impatient order as she concentrated on overcoming a fresh burst of agony.

'Aye, away with you man. I'll call you if there's anything I need.' Jeannie faced him, plump arms folded implacably across her ample breasts. A formidable sight.

Malcolm grunted and took himself off to the comfort of his wooden chair and the well-thumbed family bible.

Jeannie scrubbed her hands in the basin of cooling water by the fire and turned back to her patient. Agnes's narrow hips would never allow childbirth to be a painless process but she had already birthed three sons with less difficulty than many a bigger woman. Jeannie confidently expected that this fourth child would present no undue problems.

'Push! Harder! That's it. Come on, now. Push. Push.' Jeannie encouraged Agnes firmly, a frown of concentration marking her brow. 'Relax now. Wait for the next one.' She wiped the woman's face and moved to the end of the bed, anxious to discover what was taking Agnes so long. She had expected the child to come before midnight but now it was after two in the morning. 'Open your legs, Hen. I'm needing to do a wee check inside.'

Agnes nodded weakly, past caring about the indignities of giving birth.

Jeannie slipped a gentle hand into the vagina, feeling her way up, expecting to meet the soft, round crown of the infant's head. What she actually encountered made her withdraw her hand in sudden fear. Murmuring encouragement while Agnes fought another contraction she repeated the examination. Again the unmistakable shape of a tiny foot.

'Well, Lass. I think this is a big one,' she lied.

'Aye,' Agnes gasped. 'It surely is. The others were not half so hard to bring out.'

'Maybe I should see if Doctor Stobie is about. He could give you something for the pain. And he might be able to help you along a wee bit.' She saw the first dawnings of fear on Agnes's drawn face. 'You are just a wee slip of a thing, Agnes McLean. You were lucky with the other three but there's no point in suffering if the doctor could make it easier for you.'

'Can you not do it, Jeannie?' Even through her pain Agnes knew they could scarcely afford the midwife's fee. Paying Doctor Stobie to visit in the middle of a night as foul as this one could mean nothing but soup and turnips for another week.

'I don't believe in taking chances, Hen. Now, lie still a while and try not to push. We don't want you all torn. I'll tell that man of yours to fetch the doctor.' She was already on the stairs as she spoke the last words, leaving Agnes to sink wearily back against her dampened pillow.

Malcolm's loud protests were audible even above the storm but eventually the front door slammed. His boots rang on the greasy setts as he slipped and slithered his furious way up the narrow wynd, splashing unheedingly through rivulets of water.

Almost half an hour later he was back. Doctor Stobie, a kind-hearted, energetic man in his late fifties, a pair of pince-nez jammed firmly on the bridge of his nose, was with him. Like Jeannie Moys, Stobie walked straight through the house and was half-way up the narrow staircase before Malcolm caught up with him.

'No,' Stobie stopped him firmly. 'Stay here. There's nothing you can do just now.'

Malcolm grunted and went to warm himself at the huge, blackleaded range which dominated the room. He was tempted to slump into his old chair in front of it but knew he shouldn't sleep while the families of the men missing on the 'Pride of Fife' continued their grim vigil outside. Not that he intended to join them there, not in this wild weather. Instead he clasped his hands together, shut his eyes and prayed briefly for the boat's safe return, remembering to add a plea for his labouring wife. Then, conscience appeased, he sank into his chair and was instantly asleep.

Stobie had his top coat off before he was properly inside the mean bedroom. He noted the bare details in a glance. A wooden bed, inadequately covered with patched and darned blankets, a rickety table supporting a cracked wash-stand basin and jug, a single chair, a rag rug on the uneven floor, fraying curtains at the windows and two old oil lamps giving uneven illumination. All spotlessly clean but the very cleanliness emphasised the poverty of this household. It was unusual for a fishing family to be quite as poor as this one, but it was common knowledge that Malcolm McLean was no lover of work. The resulting loss of income was painfully obvious inside his home.

'Well, well, Agnes. What a night to choose.' His voice was brisk and friendly, giving no hint of his thoughts.

'I'm sorry you had to come out, Doctor,' Agnes apologised, carefully pronouncing her words in poor imitation of his own refined Edinburgh accent. 'I don't really think there was any need, but Jeannie . . .' She gasped and lapsed into silence as the contraction's grip strengthened.

'Don't you be worrying your head about that. I'm glad to help.' He checked her pulse as he spoke, finding it fast but strong and regular. Then, very gently, he repeated the old midwife's examination, finding precisely what she had found. 'There, that wasn't too bad, was it?'

'Is there something wrong, Doctor?' Agnes whispered.

'Not wrong. More unusual.' He patted her hand. 'Nothing I haven't come across before. Now, the first thing I want to do is give you something to ease the pain. There's nothing to be gained from wearing yourself out. You'll need all your strength for after the baby's born.'

She nodded, more weakly now. 'But can't you tell me what's wrong?' she pleaded.

'There's nothing wrong. But the child is a very large one and you are just a dainty wee thing. All I'm going to do is help him out. You leave it all up to me and Mrs Moys here. And don't worry.' There was no point in distressing her more with the truth.

'Aye,' she smiled bravely and made no objection when the light, gauze mask was pressed over her face, although her pale eyes widened in fright above it.

'This will smell strange and make you a wee bitty dizzy. That's quite normal. Then you'll feel as if you're floating away. Now, don't fight it.' He dripped chloroform onto the gauze and watched her eyes flicker and close.

'You know what to do, Mrs Moys. Just keep her nicely under and I'll see if I can turn the child.'

He positioned himself between the labouring woman's legs and worked with one hand on her distended belly, the other manipulating inside her. Minutes passed. Beads of moisture formed on his forehead. Once or twice Agnes moaned. He paused, wiping the perspiration from his face. Very gently, fearful for the delicate child, he worked for another five minutes. Finally he sat up, straightening his painful back, and shook his head.

'It cannot be done. I'll have to do what I can for her with the baby in this position.'

Working with urgency now he made a neat cut in the perineum then, measuring his actions in time with the weakening contractions, fastened a hand firmly around the emerging foot. Seconds later, in response to his firm pressure, a tiny hip appeared. The next contraction allowed him to guide the second hip and the shoulders through the birth canal. Only the head remained hidden. Gently Stobie felt round the stalk-like neck, half expecting to find the umbilical cord strangling the infant. To his relief it was clear. The next contraction expelled the baby into his hands.

'There! A girl! That'll please Agnes. And not even average weight,' he added in some surprise. He cut the cord quickly, satisfied himself that the leg and hip had not been damaged as he pulled on them and passed the squirming infant to Jeannie.

'Good Lord!' His loud exclamation made her turn quickly. 'Hurry, give Agnes another drop or two. There's another child here.'

Hastily abandoning the mewling infant to the wooden crib, Jeannie administered more chloroform to Agnes who was already coming round.

The second child slid head first into the world only two minutes after her sister and immediately set up a whimpering cry.

'Well, what a surprise. No wonder I couldn't turn the first one.' Stobie chuckled his delight. Not all breech births had such a happy outcome.

'Wake up Agnes. It's all over, lass. You've two bonnie girls.' Jeannie's plump cheeks glowed with pleasure as she roused her patient.

Agnes smiled vaguely, not quite able to focus, her head ringing strangely, feeling slightly sick.

'I'll call back tomorrow, to be sure you're all comfortable,' Stobie called as he washed his hands and rolled his sleeves down. He checked Agnes's pulse, well aware that she hadn't yet understood what had happened. 'Try and get some rest, Agnes. You're going to have your hands full this time.' He winked at Jeannie. 'I'll send Malcolm up.'

Stobie called Malcolm's name and when that failed to waken him, poked him unsympathetically in the arm. Malcolm growled and just managed to control his temper.

'Well,' he demanded. 'Is it all over with?'

'Everything is fine,' Stobie said. 'But I should warn you, you are in for a shock.'

'Shock?'

'Aye,' Stobie chuckled. 'It was twins! Both girls. Both perfect.'

'Twins . . .' Malcolm paled, mouth agape. 'Girls . . .?'

'Congratulations!' Stobie's eyes gleamed behind the spectacles, now slightly awry on his nose. 'Off you go and see that wife of yours. She'll be wondering what's keeping you.'

'Aye. Right.' Malcolm started off up the stairs, then hesitated. 'Eh . . . How much do I owe you, Doctor?' he asked in some trepidation. To have the doctor in attendance at all was an unlooked-for expense. To have to pay for the safe delivery of twins was, no doubt, twice as costly.

'Not one penny. It was a pleasure. No! I wouldn't hear of it.' Stobie raised his voice over Malcolm's objections. 'I'm only too pleased to have been here. Use the money to buy the extra bits and pieces you'll surely be needing.'

'No Doctor. Thank you but I'll pay what's owing. Like any other man.' Malcolm growled, his colour heightening at this imagined slur on his ability to support his family.

Aware that this was now a matter of pride, Stobie settled it with ease.

'Well, to tell the truth, I prefer to take my payment in kind whenever I can – if you understand me. And I'm more than partial to a nice bit of haddock. But I don't want to put you to any bother. What with your bad back, if you'd rather pay cash . . . well, I suppose.'

'No . . . that is . . . fish it is then, doctor. I'd be more than pleased to send you a good bit every now and then. When I'm back at work,' Malcolm blustered.

Stobie was through the front door and away before Malcolm could finish. Pleased with the arrangement he had made with the doctor he flew up the stairs and into the bedroom.

'The doctor has agreed to take a bit of fish for payment,' he announced proudly. 'Though why you needed to send for him in the first place . . .'

Jeannie looked up from the crib and frowned. 'Agnes and the bairns are fine, Malcolm.' The rebuke in her voice was obvious.

'Oh aye.' His wife was propped up on her pillows, her face pale, her fair hair still clinging damply round her face. But when she heard voices she stirred and held out a hand to her husband.

'I must have fallen asleep,' she slurred, her mind still fogged by the anaesthetic. Then her face froze and she turned to Jeannie with an expression of dread. 'The bairn! Where is it?'

'Lie back, Hen. Everything's fine. You had to have chloroform. Do you not remember? It takes a wee while to wear off. That's why you're so sleepy. But just look at this.'

Jeannie bent over the crib. When she straightened she held a tiny infant in the crook of each ample arm. The first one, howling lustily, she deposited firmly in Malcolm's huge, rough hands. The second, peacefully sleeping, she handed to Agnes. 'This one was born two minutes after her sister. And before you ask they're both fine, bonny bairns.'

But Agnes was beyond sensible speech and could only stare from one to the other of her tiny daughters in open-mouthed amazement.

'Now you know why you were having such a struggle,'

Jeannie laughed. 'Well, I'll be back in the morning. It's been a long night and I've my own family to see to. You get some rest now.'

'Well, Agnes,' Malcolm said after the old woman had left. 'You've given me quite a surprise tonight.' His expression left her in no doubt that the surprise had not been pleasant.

'Myself too,' she admitted and laid the placid younger baby on the bed in front of her. 'Put the other one here, too, Malcolm. I want to look at them,' she instructed, her voice heavy with fatigue and disappointment.

He did as she asked and stood back frowning down on his daughters, both now silent.

'They're exactly the same. How am I to tell them apart?' she asked with something approaching panic in her voice.

'We could tie a thread round the ankle of the oldest one,' he suggested.

'Aye, we could do that, right enough.' But she sounded doubtful.

'There's no need!' Malcolm exclaimed. 'Look, this one has a funny wee mark on its shoulder. See.' He held the youngest baby out to his wife. 'There.' His finger rested briefly on a small but clear, reddish mark, just to the side of the throat.

'I can see it,' Agnes whispered, her voice faint with horror. 'And I know what it is.'

'It's a birthmark. Lots of bairns have them. It'll fade with time.'

'Not this one. Can you not see? It's shaped like the new moon. My Granny has it. They say it's always been in our family. And they say that anyone with the mark is fey . . . like my Granny. And her mother before her. She knows when things are going to happen.'

'Rubbish! Don't go filling your head with that sort of nonsense, Agnes. It's a birthmark and that's all. And your Granny Guthrie has always been strange. Everyone knows that.'

'It's more than that, Malcolm,' she insisted.

'No it's not!' he stormed at her. 'And there's more to be worrying about. Like how are we supposed to feed and clothe two more bairns?' He made it sound like an accusation. She stared, wounded but speechless. 'Get to sleep,' he ordered harshly, taking the sleeping infants and thrusting them into the crib. 'I don't want you to be in that bed for any longer than you have to be. You know I can't see to the boys on my own.'

Agnes closed her eyes to hide the hot tears as he stomped from the room.

Malcolm checked that the boys – Hugh, still a baby, William, an energetic three-year-old and four-year-old Thomas – were still sleeping then stole downstairs, meaning to catch a few hours' sleep.

He was unbuttoning his shirt when he realised the wind had died down. He opened the front door a crack and peered towards the quayside. There, still huddled together, the small group kept their vigil, scanning the horizon for any sign of the missing boat. He shut the door quickly before his sister-in-law could see him and shame him into sharing their agonising wait.

Sudden anger drove his fist bruisingly into the heavy wooden door, but he didn't feel the pain over the bitterness of his thoughts.

What cruel twist of fate, he wondered, had imposed the unwanted burden of two daughters on him this cursed night while stealing the lives of his brother and the three crewmen, as if to even the balance?

Drained and cold he sank back into his chair.

TWO

Agnes dragged the wet cloth impatiently over five sticky faces, starting with Thomas, the eldest, and working hurriedly down the line in order of age. William, Hugh, Twi and Isobel were all treated to the same cursory wipe-over, designed to remove any lingering traces of breakfast porridge. Then she wrung the cloth out in a bowl of icy water and began again. This time ten small hands would be rubbed and scrubbed until they glowed red across the knuckles.

'Hold still will you,' Agnes snapped at eight-year-old Thomas. He still squirmed, wasting time that was perpetually running away from her, so she administered a sharp slap across the back of his chapped legs. Chastened he bit down on his lip, held back tears and offered his cracked hands to be rubbed until they seeped blood.

'I don't know why you can't let me clean you up without all this fuss. You know you only end up in trouble, and you're big enough to be setting a better example for the wee ones.' Agnes rubbed her son's hands vigorously, treating the other three no more gently until she reached Isobel. The little girl, beautiful, fair and of almost elfin build, held her hands out obediently. The pale, smooth skin, unlike that of her brothers and sister, was unmarked by the chilblains and chaps which afflicted everyone else during the long, icy winters. Agnes smiled, merely dabbing at the delicate fingers and murmured, 'There's a good wee lassie,' words of encouragement seldom heard by her other offspring.

As one the five youngsters collected their boots and coats, their degree of accomplishment with laces and buttons increasing according to age. Agnes dragged a brush through her own fine hair and struggled into a worn, old-fashioned coat, pulling a knitted shawl over her shoulders to keep out the worst of the raw morning. Finally she bent to rearrange the children's socks and coats, trying to cover as much of their exposed skin as possible.

It shamed her to see how shabby they all looked. Not one of them wore a single item of clothing which had been bought or made especially for them. Every threadbare article from coat to drawers had first belonged to some other child.

By the time Hugh got his singlets they had already been worn by Thomas, William and, before them, by their two McPherson cousins. The girls' clothes arrived via a similar route.

It was fortunate, Agnes thought, grimly, that the twins had turned out to be so different, not identical at all. Anyone who didn't know them would be astounded to discover they were in any way related. Twi, the oldest by two minutes, was already, at four, a sturdy, noisy and impatient child with her father's red hair and fiery temper. Isobel was slight and fair, her delicate appearance belying a determined and self-sufficient personality. While Twi ran wild with the other youngsters Isobel was content to sit by herself, drawing endless pictures, working doggedly until she was satisfied with the result and then abandoning it for her mother to throw away. When Twi flushed bright red and screamed with temper because her shoelaces defeated her, Isobel quietly rejected Tommy's offer of help and struggled on until she achieved a passable bow, all on her own. The practical advantage of the differences between the twins meant that Agnes could pass Twi's clothes down to Isobel, an extra economy she was forced to appreciate.

The day of the twins' birth had marked the start of a changed life for the McLeans. The addition of two extra mouths to feed in a family already struggling for a decent existence on an insufficient income had placed a tremendous strain on their slender resources. But what had really reduced them to their present, impoverished state, had been the loss of the old 'Pride of Fife'. The old steam drifter, claimed by the notorious storm of 1926, had taken the family livelihood to the bottom of the North Sea with it. The boat had been jointly owned by Malcolm and his brother George, left to them by their father. The herring they fished in winter and the line fishing in summer provided an adequate living, and they had had the status of boat-owners, been their own men. But now, with no boat and lacking the means to purchase a share in any other vessel, Malcolm was reduced to hiring himself out as a casual hand wherever he could find a day's work. His pitiful wages scarcely kept the roof over their heads.

To eke out the unvarying diet of herring and oats, Agnes had been forced to join the women in the gutting shed. Her hands, once pink and soft as Isobel's, were red and scarred from the multitude of small cuts, unavoidable as the knife slipped in the slimy fish.

This morning the boats were due in with the tide, just after nine. Agnes was in a rush to deliver the boys to school and take the girls to her Mother's house so she could be at her table in the open shed when the first boxes came ashore.

'Hurry up. Tommy, you take Twi's hand.' Agnes herded her family out onto the quayside, already busy with the motorized vans and horse-drawn carts of the local fishmongers, come early to get the pick of the catch. Holding Isobel's hand in her own she led the way, threading rapidly round lobster pots, coiled ropes, discarded crates, draped nets and steaming horse dung, savouring the pungent, ever-present smell of fish, and hurried up Harbour Wynd towards Kirkgate and the school.

'Right boys. Off you go,' she said as soon as the small building was in sight. Then, holding one small girl in each hand she rushed on along Kirkgate, turned right down Mercat Path and down again, into the Butts. This row of dilapidated houses, running towards the shore, north of and round the point from the harbour, was where her widowed mother and Granny Guthrie lived, where she herself had been raised. Nearly running now, Agnes clattered down the steep street and let herself into a house at the far end of the row, almost on the beach itself.

'I can't stay. I'm late.' She gave the twins a push in their grandmother's direction and hurried away, retracing her steps to the harbour.

The first two boats were already in. Shallow boxes holding the fish which the fishermen had managed to gut were piled up on the quayside while the trays of whole fish were thrown into the gutting shed. Ignoring the cold Agnes threw her coat and shawl onto a pile of others, knowing she would warm up soon enough. Rolling her sleeves back over rough, work-coarsened arms she took up her knife and set to work cleaning the fish, tossing the slimy bodies adeptly into the waiting trays. She worked at speed, sometimes chatting with the other women but, more often, in silence.

As she stared through the open shed the 'Annie May' chugged into harbour and tied up. Agnes caught the unmistakable flash of Malcolm's red hair as he worked to unload the catch, his huge frame dwarfing the other men. For two hours they laboured, unloading, washing decks and checking nets, lines and gear, ready for the next trip.

Agnes watched him intently, willing him to look her way just once. But he didn't. He never did. Even when he was obliged to come into the gutting shed he ignored her. His attitude amused many of the other women and hurt Agnes. After all, it wasn't her fault that she was forced to work here. She liked it even less than he did. But, with five growing youngsters to provide for, what other choice did she have?

Two hours after her husband had made his way home Agnes slit her last fish and collected her coat. Picking up the three haddock which were her due she made her way slowly across the quay, treading a path through thinning crowds, exchanging a few words with friends and neighbours as she went.

Malcolm was asleep in his wooden chair in front of the range, as she had known he would be. Even in sleep his face was set in grim, unsmiling lines.

Fearful of waking him and unleashing the fierce temper which flared at the slightest fault these days, she closed the door with exaggerated care and went through the ritual of washing, using the metal bowl at the kitchen sink, to sluice away all traces of fish. Next she checked the range was still warm and added three small potatoes and a carrot to the soup simmering for the evening meal. Tonight it would be supplemented by the fish, rolled in oats and fried in bacon fat.

That done she crept upstairs to tidy the beds. The boys slept on a rough, home-made bed in one room, the girls in the other while she and Malcolm slept in the bed recess in the downstairs room.

By the time she tiptoed tiredly downstairs again Malcolm was blearily awake. 'What were you doing, making all that noise while I was trying to sleep,' was his bad-tempered greeting.

'I was as quiet as I could be,' she snapped back at him.

'I'm waiting for a cup of tea,' he growled.

'The kettle's on the hob. It'll not be a minute.' She busied herself at the range, enjoying the glow of warmth it threw out at her.

'What's taking you so long, woman?' he rose to his feet and lurched angrily towards her.

Grabbing the teapot from the warming plate she poured thick, black liquid into his cup and offered it to him.

Snarling he pushed her aside and filled the cup to the very brim, as if she was incapable of even performing that small task to his satisfaction.

Biting back her anger Agnes grabbed her coat. 'I'll away and fetch the bairns,' she muttered and escaped.

Her progress through the village was considerably slower than it had been six hours earlier. Harbour Wynd seemed steeper and Kirkgate was bitter with the gusty east wind. The Butts were deserted.

Her mother's house was neater than most, whitewashed and fresh looking. Agnes mounted the outside steps tiredly and let herself in. Her grandmother, Granny Guthrie, over seventy and gnarled and wrinkled as any seaman, nodded her head in perpetual agreement as she dozed in her chair by the window. Agnes slipped past her and into the kitchen at the back.

Rose Mathie looked up from her floury table. 'All finished then?' she asked, poking a wisp of grey hair back under its restraining net. At nearly fifty Rose was as fit and active as ever, frequently shaming her permanently exhausted daughter with her vitality.

'Aye. Till next time.' Agnes shrugged and smiled thinly. 'Are you two ready then?' she asked the twins who were happily fiddling with bits of dough.

'Och! Bide a while. Surely you don't have to rush away. Have a cup of tea at least.' Rose was already lifting the kettle from the hob.

Agnes laughed at last, suddenly realising that she had had nothing to eat or drink since early morning. 'Thanks. I hope these two have been behaving themselves.'

'Of course they have. They're never a bit of trouble. I'll miss them when they go to the school.'

'You'll have some peace at last,' countered Agnes.

'Peace to do what?' demanded Rose. 'The bairns keep me going. Without them the days will be too long.'

Mother and daughter sipped their tea in silence while the litle girls rolled and pulled contentedly at the dough which was now a revolting shade of grey. Agnes felt herself relaxing in the warmth of the snug kitchen but when she looked up and found her mother's shrewd eyes watching her, knew she had let her defences down too far.

'What is it, Hen? I can see there's something bothering you. Would it not help to talk about it?'

'No,' Agnes snapped, too fiercely.

Rose sighed. Money again, she guessed, knowing how hard-pressed Agnes and Malcolm were these days. And money was the one thing she couldn't help them with. Her own circumstances were too strained for that.

'I'm just tired, that's all.' Agnes stood, ready to go, well aware of her mother's thoughts. 'We'd best be off or the boys will be out of school and away home without us.' She hurried away before her mother could ask any more probing questions.

By seven-thirty the children were all sleeping soundly and Agnes had taken up the never-ending mending which occupied her evenings. Malcolm sat in his usual seat. It was his habit to read a passage from the bible every evening before going to bed and the huge book was open on his knees. He seemed as good-tempered and relaxed as he was ever likely to be. She wondered if she should tell him now, reluctant to spoil the relatively contented atmosphere but knowing he would have to be told soon. She prepared for the worst.

'Malcolm . . .' she whispered fearfully.

'I'm tired, Hen. I think I'll away to my bed.' He seemed not to have heard her.

The back door slammed as he went to relieve himself in the backyard privy, leaving Agnes to draw back the curtains which hid the bed closet from view. It was nothing more than a bed-sized cupboard with a curtain instead of a door. Their double bed slotted neatly into the recess giving them a snug and draught-proof place in which to sleep.

Malcolm hurried back into the room and stripped his clothes off, his intention already physically obvious. 'Come on, Hen. Hurry up.' He slipped under the covers, grinning in expectation.

'Aye. Aye. I must just go outside first,' she muttered, wondering bitterly why he only bothered to be nice to her when this was what he wanted. She lingered outside until icy skin and chattering teeth forced her back indoors. Instead of climbing into bed she perched on the edge, keeping as far away from her husband as she could.

'I've got something to tell you first, Malcolm.' Her voice wavered.

'What?' he grunted impatiently.

Still she hesitated, dreading his reaction. 'I'm going to have another bairn.' There, it was said. She tensed, ready for the explosion.

'What did you say?' he whispered, full of menace.

'I'm having another bairn.' She breathed the words, unable to look at him now.

He glared at her, desire forgotten, then clambered out of the bed and stood in front of her. 'When?' he barked.

'September, I think.'

'September? And how the hell do you think we can afford another one?' he roared at her. 'I warned you not to let yourself get that way again. I warned you.' His voice rose until she thought her head would burst.

'It's not my fault. I told you to be careful at Hogmanay.' The words were barely out of her mouth when his hand caught her across the face, choking further argument.

'You stupid bitch.'

'It's not my fault,' she insisted rashly.

'It is so your fault. It's in your body. It was your body that made me do it to you.'

'And it's your bairn too. Not just mine.'

'It's yours! I'm having nothing to do with it. I told you to make sure there were no more bairns. You should have made sure you didn't get that way again.' He punched her shoulder, sending her backwards onto the bed. 'So you had better take care of it. Do you understand? Do you?'

'Aye,' she screamed back at him. 'I understand. You want me to get rid of it. Your own bairn. How can you ask me to do that?'

'I'm not asking. I'm telling.' He spat it at her.

'Malcolm,' she sobbed. 'Please, don't be like this . . .' She

22

looked at him towering over her, then scrambled across the bed in disbelieving horror. 'No, Malcolm. Not now.'

'Why not? The damage is already done,' he said callously, shoving her down onto the bed and lowering himself onto her. 'We might as well make the best of it.'

The first days of April were warm with the promise of spring. Twi and Isobel, with Granny Rose for the day, were well wrapped up and taken to the beach where they were allowed to run freely before finally settling to scooping sand into great piles, using shells as tiny spades.

Rose chuckled as Twi's sandcastle collapsed yet again, then tut-tutted as the small girl kicked out in a furious temper before sinking to the ground in a great sulk. How different she was from her twin. Isobel seldom indulged in fits of temper, reserving her rare anger for events of importance, overcoming obstacles with quiet, stubborn determination. As usual she was unimpressed by her sister's outburst, merely glancing up with bright eyes which missed very little before returning to the intricate picture she was drawing in the sand. Rose marvelled that this beautiful, artistic child could have come from such stock.

'Well,' Rose stood. 'Time to go. Your Mammy'll be here in a wee while.' She brushed sand from her long, black skirt and collected their things together hurriedly. If they weren't ready Agnes would snap and fret while she waited.

The Butts led directly onto the beach so they were indoors in less than five minutes. Agnes arrived only a minute or so later.

'Aw, just look at you!' was her greeting. 'All covered in sand. As if I haven't enough cleaning to do.'

'It'll brush off,' snapped Rose, weary of her daughter's continuing waspishness. 'And the sun will have done them both good. Even Isobel's got some colour in her cheeks.'

'More than likely she's running a temperature,' retorted

Agnes, determined to find fault. 'And you shouldn't have left Granny for so long.'

Granny Guthrie slept peacefully in her chair at the window, where she had been since before the children arrived.

'Away home with you. There's no point talking to you when you're like this.' Rose turned to kiss her granddaughters then stopped, a look of pure horror on her face. Agnes forgot her anger and followed her mother's gaze.

Isobel stood still as a diminutive statue, her wide, blue eyes fixed and staring, her mouth slightly open, her hands held upraised as if frozen in the act of saying goodbye.

Isobel didn't understand. Her mother had come through the door, scolding as usual and then, suddenly, she hadn't been there any more. And they weren't in Granny Rose's house, but in her own bedroom. The room looked different somehow. It was the bed! Isobel saw it had been pulled away from the wall, into the centre of the room. And Mammy was lying on it. Still and white with a pretty, white, lacy nightdress on. One she had never seen before. Her eyes were closed so she must be sleeping. Isobel smiled. Mammy looked so pretty. Like an angel must look. But, as she stared, wondering why Mammy wouldn't wake up and make the tea, something horrible happened to the bed. It turned red and sticky, as if Mammy was floating on a pond. And it smelled funny. It looked a bit like blood. Isobel swallowed, feeling sick. It was blood! She knew, without any doubt at all that her Mammy was sinking into a pond of blood.

'Mammy! Mammy! Don't go . . .' she whispered, then screamed shrilly. 'MAMMY!'

Suddenly she blinked and her eyes focussed on her grandmother and Twi, both looking at her as if she had done something very wrong. And Mammy, glaring at her as if she was rude, or dirty. 'Mammy?' the little girl asked, not quite sure if she could believe what she was seeing or if that

24

other room, the one she could still smell, was where her mother really was.

'I told you the beach wasn't good for her!' Agnes yelled at her mother.

'This has got nothing to do with the beach and well you know it! You know what it is. You've seen it in Granny Guthrie often enough,' Rose whispered, her quavering voice betraying the depth of her shock.

Agnes didn't have time to argue. Isobel fell forward in a faint.

When she revived, minutes later, she complained of a headache. Without another word to her mother, Agnes picked her daughter up and carried her home.

'The bairn's not well. I'll get her to bed and see to your tea in a minute,' she explained to Malcolm.

'What's wrong with her?' he demanded, intolerant of anything that might delay his meal.

'I don't know,' she lied. 'Likely it's just a chill. She was on the beach this afternoon. I told Mother it was too cold for her.'

'She looks fine to me.' Malcolm lifted his fragile daughter effortlessly and carried her towards the stairs. 'I'll put her to bed. You see to my tea,' he yelled back at Agnes.

'No Daddy. I don't want to go to bed.' Isobel, usually so quiet and obedient, especially when her father was around, had gone rigid in his arms. Ignoring the outburst he carried her impatiently into the bedroom and only stopped when he recognised raw terror on his daughter's face. 'Take me out. Take me out,' she screamed.

'If you're not well you should be in your bed.'

'No. No.' She covered her face with her hands and refused to look, terrified of what she might see.

Unusually patient Malcolm loosened her fingers. 'Look, lass. There's nothing here to be frightened of.'

Reluctantly she nestled closely in to her father and peeped into the room.

The bed she shared with Twi was in its usual place, hard

against the wall. She let out her breath and turned to her mother who had run up the stairs to see what all the noise was about.

'Can I see your long, white nightdress, please, Mammy?'

'My long, white nightdress?' Agnes laughed nervously. 'I haven't got a long, white nightdress, Hen.'

'Aye you have. It's all lacy and pretty,' Isobel insisted. 'Like a wedding dress.'

'I didn't even have one of those. I borrowed your Aunty Dorrie's. And it was blue. And you know my only night-dress is pink. Like your own.'

Isobel nodded, feeling sleepy now. 'But I don't want to go to bed. Not on my own. Please Daddy.'

'Och, alright. You can lie on our bed, until Twi goes to bed. Just this once mind.' Malcolm relented. 'You're prob-ably right,' he said to his wife later. 'Just too much cold on the beach.'

Agnes nodded but her face was still taut with terror.

The bus was late. Agnes stamped her feet, cold even in the continuing warm weather. The three other women who had gathered at the Tollbooth to wait for the bus on its daily, winding journey from Leven to St Andrews chatted and laughed together, unperturbed by the unreliability of the timetable. But, too nervous to stand still, Agnes wandered restlessly for fifteen yards up the road and back again, then started off in the opposite direction.

'Agnes! Come on, Hen. Here's the bus,' Annie Wardlaw called as the cream and blue single decker ground its way towards them.

The journey was interminable. The driver lingered to chat through his open window at every stop, greeting half a dozen acquaintances as they made their way through the busy village centre. But at last they were out of Kilweem and bumping along a rutted country road. Every jolt made Agnes's stomach heave until she thought she might have to ask the conductor to stop the bus so she could be sick at the roadside.

With considerble relief she saw the first houses of Wester Anstruther. Again the bus slowed, new passengers got on, others got off. The driver seemed to want to talk to a dozen different people. Then they were through Anstruther and into Cellardyke. Agnes got to her feet and waited impatiently by the door as the bus turned into Harbourhead. She jumped off as soon as it stopped, but then, suddenly aware of the other women still on the bus, waited, unwilling for them to guess her errand, hovering tensely, looking out over the sparkling sea until the bus was out of sight.

Walking slowly now she made her way along the street, finally finding the narrow wynd she sought. The clustered houses were not numbered so she counted and found number seven, small, but harled and trim, in the middle of a run of old, stone-built houses.

At the half-open door she hesitated. Once inside the house it would be too late to change her mind. But that was impossible after all that had been said over the past few weeks. Malcolm's continuing anger; his unjust insistence that this was her fault; the accusation that she was deliberately delaying, and the knowledge that he was right about one thing – they could not afford another child. Now she was more than five months into the pregnancy and it was too late for this to be done easily. She should have come weeks ago, but Cathie Struthers' fee and the bus fare had had to be pinched and saved. Even now they would all exist on watery soup and cheap fish for the next two weeks, as they had done for the last six.

'If it's Mrs Struthers you want, she's in. All you have to do is put your head round the door and call out.'

Agnes jumped. She hadn't noticed the other woman who walked on past her with a knowing look, and let herself into a house further down the street. Shame smarted in Agnes's eyes and burned on her cheeks. Shoving the door harshly aside she stepped into a dark, varnished hall and shouted. 'Are you there, Mrs Struthers?'

A heavy curtain on the far wall swept back as the door underneath it opened. A woman, in her late forties, Agnes guessed, stepped through and stopped to rearrange the curtain before turning to look at her visitor.

'You'll be Agnes McLean?' she asked in a voice artificially pared of the broader accents of the native Fifer. She stood, her hands clasped neatly in front of her, her face impassive; a tall, angular woman with greying hair scraped tightly into a bun and wearing a long, grey dress in a style popular more than twenty years ago. There was no comfort there for the frightened Agnes.

'Mrs Struthers?' she asked, but the words emerged as a sad croak.

'Well, now you are here let's not waste any more time.'

'I'm sorry if I'm late. There's only the one bus from Kilweem. It's always late.' Agnes made her excuses.

Mrs Struthers seemed not to hear. 'Take your coat off and come with me.'

Agnes fumbled with her buttons.

'Through here, Mrs McLean.' The voice was loud, ugly and commanding. Agnes hurried after Mrs Struthers and found herself in a large, square kitchen, dominated by a long, wooden table, so clean it was almost white.

'Take everything off from the waist down and get yourself up onto the table.' Mrs Struthers rolled back her sleeves and waited grimly.

Agnes paled and looked in vain for a screen of some sort where she might at least try to undress with some attempt at modesty. 'Here?' she asked at last.

'Aye. Here. You've nothing under they skirts that I haven't seen a hundred times before.' The words were brusquely said and the mouth twisted into a hard, cheerless, ghost of a smile. 'Come along. Quickly.'

Agnes backed against the range, a smaller, neater thing than her own, and felt the heat singe her backside as she undressed. Cathie Struthers' eyes never left her as Agnes removed her drawers and straightened, her private regions open to view. The other woman's eyes rested piercingly on her belly.

'So, you're showing? How far on are you?'

'It was at the New Year,' Agnes whispered, knowing how that must sound.

'Och aye!' Mrs Struthers smirked her understanding. 'Too much celebrating was it?'

Agnes flushed, feeling humiliated and exposed.

'Well, you're not the first. And you'll not be the last. Now get up there and lie down.'

Agnes hitched herself inelegantly onto the cold table and allowed herself to be pushed flat.

'You do realise you've left it far too long?' Mrs Struthers poked Agnes's abdomen roughly.

'Too long?' Agnes's heart leapt, but whether with relief or dread she couldn't tell. 'Can you not do it?' she asked.

'Oh, I can always do it. But the longer it's left the harder it is. For you. It will be painful and could take a long while.'

'I'm not frightened of pain.'

'No? Good.' Again there was that chilling smile. 'Sit up. We'll get the details sorted out first.'

'Details?'

'You have brought the money?'

'Oh . . . Aye.' Agnes scrambled down and, acutely aware of her nakedness, fumbled in her bag. Hesitantly she pressed one pound and fifteen shillings into the older woman's outstretched hand. A whole week's wages.

'Good.' Mrs Struthers counted it carefully, then stuffed the money into a commodious jar above the range. 'Get back on the table and I'll tell you what will happen.'

Shivering, Agnes perched on the table's edge, listening intently.

'It will not take me long. It will be sore but you must lie perfectly still. After that . . . well, everyone's different. With some it's all over in some three or four hours. Others

29

have to wait a full day. You'll bleed, have bad cramps and then it will come away. You will know when it has happened.' She looked at Agnes to make sure she understood. Pale and sweating Agnes could only nod.

'You may have a cup of tea afterwards,' Mrs Struthers went on. 'But you must be away from here by three. No matter what.'

Agnes nodded again. 'I have to get the three o'clock bus anyway.'

'The bus?' The grey eyebrows flew up in surprise. 'On your own?'

'Aye.'

'Och well, I suppose you'll be alright. You're young enough. In a couple of days you'll be as fit as ever.' She gathered Agnes's legs and hauled her back onto the table. 'Hold on to this and keep still.' She pressed a rolling pin into Agnes's shaking hands and eased her legs up.

At first there was nothing, just a sharp touch of coldness, high inside her. But then, just as she was starting to believe that this was going to be bearable, a skewer seemed to run into her, searing with stabs of white-hot pain which went on and on.

Through the red mist covering her eyes Agnes heard the cold instruction to lie still. She gripped the rolling pin and bit on her lip until it bled.

And then it stopped. As suddenly as it had started, leaving nothing worse than a dull ache.

'That should do it. Now sit yourself up. Slowly. Then come and sit here in front of the range.'

'Is it . . .?' Agnes stammered through chattering teeth.

'I told you. Not yet. But it should come away this evening, or maybe tomorrow.'

'Oh.' Agnes pulled herself back into her clothes, surprised that there was nothing; no blood, no sign yet of what had been done to her.

'Drink this.' A pretty cup of milky, sweet tea was pressed

30

into her hands and she sipped gratefully. Mrs Struthers took her money jar from above the range and disappeared. Agnes slipped into a light doze and woke to find herself being vigorously shaken.

'Come along, Mrs McLean. It is nearly three. Your bus will be along shortly.'

Agnes jumped out of her chair, took a shallow breath of surprise as a sharp pain, low in her abdomen, slashed into her with the sudden movement, then relaxed as it subsided into the dull ache she had felt before. Her threadbare coat was thrust into her arms and she was hustled back into the hall before she could get it about herself.

'Hurry yourself or you'll miss that bus.' Mrs Struthers shoved her out into the street. 'And remember,' she hissed. 'If you should have any trouble, if you should need a doctor, tell him you did it yourself, with a knitting pin.'

The sea air felt sharp and clean after the heat of the kitchen. Apart from a small niggle of discomfort, deep in the pit of her belly, Agnes felt quite normal. Careful not to hurry and perhaps start things off too soon, she walked back to Harbourhead, arriving just as the bus trundled up behind her.

Conscious of the other passengers, some of whom she knew, Agnes forced her face into a carefree smile and found herself a seat.

The homeward journey took half an hour. Agnes sat tensely, every nerve concentrated on the dragging sensation, terrified of some shameful mishap on a public bus, overwhelmed by sadness, already grieving for the baby she knew was dying.

But she reached the Tollbooth safely, then walked slowly home, immensely relieved when her own shabby front door came into view.

Malcolm was in his usual place in front of the range. 'Alright?' he asked, not even looking at her.

'Aye,' she answered, suddenly feeling incredibly tired.

31

'Well, hurry up and make my tea and get the tatties on. I'm starving.'

The evening dragged. Agnes tensed to every twinge but by nine o'clock the ache had become familiar and, despite her fierce concentration upon it, was not growing any more severe.

'Perhaps it hasn't worked,' she fretted.

'It had better work. And she told you it might take until tomorrow.'

'Aye, she did say that, right enough.'

'Well, there's no point in worrying about it. Let's away to bed.' He seemed hardly concerned for her.

It was pitch black in the bed closet. Beside her Malcolm snored fitfully with his back to her. For a moment after she woke she forgot. But then her visit to Mrs Struthers came back with burning clarity. Pain, like she had never imagined, cut through her, seeming to tear her apart, driving the breath from her body with the shock of it. Then, even before she had time to realise what was happening, it faded, dying away, almost to nothing. Then again, sharper, fiercer, making her cry out loud as it shoved red hot fingers deep into her abdomen.

'Malcolm,' she screamed.

'What's wrong?' Bad-tempered, still half asleep he growled his irritation then, hampered by the dark, clambered roughly over her and got a light on.

Her body arched under the onslaught of pain, ripping and shredding, making her heart hammer with terror. And the sticky rush of blood that went on coming and coming. 'Malcolm,' she whispered, already weakening.

'Shhhusssh. You'll waken the bairns.'

The pain receded, edging back, leaving her mind free. Waiting, gathering strength for the next attack.

'A towel, Malcolm. Fetch a towel,' she whispered, shoving frantically at the covers.

He grabbed a grimy one from the back of the door and came towards her with it. Then stopped, horrified by what was revealed on the bed. The sheet was no longer visible under the pumping, red stain, redness which poured from her even as he watched.

Turning he fled, slamming out of the house, pounding through the wynds to Jeannie Moys' door. A window opened above his head.

'What is it?' Jeannie's plump body filled the frame.

'It's Agnes. She's bleeding . . . real bad.'

'Wait there.' The window crashed down. Two or three long minutes passed before she opened the door.

'Now, Malcolm McLean. What's this all about?' she eyed him with distaste.

'It's Agnes,' he repeated. 'She's bleeding.'

'Why?'

'I don't know. But it's everywhere.'

Jeannie pulled the door shut and set off down the wynd at a rolling, half trot.

Agnes was lying exactly as he had left her. Her face was damp and pallid, her breathing fast and shallow.

'Good Lord!' Even Jeannie was shocked by what faced her. 'I didn't know she was expecting again, Malcolm,' she challenged him.

He turned away, sickened by the scene. Jeannie grabbed his arm.

'She's tried to do away with it, hasn't she?'

'No. She woke up like this,' he lied, unable to meet her eyes.

'Don't waste time lying to me, Malcolm McLean. You'd best run for the doctor. I can't do anything for her.'

'I can't have the doctor here!'

'Then she'll die.' It was blunt, cruel.

'Can you not stop the bleeding. Do something?' he pleaded with her.

'I don't know how. You must fetch the doctor.'

33

Still hesitating, seeing the sticky, red stain, bigger and still spreading, but more slowly now, he pleaded with her again.

'It's stopping. Look, she's no bleeding as much. Please, Jeannie, you do something for her. I can't fetch the doctor. He'll know.'

'He'll know anyway, when she dies, and she'll die alright if you don't fetch him here. And fast.'

Malcolm grunted but, at last, stormed from the house again.

Jeannie felt for a pulse, found it at last, weak and fluttering. Only semi-conscious Agnes was mercifully beyond pain and lay inertly on the soiled bed. Not knowing what else to do, Jeannie took Agnes's cold hand in hers and hoped the woman was comforted.

Stobie examined Agnes in grim-faced silence, propped her hips up with pillows in a belated attempt to stem the flow of blood, but knew it was hopeless. When it was over and Agnes no longer breathed he rounded furiously on Malcolm.

'Why? Why did she do this? My God! Why?'

Shocked into truthfulness Malcolm whispered, 'We couldn't afford another bairn.'

'You couldn't afford another child? But you could pay for this to be done to her?' In all his long years of practice Stobie had never seen damage as severe as this. He felt sickened, old. But, as shocked as he was, Stobie knew that Agnes was not the first to have resorted to such desperate measures. Some more than once.

'I told her to do it,' Malcolm admitted. 'But I never thought it would be like this. I swear I didn't know it would be like this.'

Dressed in their best, least mended clothes, the children were led upstairs to say goodbye to their mother.

Only Thomas cried. William couldn't bring himself to look and Hugh merely stared with huge, confused eyes, at

34

the beautiful lady on his sisters' bed. The twins only knew that something dreadful had happened to their Mammy and they had to be on their best behaviour.

Rose hoisted Isobel onto her hip so that the little girl could look down on her mother for the last time. Rose had aged visibly over the last three days and seemed a mere shadow of her former self.

'Don't cry, Granny.' Isobel's soft arms clasped round Rose's neck.

Rose sniffed back her tears. 'Look, Hen. See how lovely yer Mammy is.' And it was true, she thought, sadly. More beautiful than she had ever had the chance to be in life. And better dressed in the long, white nightdress, donated by the Minister's wife.

Isobel tore her saucer-like, blue eyes from the spectacle of her grandmother's tears and obediently looked at the dead woman. A faint smile played round the rosebud mouth. Mammy looked lovely. That was nice.

'I knew Mammy had a pretty, white nightdress,' she exclaimed. 'Why did she say she didn't have one?' she asked her grandmother, her small brow creased in perplexity.

Above her fair head Rose's eyes met those of her horrified son-in-law and both understood the import of those innocent words.

In those few seconds the stilted love that Malcolm had for his daughter died and was replaced by loathing. And fear.

THREE

'Granny Guthrie was a witch! Granny Guthrie was a witch!'

In the school yard a group of girls surrounded ten-year-old Isobel, taunting and jeering with the calculated cruelty peculiar to children. She stood, pale, silent and strangely dignified, understanding that any retort from her would only make matters worse.

'She was not!' Three inches taller than her sister and solidly built, Twi stormed to the defence of her family, shoving aside friends and foes alike.

'Aye, she was!' Maureen McArdle stepped into the ring, undaunted by the fury blazing from her red-headed classmate's stormy eyes. 'My Mammy says she was.'

'Your Mammy doesn't know what she's talking about,' Twi shot back at her, grabbing her twin sister's arm and attempting to pull her out of the excited crowd.

'She does so! She said your Granny Guthrie was a witch. And I heard Jeannie Moys say it, too. Granny Guthrie knew when your grandfather was going to die and she knew when King George was going to die. And lots of other things.' Hands on her hips she spat her evidence and surveyed her cronies in triumph. 'Isobel McLean is just like her Granny. Fainting and raving, *and* she's got the mark to prove it,' she delivered her punch line with relish.

'Witch. Witch. Witch. Witch . . .' They went on, following the girls as they ran for the shelter of the school building.

'Why did you not run away from them?' Twi hissed angrily under cover of the general commotion as the fifteen

36

girls were joined by the ten boys in their class, filing in from their own playground.

'You shouldn't have interfered,' Isobel shot back. 'You only made things worse. And anyway, what's the point in running, that's what they wanted me to do. They would have followed me. They'll forget in a day or two. This is only because Granny Guthrie died.' The patience in Isobel's voice, her calm acceptance of her place as a pariah hinted at a maturity beyond her years.

'It's because you fainted in the playground last week and raved on that Granny Guthrie was going to die,' Twi pointed out the obvious, but Isobel affected sudden deafness.

All afternoon Twi was aware of hostile whispering and nudging among the other girls. Once or twice she intercepted looks of pure malice directed at Isobel who worked on her sketch, deliberately pretending to be unaware of the atmosphere in the classroom.

Watching her sister as she worked, Twi felt a stirring of envy. They were twins but sometimes it seemed that Isobel had an unfair share of the good looks and talent. Her ability to draw so well was almost magical to the unartistic Twi and frequently won the teacher's unstinting praise – though Twi knew that did nothing for her sister's popularity with her classmates.

And that hair! Isobel's fell in a smooth, white-gold curtain, framing a pink and white complexion of the kind more normally reserved for fairy tale princesses. And she was slim with neat feet and pretty hands. Twi sighed and looked at her own chapped knuckles and chewed nails. Her fingers strayed unconsciously to her cheeks, half expecting the mass of freckles which matched her flaming hair to be detectable as lumps and bumps on her skin. Their eyes were the same vivid blue, but who, she wondered morosely, was going to notice hers, framed as they were by pale, sandy lashes and thin brows? Even her name was a compromise. Helen was what she had been christened, but for as long as she could remember she had simply been called Twin, or

Twi, as if no other identification was necessary for Isobel's sister. But at least no-one called her a witch.

Aware of her sister's scrutiny Isobel looked up from her drawing. 'Why are you staring at me like that?' she asked.

'I was just wondering how come you're so bonny and I'm so plain,' Twi answered with typical directness.

'You're not plain. And everyone likes you much better than me,' Isobel said generously.

'Aye, maybe.' Twi grinned suddenly, unable to hold ill-feeling for long. 'But I do wish we were identical after all.'

'No you don't.'

Twi frowned, surprised by the unusual bitterness in her sister's voice.

The teacher's sharp, 'Quiet, Isobel McLean,' brought titters of delight from the rest of the class.

'Why not?' Twi hissed when the teacher's attention was elsewhere.

'Because then they'd be calling you a witch, too,' came the toneless reply.

After lessons a crowd of chanting children gathered by the school gates. 'Witch . . . Witch . . . Witch . . . Witch . . .'

Isobel walked on, her head high, refusing to let them see her pain. Twi, flushed with anger, quickly abandoned all restraint and yelled back. Then the mood changed subtly from idle amusement to something more menacing. Now even Isobel was frightened. Instead of running alongside the sisters, the others circled them, blocking their way home, shoving them back when they tried to break through. Some of the older pupils joined in.

'Witch girl . . . Witch girl . . . Witch girl . . .' the chant grew stronger and louder.

'I'll tell our Dad,' Twi screeched desperately, knowing they were hopelessly outnumbered.

Hoots of derision greeted her words. No-one seriously feared the reclusive old bible-thumper who was as odd, in his own way, as his daughter.

Twi grabbed Isobel's hand and made a furious dash for the nearest child, red hair flying. The girl, smaller than she, held her ground for an instant then fell over, allowing the twins to forge ahead.

'Run,' screamed Twi. But Isobel stumbled and the other children were upon them again. Already Twi could feel the sting of sly thumps and pinches. But, just as she thought they were trapped, a tremendous noise from behind made all heads turn.

From the direction of the school yard came the three McLean brothers, hollering and yelling at the tops of their voices. Thomas, a well-developed fourteen-year-old with the broadest shoulders in the school led his brothers, the slightly smaller, thirteen-year-old William, with his father's irascible nature and Hugh, smaller still but stocky and full of outrage on his sisters' behalf. Reaching the nearest boy Thomas simply picked him up and tossed him aside. Some of the braver spirits stayed to make a real fight of it but most fled. Justice was delivered in the form of a few discerning punches, a couple of well-aimed kicks and a satisfying grapple in the muck of the roadway. Within minutes Kirkgate had cleared of all bar the McLeans.

'Come on then,' ordered Thomas, dusting off his ruined trousers with the air of a man completely satisfied with a job well done. 'Let's get home.'

Unfortunately for all five, Malcolm McLean was waiting for them. His fury at their dishevelled appearance and the rip in Thomas's trousers was audible all along the quayside.

'They were picking on Isobel,' Thomas explained.

'You should turn a deaf ear. There is no need to go fighting and yelling like a pack of ruffians,' Malcolm preached.

'I wasn't with them, Father,' William lied shamelessly, trying to avoid the inevitable.

'The others started it. All the boys did was get us out of trouble,' Isobel pleaded.

'Don't answer me back!' Malcolm roared. 'I'm not

interested in what started it. I'll not have you scuffling in the streets. Your Mammy would be shamed by you, God rest her soul.' He reached up to the hook on the back of the door. Five pairs of lungs sucked in cold terror as the heavy belt swung into view.

'That's not fair! Please, Daddy, don't belt them. It wasn't their fault.' Isobel braved her father's temper to try again.

'Quiet,' he thundered and she took an instinctive step back. 'You two lassies away and read your bibles for an hour and then get to your beds. There'll be no teas for any of you tonight.' They knew better than to argue.

'*Now*!' Malcolm glared at Thomas. 'You first. I'll teach you to brawl and ruin your clothes.' He flexed his belt menacingly.

'Do you not think you're overreacting, Malcolm?' Rose intervened.

'Hold your tongue woman. This is nothing to do with you,' Malcolm stormed, looking capable, in that second, of even hitting her.

Punishment was meted out in liberal fashion, leaving the boys sore and resentful.

'See what the good book tells you about obedience. Then you can get to your beds and all. And there'll be no tea for you for the rest of the week.'

'This is all your fault, witch girl,' William hammered bitterly on his sisters' door as he made his painful way to bed.

Hours later, when the house was in black silence, Isobel heard her grandmother slip into the room. Her bed was against the far wall.

'Granny?' she whispered, careful not to disturb Twi who was fast asleep.

'Aye, Hen?' Rose groped her way to her granddaughter's side.

'Are the boys alright?' Isobel asked, well aware of the pain her father's belt could inflict.

'Aye, Hen. They'll have forgotten about it in no time,' she lied.

'It was my fault,' Isobel said, her voice catching in her throat.

'No, lass.'

'They were only fighting because of me, because the others were calling me names again.'

'Oh, Hen . . .' With a sinking heart Rose listened as Isobel related the day's events.

All five children had had a hard life since their mother's death. Blaming himself, never able to forgive himself for that dreadful night, Malcolm McLean had become sterner, more harsh, as if he believed that he could atone by banning all enjoyment, all laughter and any small luxury from his home. His life consisted of work in the form of odd jobs such as tying lines or mending nets, and the Bible. Every free minute was spent in the old, wooden chair in front of the range, reading the scriptures and then imposing his formidable interpretation of God's law on his unfortunate family. If he derived any comfort from this cheerless regime it was certainly not apparent to anyone else.

Rose had watched her grandchildren recoil from their father, powerless to intervene, tied to her home in the Butts by the need to care for her own invalid mother. When Granny Guthrie's death released her from that duty she wasted no time in pointing out the advantages of a shared economy to the miserly Malcolm and relinquished her own home in the hope of being able to make life easier for the children. So far, she thought, shuddering as she recalled the vicious thwack of the belt, she had failed.

And she had failed especially badly with Isobel. Not for the first time she regretted the close, village community where everyone knew everything about everyone else. Granny Guthrie's strange but harmless ability to see the future was almost legendary in Strathannan and it was obvious that Isobel was similarly afflicted with this unwanted gift. Rose was powerless to protect her granddaughter from the ignorance and suspicion of the villagers.

'Why do they hate me?' Isobel's soft voice jolted her out of her reverie.

'They don't hate you, Hen. They just don't understand.'

'Because I faint?'

'Aye, because you faint. And because you sometimes know about things before they really happen. Just like your Granny Guthrie did.'

'They say I'm a witch, too.'

'They don't understand,' Rose repeated, sadly.

'Am I a witch?' Isobel persisted.

Rose forced a dismissive laugh. 'Of course you're not. Don't be silly.'

'Granny Guthrie said I had the mark. Like her. Did she think I was a witch?'

Rose cursed the old woman's loose tongue. Putting a hand out in the darkness she easily located the small, raised half-moon on Isobel's neck. 'Granny Guthrie had a mark exactly like this. And her mother before her. It runs in the family.'

'Does it mean I'm a witch?'

'No, it's only a birthmark.'

'Then why does everyone say I'm a witch, like Granny Guthrie?'

Rose sighed, obviously she was going to have to explain differently. 'Do you think Granny Guthrie was a witch?' she asked but Isobel, expression hidden by the darkness, stayed silent. 'Well, what do you think a witch would be like?'

'. . . Ugly . . . bad . . . and able to do strange things,' was the thoughtful reply.

'Was your Great-granny like that?'

'Not ugly. Not bad either. She was funny . . .' The young girl smiled to herself at the memory of the old woman who had slept her life away for as long as she could recall but who had occasionally wakened for long enough to tell wonderful tales of her own girlhood. 'But she was strange.

Sometimes she knew what was going to happen . . . like me . . . and she fainted like me, too.'

'Fainting doesn't make you a witch.'

'But Granny Guthrie did know when some things were going to happen! She had that fit on Jubilee day and told everyone that King George the Fifth was going to die. And she said that Mrs Simpson would never be queen. And she was right. The old King died and the new King ran away with Mrs Simpson and now we've got another new King and Queen. How could she have known all that if she wasn't a witch?'

'She was just a poor woman who, like you, had a very special gift. It made her sad to know when things were going to happen. But she couldn't stop them, and she couldn't make things happen, either. She just knew about them before other people.' Rose sighed. 'Your Granny was a good, kind person who would never hurt a fly. Just like you.'

'I wish everyone wasn't so horrible about her. And I wish they wouldn't call me a witch.'

'Och, Hen. You've a lot to learn about folk. If they don't understand something, they fear it. That's the way it is with you. These fainting fits of yours . . . they frighten people, that's all. They're just stupid children.' And stupid, ignorant adults too, she thought. 'Now, snuggle down and go to sleep. It's late and I'm tired.' She smoothed the silky hair, leaned over to kiss Twi's brow, then Isobel's. 'Anyway, I think they're mostly jealous.'

'Jealous?'

'Aye. You're so pretty and they're all so plain. They're jealous.'

'No, that's not it.' It was a simple statement of fact as Isobel slipped down into bed and closed her eyes.

FOUR

Malcolm McLean greeted his eldest son's return from the battlegrounds of North Africa with no more than a curt nod, not even bothering to rise from his chair at the fireside. Thomas flushed dangerously, opened his mouth as if to say something, then seemed to realise the futility of anger with such a stubborn, entrenched man. Shrugging he turned back to his siblings. They clustered round with tears and laughter all hopelessly confused.

Isobel smiled up into the broad, strong-boned face with adoration shining from her eyes. Thomas looked so smart and proud in his uniform. And so much older. A man! When he had left home a year ago he had been little more than a boy. His experiences since then had matured him in a way that four years on a fishing boat had conspicuously failed to do. Or perhaps it was just that away from their father's overwhelming discipline he had been free to develop his own personality.

Still limping slightly from the thigh wound which had temporarily removed him from the fighting, Thomas turned his older, male eyes on his sister and appraised her with new appreciation. What a beauty! So delicate and pale, as if she might fade away if she wasn't loved and cherished. But that was an impression dispelled by one glance into her vivid, blue eyes. Eyes which reflected her moods, flashing with anger, sparkling with humour or freezing with contempt to such an extent that words were not always necessary.

Isobel stood on tiptoe to reach her brother's rough cheek and had to restrain herself from hugging him too tightly, knowing he would be made uncomfortable by too much overt affection. As a family they rarely indulged in physical closeness. Their Grandmother Rose had been the only one who had ever hugged and kissed them but she had died in 1939, only days after war was declared.

Reluctantly Isobel released her favourite brother and watched while he kissed Twi and shook hands with his brothers. Hugh and William were only home by the greatest of good fortune. None of them had expected the family to be reunited until after the war. Both younger brothers, and the boat they crewed on, had been commandeered for the war effort and they were, for the duration, in the Merchant Navy. This short home leave was to allow their boat to undergo some urgent repairs.

The boys, eighteen and twenty years old to Thomas's twenty-one, slapped his back heartily and immediately started to throw questions at him.

'Easy now. Give me a chance. I'd like to put my bag down and have a cup of tea before you start on me,' he laughed, but Isobel wondered if she was the only one to notice the shadowed depths to his eyes and the faint lines at the sides of his mouth.

'Aye, of course. Here, sit down and the girls'll make us all something to eat.' Hugh winked at his sisters who were already at work on the evening meal.

'Aye. And after our tea we'll go to the Lobster for a wee half,' Thomas suggested.

'Indeed you will not!' Malcolm's outraged roar wiped the smile from all their faces. Thomas heard it with a familiar sinking feeling which took him back a year, as if he had never been away. He walked over to the hearth, grim and cheerless without a fire in it, and faced his father. They all saw the determination in his face, heard it in the low, even tone of his voice.

'I want to look up my old friends, Father. And I could use a drink tonight.'

'Old friends?' Malcolm scoffed. 'Well, you couldn't get away from them quick enough, could you? Getting yourself blown to bits with an English regiment in the desert is better than staying with the boats and your own kind, is it?' he snarled at Thomas, then faced his younger sons. 'As for you two, you'd be better off offering thanks to the Lord for keeping you safe than going to that Godless place. No good ever came of drinking. And this door closes at nine sharp. If you are later than that, or any the worse for drink, you had better look for a bed elsewhere.' Having said his piece he took up the huge family bible and began to read his daily passage, seeming to dismiss his family from his mind.

The June evenings were long and mild. The five brothers and sisters, four with varying shades of red hair and the strong build of their father, one with the fragile beauty inherited from her mother, wandered along the quayside. The fine weather had brought the older fishermen out to sit and smoke a pipe at the water's edge. Thomas lingered to talk with them and by the time they found themselves in Kirkgate it was already after seven.

'We'd best not be too long. Father'll not be pleased if we keep the lassies out,' Hugh reminded Thomas.

'Don't worry. He knows they're with us. He just wants to make sure they're not enjoying themselves. You know,' he added, 'you shouldn't let him treat you the way he does. You are old enough to go to war and old enough to stand up for yourselves. You have to live your own lives.'

'Like you, you mean?' asked William, an edge to his voice. 'It was alright for you. You just announced you were joining up and off you went. It was us who had to put up with his foul temper for weeks.'

'I'm old enough to decide for myself. His temper's not my problem,' retorted Thomas. 'If he had his way I'd still be coming in at nine every night. Like a wain.'

'I don't understand why you had to go off and join the army when you could have stayed with the boats. And an English regiment!' William's disgust was obvious. Of the five he was the one who most resembled their father in both looks and temperament.

'I hated the boats.'

'Not good enough for you?' William sneered.

Isobel saw the muscles at the side of Thomas's jaw clench. 'I wish you wouldn't argue,' she said. 'You are all only home for the week. Let's make the most of it without fighting.'

'Aye, William, leave Thomas alone. He's doing what he thinks is right. And he's been wounded for it,' Twi added her plea.

'Big hero,' retorted William furiously. 'Do you think we can't be hurt, doing what we're doing?'

'Alright, that's enough. Let's not all fall out,' Thomas interrupted. 'I knew Father wouldn't like it when I left, but he gave me no choice. I'm sorry if he made life difficult for you afterwards.'

'It wasn't that bad really,' Twi reassured him. 'He was just a bit quick-tempered, that's all.'

'Aye,' added William bitterly. 'Just like normal.'

'Just like normal,' Hugh echoed his brother's words then added, 'You know, Tammy, I've been thinking . . .'

'Careful, Hugh, you don't want to overdo it,' Twi teased wickedly, restoring the atmosphere somewhat.

'What were you saying, Hugh?' Thomas encouraged him.

'Well . . .' he began. 'I was wondering if I should join the army, too.'

'You!' Thomas's face distorted with horror. 'But you're a fisherman, Hugh. You love the sea.'

'No, Hugh, no. You wouldn't like the army,' Isobel shouted in a rare display of emotion. It was bad enough having her beloved Thomas serving in Africa without having Hugh so far away, too.

'I've been thinking I might just join up,' Hugh continued.

'No.' It was snapped, final and absolute. All four looked at Thomas in surprise.

'But you did it, Tammy,' Hugh challenged softly.

'Aye. And I know what it's like over there. And I'm telling you not to do it. They wouldn't let you, anyway. You're needed on the boats. You can't transfer now.'

'Is it that bad?' Hugh asked.

'Aye. And no-one in their right mind would volunteer for it. Not if they could see what it was like first. Most lads don't get the chance. They have to join up. You don't. Stay here with the boats, Hugh. Stay with the boats.'

Isobel had a tight knot of fear in her heart. For a moment his face had mirrored all the fear and tragedy of the past year. 'What's it like, Tammy?' she whispered, half afraid to know.

'Like? I can't explain. And if I could I wouldn't,' he said gruffly. Then the ready smile flashed back into place. 'I don't want to talk about it. For the rest of the week I want to relax and forget about the war.' As if to make his point he ran off along the beach, leaving them to follow.

'I've got an idea,' he said five minutes later, throwing himself down into the fine sand. 'That's why I wanted us to have this walk together.'

They gathered round him, listening eagerly. Isobel produced her ever-present sketch pad and started to draw a rough portrait of him as he spoke.

'There's a dance on Saturday night. St Andrews. We could all go. To celebrate being together again.'

'What about your leg?' Twi asked doubtfully.

'Och, it's nothing and it's almost better anyway. Well?' he demanded.

'What dance is it?' asked Twi.

'He means the one the RAF boys at Leuchars and the Poles up there with them give every month. They say it's great,' Hugh supplied the answer.

'Good, that's settled then.' Thomas flicked his cigarette away casually.

'Please, keep still, Tammy,' pleaded Isobel, bending to her sketch and working with deep concentration for a few seconds before speaking again. 'I don't think Twi and I will be able to come. Father'll never let us go to a dance.'

'No, but there's nothing to stop us going.' William had no intention of allowing his sisters to ruin a good night out.

'We'll all go. I'll sort it out with Father,' Thomas promised, a glint of anticipation in his eyes.

'We still couldn't go,' insisted Twi, a hint of sullenness in her voice.

'Don't tell me you've nothing to wear,' teased Thomas.

'That's true, too,' giggled Isobel, then added quickly. 'But we'd manage something. The truth is, we've no money. We can't afford the bus fare to St Andrews, never mind the price of a ticket to the dance.'

'No money?' Thomas yelled. 'No money? But you're both working. Surely you have a wee bit to spare?'

'Father takes our wage packets. We're not even allowed to open them,' Twi explained in a humiliated whisper.

For a moment Thomas stared at her, openly amazed before he exploded, 'That's ridiculous! You're entitled to your own money. Does he take all of it?'

'All of it,' Twi nodded. Despite the fact that both girls worked a six-day week. Twi on a local farm and Isobel in a village haberdashery, each meekly handed her unopened pay packet to their father on a Friday night.

'But what if you need to buy something?'

'Then we ask.'

'For everything?' Thomas's voice rose a note.

'Everything. And when he does allow us to buy something we have to show him a receipt and give him the change.' Isobel refused to admit to humiliation but her complexion reddened.

'But that's not right. You should at least have some money of your own. And what's he doing with all the extra cash? He can't be spending it. He's worse dressed than you two and he doesn't smoke, or drink, or anything.'

'Isobel already asked him about it. Told him we should

49

have something for ourselves each week,' Twi smiled at her twin.

'And?' demanded Thomas.

'He slapped me.' She met Thomas's appalled eyes squarely.

'At your age?'

'At my age.'

'Don't sound so surprised,' yelled William, storming to his feet in a flurry of blown sand. 'It's not that long since he was taking his belt to you. We all know that's why you joined up.'

Unable to deny the obvious truth of the statement Thomas nodded, 'Aye, you're right enough.'

The five lapsed into strained silence, uncomfortable at the exposure of so much ill feeling.

Isobel shivered and stood up, feeling the evening was ruined. 'We'd best be getting home. There's a cool wind blowing up.' She wrapped her cardigan more closely round her shoulders. 'Anyway, Tammy, thanks for trying but Twi and I won't be going to the dance.'

'Oh aye you will.' And he too was on his feet, towering over her, daring her to contradict him. 'You leave Father to me. And if he really is too mean to let you have some money, I'll pay for you both.'

None of them ever knew for sure what took place between Malcolm McLean and his eldest son but the atmosphere in the small house was so tense for the next three days that the twins assumed the worst. But, on the Friday night, there was a soft knock on their bedroom door.

'It's just to tell you,' Thomas beamed, 'that you can fix your best frocks and do up your hair. Saturday night we're all going dancing.'

'Oh, Tammy.' To his intense embarrassment, Twi threw herself at him.

'How did you manage that?' demanded Isobel, tossing aside her sketchpad.

'It doesn't matter how I did it,' he chuckled. 'But look at this.'

He held his hands out, palms upwards, offering the contents of each hand to a twin.

'My God!' spluttered Twi, earning a look of rebuke from her brother. Then she took the five pound note and shoved it quickly into her handbag. 'Thanks, Tammy. I've never had this much money in my life.'

Isobel was still looking at the money, but doubtfully. 'This money, Tammy,' she asked. 'Is it from father or from you?'

'It is yours, Hen. Just a part of what he should have been giving you. And he'll give you something for yourself every week from now on.'

'You laddies get these lassies back here by nine-thirty at the latest,' Malcolm roared as they prepared to leave. 'And no talking to strange men. And only dance with your brothers.' He stabbed a warning finger at the girls.

Thomas raised one eyebrow and winked blatantly at Twi who quickly swallowed the protest which sprang to her newly lipsticked lips.

'We'll be back about half past eleven. The bus gets in around then. There's no another one so we can't come home any earlier,' Thomas said in a voice full of authority. 'And of course we'll look after the lassies. But you could trust them anyway, Father, even without us there.'

Isobel held her breath, expecting the usual flash of temper, but to everyone's astonishment Malcolm only grunted and took up his bible.

'Good night, Father,' they chorused.

'Don't bother to wait up. We'll make no noise when we come in,' Thomas called as they closed the door.

The bus was late but then, thought Thomas, when had it

ever been anything else? But, unhampered by blackout regulations on this clear, summer night, it eventually covered the winding miles to St Andrews in good time.

'Is this the place?' Isobel exclaimed, surveying the ramshackle hall in disbelief.

'Aye,' Thomas chuckled. 'This is the place.' His words were confirmed by the number of young people who were pushing through the lopsided doors, many of the men in the uniform of the RAF, or their Polish counterparts. As far as Isobel could tell, Thomas was the only soldier there. He bought their ticket and ushered them inside, naturally assuming the role of leader.

Isobel was proud to be seen with him. He looked so very smart. Tall, straight-backed and with a suggestion of humour playing around his mouth. Even his eyes were clear and unshadowed tonight. Unlike Hugh and William he had escaped their father's brilliant red hair. Instead he had a luxuriant head of deep auburn waves. Isobel noticed two girls giggling and preening in a very obvious attempt to catch his attention and smiled to herself as he, just as obviously, ignored them.

Inside, the hall was packed. A four-piece, uniformed band played popular dance numbers, mostly borrowed from Glenn Miller, and the floor was already crowded with dancers.

Despite the handicap of clothing coupons everyone looked smart and attractive. Twi, vibrant and exciting in a renovated green print dress, her much repaired, only pair of shoes and least darned stockings, chattered nervously. Within minutes she was dancing with Robbie McArdle.

Robbie was a local boy, two years older than Twi and eldest son in the latest generation of Kilweem's largest, most rambling family. Isobel knew Twi was sweet on Robbie, and he on her. But their father's repressive rules had limited their meetings to the occasional stolen lunch-time and by Robbie contriving to spend an extraordinary amount of time loitering on the quayside. This was the very first time they had been able to spend more than an hour together.

Although Isobel recognised many people she made no attempt to join them, sensing she would not be welcome. The passing years had done little to ease her uncomfortable position in the tight-knit community. Her continuing fainting spells made her an easy target for the superstitious and the spiteful alike.

'You go and join your friends,' she said to Hugh who had remained loyally at her side. 'I'll chat to some of the girls.'

'Are you sure?' he hesitated, then persuaded by her none-too-gentle shove, joined a group of old friends.

Feeling conspicuously alone but determined not to show it, she made for a row of hard chairs that lined one wall. She sat on one, the proud tilt to her head giving no hint of her discomfort, determined to at least give herself the pleasure of watching the dancing and enjoying the music.

The crush was so great that people constantly brushed against her. She ignored them. When a resonant male voice spoke near her she automatically assumed it was aimed at someone else.

'I said,' it repeated, more loudly this time, 'would you like to dance or have you got a wooden leg that keeps you glued to that chair?'

Slowly she turned her head and was greeted by a display of the whitest teeth she had ever seen.

'Oh good. You are alive then?' The teeth multiplied into a broad smile. 'Well,' they demanded. 'Will you dance or won't you dance?'

Now she saw that the teeth were framed by a perfectly pleasant face atop a body in RAF uniform. He stepped aside, bowed comically low, then took her unresisting hand and dragged her onto the dance floor.

'You are far too lovely to be sitting on your own,' he said.

Despite herself, she giggled.

'That's more like it,' he nodded approvingly. 'I'm Michael

Rawlings. Stationed here for the duration.' When she merely smiled, offering no reciprocal information he felt obliged to go on. 'Got shot down over France. Lucky to make it back. Picked up some injuries on the way, though, so I'm likely to stay here now until it's all over. Desk-bound,' he added in disgust, making an episode of outstanding courage sound like a slight inconvenience.

Isobel looked at him with more interest, meeting his steady eyes for the first time. 'My name is Isobel McLean,' she offered softly. 'I stay in Kilweem. On the coast. I'm here with my three brothers and twin sister,' she rushed on, anxious to let him know that she wasn't as alone as she had looked.

'Twin? You mean there's another girl as beautiful as you in this room?' he asked, looking round quickly.

'No,' she flushed and laughed. 'I mean, we're not identical. Most folk say they wouldn't even take us for sisters. Look, that's her, dancing with the boy over there. She's wearing the green dress.'

'The red-head?'

'Yes.'

'My, you certainly are a good-looking family,' he quipped appreciatively. Later he bought her a drink and introduced her to some of his colleagues. Suddenly she found herself inundated with potential partners. She grinned at Thomas's mock horror as she passed him with her third partner in as many dances. Then Michael reclaimed her and after that, time passed so quickly that, before she knew it, it was time to go home. Already the crowd was thinning out.

'I'd like to see you again, Isobel,' Michael said as they danced for the last time.

'I don't know,' she admitted. 'My Father is very strict. He wouldn't approve. And it's difficult for me to come to St Andrews.'

'Then I'll come to Kilweem,' he offered, keeping a proprietorial arm round her shoulders.

Her heart sang. He really was very attractive. But surely

it was impossible? She shook her head sadly. 'He would never allow me to meet a man.'

'Perhaps, if I introduced myself to your brothers,' he suggested. 'Maybe they could help persuade him?'

Her smile lit her whole face. 'Yes. Thomas, my oldest brother, it was him who talked Father into letting us come here tonight.'

Tired but happy Isobel found her brothers and sister near the door and introduced Michael. Only Thomas was missing.

'Here he is at last,' said William, impatient to be off.

Smiling and still flushed with enjoyment, Isobel turned to watch Thomas as he strode across the floor.

But there must be something wrong with the lights. Why were they flashing like that? And the floor! It was undulating and shimmering. And why was she standing in the middle of a vast expanse of white sand with a blistering sun beating on her head? And it was so quiet. An eerie, breathless silence which was quite wrong. The strange flashes of light in the sky made her feel lightheaded and the pungent heavy smell of burning brought sudden nausea. But Thomas was still there, coming towards her, his face blackened and grim, his uniform torn and filthy. And for some reason he had his helmet on.

She smiled and tried to go to meet him, but her feet wouldn't work. So she waited, smiling as he got nearer. He was taking so long, as if he was walking in slow motion. She wanted to yell at him to hurry up and meet Michael but, as she opened her mouth to shout, a brilliant flash surrounded him, silhouetting him for a second before engulfing him in white, blinding light and swirling sand. She blinked, raised a hand to shield her eyes and felt the blast of heat on her skin. When she looked again it was dark, like dusk, and Thomas was falling away from her, a slightly surprised expression on his face. And he went on falling, spiralling away into the dark hole that had opened at her feet, tumbling into never-ending blackness until he was no larger than a pin prick.

And then there was nothing at all.

'Wake up, Isobel. It's all right now.' Thomas leant over her protectively but behind him, even through her half-closed lids, she could see the avid, inquisitive faces. And there, face ashen with disgust, was Michael. As her eyes focused on him he turned and barged away into the crowd. She knew she would never see him again.

'I'll help you to your feet. You'll feel better in the fresh air.' Thomas on one side and Hugh on the other, they lifted her bodily and hurried outside, anxious to protect her from the suspicious faces and whispered speculations. Desperate to disassociate himself with the shaming scene William had long since fled.

As soon as she felt able they propelled her onto the bus and guided her to a seat at the back. There was a sudden hush and calculating eyes followed her.

She had no memory of the journey home, or of going to bed but she woke, hours later, with a splitting headache and complete, devastating recall of that nightmarish vision. No matter how hard she tried she couldn't control the trembling which shook the whole bed with its violence.

'What's wrong? Are you not well?' Twi shot upright in alarm and threw back the curtain so the moon's gentle light could illuminate the room. 'Answer me, Isobel. What's wrong?' she demanded impatiently, far from her best in the middle of the night.

'Nothing . . . go back to sleep,' Isobel stammered.

'Was it another of your funny turns? Did you see something awful?' Twi was used to her sister's strange fits which were usually nothing more than an embarrassing faint. Only rarely had Isobel admitted to seeing something beyond the range of normality.

'No,' Isobel snapped, still too shocked to want to talk.

'Don't snap at me,' Twi retorted. 'You'd be better with an apology after what you did last night.'

Isobel raised haunted eyes, dreading what she might, unwittingly, have said.

'I don't suppose Robbie'll ever want to see me again. How could you? Lying there twitching and moaning, like something not right in the head. After me telling him it was all rubbish what they say about you.' Then she was sobbing. 'He'll never want to see me again and it's all your fault, Isobel McLean.' With that she turned on her side and buried her face in the pillow.

Isobel dragged herself out of bed and wrapped an old coat round her. Still shaking uncontrollably she slumped in the room's only chair. She stayed there, drifting between full, anguished wakefulness and horrific dreams until dawn sent rays of bright light into the room, waking both girls at the same time. Cramped and stiff, Isobel stirred then paled as memory raced back. In the bed, Twi felt a surge of guilt when she recalled her own angry words. Gathering a blanket round her she stumbled to her sister.

'I'm sorry, Isobel,' she offered at once. 'I shouldn't have said what I did.'

Isobel attempted a weak smile and failed. 'It's alright. I understand. I know I embarrass you and the boys,' she said tonelessly.

'No you don't. I was just being spiteful. I know you can't help it.' Twi smiled as brightly as she could in an effort to make up for her harsh words, but Isobel didn't respond and sat rigidly in the chair, staring sightlessly in front of her. Her appearance, so pale and bloodless, almost transparent, frightened Twi. 'Come on, find your clothes and get some food inside you. You'll feel better then.'

'I'm not hungry,' Isobel snapped suddenly. 'Just leave me alone. Please.'

Twi flushed angrily but then, realising how out of character that outburst had been, knelt in front of her sister, took Isobel's cold hands into her own warm ones and buffed them gently. 'What did you see last night?' she asked. 'You did see something, didn't you?'

'Yes.' The voice was dull, flat, the blue eyes distant and devoid of hope.

'Then tell me,' Twi begged.

'No . . . Oh no . . .' Isobel sobbed, turning her face away. 'Dear God, no.'

'For goodness sake, Isobel! You're going to make yourself ill. Tell me what's wrong . . . please.'

Slowly Isobel pushed Twi away and struggled to her feet. 'I don't know what it was. I don't understand it myself,' she lied. 'It was just . . .' her voice faltered. 'It was just a feeling. Awful . . . A nightmare. Nothing more.'

Twi eyed her doubtfully. Isobel had never been so badly affected by any of her previous turns. 'Are you sure that is all it was?'

Isobel stared out over the harbour, indecently still and peaceful at this early hour on a Sunday. What she had seen was what would happen. She understood that much. There was nothing she could do or say to alter what was already written for the future. But how could she face her family, Thomas himself, and pretend that everything was normal, that she expected to see him alive again? But that was exactly what she must do. This burden was hers alone, and not for sharing.

Swallowing hard she forced herself to face her worried sister. 'That's all it was, Twi. A dream. Just a stupid dream. I can't even remember what it was all about.'

After breakfast on Monday, Thomas left to rejoin his regiment. Grinning cheerfuly, totally recovered from his injury and, in his heart, glad to be leaving this uncomfortable little house and his father's unrelenting disapproval, he kept his farewells brief. The boys, also due to leave within twenty-four hours, got a firm handshake while the girls were treated to a peck on the cheek.

'Be good,' he said, winking at Twi. 'Keep away from those McArdles.'

She coloured and grinned back, knowing he was only teasing.

'And you,' he faced Isobel cheerfully. 'No running away with those Air Force fellas. There's better than them for you.' He stopped, his smile fading as he saw her bleak expression, the bleached skin and darkly shadowed eyes.

'Isobel, are you alright?' he asked, recalling how withdrawn she had seemed since that unfortunate incident on Saturday night.

The distant stare sharpened suddenly and she focused on his face. 'Please, Tammy, don't go back. Stay here. Please,' she pleaded with him passionately, gripping his arms so fiercely it hurt.

'But you know I can't do that. I have to go back. I'll be named a deserter otherwise.'

'That wouldn't matter. You could hide. Anywhere. Please.' Desperation glittered in her eyes, brought the cold sweat of dread under her arms, down her back.

'No, Isobel. You're being stupid.' He spoke, sternly, ignoring the sudden wrench of fear in his own gut.

'Please, Tammy. Don't go back. Please . . . Please!' Her voice rose to the edge of hysteria and she clung to him.

'Come on, lass. He'll be back in no time at all.' Hugh drew her firmly aside and she stood stiffly inside the restraining circle of his arms.

'Get a grip on yourself, Isobel. Nobody wants to look at that miserable face at this time of the morning,' William threw her a disgusted look.

'That's just like us, eh?' Thomas forced a laugh, more disturbed by his sister's strange behaviour than he cared to admit. 'Always arguing. I think that's what I miss most.' Slinging his kitbag over his shoulder he turned at last to his father who was watching from the doorway in silence.

'Goodbye, Father. I hope it'll not be long before I see you again.' He offered his hand. The older man ignored it.

'Maybe you'll have learned some respect by the time you come back,' was Malcolm's harsh comment. 'And leave your Englishified ideas behind the next time, and all.' With that he turned and shambled into the house. Thomas's last view of his father was of him settling into the old, wooden chair, the bible already on his knee.

Thomas stared, the pulse in his neck throbbing, then, with a final grin at his siblings, set off along the quayside, jumping nimbly over lobster pots and crates but not looking back before turning the corner and disappearing from sight.

Isobel lingered outside long after the others had gone indoors. It seemed to her as if she was in some sort of trance, as if nothing was real any more and she was just a spectator to everyone else's life.

It stayed like that for almost six months. When it finally came, as she knew it must, it was a relief.

She knew, as soon as she came home that night. Twi was sobbing in great, heaving spasms and rushed upstairs as soon as Isobel came in. Her father sat rigidly in his chair, his lips moving unnaturally fast as he desperately sought comfort, or oblivion, in the great book.

'Thomas?' she whispered, knowing the answer before she spoke.

'Aye.' Malcolm handed her the impersonal letter which informed him that Thomas had been killed in action, then went back to his bible. He seemed to have no need of her so she went slowly to the bedroom. Twi was huddled on the bed but when she saw her sister she got up, dried her eyes and threw her coat over her shoulders.

'I think I'll go for a wee walk,' she said coldly, leaving Isobel to stare out over the bleak harbour alone. On the windowsill was the pencil sketch she had made of Thomas that night on the beach. A laughing, animated face, an incomplete, unsatisfying sketch which was all she had left of him. She clutched it to her chest and sobbed.

It was two long hours before Twi came back. She took off her coat, changed her shoes, powdered her red nose and did half a dozen other small things, all without a single glance in Isobel's direction.

'You were out for a long time,' Isobel said, trying to break the unbearable silence. 'I was worried about you. It's too cold for walking.'

'You knew.' It was a bleak accusation. Twi spun round to face her twin with a strange, hostile expression.

Isobel blanched, startled by the cold, hard words. 'Yes.' She could no longer deny the truth.

'When you made all that fuss . . . when Tammy went back . . . I wondered then. But I didn't want to believe it.'

The girls faced each other across the room. They might have been strangers. The few feet which separated them were long, icy miles.

'I didn't want to believe it either. But I knew it was going to happen. I saw it all,' Isobel went on, her voice little more than a hoarse whisper.

'Oh God!' screamed Twi. 'Why didn't you stop him? You didn't have to let him walk away and get killed. You should have stopped him.' Tears streamed down her face.

'I tried.' Isobel choked on the words. 'He wouldn't listen. You heard me. I begged him not to go. But he wouldn't listen . . .'

'You should have stopped him. Made him stay.'

'Don't you understand? There wasn't anything I could do. I can't change things. I see what's going to happen but I can't do anything to stop it. Nothing at all.'

'But you've known. All this time,' Twi said bitterly.

'Don't say it like that . . . as if it was my fault he died.'

'I didn't say that. But you should have warned him.'

'How do you think I felt? Knowing I would never see him again . . . knowing there was nothing I could do to change it? And how could I tell you what I knew? Have you any idea what the last six months have been like for me? Waiting, knowing he was never coming home. Would you have wanted to share that knowledge with me? Would you?' she challenged her appalled twin.

Twi stared as if she was seeing Isobel for the first time. 'I never really understood about you before,' she whispered, at last.

'It's a curse,' Isobel said flatly. 'I would do anything to be rid of it. Anything. I wish I had never been born. Better it had died with Granny Guthrie.' And she turned away with such a depth of despair on her face that Twi was frightened for her.

But something bitter and unforgiving prevented her from trying to comfort her sister now.

FIVE

As soon as the evening meal was over the boys – back to being fishermen now that the war was finally over – took themselves off to the Lobster anxious, as always, to spend as much time as possible away from their increasingly morose and irritable father. The girls hurried through their chores and retired to their room.

Isobel had seen at once that Twi was bursting with excitement. As soon as the door was closed she rounded on her.

'Come on. Out with it. I can see you're dying to tell me something.'

Twi blushed, grinned, then burst out, 'Robbie's thinking of leaving the fishing.'

'But he's always been on the boats.'

'Aye. But he doesn't like it that much. He only started because his father and brothers were all there before him. And anyway, there's no future on the boats now.'

The post-war years were bringing little reward to the fishermen, many of whom had lost their boats in the war. Few had the money necessary to make repairs or buy new craft. All along the coast of Strathannan, families who had been fishermen for generations were drifting away to find employment in the coalfields, or even in factories.

'So, what's Robbie going to do?' Isobel asked.

'Well, his cousin – you know, Iain? – he works up at Waddle's farm at Backmuir. Old Waddle's looking for another hand. He's told Robbie he can have the job if he wants it.'

'Oh,' Isobel was beginning to suspect what was coming next.

'Is that all you can say?'

'I was just wondering about the pay. I've heard that some of these farmhands don't get much of a wage.'

'I don't care about money. It's safer than fishing.'

'And?'

'And?'

'And there must be more,' Isobel chuckled.

'There's a cottage goes with the job. Robbie says its braw. Two bedrooms. And an inside toilet.' To Twi's mind that was the ultimate luxury. 'Oh, and Robbie's cousin, Iain, has the cottage right next door.'

'Sounds lovely.'

'Robbie's right keen.'

'For goodness sake, Twi, hurry up,' Isobel prompted, thoroughly impatient now.

'And he says that if I promise to marry him, he'll take it,' she ended on an excited squeak. 'I said I would.'

'That's wonderful!' Isobel flew at her sister and grabbed her in a suffocating bear hug. 'I'm really happy for you. Robbie's lovely. I know you'll be happy.'

'You know?' asked Twi, raising her eyebrows and disengaging herself rather roughly. 'Come to think of it you don't seem very surprised. You didn't have one of your funny turns about this, did you? Did you already know about Robbie and me?' The excitement died in her eyes and Isobel recognised the all-too-familiar wariness there again.

'No, Twi,' she reassured her, sighing softly. 'But I guessed. You have been seeing a lot of one another. And you were so excited this evening.'

'Aye. I suppose so,' Twi conceded, still with a hint of suspicion.

'Honestly.'

'I believe you. I'm sorry I asked,' Twi snapped.

'Have you told Father?'

'Not yet.' Twi frowned. 'Robbie's coming to tea on Sunday. He'll ask him then.'

*

Robert McArdle knocked hesitantly on the McLeans' front door at Sunday teatime and was invited in by William, who gave him a rather lewd wink. Robbie fiddled nervously with his stiff collar.

'Come along in, Robbie. You're in fine time for tea.' Twi rushed to his side. 'You look grand,' she whispered. 'I've never seen you in a suit before.'

'No. And you'll only see me wearing it one more time. When we get married. It's right uncomfortable.'

'Don't stand there whispering like a pair of five-year-olds,' Malcolm yelled from his chair at the fireside.

Straightening his back, pulling himself to his full five feet seven inches, Robbie strode over to face his prospective father-in-law.

He knew, the whole village knew, what a strange, violent-tempered and reclusive man Malcolm McLean had become. In fact the McLeans were generally considered to be a very peculiar family. Isobel's fainting fits still set her apart from the other girls in the village and it was widely believed that she could see the future, like Granny Guthrie. Robbie's mother, who was deeply superstitious, was violently opposed to having a McLean for a daughter-in-law. But Robbie was determined.

'Good evening, Mister McLean.' Robbie offered his hand, then didn't know what to do with it when Malcolm steadfastly ignored it.

'Well, Robert McArdle. Sniffing round after Twi are you?' was his crude response. Still ignoring the flagging hand he dragged himself out of his chair and took his place at the wooden table.

'What's this?' he demanded, fingering the cloth which covered the scarred wood.

'It's a tablecloth, Father, and well you know it,' snapped Isobel, furious with him.

'So I see. But what's it doing on our good table?'

'To make it look nice. For our guest,' she hissed at him while Twi tried to distract Robbie's attention.

'Oh, I see! It's good enough for us to eat off the bare wood on any other day but because Mister McArdle is here you expect me to eat off something that looks like a woman's petticoat! Well,' he thumped the table making the plates rattle. 'I'll not have it. This is the Sabbath and we'll take our food good and plain, like any other day.'

'Father . . .' started Twi, flushing an angry scarlet.

'No,' whispered Robbie. 'Do what he wants. It makes no difference to me.'

'Take it off,' insisted Malcolm, tugging dangerously at the edge of the cloth.

Silently the girls relaid the table while their brothers watched, squirming with shame.

'Hurry up, will you.' Malcolm banged the table impatiently.

They had made a special effort, serving the inevitable fish, but made into a pie with potatoes, carrot and turnip, followed by a steamed pudding, a rare luxury in these days of continuing rationing. It was ruined by a lengthy grace, droned out by Malcolm, which allowed the food to cool unappetisingly. They ate in the total silence he demanded.

As soon as the meal was over William and Hugh disappeared and Isobel took herself upstairs, leaving the young couple alone with Malcolm. He retreated to his chair and took up the bible, hunching over it with such an expression of forbidding concentration that Twi faltered.

'Maybe we'd best leave it. He's not in a very good mood tonight,' she suggested, close to tears.

'No. I'm going to ask him. He knows why I'm here. He's just trying to make it as difficult as possible. But it'll not work with me. I'm not frightened of him.' Robbie's brave words were belied by his sweating palms and hammering heart.

'Daddy? Robbie wants to have a wee word with you.'

'Not now. Can you not see I'm reading the good book? If you were anything near decent you'd be doing the same,' Malcolm growled.

'We'll go for a wee walk and come back later, then, when you are ready to talk to us.' It was a rare show of determination from Robbie who would normally go to some lengths to avoid any sort of confrontation. Mild-tempered and soft-hearted he hated discord, but knew that if he didn't stand up to Malcolm now he would lose Twi's respect.

'I'll be at this all night. Like I am every night.' Malcolm didn't even raise his eyes from the text.

'In that case I might as well say what I've come to say now.' Robbie stepped closer, making it plain that he wasn't going to be defeated. In that moment Twi loved him so much that she would gladly have died for him.

'I told you. Not now,' Malcolm hollered.

'It'll only take a minute,' Robbie insisted, forcing his reluctant body to stay where it was.

'It seems I'll get no peace until you've had your say,' Malcolm relented at last.

'Twi and I want to get married. I've come to ask your permission.' Robbie came straight to the point, anxious to get this ordeal behind him.

'Oh you have, have you?' Malcolm sneered. 'And what makes you think you're good enough for her?'

Twi gasped.

'The McArdles are as good as the McLeans, any day,' Robbie bridled at once.

'Oh aye? If you're that good where are you going to live? Not here that's certain and there's no room with your own mother and father, not with all the brothers and sisters you've got.'

Robbie played his trump card. 'I've got a house all arranged.'

'Where? There's nothing in the village.'

'We're not planning on staying in Kilweem. I've got a job on Waddle's farm. And there's a braw wee house goes with it.'

'You're going to work as a farmhand?' Malcolm asked, genuinely astounded.

'Aye.' Robbie was defiant now. 'How can I be a fisherman now? My father's boat was drafted into the Merchant Navy for the war. She's still at Fleetwood. Ruined. It needs a small fortune to refit her. We can't afford that. Father'll have to sell her. No, there's no future for me in the fishing.' His voice was bitter but his wasn't the only family who had seen their livelihood destroyed by the government's lack of gratitude for their war effort. 'So, my cousin already works on the farm. He suggested me for the job. Waddle wants me to start next week so Twi and I want to be married as soon as we can.'

Astonishingly Malcolm seemed to lose interest. Very carefully and deliberately he fumbled with his bible until he found his place and started to read again.

'Do we have your permission, Mr McLean?' asked Robbie, his voice a shade louder than he had intended it to be.

'Permission? I su ̦pose so. Not that you need it. Do what you like.'

Tears of humiliation flooded Twi's eyes. 'Is that all you can say? Aren't you even going to wish us luck?'

'You'll make your own luck. And don't bother asking me to pay for your wedding. You want to get married so badly, you pay for it yourselves.'

Four weeks later, in a simple ceremony at Kilweem kirk, Twi became Mrs Robert McArdle. Inside, Robbie's vast and rambling family outnumbered and overwhelmed her own. But at least her father had put in an appearance. She had half expected him to stay at home, crouched over his bible.

As soon as the service was over and the photographs taken, by one of Robbie's seven brothers, they all piled into a hired bus for the journey up to Waddle's farm. There, in a disused barn heated by two braziers, long tables were set up, loaded with the most magnificent array of food Twi had ever seen.

'Congratulations,' Farmer and Mrs Waddle greeted the

newlyweds inside the doors. 'I hope you'll be very happy.' His weathered face was creased in delight as he claimed a kiss from the bride who was radiant in a dress loaned by yet another McArdle relative.

'Well then, take your places and we can start on the meal,' Mrs Waddle led them to their seats.

As she waited for the guests to settle down Twi stared in open amazement at the spread of food before them. After the austerity of the war years she was sure there could be nothing better on offer at Buckingham Palace itself.

'Look,' chuckled Robbie. 'Not a fish in sight.'

She giggled. 'I've never seen anything like it. And just look at the cake!' A magnificent, three-tiered edifice waited on a side table. 'How on earth did your Mammy manage all this?'

After Malcolm's adamant refusal to contribute, even to a present, Robbie's huge family had rallied round to provide the best feast in living memory, shamelessly resorting to the black market and willingly donating part of their scanty rations to start the young couple off in style.

Along the table from her sister, in her place as best maid, Isobel had the sour-faced minister on one side and an empty seat on the other, effectively isolating her. She looked out over the company and won an encouraging wink from Hugh. Across the table from him, William was deep in conversation with his girlfriend, Maggie Cameron. When he caught his sister's eye he glowered at her, reminding her frighteningly of their father. Of him there was no sign. But no-one had seriously expected Malcolm to put in an appearance at the reception. Isobel, for one, was glad he wasn't there to cast his grim shadow over the celebrations.

She ate her meal in silence, keenly aware of the fact that her position as best maid was resented by every McArdle there. Twi had fought long and hard for the right to have her own sister attend her, despite the open objection of the minister and the anger of Robbie's mother who had insisted that one of Robbie'e three sisters should have that honour.

But at last it was over and Iain, Robbie's best man, cousin and new neighbour, launched into a rambling, disjointed speech.

Isobel's attention wandered until her eye was caught by a stranger, a man she had never seen before, who sat at one of the tables furthest from the bridal party.

Only the top half of his body was visible but Isobel could see how he dwarfed his neighbours with his big-boned, well-muscled torso. His hands, clasped round his glass and completely engulfing it, were huge and red, the hands of a man accustomed to manual labour, but they were strangely at odds with his immaculate white shirt, dark tie and obviously expensive suit jacket. Completely unaware of how open her scrutiny was, Isobel allowed her eyes to settle on his face. His strong features, dominated by a large nose, a generous mouth and eyes which were pools of darkness under heavy brows, were impassive as he, like most of the other guests, stared dutifully at the speaker. Even from that distance Isobel got a picture of a man who cared little for the impression his appearance made on others, of a man with little vanity. His hair certainly conveyed a careless image, and brought a smile to her lips. It was longer than fashion dictated and was beginning to stick out in places, as though it had been tamed, with difficulty, for the occasion – like him. In all, she decided, he was far from handsome, but there was something . . . something almost magnetic about him.

Suddenly he turned and met her gaze, then smiled, not at all perturbed by her examination, displaying a flash of even, white teeth before winking wickedly with humorous, dark eyes.

Isobel felt the blood rush to her cheeks. Acute embarrassment dropped her gaze at last and she once more fastened her attention resolutely on the best man who was stumbling to the end of his speech. But only with the greatest of difficulty did she resist stealing another glace at this charismatic man.

The guests chinked their glasses enthusiastically as they toasted the bride and groom for the last time. The trestle tables were eagerly cleared away and a fiddler, a pianist, a trumpeter and an accordianist took their places at the far end of the barn. Despite this strange assortment of instruments they soon filled the place with lively music.

'Bride and groom. Bride and groom.' Composure regained, Isobel joined in the hand–clapping and shouting.

Looking self–conscious and uncomfortable in his smart suit, Robbie pantomimed a bow and offered his arm to Twi who blushed furiously and allowed herself to be led onto the floor, still littered with hay.

Fortunately for them the makeshift band changed their tempo to approximate with the rhythm of a waltz and the young couple managed a creditable performance as they opened the dancing. When they had circled the floor a couple of times to shouts of encouragement from Robbie's younger, male relations, Isobel was surprised to find Iain at her side, offering his arm.

'The best maid and the best man always dance next. It's the custom,' he informed her, wondering if this very lovely girl could really be as weird as people said she was. 'I'm not much of a dancer mind, but I believe I could manage to get round the floor without falling on my face.'

By now several people were looking at them expectantly. Knowing there was no way to get out of this, Isobel smiled softly and took his arm.

'Go on, Isobel. Iain'll not eat you. But no fainting, like you did that time at St Andrews.' Janet McArdle, Iain's wife, had seen the admiration in her husband's eyes and called out spitefully, completely ruining the moment for Isobel.

In fact they made a very attractive couple. Smartly suited and craggily good looking, with the same dark colouring as Robbie, Iain made the perfect foil for Isobel's pale, pink loveliness. As she glided around the rough floor, following Iain's gentle lead, her soft pink dress – also borrowed from a McArdle – floated with her movements making her seem ethereally beautiful. The faint blush that stained her cheeks again when she passed close to the strange young man and saw him watching her, only enhanced that beauty.

'I never realised just how lovely Isobel really is,' the bride exclaimed generously. 'Look, Robbie, doesn't she look wonderful.'

'Aye.' Even loving Twi as deeply as he did, Robbie could still appreciate the exquisite beauty of the mysterious girl who had the attention of so many of his guests. 'But,' he added gallantly, 'she's not a patch on you. She's too peely wally for my taste.'

All attention was drawn away from Isobel and Iain as the bride and groom kissed, deeply, proudly, right there in the centre of the dance floor.

Taking advantage of the temporary halt to the dancing, Isobel plucked up the courage to ask Iain the question which was burning in her mind, striving to sound as casual as possible. 'Who's the man with Farmer Waddle?'

Iain glanced across the barn. 'Him? He's the manager of that big estate at Brighead. Name's James, I think . . . or John. He lent some of the tables.' Iain imparted this information easily enough, leaving Isobel little wiser, then whisked her off round the floor again as the dancing resumed.

At the far end of the barn James Dryburgh laughed and suspended his conversation with Farmer Waddle to turn his attention back to the fragile vision and her handsome partner.

'Who's the best maid?' he asked.

Waddle nodded. 'Aye, she's a beauty that one. And just as well. She'll need all her looks if she's to get a man of her own.'

Dryburgh raised a disbelieving eyebrow.

'She's young Twi's sister. Have you not heard about her?'

'I don't know any of the fishing families.'

'You know this one. You've heard of Granny Guthrie?'

'Everyone in Strathannan knows of Granny Guthrie.'

'Well, Twi and Isobel are her grandchildren. Those two are twins, though you'd never think it to look at them.' Waddle took a long draught of his beer.

James looked again at the bride and her sister. The difference was incredible. Twi was attractive enough in a sturdy, fresh-faced way and looked ideally suited to farm life. But Isobel seemed too fine, too lovely for such mundane surroundings.

'According to the village folk, Isobel has inherited her Great-granny's ways,' Waddle went on. 'They say she sees the future.'

'And does she?'

'I couldn't rightly say. I only know what the wife says and she seems to think there's something in it. But I do believe what they used to say about Granny Guthrie.'

'They called her a witch,' James said, a frown marring his strong features.

'And they say the same about this one. Most people keep clear of her,' was Waddle's gruff reply.

Having no real liking for these well-lubricated affairs, James Dryburgh had intended to leave as soon as he decently could. Instead he found himself lingering, watching the young McLean girl intently. He soon saw that she had few friends, that some of the guests were openly hostile towards her. But, far from inspiring pity, her calm composure, the high, almost aristocratic tilt to her head and her refusal to let the animosity of the McArdles mar the occasion, demanded admiration.

'Can I fetch you a drink?' he found himself asking her, wondering what on earth had got into him. Friendly and relaxed with those he knew well James Dryburgh was reserved, even shy, with strangers. It certainly wasn't his way to accost strange females.

'Eh . . . no . . . no thank you.' His unexpected approach startled her, reviving her earlier embarrassment, turning even her ears pink.

73

'You look warm,' he said, only his eyes betraying the incipient laughter. 'I'll get some lemonade.' Ignoring her embryonic objection he shouldered his way through the crowd to the bar, towering over everyone.

When he brought her drink she could think of nothing to say which could conceivably be of interest to this disturbingly, illogically attractive man, but she relaxed fractionally when she saw he was content to stand and watch the dancers, laughing when someone missed a step or fell.

She felt his presence beside her, a mere twelve inches away, as an electric field which was drawing her into it.

The band swept into a noisy jangle which they announced as an eightsome reel.

'We might as well join in,' he said casually, taking her agreement for granted and fixing a firm hand round her bare upper arm to steer her into the centre of the floor.

When he took her hands in his strong, warm grip she felt as though they were burning. Every time the pattern of the dance brought him to her again he smiled into her eyes, making her heart sing and her mouth go dry with excitement. Too soon it was over and he was returning her, amid many interested glances, to her chosen spot against the wall.

She smiled up at him now, happy, relaxed and excited by the prospect of flirting gently with him. But he avoided her eyes, seemed absolutely disinterested in her. Isobel's heart fell with a painful lurch leaving a churning blackness in her chest. With scarcely another look at her he muttered a brief, formal word of thanks and strode purposefully away.

Angry and hurt at being so publicly discarded she glared at his back while he took his leave of the bride and groom. As he went through the wide doors he turned and briefly bowed his head at her, mockingly she thought, before finally disappearing into the night. She tossed her head and turned away to show she didn't care, masking her injured feelings with the indifference she had become so good at.

Isobel suddenly found she was very much in demand.

Girls who had never spoken to her appeared at her side as if they were her best friends.

'And what did James Dryburgh say to you, Isobel?' asked Janet McArdle, anxious for gossip to pass on to her cronies.

'Nothing,' Isobel retorted, seeing this false friendliness for what it really was.

'He must have said something,' Janet insisted.

'He asked if I wanted a drink and then asked me to dance, that's all.'

'What did he say when he was going?' Janet persisted avidly.

'Goodnight! What else would he say?' snapped Isobel, thoroughly irritated by now.

'Come on, Isobel. Time to give me a dance.' Hugh, who had witnessed the whole thing, rescued her swiftly. 'Well, you certainly put their noses out of joint,' he chuckled. 'James Dryburgh is quite a catch and he's never been known to dance with a local girl before. You'll be the envy of the village.'

'I doubt it,' she smiled thinly at him. 'He only danced with me because he felt sorry for me, standing on my own.'

But how she wished it had been otherwise.

With his mind full of the enchanting creature he had encountered at Twi and Robbie McArdle's wedding, James Dryburgh had difficulty concentrating on the road.

Never had he seen anyone so beautiful. Isobel McLean had an aura which separated her from her peers, reducing them all to sepia shadows by comparison. Her beauty, her dignity, her mystery entranced him. He remembered every small detail; the way her dark lashes curled onto her cheeks, hiding the gloriously blue eyes; the way the faint, pink blush blossomed on her skin; the astounding depth of those eyes when she did, finally, look at him; the fragile wonder of her slim, graceful neck and the shining, floating drift of golden hair.

75

But, she was little more than a child. The slender build of her body and her diminutive height – reaching barely to his shoulder – reminded him that she could be no more than twenty while he was already thirty. It was obscene for a man of his years to be thinking in such intense terms of such a young and obviously inexperienced girl. The good-humoured lines faded from his face. He had better take himself home and back to work, keep his mind occupied with other things, away from these errant thoughts, before he was tempted to pursue them.

SIX

*W*ithout Twi's tempestuous presence the Kilweem household was a miserable one. William, who was growing more and more like his father, seemed to think that Isobel was some kind of unpaid domestic servant. Malcolm himself seldom said more than three disapproving words at a time. Then Hugh, saving up to get married to May Rennie, a local girl, found himself a job at Rosyth dockyard, west along the Forth. He took lodgings in Dunfermline and only returned to Kilweem to visit his fiancée. Isobel missed him dreadfully.

Meanwhile, Twi was too busy with her new husand and his enormous family to spare many thoughts for her sister. It was early March before conscience prompted her to invite Isobel to the cottage.

She welcomed her sister with a proud sparkle in her eyes and dragged her hurriedly across the doorstep before her neighbour, Janet McArdle, could see her. None of the McArdles, apart from Robbie himself, bothered to hide their dislike of Isobel, which was another reason why Twi hadn't asked her sister here before now.

From the disparaging remarks William constantly made, Isobel had expected Twi's home to be primitive, but that was far from the case. It was a single-storey house, the last in a row of three and typical of its kind. The front door opened directly into the farmyard but there was a small vegetable plot and drying green at the back. Isobel duly admired the kitchen, which was far better equipped than her own and even boasted a brand new electric cooker in place of the erratic, black-leaded range which was the bane of

Isobel's life. The traditional double sink looked out over open farmland, a vast improvement over the tumbledown, outside toilet which was the uninspiring view from the Kilweem kitchen. And, of course, there was the inside bathroom.

'This is wonderful,' Isobel gasped with a rare touch of envy. 'And William said you didn't even have running water up here.'

'Och, take no notice of him. He's just jealous that Robbie and I managed to get a house. It'll be much more difficult for him and Maggie Cameron to find something in Kilweem. Come on, I'll show you the other rooms.'

Isobel followed her into a large, dark bedroom, furnished with a bed and a huge, ugly wardrobe. 'It's got a full-length mirror. Look.'

Isobel glanced fleetingly at her own reflection and felt the usual surge of disappointment. If only she was bigger and more vibrant-looking, like Twi, she might be able to find a husband of her own, she thought as Twi steered her into the sitting room. Marriage was her only escape route from Kilweem. But who, she thought angrily, would want to marry someone as odd as she was?

'Where's Robbie?' she asked, determinedly pulling her mind away from self-pity.

'Working. He doesn't get a lot of time off. They're busy ploughing the big field. After that the cows need to be milked. He won't be home until after eight tonight.'

Twi chattered on, describing her new life in minute detail until, at last, she ran out of things to say. 'I'd better get the tea on the go,' she said then.

'I'll help,' Isobel offered at once.

'No you won't. I daresay you spend your time running round after William and Father. So, while you're here, you're on holiday for the day. Sit still and make the most of it.'

Isobel complied willingly enough and settled comfortably back in the soft chair in front of a blazing fire, feeling happy and relaxed. But, as Twi turned to go, Isobel tensed in horror as she recognised the familiar, dreaded sense of lightheadedness which always preceded one of her attacks. Desperately trying to fend it off she clenched her fists and closed her eyes. Every time this happened she had a glimpse of some awful tragedy. She couldn't bear the thought that something dreadful was in store for Twi.

But, instead of the usual feeling of confusion and the dislocation of her senses, Isobel knew precisely where she was and what was happening. And, above all, she felt a powerful surge of joy.

When Twi came back into the room she was smiling softly, although she didn't appear to be aware of Isobel. Instead she went to Robbie who was now standing by the fire and handed him a shawl-wrapped bundle. From where she sat Isobel could just see two tiny, blue-booteed feet, a hint of dark hair under the knitted bonnet and smell the distinctive baby scent of warm milk and damp skin.

'No, Isobel! Not here! Wake up! Do you hear me? Wake up, Isobel.'

Isobel opened her eyes and looked straight into her sister's angry face. 'I'm alright.' She pushed Twi aside and struggled to sit upright.

'You nearly fell out of the chair,' Twi admonished. 'It was one of your turns, wasn't it? Oh, Isobel, why do you have to be like this? What was it about? Tell me . . . Was it about me . . .? About Robbie?'

'No . . .' Isobel sounded hesitant.

'It was! Tell me, Isobel. Please.'

'Don't get upset. It's nothing awful. Honestly.' Feeling much better than she normally did after one of these attacks, Isobel leaned forward to comfort her sister, but Twi backed away.

'You're just saying that,' she screamed. 'It's Robbie. I know it is. Something terrible . . . you're just not telling me.'

Isobel recognised real fear in Twi's face. 'It was about you and Robbie,' she admitted reluctantly, 'but it was good. Please believe me.'

'How can I? After what happened with Thomas?' Twi was verging on hysteria now.

Dismayed, Isobel realised there was only one thing she could do now. 'If I tell you, will you promise not to tell anyone I told you. Not even Robbie?'

'Yes,' Twi agreed, still shaking.

'Sit down then. This could come as a shock.' Now Isobel was in charge. She shoved her distraught sister into a chair and, kneeling in front of her, took Twi's hands in hers. 'This is personal. Between you and Robbie. I hope you won't be too upset about me knowing,' she began, wondering if Twi would guess.

'Stop talking in riddles, Isobel McLean, and tell me what you mean.' Twi was fretting with impatience.

'I saw you and Robbie.'

'Where?'

'Here. And you had a wee baby. Your baby.'

'My baby?' Twi paled and gaped at her sister.

'Yes. So you see, it was good news.'

'I'm not even a fortnight late yet,' Twi whispered. She stood up and wandered to the window, then abruptly rounded on Isobel. 'My God,' she screamed. 'What sort of person are you? How do you know these things? It's not right . . . It's . . . it's unnatural. And what gives you the right to spy into my life? What else did you see? What else do you know about Robbie and me?'

'No . . . Twi, please. It's not like that. You know it's not.'

'So, it's true! You are a witch!' The scornful, hostile voice made them both jump.

'What are you doing here, Janet?' Twi demanded furiously.

'I heard you shouting and yelling. I came to make sure you were alright.' Janet McArdle kept her cold, pale eyes on Isobel.

'You should have knocked. You've no right to walk into my house. That was a private conversation,' Twi stormed.

'Private? The whole world could hear you two screaming at each other. So, you're in the family way, eh? And what a way to find out.'

'It's none of your business, Janet, so don't go repeating what you heard,' Twi warned.

'I'll have to tell the family.' Janet's thin face twisted with malicious delight.

'I'll tell them myself. After I've told Robbie.'

'Be quick about it, then, because I'm going to tell everyone exactly how you found out. I think they're entitled to know what a weird family you come from.' Janet grinned her delight. 'Don't you?' she asked as she turned on her heels and stalked out in triumph.

'Oh, Isobel,' Twi sighed. 'What have you done? Why couldn't you be a normal sister? You're nothing but trouble.' But she seemed more sad than angry now.

'I'm sorry.' Isobel's face had drained of colour. Her head thumped and her stomach churned.

'It's not your fault.' With a huge effort Twi managed to ban the resentment from her voice. 'Janet's a spiteful piece of work. And she had no right to be here in the first place.'

Somewhat subdued, Twi returned to her kitchen while Isobel, totally exhausted, fell asleep in the chair. The sound of Robbie's raised voice woke her.

'How come everyone seems to know you're in the family way, except me?' he demanded angrily.

'I didn't know myself,' Twi attempted an explanation, but Robbie was in no mood to listen.

'Angus's missus brought him a flask of tea and congratulated me! And I didn't even know what she was talking about. Then she started telling me to check for the witch's mark when it's born, because it runs in your family.' A thump and a crash followed as he brought his fist down on the table. 'Why didn't you tell me?'

'I didn't know.'

'You didn't know when I went to work this morning but you know now?'

'I only found out this afternoon. I was going to tell you later. After Isobel's gone home.'

'Isobel's here?'

'Aye. Keep your voice down and I'll tell you what happened.'

Then Isobel could only hear a low murmur. When there had been complete, tension-laden silence for a couple of minutes she picked up her coat and slipped it on.

Hearing movement Twi bustled into the room. 'You're not going? I'm making tea for you.'

'I think I'd better.'

'Aye. I think you'd better and all.' The normally placid Robbie scowled at her. 'It's true what they say then? You are a witch?'

'I'm not a witch, Robbie. I just sometimes see things about other people. And I would do anything to stop it happening,' she choked, close to tears.

'Well, it won't be happening in this house again. Stay away from here. Do you hear me?'

'That's not fair, Robbie.' But Twi's defence of her sister was half-hearted.

'It's not fair that folk will think our bairns will be like her.' He turned to Isobel with a long sigh, his face a mask of conflicting emotions. 'I'm sorry, Hen. I've nothing against you myself, but I can't risk them treating my wains the way they treat you.' He spoke to his wife again. 'She's not to come here again, and that's final.'

At first Isobel thought she was being over-sensitive. After all, she had always been an object of curiosity among the more superstitious and ignorant villagers, who often turned to stare at her. But now the looks were openly hostile, the whispers louder.

When she stood in the fleshers queue for twenty minutes,

only to be told that there was no mince left when a whole fresh trayful lay on the counter, she knew she was facing outright rejection.

'But there is plenty of mince, Mr McLaren,' she insisted, offering her ration book. The sniggers from the other women in the queue almost drowned his reply.

'It has all been ordered. By these other ladies,' he said curtly, serving the woman behind her.

Isobel's face flared scarlet with humiliation and it took all her courage to turn and walk calmly from the shop, refusing to give in to the urge to run away in shame, which she knew would delight them. With firm, even steps, she marched down the street to the bakers. Mercifully it was empty.

'A pan half please,' she smiled at the young Stobbart girl. To her dismay the child, little more than ten years old, bolted to the back of the shop and returned with her father.

'I would like a pan half please,' Isobel repeated, pointing to the freshly baked loaves behind him, ignoring the clutch of smirking women clustering into the shop behind her.

'They're all ordered.' It was terse and sharp.

'A plain one will do then.' There were at least two dozen of the taller, crustier loaves on the other side of him. Again she offered her ration card, again it was ignored.

'They're all spoken for, too,' he glared at her and shoved his daughter back into the recesses of the shop.

Isobel forced her way through the silent, grinning women and slipped into Cross Wynd, a narrow alley behind the shops, lingering there until she felt calmer. 'You can't let them get the better of you,' she told herself sternly. And besides, she still needed her messages.

Striding purposely she left the shelter of the Wynd, crossed the main street and made for the greengrocers, well aware of the small knot of women still following her. Picking a turnip from the shelves outside she went in.

'I'll have this please.' She handed it over to be weighed.

The middle-aged woman frowned, clearly not liking what

she had to say. 'It's like this, lass,' she said, but not unkindly. 'If we serve you, no-one else will buy from this shop.'

'I'm sorry, Hen. I wouldn't have agreed myself, but I've my business and the bairns to think about.' Ernie Moys, son of the old midwife, seemed almost apologetic. 'If all the McArdles and their friends stop buying from me I'd have no customers left.'

Isobel's shoulders drooped momentarily but angry pride made her pull them up. Straightening her back and holding her head high she left the shop. The crowd of avid observers, intimidated by her angry stare, parted to let her through but then she found her path blocked by Maureen McArdle, her old adversary from school.

'Have you got the message, Isobel McLean?' she spat. 'You're not wanted round here. You and your creepy ways.'

'Let me through,' Isobel was restrained by Maureen's hand digging viciously into her shoulder.

'We don't want you in our village, witch girl.'

'I've as much right to be here as you have, Maureen McArdle, and I'm no witch and you know it.'

'Witch girl. Witch girl. Witch girl. Witch girl,' they chanted, taking her back ten years, but then they moved back, laughing and jeering as she forced her way through and started towards home, her rigid back and unhurried steps giving no hint of her inner turmoil.

She burst through the front door and, dropping the façade of indifference, leaned against it, swallowing tears in great noisy gulps.

'And what's wrong with you?' William challenged brutally.

'The women at the shops . . . they're all calling me a witch again.'

'Well, it's true isn't it? You're right funny in the head. Everybody knows that. The whole village knows what you said to Twi. Telling her she was in the family way before she even knew it herself!'

She could only gawp at him, horrified by the bitterness she saw in his face.

'You're not the only one to get it,' he went on, ruthlessly. 'We all get a hard time because of you. Twi's in-laws are making her life a misery because they reckon this bairn of hers could be like you. Aye, we all suffer because of you.'

'What have I ever done to hurt anyone?'

'You're my sister. That's enough. But if you really want to know, Maggie Cameron's father has told her to stop seeing me. They think like the McArdles. They're frightened their grandchildren could inherit your ways from me.' His mouth twisted into an angry snarl and she turned away, defeated.

It was already dark that chilly October evening when she set out for a lonely walk, her mind in turmoil. First the village and now her own family had turned against her. There was only one solution. If she was to have any hope of living a normal life, of finding peace of mind and happiness, she must get away, escape from the superstition and suspicion that surrounded her, make a new start somewhere where she wasn't known. But to do that she needed money, money she could never hope to save from the meagre allowance her father made her.

Wrapping her coat tightly round her in an effort to keep out the blustery breeze, she threaded her way through the scattered remains of the day's work still littering the quayside, and headed for the beach, deep in thought.

The wind whipped the sand, throwing it in stinging bites against her legs, but she walked on, relishing it, enjoying it, defying it, as if it might scour the anguish from her heart.

On and on she walked, past the last houses of the village and on towards the rocky headland where the sand finally petered out into slimy rocks. Far in the distance, where grey sky met greyer sea, the lights of a ship were just visible as it made its slow way up the Firth of Forth to the shelter of the dockyard at Rosyth.

She sat under the dunes, watching and listening, her ears filled with the sound of breakers crashing on the shore and with the screeching of the gulls. Slowly, inevitably, the sea had its extraordinary effect on her. Always, ever since she was an infant, she had loved the sea, finding comfort in its raw power, especially when it was angry and threatening, as it was tonight. Gradually the tension fell from her body and she started to relax.

She could never recall what, exactly, alerted her, never knew whether it was some out-of-place sound or perhaps a fleeting movement on the edge of her consciousness. Or maybe it was her unique sensitivity. Whatever it was, she knew she was no longer alone.

Straining her ears for some other noise above the crash of the ocean she got to her feet, every sense alert with the premonition of danger, and began to walk back to the village.

The lights danced hazily, still two miles away, when she caught a glimpse of a shadowy figure in the dunes.

Truly frightened now she moved out, away from the shelter of the sand hills, to the damp surface where the tide had recently washed the shoreline. It was firmer here, allowing her to move more quickly. Again she saw the unmistakable shape of someone moving through the dunes, parallel with her. She broke into a trot and, as she ran, caught the drift of the familiar, dreaded chant. 'Witch . . . witch . . . witch . . .' It was broken and distorted by the wind but growing stronger, bolder with every second. Sure-footed on the firm sand she raced towards the lights, still so far away.

She was no more than half-way there when two figures emerged from the dunes and cut off her flight. They were followed by two more, all shouting the awful taunt. 'Witch . . . witch . . . witch . . .'

She stopped, half stumbling, and turned to make a dash

tor the dunes. More figures appeared, blocking off her escape and encircling her. She recognised most of them. Village boys all. Some she had gone to school with, others were friends of her brothers. All wore the same, intense, excited expression which turned her blood to ice.

'What do you want?' she confronted them bravely, her breath coming in sobbing pants.

'Witch . . . Witch . . .' they chanted, leering at her through the darkness, getting closer all the time.

'Get away from me,' she screamed, trying to dodge past. But they enclosed her, coming close enough to touch her now. One of them poked her arm, another jabbed her sharply in the ribs from behind, making her spin round.

'Let me go,' she demanded. 'What do you want with me?'

'You should know that. You're the one who can tell the future.' A tall, heavy youth stepped forward. She recognised him at once as Henry McArdle, one of Robbie's brothers.

'I cannot tell the future.'

'Oh, but you can. You told your own sister she was going to have a bairn even before she knew it herself.' There was challenge and undisguised menace in his voice. She stepped back but was caught from behind by strong arms.

'You are a witch, Isobel McLean,' Henry McArdle accused.

'I am not!' She struggled to break away but failed. 'I'm no different to anyone else.'

'That's not what we heard.' Another boy, smaller but just as dangerous, joined the first. 'I've heard you've got a mark that proves you're a witch.'

'Aye.' There was a general growl of encouragement from the five or six other youths.

'Have you got the mark, Isobel McLean?' McArdle hissed, grinning at his cronies.

Now the moon came from behind a cloud and she could see them all clearly, could read the cruelty in their eyes, see the power of their young, almost adult bodies.

'Leave me alone.' Time and again she backed away, always to be grabbed and shoved forward again.

'I asked you if you had the mark,' Henry shoved his face into hers.

'No,' she lied desperately. 'No!'

'Then prove it! If you've not got a mark, you're not a witch. But you'll have to prove it to us.'

'*No!*' She ran at them but again they caught her.

'Come on, Isobel,' he adopted a thin, wheedling voice. 'Let us see. Show us there's no mark.'

Now they were so close she could feel their breath on her face. '*NO!*' she screamed in panic.

But their hands were already on her. She thrashed, kicking out with sturdy shoes and sharp elbows. The surprised grunts and angry shouts told her she had found her target.

'Don't be like this, Isobel. We're only trying to help,' someone jeered.

She fought bravely but they simply overwhelmed her. Felled by a huge shove she was on the ground, lying there with her mouth full of sand while a dozen hands tugged at her clothes. Strong arms pinned her down while others worked purposefully at her skirt and blouse.

'Aye, that's right, Hen. Scream away. Nobody can hear you. Not above the wind. And we're miles from the village. Go on, scream yourself sick,' Henry taunted.

Now she had nothing on except her shoes and under-clothes. Pulling her by her hair Henry yanked her to her feet. Shame and terror vied within her as she tried to cover herself with her hands.

'Now,' whispered Henry. 'Take the rest off. Then we can look for the mark.'

She heard the way his breath came in fast pants, felt the heat of his hands as he fumbled with her underwear. Then she was naked, open to the freezing wind and the hushed stares of the young animals who were surrounding her. Silence fell. The mood of cruel bravado was replaced by something infinitely more threatening, more horrendous, more shameful.

She shivered convulsively. 'Stand still,' Henry ordered. 'I want to look at you.'

Held from behind she couldn't move as he ran his hands over her trembling skin. She clenched her teeth as rough hands fumbled with her breasts and gasped with revulsion when he forced his way up the inside of her clenched thighs, lingering in the private reaches at the top before suddenly pulling away from her. Now his questing fingers located the small, raised mark at the base of her throat.

'Here it is!' he yelled his triumph, peering at the crescent-shaped mark.

'Leave me alone,' she begged. 'Please.'

'Why should we? We can do what we like. Nobody would take your side even if you told them about this.'

Realising that what he said was perfectly true, she tried to bargain with him. 'But I won't tell anyone, if you let me go.'

He guffawed and squeezed her breasts so hard that tears of pain flooded her eyes.

'I think we should see if a witch is the same as any other woman,' he whispered chillingly.

Fear welled with new force inside her. Instinct warned her of a new danger which, in her innocence, she couldn't fully comprehend.

'That's enough, Henry.' One of the youths moved away, not willing to be a part of what was coming next.

'Go on then, Jimmy Burns. If you're not man enough to do it then away home to your Mammy. Leave the witch to those of us who are.' He fumbled with his trousers as he spoke, then dropped them round his ankles. Isobel swallowed hard, shame bringing heat to her chilled body, fear and horror rooting her eyes to the swollen thing rearing at her.

'Lie down,' he advanced, holding his manhood in his right hand. When she tried to move he shoved her so hard that she fell, sprawling inelegantly on her back, splaying her legs, exposing the area she instinctively sought to protect.

Before she could move he was on top of her, straddling her. The others fidgeted, watching with hot-breathed excitement. His hands gripped her shoulders, making her gasp with pain. But then she realised that his engorged organ was thrusting at her private parts with unbelievable force. She knew then, in a moment of blinding clarity, that this was the answer to all the girlish speculation in which she and Twi had indulged; that this was the secret thing that happened between men and women. Then all thoughts perished under the searing pain of forced penetration.

Like an animal he rocked over her before grunting and shuddering into rigid stillness. Rough, impatient hands pulled him away from her and his place was taken by another of the youths. His time was mercifully short. With a jerk and a groan he spent his seed before he pulled out of her and rolled away, leaving room for the next boy. She was aware of throbbing pain, of oozing, despicable stickiness, of raw soreness. And then of nothing but blissful, welcoming blackness.

When she opened her eyes and moved her aching, bruised limbs she was shocked to see scudding dark clouds silhouetted against the moon's luminescence. Then, seeing the fleeing bodies and remembering it all with chilling clarity, she sat up stiffly and retched into the sand. In a guilty act of charity someone had covered her naked body with her coat but she was already icy to the point of numbness, her teeth chattering in her aching head, making her eyes pulse with pain. Sand adhered to her sticky legs and as she rose, staggering dizzily to her feet, a rush of thick liquid flowed down her thighs.

Swallowing new nausea she scrambled to the water's edge. There, in a frenzy of shame and disgust, she plunged her naked body into the freezing waters, oblivious to the cold, as she tried to sluice the odious traces of the assault from her body.

Three times she emerged from the water, only to dash back again as the treacherous trickle from deep within her soiled her legs afresh. Using fistfuls of sand she scoured her thighs and breasts until they bled, then plunged back into the pounding, cold waters of the North Sea. At last, exhausted, sore and on the point of collapse she dragged her clothes on and forced herself to limp along the beach.

An hour later she reached the bottom of the Butts. By now all the lights in the village were extinguished and she had no idea what time it might be. She couldn't risk walking through the village where, if she happened to meet someone, they would surely be able to tell what had happened simply by looking at her. No, better to chance the rocks on the promontory which separated beach from harbour.

The tide was out and the moon shed a fitful light over the slimy headland. It took her fifteen minutes to negotiate the two hundred yards of slipperty, weed-strewn rocks and clamber onto the end of the harbour road. Everything was still and calm, even the wind had dropped. Apart from the constant churn and splash of the sea there wasn't a sound to be heard.

Wincing with pain from her battered limbs Isobel hobbled down the back wynd and slipped into the house through the back door.

Her father's regular snoring echoed from behind the curtained bed recess. She crept past him and hauled herself upstairs to the sanctuary of her own room.

Using the jug of cold water on her table she washed again, scrubbing at the torn and violated skin until she bled anew.

When she finally fell into bed her pounding head, aching limbs and the persistent throb in the secret recesses of her body kept her from sleep for most of the night.

Dawn sent wispy tendrils of mist into the cold bedroom. Slowly she dragged herself downstairs to light the fire before her father and brother got up. Every movement seemed to tear into her.

Malcolm hawked and stumbled to the outside toilet. Then came the thud of William's footsteps on the stairs.

'Bring us our tea,' he demanded as he and Malcolm stood in front of the range in baggy, woollen long johns. This ritual of dressing in the relative warmth of the kitchen area had been part of her life for as long as she could remember. Never before had the sight of them in their underwear disturbed her. Today her face burned with shame and she thrust their cups at them with averted eyes.

Unable to face her job that day she performed the necessary household chores with painful slowness, feeling that every last ounce of energy had been leeched from her. By the time the men came home again she had at least stopped shaking and the sharpest edge of pain had gone from her injuries. Anger was replacing self-pity.

She was still so preoccupied that she failed to notice how grim-faced and taciturn her father and brother were. She was totally unprepared for her father's attack. Dropping his lunch box on the floor he strode up to her, pulled her round to face him and struck her viciously across the cheek. The venom in his voice stunned her.

'I never thought a daughter of mine would bring such shame to this house. Everyone in the village knows about you.'

'What?' she whispered, tasting blood from her nose.

'You and Henry McArdle! Selling yourself to him. On the beach. A common whore!' His voice rose in fury. She could only gape at him.

'He's telling everyone that my sister can be had for a few coppers,' William roared, hatred gleaming in his eyes.

'That's not true. He's lying.' She found enough voice to defend herself at last, begging them to believe her but seeing, from their eyes, that she was failing.

'You're denying it then?' Malcolm asked, sternly upright, holding the bible in front of him. 'You'd swear on this bible that you didn't sell yourself to him?'

'Yes. Yes I would.' She reached out to take the book but he yanked it away as if frightened she might defile it.

'And damn yourself forever,' he roared.

'No, I'll swear. Let me, please. Then you will have to believe me.'

'You were with him alright,' William closed on her. 'He was crowing about seeing your mark. How else would he know about that? You're always so careful to keep it covered up.'

She blanched, felt sick.

'Can you truthfully swear that you didn't lie with him? Can you put your hand on the Lord's book and swear you are still intact?' Malcolm held out the Bible.

'No,' she whispered. Another blow from the back of his hand sent her staggering back against the wall.

'So it is true? You were selling yourself.'

'*No*,' she screamed at him. 'He forced me. On the beach.'

'I don't believe you.' Malcolm struck her again. 'Too many others saw him with you. Whore! Harlot! This is a decent, God-fearing house. Have you no shame?'

'I told you it wasn't like that. Why won't you believe me?'

'Get out of our sight,' William shoved her roughly towards the stairs. 'Everyone's talking about you. All the men.

'You should see how pleased they are to tell me about my own sister. Slut!' he yelled, sending spittle into her face.

It came as no surprise when Mr Truscot, manager of the haberdashery, gave her a handwritten note telling her she had been fired. He gave no reason but she knew he must have heard the rumours.

Without a job and with no hope of finding one locally, Isobel's situation was desperate. There was no longer any future in Kilweem. She had to get away, to build a new future for herself somewhere where she and her family weren't known. Dundee perhaps, or Edinburgh. But she didn't even have enough money for the bus fare to either of these places. Without money she was trapped. Her faltering request for a loan was met with outraged refusal by both William and Malcolm.

Finally, in desperation, she walked the five miles to Waddle's farm, hoping her sister would be able to lend her a few shillings. Since that dreadful day, six months ago, Twi had only come to Kilweem twice and had had little to say to her sister. Isobel of course had not been back to the farm. It was a tired and nervous young woman who plodded up the muddy track to the cottage.

Sensing eyes on her from the other cottages and seeing the curtains of the neighbouring house twitch, Isobel rapped fiercely on Twi's door. She was rewarded by the sound of hurrying footsteps.

'Isobel!' Twi gasped. Then, recovering her wits. 'You'd better come in.' As aware as Isobel of the watching neighbours she grabbed her sister's arm and yanked her over the doorstep.

'How are you, Twi?' Isobel asked uncertainly.

'I'm fine.' Grim-faced but surprisingly quickly considering the bulk of her pregnancy, Twi led the way into the sitting room.

'Robbie's working. He'll not be back until tonight so sit yourself down and I'll make a drink.'

'Thanks,' Isobel muttered, dropping thankfully into the nearest chair.

Twi stopped in the doorway, frowning as she saw the strain in every line of her sister's body. As usual her reaction to her twin was confused, half resentful, half loyal. 'Surely you didn't think I'd turn you from my door?' she asked in a softer, kinder voice.

'Robbie told me not to come here. I don't want to cause any more trouble for you.'

'You've caused me trouble all my life,' sighed Twi. 'I don't think he would be happy to come home and find you in his best chair,' she admitted. 'But it's not that he doesn't like you. It's the bairn he's thinking of. And the things his family say about you. You know what they're like.'

Later when they were both revived by the scalding brew, Isobel haltingly told Twi what had happened, her face burning with shame but finding some relief in being able to share it with someone else.

'I heard rumours,' Twi admitted. 'You know what it's like for me. Robbie's family is so big. They hear about everything first. And they were only too happy to tell me about this. But,' she added quickly, 'I didn't believe it. I never thought you would go with Henry willingly.'

'It doesn't make any difference. The damage is done. Father and William believe it. They had made up their minds before they even asked me about it. They're delighted to believe the worst of me. As far as they're concerned I'm a whore. I've disgraced them. I'm nothing but an embarrassment to them . . . I've got to get away, Twi, I hate Kilweem.'

'You're going to leave the village?' Twi asked, her voice sharp with shock.

'Yes . . . after what happened. I'll never be allowed to forget it. Every time I see one of them . . .' she shuddered, then smiled wistfully at her sister. 'But I had already decided to go anyway. Don't you understand? All the time I stay here my life isn't my own. The villagers have never accepted me, Father and William think they own me. You and Hugh have your own lives to lead . . . I need a life of my own, too. I'll never make anything of myself all the time I stay in Kilweem. I'll go to Dundee, find a decent job and I might even take some art classes. I want my own home. Maybe even a husband one day. I'll never get all that here.'

'You'll be all on your own.'

'I've been on my own all my life,' was the hard retort. 'But . . .'

'But?'

'I haven't even got the bus fare to go to Dundee. Father

95

won't lend it to me and neither will William. If you could just lend me a few shillings I'll send it back to you as soon as I can.' She felt like a beggar.

'I haven't got it,' Twi muttered, her eyes on the floor. 'There'll be no money until Robbie comes home with his pay tonight. He doesn't get much of a wage. By the time I've bought the messages and paid the clothing club man there's nothing left until the next payday. I'm sorry.'

'Oh no,' Isobel whispered. Twi had been her only hope.

They sat in tense silence until Twi recovered from her embarrassing admission. 'So, what will you do now?' she asked.

'I don't know,' Isobel admitted. 'But I'm leaving Kilweem, even if I have to walk to Dundee.'

'Look . . . I don't think you've got much chance, but there is something you might try.' Twi sounded uncertain.

'What?' Isobel's head shot up.

'Don't get excited. I don't think anything will come of it. I'm likely raising your hopes for nothing.'

'Anything's worth a try.'

'Well, they're looking for a new housekeeper up at Netherdrum. Mrs Waddle told me yesterday. But you're too young for that kind of job.'

'Netherdrum?' The name sounded vaguely familiar. 'Where's that?'

'You're not seriously thinking about going after it?'

'Why not? I've got to do something and a live-in job would be ideal until I've saved enough money to move on. The sooner I get away from home the better.'

'I suppose so,' Twi conceded. 'But Netherdrum's a long walk from here and you know I can't give you the bus fare.'

'Just tell me how to get there.'

'It's on the Cupar road. At Brighead.'

Isobel shook her head, still unable to place it.

'Big white gates. You can't miss it.'

'Oh . . . I remember. We used to pick rasps with Granny Rose up there.'

'That's right.'

'That's six or seven miles from here.'

'I told you it was a long walk.'

'If I leave now I should get there this afternoon some time.' Isobel was already on her feet, reaching for her coat, determination solid in her face.

'Wait a minute,' Twi raked in a cupboard and produced a clean duster which she shoved into a small, clutch handbag. 'Here, take these. Polish your shoes and comb your hair before you go in. And pinch some colour into your cheeks. You'll not get a job in a big house like that in the state you're in. You don't look strong enough to lift a cup of tea, never mind work for a living.'

'Thanks,' Isobel dropped a light kiss on her sister's freckled cheek.

'Isobel . . .' Twi hesitated.

'What's the matter?'

'I was wondering if you knew . . .' she blushed and dropped her eyes. 'After what happened . . . on the beach . . .'

'I don't want to talk about that anymore, Twi.' Isobel coloured hotly.

'This is important, Isobel,' Twi persisted. 'You do understand what can happen, don't you. After you've been with a man?'

'What . . .?'

'Oh, God, Isobel!' Twi groaned. 'Wake up ! You could be expecting.' She watched as her sister digested the information, saw the eyes close in shock, saw the blush fade with alarming speed.

'Of course I know that!' Isobel shook her head, trying to clear it. 'Why didn't I realise . . . I never even thought . . .'

'You'll most likely be alright. But I thought I should warn you.'

'Yes. Yes, of course. Thanks.' Still looking shocked, Isobel opened the front door.

'Good luck,' Twi whispered as she stepped into the farmyard. Then, 'Look after yourself, Isobel,' she shouted in defiance of Janet McArdle who was, she knew, watching.

SEVEN

*B*y mid-afternoon the seven miles which had seemed so trivial that morning had become an almost impossible distance. But Isobel strode along on legs which screamed for rest, determined to reach her goal. Never slackening her pace she approached each corner praying it would reveal Netherdrum's white gates, but discovered only disappointment after disappointment. She forced herself on, telling herself she would never succeed in building herself a new life if she let herself become discouraged at every small setback.

At last she sank onto the grass verge for a few minutes' rest and massaged life back into her aching feet and cramped calves. Already the sky was darkening with the threat of evening and she was unhappily aware of the very real danger of being stranded in open countryside after nightfall. But she wouldn't turn back to Kilweem now. Isobel's heart lurched at the thought and sent her rapidly back to her blistered feet.

The first glance around the next corner showed a narrow, exposed road which seemed to stretch ahead forever. But then, through a break in the hedgerow, she glimpsed the grey stonework of a large house. Her heart hammered and her step smartened with an unsuspected reserve of energy as she limped down the road in search of the all-important white gates.

She found them at last, set back a little so they weren't visible until she was almost on top of them. Carved into each of two vertical stone posts was the word Netherdrum.

Relief made her legs tremble but it was late and there was

no time to waste. Remembering Twi's instructions she took five minutes to tidy herself and ruthlessly pinch some colour into her white cheeks. Then, settling her hat on her head at a jaunty angle she walked rapidly through the gates, holding her head high and ignoring the pain of her blistered heels.

The house revealed itself gradually as she walked up the curving driveway. As she got nearer she realised, with some relief, that it was not as grand as the imposing gates implied. It was more a large, rambling farmhouse than the impressive mansion she had half expected. The grey, weathered stone-work, partially clad in clinging ivy looked old and welcoming while the windows, draped in red velvet with pot plants on the lower sills, gave the place a warm, homely feel. This, she knew suddenly, the feeling so overwhelmingly strong that she stopped for a minute, astounded by the intensity of it, was where she belonged.

On a surge of hope she walked boldly up to the front door and knocked with the huge, brass ring. She waited a minute, then repeated it.

'Oh no,' she whispered, hope draining even more quickly than it had risen. Even in the rapidly falling dusk the house remained in darkness.

But perhaps she had been knocking at the wrong door. There was certain to be a back entrance which she, as a prospective employee, should use.

Hurrying now she skirted the side of the house. Sure enough, sheltered by a clutch of outbuildings, she found a rear door. And light filtered from behind it.

Using her fist this time she hammered on the black-painted wood. Almost immediately she heard a man's voice, low and indistinct, and heavy, slow footsteps. The door was flung open to reveal an elderly man, dressed in muddied overalls, peering at her through myopic eyes.

'What do you want?' was the peremptory demand.

'I . . . I . . .' she stammered, completely thrown by his rough appearance.

'Well?' he roared.

'I've come about the job.'

'You'll have to talk up. I'm a wee bitty hard of hearing,' he bellowed, cupping a gnarled hand behind one ear.

She repeated herself, louder this time.

'Oh . . .' he seemed surprised. 'At this time of the day?' His old eyes examined her critically. 'You're not very big, are you?'

'I'm nearly twenty-one,' she began defensively, then changed her tone. 'Just because I'm small doesn't mean I can't do the job,' she yelled back at him.

'What did you say?'

Isobel sighed in exasperation. 'Is there anyone I can talk to about the job?' she mouthed each word slowly.

'The now?'

'Yes. Now.'

'There's no-one here bar myself and I'm just off home.'

'Just a minute,' she begged at the top of her voice. 'Isn't there anyone I can talk to?'

'I already told you. No. I'm just the gardener.'

'When will someone be here?' she persisted.

'Don't ask me, Hen. As far as I know he's in Kirkcaldy, at his factory. He doesn't tell me his plans. I don't know when he'll be back.' With those discouraging words he closed the door and walked away, his bowed legs giving him a strangely rolling gait.

Slowly, feeling each leg as a dead weight, Isobel dragged herself back down the drive. By the time she reached the gates it was dark and the temperature had dipped alarmingly.

Totally dispirited she started to retrace her route, her blistered feet burning with each step and hunger gnawing at her stomach. How stupid she had been to come here on the off-chance, chasing a job she wasn't even sure existed.

Seven or more miles to Twi's and another four to Kilweem. America seemed closer. But there was no alternative. Unless she wanted to spend the night in the open. She had barely reached the first corner when the rain started, coming in steady, soaking drizzle that seeped its way through to her skin in less than five minutes.

And then it happened, catching her as it so often did when she was tired or upset. The road wavered, turning into an undulating sea of gravel and her feet seemed to lose contact with the ground. Frightened of falling on the hard surface she had just enough time to fling herself onto the wet, grassy verge.

When she looked up the skies had cleared to vivid, azure blue and she could smell the delicious aroma of new-mown hay. A movement behind her made her turn towards the hedgerow where a young woman, wearing a floating summer dress, her long hair rippling in the light breeze, was picking ripe raspberries from the bushes, placing the fruit in a bowl perched on the front of the pram she pushed. The infant inside slept peacefully as the woman ran a loving hand over the downy head. They moved on, coming directly towards Isobel. There was a moment when the woman seemed to look straight at her. Isobel gasped, reeling with the shock of recognition. The face which had looked so calmly through hers was her own. But when she turned to follow the woman as she moved on down the road, she had disappeared.

When Isobel regained her senses she was spreadeagled on the verge, the rain pouring over her, drenching her until she could feel rivulets running down her back. Her saturated hair clung to her head like a great, waterlogged sponge. Still confused she tried to struggle to her numbed feet but her head spun appallingly and there was no strength left in her legs which trembled treacherously beneath her. Using the dripping hedge for support she hauled herself upright, shivering as the damp seeped into her very soul.

The sky was an unrelenting black, the moon and stars obscured by heavy cloud. Instinct warned her that the evening was well advanced. Common sense and her saturated condition told her that she must have lain on the verge for at least an hour, probably longer. Shivering uncontrollably she attempted to leave the partial shelter of the hedgerow but stumbled in the darkness and landed on her knees in the sodden grass. Truly frightened now she knew she had to get help and scrambled to her feet, trying to recall where the nearest house was. Hunching her shoulders she set out towards the coast.

She had travelled less than half a mile, had seen no sign of any house, was chilled to the marrow of her slender bones, when a car tore round the corner, seeming to bore straight at her. Stunned by the unexpected glare from the headlights, she froze, like an animal, but as the vehicle closed on her with undiminished speed she managed to flatten herself against the hedge. The headlights caught her in a dizzying swathe of light as the car shot past. Still startled Isobel waited a minute before stepping out of the muddy ditch she had landed in. The grinding of the car engine as it reversed back towards her threw her into a tangle of confusion, torn between relief at imminent help and anger with anyone who could drive so recklessly fast on such a narrow road.

'Are you alright?' The passenger, a man well wrapped against the cold, shouted through his window. The driver, similarly well protected, peered at her from the far side of the vehicle.

'Yes,' she shivered through chattering teeth, unwilling to meet his eyes, feeling increasingly ill and disorientated.

'But you are not!' It was an outraged statement made as he clambered onto the road, followed rapidly by the driver, who hung back a little as if he was the other man's subordinate. 'You are absolutely drenched. What on earth are you doing on this road on a night like this?' It was a shouted accusation. Now she could see he was elderly but tall and imposing, his manner bad-tempered and impatient.

'I'm on my way home,' she retorted, aggravated by his tone, then stepped back a pace, wary of this overpowering man on such a lonely road.

The driver, younger but taller still, stood close behind the older man. His upturned collar and the hat, pulled well down, hid an expression of complete astonishment which was rapidly replaced by concern as he made an appraisal of her condition. Now he spoke in a deep, gravelly voice which she recognised instantly.

'Going home? But you are miles from anywhere.'

But she was already moving away from him, her horror when she realised who he was adding to her determination to avoid being recognised.

'Wait! We're trying to help. At least let us take you home.'

She broke into a run before he finished speaking, shouting back something that drowned in the rain. James Dryburgh sprinted after her but as he closed on her she stumbled, sprawling painfully in the road and losing her felt hat before hoisting herself to her knees and collapsing again when her legs refused to support her slight weight.

'Get away,' she screamed, seeing only Henry McArdle, feeling the sand of Kilweem beach between her toes. 'Leave me alone, Henry McArdle.'

James froze. He had no idea how to deal with this hysterical female. But, now that her hat no longer hid her features he saw something familiar in the face, dripping with water and distorted with terror though it was. Appalled he dropped onto his heels, staying well back, striving not to alarm her further.

'Miss McLean? It is Isobel McLean, isn't it? Twi's sister? I don't expect you remember me. We met at you sister's wedding. We danced a reel together.' Rain seeped into his shoes, trickled under his collar.

Soothed by his calm, even tone, Isobel gathered her fevered senses sufficiently to banish Henry McArdle from the scene. Still wary and uncomfortably aware of her bedraggled appearance she rose unsteadily to her feet but swayed precariously as her head swam. And why were her teeth chattering when she was so hot? 'I'm just on my way home,' she repeated, backing slowly away.

'Kilweem is more than ten miles from here. You can't

possibly walk all that way and certainly not in this weather.' James eased himself upright, wondering what had happened to terrify her so badly.

'I walked here and I can walk back,' she said defiantly.

Now the older man spoke again, his voice snapping with impatience.

'Rubbish! Stop wasting everyone's time, young woman and get in the car. We can have you home in ten minutes.'

'No!' Visions of her father's reaction if she turned up in this condition with two strange men made her yell it at them. 'I can't go home. Not like this.'

'Then we'll take you to your sister.' Still calm and reasonable James flashed a warning glance at the angry older man and inched forward, matching her backward retreat step for step.

'No.'

'Why not?' he demanded, exasperated by her irrational refusal. 'We're not going to hurt you. We're trying to help.' Something in his warm, deep voice, in the steady kindness of his eyes, halted her. For a moment she wanted nothing more than to climb into the warm interior of his car.

He sensed, rather than saw, the hesitation. 'Come on, get in.'

His touch, light though it was, burned her. She jerked away. 'Please, don't touch me,' she said, a note of hysteria creeping back into her voice.

He hesitated, startled and upset by her hostile reaction, unable to know that it wasn't him but Henry McArdle that she saw.

Abruptly she broke into a run but the spinning in her head became so violent that it lifted her from the ground. As the blackness of the road reached up to engulf her she felt as if she was floating off into space.

James Dryburgh caught her before she could hurt herself. He stood with her limp body held easily in his strong arms, seeming undecided.

'Don't just stand there! Put her in the car, for God's sake.

Before we all drown.' The older man hunched further inside his coat and strode back to the car.

James hoisted her more securely in his arms, then carried her quickly to the car, arranging her limbs gently along the back seat.

'What do we do with her now?' he asked as he slid behind the wheel.

'My God!' Campbell Geddes exploded. 'Why couldn't you have just driven on, like anyone in their right mind would have done?'

James ignored him. 'Shall I take her down to Kilweem?'

'Kilweem. And what then? Knock on doors until we find someone to claim her?' Geddes turned stiffly in his seat and glowered at the inert figure on his fine leather upholstery. 'Take me home. It's been a long day and I need a drink. As for that blasted young female, Mrs Mac can see to her.'

Five minutes later James Dryburgh deposited the dripping, semi-conscious body on the watered silk of Netherdrum's drawing room sofa.

'Oh my! She is in a state, isn't she?' Eleanor McLachlan, Geddes's housekeeper stared at the sodden girl, wondering just how she came to be in this condition.

'We found her wandering about on the road. Soaked through and frightened as a rabbit. I don't know what young women are coming to these days. In my time . . .' Geddes left the rest unsaid and stomped over to a sideboard where he poured himself a generous shot of whisky, then took himself over to the fire where he warmed his ample backside at the roaring flames.

The well-lit room revealed him as an elderly but upright man with ruddy complexion and a shock of snow white hair. A well-trimmed white moustache gave him a humourless look, exacerbated by his abrupt manner and habitually stern expression. His presence dominated any room, his personality, blunt of speech and impatient with those who lacked his own decisiveness, intimidated his acquaintances.

Campbell Geddes was a self-made man and proud of it.

The need to succeed had dominated his life and cost him two marriages in an age when divorce was still a drastic last step. Over seventy now he still refused to relax his hold on his business, a prosperous jute works in Kirkcaldy. This fine house and a modest fortune were testimony to his success.

'Poor lass.' Mrs McLachlan, a tall, thin, heron-like woman, put a work-worn hand to Isobel's forehead. 'She's running a temperature. These wet clothes will have to come off or she'll catch her death.' Her deft fingers were already working on the stiff buttons of Isobel's coat.

'I'll see if I can find something for her to wear,' Geddes blustered, hastily abandoning the fireside. 'James, before you go you'd better light a fire in the small guest room.'

By the time Geddes had irritably unearthed an old nightdress which had belonged to his last wife and a pretty bed jacket to go with it and Mrs McLachlan had struggled to dry the long, blonde hair it was already nine o'clock.

'The bedroom should be warm enough now and she'll do better in bed,' said James, lifting Isobel's unresisting body.

'And so would I,' grumbled Geddes, pouring himself another generous shot of whisky but still not offering the younger man one. 'Carry her up then get off to your own home, James. Mrs Mac can see to her for tonight and I've got more important things to think about than fussing around after stray females. And so have you.' Dismissing them all he turned round and held his hands out to the flames.

'Yes, Sir. Goodnight.' James led the way, followed by the silent housekeeper, up the staircase and down a long, narrow passage to a small bedroom where he deposited Isobel in a warmly covered bed.

A red flush stained Isobel's cheeks and she moved her head restlessly from side to side, muttering in delirium.

'Listen,' Mrs McLachlan said sharply. 'What's she saying?'

The words were disjointed and so indistinct that they had to strain to hear.

'No . . . No . . .' Isobel muttered. 'Leave me alone. Leave me alone, Henry McArdle.' Sobs shook her body and the words became incomprehensible. Mrs McLachlan frowned and patted the feverish hands, hoping this strange girl would be comforted in some way.

James's face whitened as a dreadful suspicion of what had happened formed in his mind.

'Witch. Witch. Witch,' she sobbed. Then, 'No . . . please no,' tossing herself around as if trying to escape.

'It's alright now, Isobel. You're safe here,' James whispered.

'Isobel? So you do know this lassie?' Mrs McLachlan was so surprised that she spoke without thinking.

'Yes. I know her,' he admitted. 'But not well. She was a bridesmaid at a wedding down at Waddle's farm last year. She's a Kilweem girl.'

As he spoke Isobel began to mutter again, thrashing from side to side, obviously reliving something traumatic. Mrs McLachlan wiped the burning forehead with a cool cloth and stroked the damp hair back from the lovely, flushed face.

'No. Please . . . leave me alone. It's not true . . . No . . . Leave me . . . Let me go.' There was a long pause and suddenly she screamed. 'No. It's not true. He forced me, Father . . . not true . . . No . . . no . . .' The rest of her words were lost as she subsided into a restless silence.

'Poor lassie.' Mrs McLachlan watched her with troubled eyes then, looking uncomfortable, cleared her throat several times before finally speaking. 'I don't know whether I should rightly say this to you, Sir.'

'Yes?' He caught the flush of embarrassment on the housekeeper's thin face. 'What is it, Mrs McLachlan?' he asked kindly.

She took a deep breath and glanced uncomfortably at James, visibly preparing to say something which was obviously distasteful to her.

'Well, Sir. You heard what the young lassie said.' He nodded.

'Well, I could be wrong, putting two and two together, but it sounded to me as if she'd been attacked.'

'Attacked?' James was carefully noncommittal, wondering if Geddes hadn't been right after all. Perhaps it would have been better to have left Isobel where she was. He was instantly ashamed of the thought. Never had he seen anyone in so much need of help as that poor girl on the roadside.

'When I was taking her wet clothes off . . . I noticed bruises.'

'Bruises?'

'Aye. Not new ones, though. Yellowing. Like they were three or four days old. On her arms, at the top, as if she'd been held, very hard. And . . .' she flushed.

'Go on, Mrs McLachlan,' he encouraged her softly but she saw the way his jaw tightened in anger as he spoke.

'More bruises, and scratches. All up her legs . . . Right up her legs . . . Black and blue she is, poor thing. As if . . . as if it was more than just a beating . . . Something more awful . . . if you understand me, Sir.'

'Yes, Mrs McLachlan. I understand only too well.'

'And another thing, Sir.'

'Yes?'

'George, the gardener, called back tonight and said there had been a young lassie at the door, asking about a job. About five-thirty. Just as he was going home for his tea. A wee thing with fair hair, he said. I think it must have been her.'

James gazed at the still tossing Isobel. 'That would certainly explain what she was doing out here. But I don't suppose we'll get to the bottom of it until she feels better.' He touched the burning cheeks lightly and was startled when she drew her head away sharply, muttering, 'Don't touch me. Don't touch me. Leave me alone.' Dismayed he withdrew his hand. Why did she react so violently to him?

'Better to leave her to me now, Sir.'

'Yes.' Much better. He'd done his Christian duty and now he would be wise to stay out of it. And she'd made her opinion of him plain enough. 'Goodnight, Mrs Mac.' With one last, puzzled glance at Isobel's unhappy face he hurried away.

All through the night Mrs McLachlan watched over Isobel, sometimes dozing in her chair but frequently jerked into wakefulness by Isobel's feverish tossing and occasional sobs. But, as dawn broke damply, the girl seemed to settle. Her colour lessened and she breathed more lightly. The long, dark lashes fluttered on alabaster pale cheeks and she fell silent.

'There,' said Mrs McLachlan. 'It was no more than a wee chill. She's a lot cooler and she's sleeping peacefully now.'

'Thank God for that!' Geddes, who had felt duty-bound to enquire after his uninvited guest was audibly relieved. 'I'm off to the factory, Mrs Mac. This young woman will, I hope, have made herself scarce by the time I get home tonight.'

He was escaping gladly, was already half-way through the door when his housekeeper stopped him. 'I don't think she'll be able to go just yet, Sir.'

'Oh? And why not? You have just told me how much better she is.'

'It's not quite that simple, Sir,' she insisted. 'If I could explain?'

He sighed loudly. 'Quickly then, woman.' He glanced pointedly at his fob and waited impatiently while she repeated the gist of last night's conversation with James. But, when she had finished he walked slowly to the bedside and gazed thoughtfully down on the pale, insubstantial but undeniably lovely girl who still slept there. The lines on his face seemed to soften, just for a moment. Then he seemed to collect himself. 'Well, I suppose she'll have to stay until she's recovered,' was all he said as he marched from the room.

'Yes, Sir.' Mrs McLachlan beamed, then resumed her chair by the bed where, exhausted from her broken night, she fell quickly into a light doze.

'Who are you?' The note of panic and the frantic scrambling to sit up had the housekeeper on her feet again within seconds.

'It's alright, Hen,' she said, pressing Isobel back into the pillows. Confused and still far from well Isobel was unable to resist the gentle pressure and subsided with a sigh. 'But where is this?' she asked, memories of last night hopelessly confused with her awful ordeal on Kilweem beach.

'This is the home of Mr Campbell Geddes.'

'Mr Geddes?' The name meant nothing. She shook her head, wincing at the pain the slight movement caused. 'But where? How far from home am I?'

'This is Netherdrum house, lass. Just outside Brighead.'

'Netherdrum . . .' Isobel closed her eyes and let the tide of remembrance take her with it. 'How did I get here?'

'You were found outside. Collapsed. You were soaked to the skin.'

Isobel's eyes flew open in new panic as she surveyed the warm nightdress and the generously covered bed. 'My clothes?' she croaked.

'Don't fret, Hen. They're in my kitchen drying off. Those things belonged to Mr Geddes's wife. You never opened your eyes when I put them on you last night.' She chuckled at the obvious look of relief which spread over Isobel's face. Judging by that reaction, whatever might have happened to her, the girl was decent enough. 'Just you try to rest.'

Isobel nodded sleepily and couldn't resist the lure of the soft, warm pillows.

An hour later she woke to find Mrs McLachlan offering a tray of toast, scrambled eggs and tea.

'Do your best to eat this, Hen,' she instructed, helping her patient into a sitting position. 'How do you feel?'

'Alright,' Isobel answered cautiously, trying to ignore the upsurge of pain in her skull.

Mrs McLachlan watched her eat, talking quietly, telling Isobel a little about herself, Netherdrum and her host then, motivated as much by open curiosity as genuine kindness asked: 'Tell me, lass, what were you doing so far from home on such a dreadful night?'

Vainly Isobel searched for some plausible reason but found none. And the truth was the very least she owed this immensely kind woman. 'I came to Netherdrum because I heard you needed staff,' she admitted reluctantly.

Mrs McLachlan nodded her grey head. 'So it *was* you who spoke to the gardener last night?'

'Yes.'

'Why on earth didn't you write, lass? That would have been the sensible thing to do.' But it was kindly said.

'I know. It's just that . . . well, I need a job . . . desperately. I hoped . . .'

'It's alright, lass.' Mrs McLachlan patted the thin hand which was clutching at the blankets in agitation. 'I don't mean to pry: I'll leave you to sleep now. The more rest you get the sooner you'll mend.'

The small effort of talking and eating the deliciously creamy eggs had exhausted Isobel and she let herself slip easily into the comfortable world between sleep and wakefulness.

The room delighted her. Decorated in pale peach it was a soft, warm, safe place. The window opposite the bed looked out over the gardens, sparkling as the sunlight caught water droplets on the grass. But, undeniably peaceful and beautiful though it was, it could not banish the horror which pushed its way repeatedly into her mind. Her father's face, grim and accusing; William, aggressive and hostile; Henry McArdle.

And the dream of escaping to Netherdrum had been extinguished in the most humiliating way. Her recollection of last night's events was dim and hopelessly confused. But she did know she had disgraced herself, that her behaviour must have shocked her rescuer. Now, even if he did need extra staff, after last night's performance she would be the last person Campbell Geddes would want to employ. Rare tears slid down her face, dampening the fine, lace-edged pillow until, exhausted, she sank into dream-wracked sleep.

The next morning Isobel awoke to the certain knowledge that she could remain here no longer. The urgent need to find a job and somewhere to live would not be resolved while she lingered at Netherdrum. Resolutely ignoring her still-throbbing head and resisting Mrs McLachlan's well-intentioned efforts to keep her there for at least another day, Isobel insisted on donning her own shabby clothes, now cleaned and freshly pressed.

'I would like to thank Mr Geddes. He has been very kind to let me stay here,' she suggested to the hovering, older woman.

'Mr Geddes is in Kirkcaldy, lass. At work. He won't be back until this evening.'

'Oh,' Isobel's face was a mirror of disappointment. But she also felt a measure of relief. Good manners demanded that she thanked her elusive host but the knowledge that she had let herself down badly in front of him and an image of a stern, impatient man made her reluctant to face her rescuer. She would, she resolved, write to him as soon as she got back to Kilweem, and thank him formally.

'You really should stay, for at least another day,' Mrs McLachlan tried again, but could see, from the set line of the surprisingly firm jaw, that the girl had already made up her mind.

'But I'm perfectly alright now. There's no reason for me to stay. You've been so kind . . .' she trailed off into silence.

'And?' Mrs McLachlan prompted, intrigued by the air of sadness and mystery which surrounded this girl.

'I have things to do,' Isobel finished lamely and looked away.

'How are you going to get back to Kilweem?' Mrs

McLachlan asked, giving Isobel her handbag, empty except for the strange assortment of duster, comb and compact, without a purse in sight.

'I'll manage.' Isobel's pride wouldn't allow her to admit how much she dreaded the long walk to her father's hostile reception.

'If you turn left at the gates and walk through Brighead, you'll get a bus on the St Andrews road.'

'Thanks.' Isobel turned up her collar.

'Here, Hen.' Mrs McLachlan dropped a handful of coins into Isobel's pocket. 'Now don't make a fuss. I know you've no money and I can't let you walk all that way.'

'I can't take your money, Mrs McLachlan,' Isobel whispered, touched but appalled by her beggarly status.

'Aye, you can. It's a loan. Pay me back when you're able.'

'Thank you,' Isobel said softly. 'You are very kind. And I will let you have it back. I promise.'

Minutes later she was passing through the imposing white gates on her way back to Kilweem. Already the last twenty-four hours felt like a dream.

EIGHT

*I*sobel's reception at Kilweem could hardly have been colder. Her refusal to offer any explanation for her absence only succeeded in infuriating her father even more. Now he wouldn't speak to her. The atmosphere in the house was unbearable, and in the village she was greeted with venomous stares and hissed insults.

Her determination to get away increased with every passing minute and, at last, with the arrival of the balance of wages due to her, she had the means to leave. By the time she had given her father the half he demanded and purchased a postal order to repay Mrs McLachlan, she had just enough money left to get her to Dundee.

The very thought of being alone in such a large city with no job and nowhere to live was daunting, but somehow she would manage. She would have to. This was her one chance of a new start, away from the prejudice and hate which was ruining her life.

On her last night in Kilweem she assembled her things. Apart from her few items of clothing there was very little. Penned in her cold room while her father and brother basked in the heat of the house's only fire, relief came with the sudden, flooding knowledge that she had escaped pregnancy. She welcomed the cramps which went with this monthly event. They seemed like an omen to her, a sign that everything would, after all, work out well. The future, which had seemed bleak and frightening, now beckoned with the irrational promise of happiness. Instead of trepidation she felt excitement. In place of sadness she felt elation.

There was no explanation for it, nor logical reason for this peculiar lift in spirits but, trusting her instinct, she looked forward to the new day with barely contained impatience. For the first time in weeks she went to bed and fell immediately into a deep, dreamless sleep.

She was up by seven the next morning, refreshed and alert, to a house which was already deserted and cold. Lingering only long enough to help herself to breakfast, she was on the point of leaving when there was the drop of a letter through the box.

To her amazement it was addressed to her, in angular, very masculine writing. Hurriedly she tore the pale cream envelope apart and withdrew a single sheet of paper. When she had finished reading she crumpled against the door-frame, her hands pressed to her face. When her heart stopped hammering she read through it again, still afraid to believe the evidence of her own eyes. Then, convinced at last, she did a sudden ecstatic twirl of sheer joy.

The letter, on pale cream paper, was from Campbell Geddes himself. It was short and formal but the message it contained was the most welcome she would ever receive.

After brief, slightly stilted and very formal wishes for her good health he informed her that he was indeed looking for 'general assistance for my housekeeper', and invited her for a formal interview that day, if she was still interested.

Isobel instantly and gladly abandoned her plans to flee to Dundee and in less than half an hour was on the bus wending its way up the soft, green valley of Strathannan towards Netherdrum. It set her down within a mile of the house and she walked the remaining distance with a spring in her step. When the white gates came into view she felt her throat tightening with emotion.

In the late morning sun the old house looked mellow and welcoming. Again she had the distinct feeling that her future was here. This time, when she knocked at the kitchen door, it was thrown open to reveal Mrs McLachlan's familiar, friendly face.

'Come along in, Hen,' she welcomed Isobel. 'I'm right glad you decided to come. Mr Geddes is expecting you.'

Fifteen minutes later, refreshed and tidied, Isobel was led to Mr Geddes's small study.

Seated at the huge mahogany desk which dominated the room he looked more imposing, more severe that Isobel's blurred memory could recall. In his 'home clothes' of well-worn tweed suit and buff-coloured waistcoat he looked, she thought, like her idea of an army colonel. His booming voice strengthened that impression.

'Come in, Miss McLean.' He neither rose from his chair nor offered her a seat, contenting himself with fixing her with a slight scowl. His housekeeper had been remarkably insistent, even over his own reluctance, that he should interview this girl, despite having several other applicants for the job. But her polite and punctual letter of thanks had proved her to be educated and the rapid return of Mrs McLachlan's small loan had shown her to be honest, both qualities he valued. And, despite the unfortunate outcome, she had shown remarkable determination in walking all the way from Kilweem in the hope of finding work. Nor had she taken advantage of his hospitality for a moment longer than was necessary.

His piercing blue eyes watched her intently as she walked steadily towards him. Isobel coloured slightly but met his gaze levelly.

'I would like to thank you, Sir, for helping me . . .'

'All in the past,' he interrupted, dismissing her thanks and unwittingly saving her from further embarrassment. 'You are here to apply for a job, are you not?'

'Yes, Sir.' She clasped her nervously restless hands firmly in front of her.

'The work is hard, mind. And I expect anyone who works for me to be diligent, loyal and honest.' It was blunt, challenging. 'Do you think you can be all of these things?'

'Yes, Sir.' She answered firmly, meeting those keen eyes steadily.

'And you will be required to help in the kitchen. Can you cook?'

'I cook and keep house for my father and brother, Sir. And I am willing to learn.'

'You don't look strong.' His eyes ranged over her slight form critically.

'I am small but I am used to hard work, Sir.'

He shot half a dozen other questions at her. She replied truthfully until he asked her why she wanted to leave home. 'A daughter usually stays with her family.'

'Ours is a small house, Sir. My brother is being married shortly. He and his wife will live with my father. It would be better if I left before then.' It was not a lie, precisely; more an expectation of what would, no doubt, happen. And there was no way she could ever admit to the real reasons for her need to leave Kilweem.

Now he surveyed her in silence, recalling what Mrs McLachlan had told him about this girl's condition. 'Remember,' he barked suddenly. I'll stand for no . . . er . . . fraternising. Any men hanging around you and you'll be out. Understand?'

'Yes, Sir.'

'Right. Well, Mrs McLachlan seems to have taken a liking to you. She's a good judge of character. You can start tomorrow. For a month's trial. If you are satisfactory you can stay.'

'Thank you, Sir.' Surely he must have seen the great leap her heart had made.

'In addition to your wages you may take your meals in the kitchen. You may have two half days off in every week, provided that Mrs Mac can spare you, and you will do as she says in all things.'

'Yes, Sir.' She was willing to accept any terms.

The following day found Isobel repeating her journey. She left the Kilweem house, leaving a brief note for her father, and made her way to the bus stop without a backward glance at her childhood home.

'Well, lass, I'm busy right now so I'll show you to your room and leave you to get yourself sorted out. Come down for your meal at one. You can start work after that.' Mrs McLachlan wiped floury hands on her apron and led the way rapidly to the attic region.

The room was small and sparsely furnished. An iron bedstead took up most of the available space. The floor was bare, dusty boards and the tiny window was so dirty that Isobel could see nothing of the view. In one corner stood a small chest of drawers, in the other was a worn easy chair. An uncovered bulb was the only source of lighting and, as yet, the bed had no covers.

'Don't fret, lass,' Mrs McLachlan chuckled. 'There's plenty of blankets and sheets. I've got them in the kitchen airing off. Now, I'll show you where the storeroom is. Mr Geddes said you were to help yourself to a wee rug for the floor and you'll maybe find some curtains for that window, too.'

Isobel's initial dismay was replaced by pleasure. The room was grimy and uninviting now, and incredibly cold, but it wasn't so much worse than her room at Kilweem and she was confident she would be able to transform it into something much more attractive.

'Follow me,' Mrs McLachlan almost ran to a door at the end of the corridor, clearly in a hurry to attend to her other duties.

The attic storeroom was dark and cobwebby with old furniture and storage trunks strewn untidily. 'You'll just have to hunt for what you need. Now, I've other things to do so I'll leave you to it. Leave your door open and you'll hear the bell for lunch. Just follow the stairs right down, they'll bring you right into the kitchen.'

The kindly woman rushed away, leaving Isobel to rummage through the overflowing trunks. Eventually she discovered a single bright curtain, complete with brass rings, which would be ideal for her room. Rolled up behind a trunk she found a small rag rug and buried among a pile of broken chairs there was a small, rickety table which she could place beside her bed.

Her few personal things stowed easily in the chest of drawers. By the time she had hung the curtain and cleaned the window as best she could with a piece of old rag, the room was transformed. She stepped back into the doorway and viewed it with satisfaction. As she stood there a bell jangled faintly from somewhere at the bottom of the house.

Anxious not to be late she flew down the bare, stone stairs and emerged into a large, warm kitchen, full of the smell of frying bacon.

'Come on in, lass and meet Lizzie. She comes in every day to help out.' Mrs McLachlan turned from the range and waved cheerfully at a girl of about Isobel's own age who was pouring steaming tea into large mugs.

She was as tall as Isobel was small and just as slim. There the similarities ended. Lizzie was dark-haired and rosy cheeked. Her movements were quick and full of energy, as was her tongue. Invariably cheerful, woefully clumsy but compensatingly industrious she was glad to welcome someone of her own age into the household.

'Sit down here, next to me,' she grinned. 'Afterwards I'll show you round the house and tell you what you're supposed to do.'

Isobel smiled, overwhelmed by the girl's energy and by the huge plateful of food which was placed under her nose. Three thick slices of succulent gammon, a huge slice of bread fried in beef dripping and two golden eggs awaited her attention. Half a pint of hot tea was already in place.

Lizzie laughed. 'Mrs Mac has been trying to fatten me up for years. Now she'll do the same for you.' Already her own plate was almost clear.

'Less of your cheek, my girl. If you've finished there you can take over here while I eat my own meal.'

Lizzie obediently replaced the housekeeper at the range

while the older woman settled at the top of the long, scrubbed wooden table and applied herself to disposing of her own generous serving in the same hurried manner in which she seemed to approach every task.

While Isobel was still eating, valiantly trying to get to the end of her plateful, the outside door crashed open and a tall man dressed in a weatherproof jacket, leggings, muddy boots and a very battered cap, came in, blowing on his hands.

'It's cold enough to freeze,' he said, lobbing the cap accurately onto a spare chair before striding to the range to inspect his lunch. Isobel, who had her back to him, jumped at the unmistakeable sound of that deep, resonant voice and couldn't bring herself to look round.

'James Dryburgh,' Mrs Mac scolded. 'Just you take those boots off in my clean kitchen.'

Winking wickedly at Lizzie who giggled back he retreated to the door. He padded back in his stockinged feet and to Isobel's absolute horror, walked round the table and folded his long body into the seat directly facing hers.

'Isobel McLean!' His voice seemed to come from a long way off. But it was clear enough for her to hear the dismay and astonishment in it.

'Hello, Mr Dryburgh,' she muttered, hoping no-one would notice her scarlet face.

'Isobel is working here now,' Mrs McLachlan explained.

'Do you two already know one another?' asked Lizzie who had been quick to see Isobel's discomfort.

James continued to stare at her in silence while Isobel paid extravagant attention to the remains of her meal, remembering how attractive she had found him on the night of Twi's wedding, and also recalling how abruptly he had abandoned her that night.

'Remember, Lizzie,' Mrs Mac said impatiently. 'I told you. It was he and Mr Geddes who brought Isobel here that night.'

Isobel gasped audibly. 'You were there?' she stammered,

horror draining the blood from her face, leaving her white and shocked.

'Aye, lass.' Mrs McLachlan saved James the trouble of replying.

'You live here?' This was too awful.

'I'm the estate manager. But I don't live here. I have a cottage at the end of the estate road, on the Backdrum side,' he answered curtly. The horror in the girl's face when she recognised him had said it all. The attraction he felt for her was obviously not reciprocated.

'James eats with us,' Lizzie confided.

'Aye,' he said bitterly, wondering what on earth he could have done to so offend this strange creature. All he had tried to do was help. But he would never understand women, and this one was altogether too odd for his taste. 'So, don't worry, you won't have to put up with my company for more than half an hour a day.'

The other two women stared in amazement at this unusually curt comment from a man who was generally cheerful and even-tempered. Cut to the core, Isobel scraped back her chair and rose hurriedly from the table. 'I'll just wash my hands and then I'll get to work,' she stammered as she fled.

The water was freezing on her hands and face but she hardly noticed. Of all the people to be here, ruining what had promised to be a wonderful place to live and work. Why did it have to be him? She couldn't bear to contemplate what he must think of her after that dreadful night. But he had certainly made his attitude plain. Those few bitter words bit painfully into her heart.

Isobel's duties were far from onerous and she soon mastered them, falling happily into a routine which filled most of her day.

Rising at six to clean the grates and start the fires, as well as making sure the outdated but still serviceable range was warm and ready for Mrs McLachlan to cook on, the worst of her tasks were completed before breakfast. When that was cleared away, she and Lizzie chatted happily while they prepared the day's vegetables. That done, all the rooms had to be cleaned and dusted to Mrs McLachlan's exacting standard. Every day, at eleven-thirty, she inspected the girls' work. If there was a speck of dust lurking anywhere they were subjected to a fierce tongue-lashing which, on the first occasion, reduced Isobel to silent, private tears, mortified to think she had been found lacking.

The main chores of the day over, the afternoons were more relaxed. There was usually an hour or two of free time before the evening meal, which she spent mending or washing her personal clothes.

After supper the kitchen was scrubbed until it gleamed. Only then did Lizzie go home to her parents and seven brothers and sisters, while Mrs McLachlan and Isobel invariably settled near the heat of the range and switched the radio on.

Mr Geddes had a hot drink at half past nine. When his cup had been washed and the fires made safe, Isobel was free to go to bed.

It was a busy routine but, strict though she was, Mrs McLachlan was a fair and motherly woman to work for. More than once, when the weather was fine, she chased both girls into the grounds, insisting that the fresh air would do them good. Twice they came back to find her dozing in front of the range.

Isobel loved the grounds. Her two free half days every week were generally spent exploring them, or the gentle surrounding countryside, though she was very careful to avoid the direction of Netherdrum's farm behind the main house, at Backdrum. Her naturally artistic eye appreciated the beauty of the gardens and the subtle colouring of the mature trees and shrubs. Her very first wage had been spent on a sketchpad and new charcoal which she used at every opportunity, frequently drawing sighs of admiration from the rarely silent Lizzie.

The oldest of a large, boisterous family, Lizzie revelled in the novelty of having a friend of her own age. A strong bond quickly grew between the two young women, a thing greatly cherished by Isobel who had never known this kind of unselfish affection before. Even when Isobel gradually revealed a limited version of her own, unhappy past, Lizzie was intrigued rather than shocked, viewing Isobel's gift as something wonderfully strange and mysterious and, above all, God-given.

Of her employer himself Isobel saw surprisingly little. She took her turn, with Lizzie, to serve his meals but this was done in strict silence. Other than that she rarely saw him. When their paths did cross he was scrupulously polite but very formal and unapproachable. Only once had he spoken to her to ask if she had settled in and to inform her that, Mrs McLachlan having furnished satisfactory reports of her work, her trial period was successfully completed.

James Dryburgh was a different matter. For the first month Isobel dreaded lunchtimes and sat in miserable silence, matched only by his own taciturnity. But gradually, as they both became used to the other's presence, the atmosphere lightened and James reverted to his more usual, good-humoured character. He teased Lizzie and Mrs McLachlan mercilessly and, more and more frequently, tried to include Isobel in the cheerfulness of their shared mealtimes. But Isobel could never completely relax when James was in the room. There was something incredibly disturbing about him. An animal-like magnetism, an attraction which drew her eyes to him far too often for comfort. Especially when she so frequently found him already looking at her.

'If you ask me,' snorted Lizzie, from whom she could hide very little, 'you've fallen for him.'

'Rubbish!' Isobel shot back, a little too quickly.

'You're blushing,' accused Lizzie.

'He seems nice, that's all,' Isobel replied, inadequately.

'Aye, he is that.' Mrs McLachlan laid aside her mending and nodded sagely. 'But he's not for you, lass, so don't go losing your head over him.'

'Why not, Mrs Mac? He's young, he's rich and he's not married. Perfect!' Lizzie goaded the older woman wickedly.

'Rich?' echoed Isobel, unable to help herself.

Mrs McLachlan glanced at her sharply. Could it be that the girl didn't know? 'He's Mr Geddes's younger son, Isobel. I thought you knew that.'

'His son . . .' she was stunned. 'But his name . . . Dryburgh?'

'Mr Geddes was married twice. James Dryburgh is the son of his second wife. He took his mother's name after the divorce.' Mrs McLachlan settled her bony frame more comfortably in her sagging chair and set out to tell her tale, somewhat relishing her role.

'They were difficult ~imes. Mr Geddes, he was busy with his business, working all hours, never at home. Lilian, his first wife, well, she was a bright spark. She wanted to be with her friends in Edinburgh, not stuck out here at the back of beyond with just a baby for company. In the end she couldn't stand it any more. She just packed up and left.'

'What happened?' asked Lizzie who had never heard this particular tale before.

'Well, it wasn't common knowledge mind, though there were rumours in the village, but she met someone else and went off with him.'

'And took the baby with her?'

'No. She wasn't the type to be saddled with a child. No, he stayed here. Raised by nannies until he was old enough to be sent away to school. Best place for him, too. He was a wicked little boy.'

'James?' whispered Isobel, thinking of the generous smile and ready laugh. 'Wicked?'

'No. Not James,' said Mrs McLachlan irritably. 'I'm talking about his older brother. Mind you, the story was much the same with James's mother. I was younger than you two at the time and just a kitchen maid, but I mind it as if it was yesterday.' She sighed her nostalgia and went on. 'Those young women, they weren't prepared for a place like this. He had only just bought it then and it was cold and run down. As for him, well, it was work, work and more work. Sometimes he was away from one week's end until the next. I remember her well, the second Mrs Geddes. Lovely she was. But so unhappy. The arguments! She left him, too, in the end, just like his first wife. But she took James with her. He only came back here when she died. Wouldn't come before because of Alisdair. Those two don't get on. Never did.' She was half talking to herself now.

'Alisdair?' asked Isobel.

'Mr Geddes's oldest son,' Lizzie supplied the answer with an expressive shudder and grimace.

'Mr Geddes wanted Alisdair to stay here and run the estate with him, get involved in the business. You see, all this will be Alisdair's one day and Mr Geddes wanted him to know all about it by then. But Alisdair was having none of that. Spoiled he was. Posh school in England, rich friends, bad habits. Thought he was too good for Strathannan. He married a girl with money and went off looking for a soft life – not at all like his father that one. By all accounts they've got through all their money now, though. Gambled it away. Mr Geddes is very disappointed in him. You should hear the rows they have about that . . . In the end it was James who came and took over the farm . . . thank goodness.'

'Does this Alisdair ever come here?' Isobel asked.

'Oh yes,' Mrs McLachlan sniffed. 'Don't worry, you'll meet him soon enough!' She gazed at Isobel thoughtfully, then seemed to suddenly collect herself. 'There,' she scolded. 'You've made me say far too much. Just you make sure you never repeat anything I've said. It was just so you could understand the situation here. And I've no time for gossips.'

'No, Mrs McLachlan,' they chorused in giggling unison.

'And Isobel, lass, you do see, don't you, that James isn't

126

tor you? That is . . . well, he might be attracted, but it could never end . . .' she searched for the right word, '. . . decently.'

Isobel nodded mutely. Mrs McLachlan was right. With a father as wealthy as Mr Geddes obviously was, James Dryburgh would set his sights on someone far more suitable than a mere domestic in his family home. She retreated into unhappy silence, dreaming of what might have been.

But that conversation marked a rare black spot in Isobel's new life. From the security of Netherdrum, freed from her stern, accusative father, released from the hostility of the villagers, revelling in Lizzie's friendship and enjoying easier relationships with Twi and Robbie, and with Hugh and his new wife, May, Isobel blossomed. Her confidence soared, her skin bloomed and she put on just a little weight, giving her slender figure definition.

More than once James Dryburgh found himself looking at her with a keenly appreciative eye. But the cold look she seemed to reserve for him alone would be enough to dampen anyone's spirit. His enduring wish was to be able to put her from his mind, but she seemed to have taken possession of his soul.

NINE

*I*sobel's curiosity about James's mysterious half-brother was soon satisfied. Warned in advance that he and his wife would be guests for the weekend she had spent the morning preparing their room. Now, when she heard a car draw up, she hurried to open the front door.

Geddes stomped into the house, carrying an atmosphere of fury with him that was so intense that Isobel involuntarily stepped back a pace. A younger man followed him, flanked by a woman of startling appearance.

'Come on, Father! Don't let's argue,' the man said, shrugging his elegantly clad shoulders and smiling at his wife to reveal even, white teeth. 'I'm asking for almost nothing.'

Isobel stared at them, stunned into immobility. Alisdair Geddes was so like his younger half-brother that for a second she had thought that it was James who had marched past her. Alisdair had the same breadth and strength to his figure and gave a similar impression of careless charm. But, as he turned to follow his father into the dining room she saw that of the two brothers, Alisdair was the more classically handsome. His strong, dark features were symmetrically arranged without the slight imperfections which characterised James. Even so, the resemblance was startling.

'I do not call two thousand pounds nothing,' Geddes roared back, ignoring his son's apparent good humour. 'And it's not as if this is the first time you've come begging to me.'

Alisdair Geddes flung his heavy top coat into Isobel's

surprised arms. 'Coffee,' he said, subjecting her uniformed body to an appraising look, then smiling at her in an unpleasantly insinuating way which was unnerving in a face which bore such an uncanny similarity to James's. 'Who is this?'

'This is Miss McLean, Mrs McLachlan's new assistant,' Geddes answered, barely glancing at her.

'You hardly need extra help, Father. Surely that girl from the village can manage? It seems like a waste of good money to me.'

Alisdair's wife looked Isobel up and down as if she was a stray cat. 'You were told to bring coffee.' The cold, imperious voice shook Isobel who had been rooted to the spot by the venom in the other woman's stare.

Fiona Geddes, tall, immaculate and bejewelled, was the most striking woman Isobel had ever seen. The contrast between the inky black hair, white skin and crimson mouth was shocking. But the slight sneer on the parted lips, the severe pull of the tightly-drawn-back hair and the haughty lift of one, finely pencilled eyebrow gave the chilling impression of unapproachable arrogance.

'Yes, Ma'am,' Isobel answered, coldly polite, her calm dignity plainly infuriating the other woman.

'Get a move on, girl,' Geddes himself spoke sharply, his temper thoroughly roused by having been obliged to endure the combined pressure of his favourite though undeserving son and his unpleasant wife for the best part of an hour in the unescapable confines of their car. 'After a hard week at work I want to be able to have a weekend of peace and relaxation in my own home. I do not expect to be pestered and insulted by you, Alisdair.'

Alisdair fixed a rueful smile on his face. 'Oh, Father! I'm not pestering you. I'm your son. Where else should I go for help? Please be reasonable.'

Geddes's voice followed Isobel into the kitchen. 'Reasonable!' he bellowed, the veins on his neck bulging under a puce face. 'What is reasonable about you expecting me to support you?'

'I am not asking you to support me, Father. I just need a little temporary help.' His voice had lost some of its controlled good humour now.

'Again!' Geddes retorted furiously. 'Good God, Alisdair, you have a very generous allowance in addition to the small fortune you got your hands on when you married Fiona . . .'

'I hope you are not suggesting what I think you are,' his son said, the façade of charm disappearing under a tide of fury.

'Think what the hell you like,' his father yelled. 'The plain truth of the matter is you have gambled everything away. This gambling, Alisdair . . . it's out of control. Can't you see that?'

'Don't be ridiculous. It's a pleasant pastime. That's all. And I simply had a run of very bad luck.' Alisdair had the grace to look uncomfortable. 'I'll win it back before long.'

'Win it back!' Geddes spluttered. 'What the hell do you think you're doing, Alisdair? Why don't you get yourself a decent job? No self-respecting man would be content to live on his wife's money the way you have.'

Isobel crept back into the room in time to see Alisdair take a threatening step towards his father. For a moment she thought he was actually going to hit him. Far from backing away, Geddes took a step forward, almost as if daring Alisdair to do it. Drawn up to his full height, a snarling, towering mass of fury, Campbell Geddes, even at his advanced age, was not a man to be challenged easily. Alisdair hesitated, made a strangled noise deep in his throat and turned abruptly away.

'That's right,' Geddes taunted his retreating figure. 'Run away. Where are your guts, boy?'

From the relatively safe distance of the doorway, Alisdair spun round to face his father, a hard, twisted smile destroying the superficial likeness Isobel had seen between himself and James. 'Don't push me too far, Father and remember, one day, not too far away, all this will be mine.'

'Get out!' Geddes thundered. 'Get out of my sight!'

'Your coffee, Sir.' Isobel arranged cups and jugs on a low table, acutely embarrassed to have witnessed such a scene and eager to escape.

'Leave it,' Geddes rounded on her angrily. 'Can't a man get any peace in his own home?'

Isobel left the tray and fled.

It's always the same when they're here,' Lizzie said later. 'Alisdair only seems to come here when he wants money. But he wants other things, too,' she added cryptically. 'Just make sure he never gets you on your own.'

The whole weekend was extremely uncomfortable. The strained atmosphere even permeated the peace of the gardens where Isobel had escaped with her sketchpad for an hour after luncheon on Sunday. Picking a careful path along the occasionally muddy track through a patch of woodland at the back of the house, she made her way to her favourite place in a sun-dappled grove. Selecting a secluded spot she spread her blanket on the ground and sat with her back against a huge oak tree, looking away from the house over open farmland, her sketchbook open on her knees. The sun played gently on her face, filling her with its warmth. Soon the charcoal fell from her fingers and her eyes closed. The sound of voices nearby woke her.

'I tell you, Alisdair,' Fiona's deep, insistent tones reached Isobel clearly. 'You simply have to be firmer with him.'

He laughed, a low throaty chuckle. 'No, Fiona, you don't understand my father at all. He won't back down now. I don't think I'll get anything out of him this time. I'll have another go at him but we must be careful not to push him too far.'

'But you must think of something, Alisdair. You're the one who got us into this mess and you are the one who is going to have to get us out of it. We must get that money from somewhere. If your father is too mean to help, then you will have to find another way.'

Isobel sat as if paralysed. Already she had heard too much to reveal herself. She daren't even look round to see exactly where they were standing. The slightest movement might betray her.

'I'll think of something,' Alisdair said, running his fingers through his wife's silky hair.

'There are always the shares,' she suggested quietly.

He looked down at her thoughtfully. 'No, I can't sell those. Not yet. He would never forgive me. There's no point in alienating him over something as paltry as this.'

'But Alisdair. Your father's factory is highly profitable. He has had many offers.'

'And turned them all down.'

'So sell them back to him.'

'No, I've already tried that. Last year. He refused.'

'Then sell to the highest bidder and he'll only have himself to blame. There would be no shortage of interest.'

Alisdair sighed loudly. 'Do try to understand, my love. If those shares got into the wrong hands Father could lose everything, including my inheritance. Caulay's already hold twelve per cent and have made it clear they're on the market for more.'

'There's your answer. Sell to them. You'd get a very good price. As for your inheritance, you'd still get Nether-drum and all your father's other investments.'

'Father is absoluely determined to keep the factory as a family business.'

'But you are not interested in the factory. And *you* will never have a son to leave it to.'

'That was your decision, not mine,' Alisdair's voice was suddenly bitter.

'Yes. My body. My decision. The fact remains that you will never have an heir. Can't you see what will happen then?'

Isobel shuddered at the malignancy in her voice.

'James.'

'Yes, Alisdair. James. If your father ever realises that there will be no grandchildren from us he may well decide to leave the factory to James, especially if he ever marries. Look how quick he was to put him in your place here.'

'Never!' Alisdair took the bait. 'James will never get anything. I am the eldest. It's mine. By right.'

'If Caulay's took over the factory there would be nothing for James to have. You will get Netherdrum, you'll already have had your share of the sale of the factory. He will get nothing. Just think, Alisdair, a chance to clear all your debts and take care of James in one easy go. With a lot of money left over.' Ruthlessly she manipulated her husband. 'And, if you don't do something soon, you will be declared bankrupt. You do know, don't you, Alisdair, that I could never live with that. You'd be branded a failure. We'd lose all our friends. You'd be expelled from your club. I couldn't stand the disgrace of that, Alisdair.'

Alisdair Geddes stared down at his wife for a moment, then grinned. 'You're a scheming little bitch, Fiona. But don't you worry your pretty little head. I'll take care of it. I've plenty of useful contacts and one or two of them owe me a favour. I'll get the money.'

'And the shares?' she persisted.

'Later, Fiona. I'll sell them when I'm good and ready and not before,' he said, lowering his face to hers.

There were long minutes of muffled gasps and frantic rustling when Isobel could only imagine what they were doing. But, at last, she heard lowered voices and slow footsteps as they made their way back to the house. Stealing a cautious glance round the side of the tree she saw them making their way, arm in arm, along the woodland path.

Shivering despite the warmth of the bright sunshine, Isobel gave them five minutes, then gathered her things together and made her own thoughtful way back through the woods.

'Really, I am surprised you have the time to go creeping about the grounds.' The cold, low-pitched voice startled her. Fiona was sitting on an old wooden bench near the end of the pathway. In her abstracted state Isobel had failed to see her until it was too late.

'I usually have a free hour in the afternoons.' Isobel tried to walk on.

Fiona planted herself firmly in the middle of the path. 'Well, please do not come into the grounds. They are private.'

'I have Mrs McLachlan's permision,' Isobel defended herself a touch defiantly.

'Mrs McLachlan is merely the housekeeper. I am sure Mr Geddes would not approve, especially when the family is here.' Levelling a look of utter contempt at Isobel, Fiona turned on her elegantly shod heel and walked smoothly towards the house. Angrily Isobel watched until she disappeared round a corner. But, when she tried to resume her own journey, she found the narrow path twisting and writhing beneath her, making her dizzy to look at it. With a gasp of despair she sank onto the bench while the trees and lush undergrowth blurred and disintegrated to reform into harsh, heather-strewn moorland.

She blinked and peered into the mist which now swathed the area, shivering in the pervading damp chill that ran through her body. The silence was eerily, unnaturally still. Gradually the mist cleared until she could just make out the forms of two men, still too indistinct for her to be able to identify them. Swirling mist obliterated them for a moment and, when it thinned again, seconds later, she glimpsed dogs and guns, as if this was a shooting party. The animals ran excitedly round the men but although she could see they were barking, no sound reached her ears. Now she realised that the two men were arguing. It was obvious in their posture, in the rapid motion of their hands, in their abrupt, jerky movements. Abruptly one of the men broke away and strode into the enveloping mist, everything in his manner indicating extreme anger. As Isobel watched, powerless to intervene, the second man raised his gun to his shoulder and took careful aim. Only a few yards away the first man turned, as if answering a call and as he did so the gun went off. Acrid smoke burnt Isobel's nostrils and she watched in terror as the first man crumpled to the ground. In vain she struggled to get to her feet and go to his aid but now the area was so thickly shrouded in dense, choking fog that she could no longer see her own body. And then, without warning, coughing the bitter taste of gunsmoke from her mouth and throat, she was looking at Netherdrum again, bathed in gentle sunlight, calm and undisturbed.

For long minutes she was unable to move, lost in the horror of what she had witnessed. When she did glance at her wristwatch it was already twenty-five minutes since her encounter with Fiona. Shakily she got to her feet but spinning, crippling vertigo made her sway while bitter, rushing nausea forced her to retch painfully into the grass. It was another half hour before she was fit enough to make her way slowly back to the house.

James joined his family for dinner that night. Isobel, still pale and tired after the trauma of the afternoon, helped Lizzie to serve the meal and could scarcely take her eyes off him. Used, as she was, to seeing him in well-worn and often muddy working clothes, the transformation in his appearance was startling. Nothing could have made the gulf in their relative positions more obvious.

A dinner jacket, white shirt and bow tie seemed absolutely natural on him. He wore them with ease and assurance, appearing quite comfortable as he sipped his wine with the air of someone accustomed to the more luxurious things in life. To Isobel, the slightly unconventional length of his hair and the careless way he wore it only added to his enigmatic charm.

As she moved cautiously between the diners to serve the main course, Isobel was struck by the similarities between James, his father and Alisdair. All three were big, imposing men with a shared sense of self-assurance. But James's manner had none of the testy truculence which marked his father and lacked the smooth urbanity with which Alisdair cloaked himself. Half-brothers, their features were really remarkably alike. Only their eyes were different. James's were dark, velvety brown, deep and unfathomable; Alisdair's were lighter, always shifting and watchful.

Despite James's apparently nonchalant manner, the atmosphere at the table was tangible, so acrimonious that she longed to retreat to the relative placidity of the kitchen and Mrs McLachlan's industrious regime. The raised voices which had marred the late afternoon and early evening had obviously resulted in this tense, resentful silence – silence punctuated only by the sound of cutlery on china and the loaded glances passing between Alisdair and his wife. Campbell Geddes ate his meal with determined, black-faced deliberation while his eldest son glowered and sulked like a child. Only James was outwardly unaffected, seeming to have deliberately distanced himself from them all as he concentrated firmly on his food.

'Clear these plates away,' Fiona barked at Isobel. 'Really, you are quite impossibly slow. I don't know why you tolerate this slackness, Father.' Her lips curled in sleek satisfaction as the unfair criticism brought floods of hot colour to Isobel's white cheeks. 'You should get rid of this girl. I'll see if I can find someone else.'

Isobel actually thought her heart had stopped beating.

Campbell Geddes dropped his fork with a clatter. 'I realise things are not done here in exactly the way you would arrange them, Fiona,' he said with all the calm of a simmering volcano, 'but you are a self-invited guest in this house and hardly in a position to criticise.'

Isobel let out the breath she had been holding and raised her head to find herself looking directly at James. To her utter consternation he closed one eye in a wicked wink and grinned broadly, openly showing his delight at his sister-in-law's discomfiture.

Flushing to the roots of her blonde hair, Isobel hastily grabbed a pile of dirty plates and practically ran to the kitchen.

James stared after her, completely perplexed. He had seen the way her eyes widened and her mouth curved into a natural, responsive smile to that wink. Why, then, had she made herself scowl and run away like that? He sighed and sipped the slightly bitter coffee his father preferred. It seemed that Isobel was determined to rebuff even the slightest sign of friendship from him, no matter how hard he tried.

Reluctantly putting Isobel out of his mind, he pulled his attention back to the argument which was once again starting to simmer around him.

It was the usual one. Alisdair wanted money; their father had said no.

James frowned, deeply resenting his father's insistence that he be here tonight, forced to listen to something which was, essentially, none of his business. He suspected their father had done it deliberately, to irritate Alisdair.

Campbell Geddes was well aware of the fact that there was no affection between his sons. On the rare occasions when they had been obliged, as children, to spend time together, they had been totally unable to co-exist peacefully.

The passing years had done nothing to ease the situation. Geddes had always honestly admitted that it was Alisdair he really wanted at his side, at Netherdrum, learning to run the estate which would one day be his. But Alisdair didn't share James's appreciation of the soft, Strathannan countryside and complained that the beautiful old house was damp, draughty and inconvenient. His interest in both Netherdrum and the business was limited to an assessment of its potential in terms of his own future. His education, at a reputable English public shool followed by three years at University, had brought him into contact with a stratum of society which saw no particular merit in working for a living and had given him a taste for a lifestyle which was beyond even his father's considerable means. As soon as he could he had taken himself off to Edinburgh where, on the strength of his much-vaunted inheritance, he had found himself a wife with a wealthy father and a large dowry.

Reluctantly, Campbell Geddes had asked James to run the farm and manage the estate while he continued to oversee the business. But it was, they all knew, a temporary solution. No doubt there would be some financial provision for him when their father died, after all there was genuine, if impatient affection between them, but it was no secret that the bulk of the fortune would go to Alisdair.

James fervently hoped that this inevitability was still a very long way off. He loved Netherdrum and managed the farm with an efficiency born of a genuine love of the land and, he thought, looking at his father, Campbell Geddes seemed indestructible, as strong and indomitable as he had always been. The unpalatable fact remained that one of Alisdair's first acts on inheriting would be to oust his younger brother. And everyone sitting at that table knew it.

The voices round him, heated and loud now, stopped suddenly. James refocused his persistently wandering attention in time to see Alisdair rise and leave the room, closely followed by his awful wife.

Their father, evidently the victor, leaned back in his chair and lit a cigar, a smile of contentment on a face which was still mottled red from the strain of argument.

'Well, that's that,' he growled. 'That's the last we'll hear about that, you mark my words.'

'Yes,' agreed James, tired of it all. 'Until the next time.'

Campbell Geddes looked at his son through pungent, blue smoke as if he might have taken issue with him, but then, 'Aye, I daresay you're right, lad. Until the next time.' All trace of the contented smile had disappeared.

Much to Isobel's relief, Alisdair Geddes and his acidic wife decided to return to Edinburgh a day earlier than they had originally planned. After lunch Mrs McLachlan sent her to their room.

'Start packing, will you,' Alisdair smiled charmingly and gestured to the clothing scattered carelessly around the room.

'And make sure you do it properly,' Fiona, elegant in a grey silk dress and matching court shoes, turned from the dressing table.

Isobel, who had thought she was accustomed to the other woman's harsh beauty, was stunned. Fiona was immaculate, dressed and made up as if ready to go to a gala performance. Used as she was to her own plain but functional clothing and hampered by continued rationing, she was astounded by the sheer luxury of Fiona's wardrobe.

'Well, are you going to stand there and gawp all day?'

Isobel retrieved dresses, skirts and expensive silk under-wear from the floor and busied herself folding and repacking them, marvelling at the richness of the materials and wondering how Fiona had managed to acquire such a wide range of high-quality clothing when most people thought the possession of a single pair of nylon stockings to be the ultimate in extravagant good fortune.

While Isobel worked Fiona sat on a stool, brushing her glossy hair in slow rhythmic strokes, watching everything through her mirror.

'Let me do that,' Alisdair fumbled for the hairbrush. Only then did Isobel realise that he was very slightly drunk.

'Go away, Alisdair,' Fiona said without conviction. 'You are quite disgusting.'

Laughing, he grabbed her from behind and, seeming to forget Isobel's presence, fondled his wife's breasts. Isobel flushed scarlet, then fixed her eyes firmly on her task. Fiona's peal of delighted laughter deepened the flush to a deep, uncomfortable crimson.

'We're embarrassing the girl, Alisdair.' She waited until Isobel's eyes met her own in the mirror then snapped. 'Get on with your job.'

Now Alisdair's hand was working its way up her thigh but, abruptly tiring of the game, Fiona shoved him away.

'Get away from me, you're drunk,' she accused, rising to her feet and flouncing from the room.

'I am not,' he retorted, starting to follow her but tripping over the edge of the trailing bedspread and almost falling on top of Isobel.

'Well, well, Isobel,' he said, righting himself. 'You are a pretty little thing, aren't you? Let me have a closer look at you.' He grabbed her by the arm and tried to pull her nearer.

Flaring red anger surged through Isobel, fed by the brutal, raw memory of Henry McArdle. Never again would she allow herself to be abused, by anyone. Summoning all her strength and using both hands she shoved him. He was just drunk enough to have to fight to retain his balance, giving her time to scramble for the open door. But she wasn't fast enough. He cornered her there, slamming the door and pinning her against the wall, holding her face deliberately cruelly with one hand and squeezing her breasts with the other.

'Come on, Isobel,' he smiled, looking obscenely like James.

Acting quite instinctively, she scratched him, raking sharp fingernails down one cheek, then bit the hand which held her face. While he still stared at the wound in childlike surprise she pushed him away from her, sending him sprawling back into a table with a harsh jangle of breaking glass and crashing furniture. Not pausing to see if he was seriously hurt she stormed from the room, and cannoned straight into James and his father, come to investigate the noise.

'Isobel! Are you alright?' James asked, trying to catch her.

Too angry to be concerned with politeness and certainly not wanting his pity she barged past him and ran to the safety of her own room. Only when she got there did she realise how badly she was shaking.

Meanwhile, one glance at the tell-tale marks on his son's face was enough to tell Campbell Geddes what had happened.

'For God's sake, Alisdair,' he bellowed. He got no further. James pushed his way into the room and elbowed his father out of the way. Grabbing Alisdair by the collar he dragged him to his unsteady feet and glared at him with undisguised contempt.

'Isobel McLean is a good, decent girl. You keep your dirty hands off her,' he snarled.

'Isobel McLean is a cheap little tramp,' Alisdair snapped back, anger sobering him. 'I really can't see why you're so upset, James. Unless you want that little piece for yourself.' The malicious remark fell on unexpectedly sensitive ground. But before Alisdair could appreciate his success James's solid fist hit him squarely between the eyes, snapping his teeth on his tongue, jarring his brain and momentarily stunning him. James grunted with the force of it and drew back his fist again but Campbell imposed his own solid body between those of his sons. Without a word he pushed Alisdair back on the bed where he laid whimpering and clutching his head. Then, with a vice-like grip on James's upper arm, he dragged him out into the corridor and rounded on him furiously.

'Calm down, James,' he roared. 'By God, I'll have that girl out of this house within the hour.'

James banged his father's hand away and yelled back. 'No! It wasn't her fault. You know what he was doing to her.'

'It seems to me that she more than took care of that for herself. There was no need for you to make such an ass of yourself over a servant.'

'Sssss . . . servant?' James spluttered. 'My God! This isn't the eighteenth century!' Somehow he had never really thought about Isobel in those terms and the word shocked him deeply. 'Alisdair doesn't have the right to behave like that with anyone,' he added, more slowly. 'You can't turn her out because she tried to defend herself. She did what any

141

decent woman would have done. Or would you have been happier if she'd just kept quiet and let him get on with it?' he challenged.

'That's enough!' Geddes spluttered then looked at his younger son, one eyebrow raised in cynical speculation. 'Alright,' he agreed at last. 'She can stay. But,' he went on, his voice hissing, 'if you have any designs on that girl, forget them. She may be decent enough but she *is* a servant in this house and I will not have you, either of you, associating with her. Is that clear?'

'Yes. Thank you, father,' James said gruffly.

'And remember, James. I may be old but I am not senile yet. And that young woman will not get a second chance.'

For a full week James claimed he was too busy to eat lunch as usual in Mrs McLachlan's fragrant kitchen. Isobel, who was very well aware that she was the reason for his absence, was relieved. The last person she wanted gloating over her shame was James Dryburgh.

The Sunday after that dreadful weekend was one of those warm, lazy, late summer afternoons which begs to be savoured in the open air. Mr Geddes was sleeping off the effects of a heavy lunch in a chair on the front lawn, a panama hat shading his face. Mrs McLachlan was following his example at the back. Lizzie had gone home.

Dressed in a home-made, light summer dress Isobel carried her charcoal and sketchpad to the very edge of the formal gardens where Netherdrum was divided from its own farmland by a picturesque stream. Finding partial shade under a young tree she sat on a grassy hummock, slipped off her shoes and dangled her feet in the water. It was deliciously cold and wonderfully clear. From time to time the sun glinted on silvery scales as fish flashed through the water.

For about half an hour Isobel sat, content to relax and enjoy the dying days of a wonderful summer. But, when she felt herself becoming drowsy, she deliberately got up and splashed cold water on her face. Days like these were too precious to waste in sleep. Happily she took up her sketchpad and settled down to work. Knees drawn up under her skirt to support her pad, neat ankles and bare feet peeping from beneath, her fair hair falling softly over her face as she concentrated on her drawing, she presented a very lovely picture.

'That is a superb drawing!' The honest praise was out before James could stop it.

Isobel jumped violently and spun round, dropping her charcoal and allowing her sketchpad to slide off her knees, almost into the water. He caught it before it was damaged.

'Here. Take care of it. It's much too good to lose,' he said, grinning broadly as it handed it back to her.

She accepted it silently.

'Look,' he offered. 'I'm sorry I made you jump. I couldn't resist it.'

His expression was so contrite that she had to smile back. And anyway, she thought, the day was too lovely to spoil with bad temper.

'You deliberately scared me,' she laughed, anxious that he wouldn't think badly of her, especially after what he had done to Alisdair on her behalf. Despite her embarrassment to discover that the whole household had overheard the ensuing argument with his father, Isobel was secretly thrilled to know he had felt strongly enough to act as he did.

James settled casually on the grass below her own tussock, rolled his trousers up over his calves and stretched out in the sun.

'Ah, wonderful,' he murmured, closing his eyes.

He looked so relaxed, as at home in the shabby working trousers, loose shirt and bare feet as he had done in the formal dinner suit. As she stared at him he opened one lazy eye and squinted up at her. 'Do you mind if I stay here?' He half expected her to say she did. Any friendly overtures on his part had been firmly rebuffed in the past.

'No,' she laughed again, her blue eyes sparkling, feeling her heart hammering with excitement at having him so close.

He shut his eyes again. 'Go on with your drawing. I won't disturb you.' Then he appeared to go to sleep, as easily and completely as a child. Isobel stared at him for a full minute, suspecting that he was shamming, but his face didn't even twitch and his hands, folded loosely over his flat stomach, seemed perfectly relaxed.

Eventually she took up her materials and started to draw again, concentrating so fiercely that she never caught him watching her from under half-closed lids.

After an hour he stretched languorously, then grabbed the sketch-book from her hands. The jolly, half-teasing comment which had been on the tip of his tongue died, unspoken, and he came closer, crouching so near to her that their bodies were almost touching. By some magic, using only crude charcoal, she had succeeded in drawing a very good likeness of him, perfectly capturing the balmy feel of the day in an intricate pattern of light and shadow over his face.

'This,' he said softly, 'is marvellous. Who taught you to draw like this?'

Writhing with mortification she whispered, 'No-one.' That picture had been for her. She had never meant him to see it.

'You've never had a lesson?'

'At my school we were taught to read and write, do sums and knit.'

'But someone must have shown you,' he insisted, ignoring the flat sound of her voice. 'Look at the way you've caught the light here . . . and here. I could never do that. Pity about the subject, though.'

'I've always loved drawing,' she admitted, allowing herself to smile again. 'But I couldn't get my hands on much paper when I was little. It was too expensive,' she added pointedly, some part of her wanting to make the difference in their backgrounds plain.

'I suppose so,' he said, feeling clumsy.

'I used to draw in the sand on the beach sometimes,' she went on, feeling his discomfort. 'But I gave up because the tide always washed it away.'

Now they laughed together.

'Have you ever used paints?' he asked.

'Once I had a small tin of paints for Christmas. But I had to share them with Twi. They didn't last long.'

'I have some,' he said excitedly, moving round to face her. 'You can have them if you like.'

'No!' then, realising she had sounded ungrateful, 'I couldn't.'

'Of course you could. I never use them. I don't have time to paint. I was never any good anyway.'

'You paint?' she asked, wondering how those broad, capable hands could wield anything as delicate as a paintbrush.

'No,' he admitted, chuckling. 'But my mother was artistic and she was determined that I must have some talent hidden somewhere. She and my grandmother paid for me to have lessons.'

'I wish I had had that opportunity,' she said wistfully.

'I don't,' he retorted. 'I never felt so useless. No matter how hard I tried nothing ever turned out the way it should. But I do remember some of what I was taught. If you like I could show you the basics of watercolours. The washes and things like that.'

Now they were so close that she could feel the warmth of his breath on her face, clean and gentle. 'I would like that very much,' she whispered.

James moved a fraction closer. Her skin was melting, her eyes half closed, waiting for the kiss which must surely come. But, 'Sure. Just let me know when your next half day is.'

Before she knew what was happening he was on his feet

and backing away quickly. He couldn't let this happen. She was too young, too vulnerable. It simply wouldn't be fair to her.

The flush on Isobel's cheeks as she watched him cross nimbly over the stream was one of anger and humiliation. How stupid she had been to let him see her reaction to him so plainly. And how could she have misinterpreted so badly? He offered friendship and genuine admiration for her work, but that was as far as it went. She suspected that she had embarrassed him, too, and believed that even that tenuous offer of friendship would be withdrawn. Tears glistened in her eyes. Viciously she tore his portrait from her pad, screwed it into a tight ball and hurled it furiously into the water.

At lunchtime the next day James turned up as cheerfully as if he had never stayed away. In his arms he carried a wooden box which he deposited on the table in front of Isobel, without comment. Feeling the treacherous blush already warming her ears, suspecting what was inside, she muttered 'Thank you,' knowing she sounded particularly ungracious.

'What is it, Isobel?' Lizzie cried, running over to examine the box.

Even Mrs McLachlan turned from her cooking and gave James a quizzical look. He rewarded her with an innocent smile.

Knowing she could do nothing else, Isobel drew the box towards her, slipped the tiny brass hooks and gasped her delight.

Inside the box were at least forty tubes of paint, mostly unused, two shallow pots and four brushes. Clipped snugly into the lid was a slightly stained palette. Lovingly she fingered the tubes, imagining what she might do with them, oblivious of the three pairs of eyes, all fixed on her.

'Paints!' exclaimed Lizzie, breaking the spell.

'My, my,' said Mrs McLachlan. 'That is very kind of you, Sir,' There was a soft emphasis on the 'Sir'.

Her words made Isobel recall her manners. 'Yes . . . they're . . . they're wonderful. Thank you James,' she said softly, smiling at him now, still not knowing whether to love or hate this man who played such havoc with her emotions.

Mrs McLachlan stopped the automatic correction which sprang to her lips, knowing that to ask Isobel to call James 'Sir' now would be pointless.

James merely grinned and bent to his meal. But his brown eyes sparkled with pleasure.

Much later Isobel tidied the kitchen ready for morning. Mrs McLachlan had taken herself off to bed so she was quite alone. She moved slowly, her mind still full of James and her confused feelings for him. She heard the back door open and spun round, unnerved by a caller at this late hour. But it was James himself who stood in the shadowed doorway, filling the frame. 'Are you almost finished?' he asked, his deep voice sending quivers through her skin.

'Yes.' She busied herself at a cupboard. 'Do you want something?' She knew she sounded cold, knew too she should thank him properly for the paints but she couldn't even look at him.

'I've got something to show you,' he said, strolling into the room and settling himself comfortably in Mrs McLachlan's chair.

He waited in silence while she made unnecessarily hard work of completing the simplest tasks until at last she could delay no longer. 'I'm finished now.'

'About time. I thought I was going to have to sit there until dawn.' He smiled at her and she had the uncomfortable feeling that he had read her confusion and was laughing at it. 'Come with me, Isobel.' He walked briskly into the yard. After a moment she followed him. He was leaning non-chalantly against the wall without the least sign of impatience. 'Come here,' he laughed.

She obeyed, powerless to resist but not knowing what to

expect and wary of another rebuff. 'What do you want, James?'

'I have something for you.' In the fading light she could see him smiling softly at her. 'Come on, have a look.' He stepped aside to reveal a tall, wooden contraption, propped up beside him.

She peered at it, not knowing what it could be. Confused, she looked up and saw at once that this time he really was laughing at her. She was instantly defensive.

'Is this some sort of joke?' she snapped.

'No!' Now he guffawed aloud. 'I'm sorry . . . but you seem so suspicious. It's quite harmless. Honestly. Look.'

He yanked at the thing, revealing four legs, tapering together at the top to form a steady frame. 'It's an easel. You'll need it if you are going to paint properly. See, these pegs support the board. You pin your paper to it.'

'But,' she was speechless for long seconds. 'I can't take this. It's yours.'

'It's not mine. I made it specially for you this evening.'

After what had happened on Sunday afternoon he had spent his precious free time making this for her? She felt hopelessly confused. 'I don't know what to say,' she admitted, sounding slightly hoarse.

'Then don't say anything.' Despite all his good intentions he couldn't help himself. So swiftly she had no time to avoid him, he pulled her into his arms. Briefly, very briefly she struggled, perversely wanting to repay him for her previous disappointment. But when his lips found hers she stilled, her senses only aware of his mouth on hers, the warmth of him, the infinitely masculine smell of him, the taste. Softly he kissed her, sensing without being aware of it that he must treat her gently. Gradually she responded, returning the pressure and opening her mouth to his questing tongue. When he drew her even closer her arms slipped round his shoulders.

'Isobel,' he whispered, breaking free at last and running

trembling hands through her silky hair. 'You don't know how long I have been wanting to do that.'

In response she laid her head against his shoulder, feeling safe and protected, as if this was where she belonged. Only very reluctantly did she pull away. 'I have to go in.'

'I know. I know.' He kissed her lightly on the cheek and waited until she had safely locked and bolted the door behind her before sagging limply against the wall.

Sleep, normally so effortlessly found, just would not come. James Dryburgh seemed to have taken possession of every fibre of her being. When she did, finally, drift off, a bare hour before she had to get up again, her dreams were restless and hot. She woke with heat between her legs and excitement bubbling through her veins, yearning to see him again.

A scant quarter of a mile away, in the small cottage he occupied in stark, lonely solitude, James's light burned far into the night. He knew he had embarked on a dangerous course but it was one he seemed powerless to avoid. The obsession he felt for this stunning girl was dangerously close to love. But he also knew that no matter how strongly he felt about her, his father would abhor his attachment to Isobel McLean. Well, his father had had his own way over too many things. It was long past time to stand up to him.

Isobel lived only for the moments when she saw James. His ever-lengthening lunch breaks, the lingering, loving looks which passed between them could not fail to go unnoticed by both Mrs McLachlan and Lizzie. Deeply disturbed, the older woman was torn between loyalty to her employer and a genuine affection for Isobel. But her over-whelming feeling was fear. Fear that Isobel would be badly hurt. James Dryburgh might frequently look like a farm labourer and his relaxed manner made his real position easy to forget. But, younger son of a very minor land-owning businessman though he might be, he was still out of Isobel's class. Mrs McLachlan knew that Campbell Geddes's fury would be uncontrollable when he discovered, as he surely must, what was going on between his son and Isobel McLean.

On her next half day, when the weather was fine, Isobel met James, as arranged, some distance from Netherdrum House. Hand in hand, he carrying the easel slung effortlessly over one shoulder, she with the precious paints, they clambered over fences and gates until they found a sheltered spot, looking down on his own modest home from the top of a small rise.

Quickly she made a rough sketch while he set up the easel.

'I'm not an expert by any means but I can give you some idea of how to apply a colour wash,' he said.

She watched intently as he squeezed blue paint from one tube and mixed it with white and then a dab of black until he was satisfied with the shade. Using the brush as a scoop he added water from one of the pots, then spread the thin mix over the top half of the paper. 'Sky,' he announced unnecessarily.

The process was repeated with a dark bluey green over the lower part of the paper, overlapping the blue. 'Trees and grass.' He grimaced at his efforts. 'It's supposed to be a background. To build on.'

'Yes. I see. Can I try?'

'Sure.' He abandoned the easel to her and saw that she mastered the technique a great deal more easily than he had been able to. Impatient to experiment, she soon had other colours on the palette and a passable impression of his distant house on the paper.

'It's harder than I thought it would be,' she admitted, surveying her first efforts without any pleasure.

'You're telling me?' he laughed. 'But this is really excellent for a first try, Isobel. But look, I can't demonstrate very well, but with watercolours you don't have to make the lines hard, as if you were still using a pencil or charcoal.

Everything can be indefinite, softer, almost smudged. See.' He rubbed a finger over the still damp paint. 'Damn it, that's not what I mean! I never could do this even though I was shown it a thousand times.'

'I think I know what you mean.' Deftly she used the brush to paint a few light strokes. A gate appeared, insubstantial but more realistic than anything she had so far accomplished.

'Yes . . . I can see I'm wasting my time.'

She jerked her head up, horrified.

A firm hand tilted her chin and he kissed her firmly. 'Don't be so ready to be hurt, Isobel. All I meant was that you clearly don't need me to explain this to you. I'll probably ruin your natural style. All you need is time to experiment and practise. You are already better than I could ever be.'

The brush dropped from her hands, the easel was forgotten. Nothing mattered but the two of them together, as they sank onto the grass.

As winter placed its chill hand over Strathannan it became more and more difficult for Isobel and James to have time and privacy together. Not entirely trusting himself to be alone with her, and well aware of the damage which might be done to her reputation if they were seen, James had resisted the temptation to take her to his own home. But the day came when, frustrated by the limitations placed both on her painting and on their maturing relationship by the weather, Isobel herself broached the subject.

'The light in my room is too poor to paint by,' she complained. 'Do you think I could set up my things in one of your spare rooms?'

'Well . . .' he considered it.

'Please, James,' she begged. 'Just until the weather clears. I'll make sure no-one sees me. And it'll only be for one or two afternoons each week.'

'Okay,' he capitulated easily enough. After all, it was the first time she had actually asked him for anything. 'But I'm warning you, you might not actually get a lot of work done if I'm anywhere near.'

She giggled happily and let him pull her close enough for her to feel the hard proof of his desire. Always before she had pulled away a little, wary of making what she knew would be, for her, a final commitment, but increasingly she needed more than hot kisses and the frustrating fondling they had both limited themselves to. Like him she yearned for fulfilment; a fulfilment they were edging towards as the natural progression of a warm and loving relationship. Tonight she pressed into him, rousing him almost past self-control. Almost. The dark back-yard of Netherdrum House was no place for intimacy.

It was inevitable that the time would come when their self-imposed control would shatter. On Isobel's first half day in over a week she had painted in James's spare bedroom until the light had failed. But, unusually, her heart had not been in it.

It seemed so long since they had been together. Their brief contact at lunchtimes, always under Mrs McLachlan's eagle eye, had made their separation even harder to bear. Restlessly abandoning her work Isobel went into his sitting room to wait for him. He was late. A fall of snow and the promise of more to come had him and his three hands fully occupied in bringing the cattle into shelter. It was after eight before she heard his heavy footsteps.

'Isobel,' he stripped off his damp outer clothes hurriedly and rushed to her, his aching limbs and frozen hands forgotten in the pleasure of finding her still there. 'I thought you would have given up by now,' he said, kissing her greedily even while he spoke.

'I would have waited all night,' she whispered into his hair, inhaling the heady smell of him. 'But look, James. I've got something for you.'

'For me? You don't need to buy things for me,' he scolded.

'I haven't bought you anything,' she laughed back. 'But I did want to say thank you for giving me your paints. I don't think you really understand what a wonderful gift they were.'

Shyly now she handed him a brown paper-wrapped parcel. Intrigued he broke the string with his pocket knife and carefully peeled back the paper.

On his own admission James was not artistic. He was a strong, capable and severely practical man whose deep love of the land he farmed grew not out of any great appreciation of its beauty, but from the satisfaction of being able to make it work for him. His own rather austere house and his personal appearance, dedicated to comfort rather than fashion, were firm indications of his attitude to life. But the two small pictures revealed when he opened the package both stunned and delighted him. The first, a later and infinitely more proficient version of the scene she had attempted on her first lesson, pleased him beyond words. It was expertly done, a real testimony to her undeniable talent. The second was its companion, a view of Netherdrum House itself, hazy in the late summer sun. Both pictures showed a unique use of colour and appreciation of the subtleties of light and shade which were becoming her hallmarks.

'These are wonderful, Isobel . . . Thank you . . . I'll always treasure them.' He held them out, lost in admiration. 'I'll hang them in here so they will remind me of you even when you're not here.'

'You need reminding?' she teased.

At last he laid the paintings down and pulled her towards him. 'You are a remarkable woman,' he said as he started to kiss her, gently at first. But it was no longer enough for either of them, and they both knew it. Their kisses grew increasingly passionate, their embrace more intimate and demanding as their bodies entwined.

Their clothes were discarded naturally, without shame or

embarrassment until, for the first time, they saw each other naked. For a long moment he looked at her, openly enjoying the ripeness of her smooth body. She looked back proudly, feeling nothing but her love for him and the absolute rightness of what they were about to do.

When he took her it was with genuine love, a gently sharing act that, for him, was like nothing he had ever experienced before. For the first time in his life James was concerned that his partner should be equally pleasured. He was gentle and patient, waiting for her to show him that she was ready. Trusting him completely Isobel surrendered to her surging emotions and gave herself to him with joy to emerge shaking from the violence of her own response. In a glorious hour of intense, satisfying intimacy, James wiped away the violation of Kilweem beach so that it could never return to haunt her. Afterwards they lay snug and secure, content and silent. And without regret.

'I love you, Isobel,' he whispered into her tousled hair.

'And I love you, James,' she said, stirring regretfully but knowing that she must return to Netherdrum before Mrs McLachlan locked up for the night, or face dismissal.

'We will have to tell Father,' he said, hoisting himself onto his elbow and frowning, the thought fracturing the idyllic interlude. 'I refuse to go on meeting you in secret. It looks as though I'm ashamed to be seen with you.'

'No, James! I'm just a maid in his house. He'll never . . .'

'I don't care. I'm proud to be with you. Proud that you want me. I want everyone to know about us.'

'Not yet, James,' she said quietly. 'Not yet. Don't spoil it.' Because she knew that when Campbell Geddes discovered their secret it would be the end.

Although Isobel and James did their best to be discreet, the feeling of joy which had exploded on that first night swept gleefully into every corner of Netherdrum House. Lizzie and Mrs McLachlan could not be unaware of the new intimacy between the golden-haired girl and her strong, dark lover.

James wore his happiness not only on his face, which was suddenly five years younger, but in the warm depths of his eyes, in his more relaxed manner and in his tendency to hum, rather tunelessly, when he thought no-one else was within earshot. He felt released, renewed, as if his life was beginning all over again. He treasured every second he spent with Isobel. The more he learned of her, sharing her account of her past life with anger, shock and sympathy, the more he longed to give her the pure, uncritical love she deserved. She was everything to him. His love for her was apparent in his eyes, his hands, his voice, his body. In everything he did. It was matched only by the love she felt for him.

All her life Isobel had faced rejection. Even with her twin sister there had been a distance, a separation, caused by the dreadful burden of her supernatural gift. The taunts and jeers of her peers, the hostility of her own family had turned her inward, making it impossible for her to share herself wholeheartedly with anyone, always on the alert for the first signs of suspicion and coldness. With James, as he gradually coaxed her story from her, drawing some of the pain and anger with it, she finally found someone on whom she could rely, in whom she could trust.

His reaction to her halting admission of her ability to see snatches of the future brought no hint of repulsion but rather admiration, gentle sympathy and the steady encouragement to see it as a true gift and not the curse she had always felt it to be. In truth, it seemed to him quite natural that such a unique and beautiful creature should be so different from all others. Because of him her fear of these strange attacks lessened and then disappeared. As the apprehension waned, so too did the actual occurrences.

Isobel's love for James was so intense it was frightening in its potency. A smile from him, a glimpse of him in the grounds, watching him while he slept, hearing his voice, all caused a surge of love which was devastatingly strong. From the very beginning they were perfectly attuned to each other, intuitively understanding one another's need. There was never any doubt in either of their minds that this unlikely relationship was permanent.

The only thing which marred the perfection of Isobel's life was the continuing rift between herself and her father. Some eighteen months after she had fled from Kilweem he still stubbornly refused to see her and ignored all her many letters. William, too, married now to Maggie Cameron and the father of a baby son, made no attempt at reconciliation.

'You don't need them any more,' James insisted as she sat in the warm circle of his arms. 'You've got me. Your sister and brother, Hugh, keep in touch and Lizzie is a good friend. After the way they treated you, you shouldn't be making yourself unhappy by worrying about them.'

'I know. But I can't help wishing I could do something to put things right between us.'

But she had so much to be grateful for. She had James and that was all that really mattered.

TEN

*I*t was the dawning of a new decade. A decade in which the ravages of war would finally be repaired; a decade which, it was hoped, would bring peace and prosperity.

But for James Dryburgh and Isobel McLean the first days of 1950 would always be recalled with a sense of nightmare.

'My God!' Campbell expressed his pleasure with his customary loud rumble. 'These are pictures of Netherdrum!'

'Yes.' Too late James saw the danger. He had never given Isobel's paintings a minute's thought when he had suggested sharing a bottle of whisky in his home while he and his father went over the accounts, though Isobel herself had been careful to take her paints and easel back to the main house.

'Where did you get them?' Geddes demanded, adjusting his steel-framed glasses for a closer look. 'They really are excellent.' He was no connoisseur, but collecting pictures had become his one extravagance. The walls of Netherdrum House displayed several works by lesser-known artists which he hoped would, one day, prove to be shrewd investments. These, though they had a softer, more feminine feel than would normally appeal to him, were undoubtedly by a very gifted artist. He wondered if it might be worthwhile buying some for himself.

James remained uncomfortably silent, aware that the moment of judgement had arrived before he was fully prepared for it.

'Well,' his father persisted. 'Where did you get them, James? Who is the artist? I.M. means nothing to me.' He peered at the initials in the right-hand corner.

'I.M. stands for Isobel McLean,' James said, standing in preparation for the imminent explosion. 'Isobel painted these . . . she is a wonderfully talented artist, as you can see. In fact,' he blustered on, hoping to overwhelm his father with Isobel's accomplishments, 'this was painted with that box of paints you gave me. Remember? When I . . .'

'Isobel?' Geddes bellowed. 'You surely can't mean the Isobel McLean who works for me?'

'Yes. Isobel McLean. She spends nearly all her free time painting. I'm surprised you haven't seen her at work yourself.'

Geddes turned from contemplating the pictures to glare at his son, his expression one of disgusted anger. Dreadful suspicion brought the veins bulging from his neck and sweat beading on his forehead. 'And why,' he barked, 'would a servant in my house be giving you paintings?'

'Because I gave her her first paints . . . and because she is a very special person.' James was unhappily aware that he sounded like a guilty schoolchild. Taking a second to compose himself he straightened his back, giving him an extra two inches with which to dominate his father's impressive height and said, in a low but perfectly clear and controlled voice, 'I love her father. And she loves me.'

It was said but there was no relief in the confession. For a full minute James thought his father was going to succumb to a stroke.

His face was impossibly red, his eyes bulged and he seemed to have lost the power of speech. It was a temporary loss. He recovered to blast his son with an expletive which he had last used some forty years ago, before relegating it, along with his own impoverished background, to the convenient recesses of his selective memory. 'After all I said to you,' he panted, 'you have the nerve to stand there and tell me you are in love. Love! Damn and blast it all, James. She's a fishergirl. As common as seaweed.'

'She is not common.' James hung onto his temper knowing that losing control now could only do more harm.

'Guttersnipe! We even found her lying in one. By God, if this gets out there's no decent person would pass the time of day with you.'

'You are being ridiculous. This is nineteen–fifty . . .'

'She's pregnant. Is that it? I'll take care of it . . .'

'No! Of course she's not . . .' coherent speech deserted James.

'Then she's out for what she can get . . .'

'Don't speak about her like that!' James took a menacing step towards his father. 'I don't care about where she was brought up, or who her parents were. None of it matters. I love her. And I have every intention of marrying her. If she'll have me.'

Geddes stared at his son, reduced for the second time in minutes to speechlessness.

'Over my dead body,' he managed to splutter. Crashing his glass down on the table so hard that it shattered he stalked from the house, not even bothering to slam the door after him.

Always a man of decisive action, Campbell Geddes was yelling for his housekeeper as he blasted through his own front door, minutes later. She followed him into his study already knowing what to expect.

'Do not think,' he said when he had vented his temper on her for a full ten minutes, 'that I will forgive you for your part in this. That little tramp is your responsibility and your laxity has allowed this to happen. Now, if you wish to continue as houskeeper here, go and do as I have said. At once.'

'I'm sorry, Hen. Mr Geddes wants you away from here first thing in the morning. There's nothing I can do, lass. He'll put me out, too, if I argue with him.' Too upset by the shocked pallor of the girl's face to continue, she turned and busied herself at the hob, going through the safe routine of tea-making quite automatically.

'Where am I supposed to go?'

'Back to your father, Hen.'

'I can't,' Isobel's mind was in turmoil. But what other choice was there? Miserably she acknowledged that the thing she had most feared had finally happened. But she had always had such faith in James, believing that he would convince his father that what they had was a very special kind of love. 'James would never agree,' she stammered.

'Best to forget him, lass. We both know that it would never work out. He has his future to think about and that future is in his father's hands. He can't afford to get on the wrong side of him. I did try to warn you.'

Isobel stared, beyond speech, seeing her happy future dissolve in the steam from the singing kettle. And still she couldn't believe that James would let her go without standing up to his father. Not James who was so gentle; who loved her; who worshipped her with his strong body and made her feel safe and cherished, beyond all outside interference.

'There's nothing to be done, Isobel. It's all for the best. You'll see. James Dryburgh was never for you. You'll find someone else. Someone of your own kind.' She was trying to be kind but unwittingly drove the thorn deeper into Isobel's heart. 'If you really love James, don't make this even harder for him than it already is. If you force him to make a choice, and he chooses you, you'll cause a rift in this family which will never heal. You, of all people, should know how hurtful that can be. Don't do it to James.'

Blindly Isobel walked to the door and dragged herself to her room, those last words sitting like lead on her heart. Numbed she threw her few things into a bag, deliberately leaving behind her paints and easel. There was nothing to stay here for now. Without even being aware of making the decision she put on her coat, ready to leave. Even one more night in this house would be too much to bear.

Downstairs Mrs McLachlan fidgeted restlessly in her chair in the kitchen. She had known it would come to this, had done her best to warn Isobel of the inevitable outcome. And deep down she knew Mr Geddes was right. Isobel was no match for James. Brought up, as she had been, in an earlier era, when household servants were expected to know their place, her instinct was to agree with her employer. She nodded her birdlike head jerkily as if to reinforce her own point, but her eyes were misty with emotion.

Her own husband had been dead for many years, killed in the first war after only two years of marriage. But what wonderful years they had been. She could still recall the heady ecstasy of those too short years as clearly as if they had been yesterday. It was a love she had seen mirrored too clearly in the eyes of both James and Isobel. With a sudden return to her more characteristic urgency of movement she sprang to her feet and shrugged herself into her old coat. Taking a large torch from the shelf above the range she let herself out into the yard and started the quarter-mile walk to James's cottage.

Minutes later Isobel crept down the stairs and peered into the darkened kitchen. Reassured that Mrs McLachlan had retired for the night, she too let herself quietly out of the back door. Keeping well into the shadows she edged down the driveway towards the road, confident that no-one would see her at this hour of the night. Dry-eyed but infinitely sad she began to walk with no clear idea of where she was going, knowing only that she had to get as far away from Netherdrum and James Dryburgh as she possibly could.

Twenty minutes later James Dryburgh's car screeched to a halt outside his father's front door. Getting no reply to his insistent hammering and ringing he then followed Mrs McLachlan who had hurriedly made for the back door and the relative safety of her own room. Bursting through the kitchen he stormed upstairs to the attic and Isobel's room.

He knocked but there was no response. Fear clutching at his heart he threw the door open and switched on the light. It was the first time he had seen where she slept and for a moment he was stunned by the bareness of the small, cold room. It was, he thought fleetingly, more like a prison cell than anything else. Gradually he saw that the room was empty, not only of Isobel herself, but of everything that was hers. Angrily he hauled the covers off the bed as if hoping to discover her beneath them, then heaved the drawers out of the small chest. He found them all quite empty. And then he saw the paints, abandoned in the corner. Furious now, understanding too clearly that she had wanted to get away as quickly as possible, suspecting that she thought he had agreed to let her go, he crashed out of the room and down to his father's bedroom. Geddes met him in the doorway.

'What the devil?' he roared, knowing very well what had brought his son storming into the house at this hour but choosing to pretend ignorance.

'Where is she?' James bellowed. 'Where has she gone?'

'Who?' asked Geddes, pulling himself up to his full height ready to impose his will on his stubborn son.

'Isobel. Where is she?' James took one step closer to his father and for the first time in his life Campbell Geddes backed away from a challenge, awed by the naked fury he saw in his son's eyes. The first seeds of doubt about the wisdom of his actions seeped into his mind and were stubbornly refuted.

'In her room as far as I know,' he thundered, giving James no hint of that brief moment of self-doubt.

'She is not there.' James's voice, deep and strong at any time, seemed to roll round the old house.

Geddes shrugged. 'Then how should I know where she is? But I certainly haven't turned her out into the night if that's what you're thinking.' He ignored James's warning grunt and went on. 'If she's gone, good riddance to her. Run back to her people I should think if she's got any sense. Now go home James and let me get some sleep.' Smiling grimly now, heartily cheered by the knowledge that the girl had taken herself off before James could do anything rash, he stepped back into his room. Very deliberately he closed the door in James's face, and bolted it.

James's fists balled into solid rocks as fury got the better of him. Ignoring the pain he drove one hand into the solid wood and lashed at the bottom with booted feet. 'If anything happens to her I will never forgive you,' he yelled at the inert wood, beyond sense for a long, red minute.

The blinding anger left him so suddenly that he sagged limply back against the door, breathing heavily. Then, in command of himself again, he marched back to his car. Seconds later he was speeding through the white gates, lights blazing.

She was easy to find. Stumbling unheedingly along the road, she was little more than a mile away, so wrapped up in her own misery that she didn't even hear the car. He stopped and got out, facing her grimly.

'Isobel. Where the hell do you think you are going?' The residue of his anger was strident in his voice, effectively hiding his overwhelming feeling of relief at finding her so quickly.

Isobel stopped, stared blankly. So convinced was she that he would be relieved to find her gone that for a moment she simply couldn't believe he had come after her. 'Kilweem,' was all she muttered, although, until that moment she hadn't known that was where she was making for.

'No,' he shook his head decisively. 'You are coming home. With me.' He held his hand out to her and now he smiled.

'I can't . . . your father,' she whispered, realising just what he was risking for her sake.

'To hell with my father,' he roared, anger resurfacing with astonishing ease. She stepped back a pace, witnessing the strength of his rage for the first time, seeing a new side to the man she loved. He shot forward and caught her roughly by the shoulders. 'Isobel.' Now his voice was even more gravelly than normal, hoarse with emotion and the crushing knowledge of what it would mean to lose this wonderful woman. 'My father doesn't matter. You are the only one I care about. Don't you understand that yet?'

'I thought . . .'

'I know what you thought!' He held her away from him, glaring at her. Even in the dark she could see the intensity in those dark eyes. 'My God! How could you even begin to think that I could put my own ambition, or what my father wants, before you?'

'I didn't know what to think.' She was weeping now, tears of relief, and shame, and love. 'I didn't think at all.'

He sighed, deeply hurt that she could have ever doubted him then, regretting his harshness, pulled her into his strong, warm arms. She came gladly, resting her aching head on his broad shoulders, struggling to contain the tears which threatened to spill down her face.

'Isobel. I love you. I love you more than anything in the world. I will never let you go. Never.'

'And I love you, James,' she managed to croak.

'Never doubt me again.'

She shook her head, mutely, past words. He rocked her in his arms, like a child.

ELEVEN

'I'm sure he'll come round, in time,' James said, with less assurance every time. 'Give him a chance to get used to the idea. Father is an old man, set in his ways, and too proud and stubborn to admit that he was wrong. He likes to forget that his own background is very similar to yours. His parents were far from wealthy. They lived in an old tenement in Edinburgh. I can remember going to visit them there.'

It was a conversation which was repeated at least once a week when James tried to persuade Isobel to marry him. The rift with her own family had left a scar which she had no wish to see repeating itself on James's heart. When they did eventually marry she dearly wanted it to be with Campbell Geddes's approval and she was prepared to wait for that. She and James were together and, for the moment, that was enough.

The disapproval of the small community for their unmarried cohabitation failed to move her. Nor did the vitriolic, unforgiving letter, the very first she had had, from her father, alerted to the situation by a careless Twi. Even Twi herself, who was glad to see her sister happy at last, couldn't bring herself to visit, although she did arrange to meet Isobel about once a month. But Hugh, Isobel's ever-loyal brother, gave her the added support she valued so much. He and his gentle wife, May, made a point of visiting Isobel and James. May even shyly told Isobel that she thought she was doing the right thing in waiting to see if Campbell Geddes's attitude would soften, a gesture which warmed Isobel's heart towards the sister-in-law she barely knew and ensured a warm friendship between the two young women.

But it was Lizzie, delighted by the romance, who was her most steadfast supporter, a ready ear for Isobel's doubts and offering uncritical support in the face of almost universal condemnation.

To Isobel's deep sorrow one of her most unrelenting critics was Mrs McLachlan, whose fiercely Calvinistic upbringing would not even allow her to speak to James or Isobel while they continued to live in a state of such blatant sin.

Campbell Geddes, himself untroubled by religious scruples, was immovable. But the businessman in him rapidly made him realise the folly of following his first instinct and ordering James to leave Netherdrum. The younger man's expertise both on the farm and as financial manager to the estate as a whole would have made such a drastic course of action irrational and self-defeating. Geddes was too astute for that.

Unbeknown to James, one of his father's first actions on realising that Isobel was in residence in James's cottage had been to contact Alisdair and try first to persuade, then to bully and finally to bribe his elder son to return to Netherdrum and shoulder his responsibilities, so releasing James to continue with his highly unsuitable liaison somewhere well removed from his father's social circle. But Alisdair's interest was limited to sneering contempt for his half-brother. He had no intention of returning to Strathannan and the dreary lifestyle that seemed to content his father and told Geddes so in terms which could not possibly be misinterpreted.

Campbell Geddes, always pragmatic when it came to profitability, accepted defeat with loud bad temper and contented himself with making life as uncomfortable for James as he could.

Conversations between the two men were limited to the necessary business discussions. Even so these were invariably conducted in resentful grunts, at least on Campbell Geddes's part. Despite repeated resolutions to ignore the relentless goading, James usually found his temper fraying and retorted in kind. He lost count of the number of times he attempted to discuss Isobel with his father, eager to break through the older man's hostility, but Geddes's unvarying response was to simply leave the room at the first mention of her name.

It was as if these difficulties brought James and Isobel even closer together. Winter softened into spring and then summer, finding them secure and utterly content, wanting no-one but each other and able, at last, to ignore the continued animosity from James's father.

With time on her hands Isobel painted, throwing herself into her hobby with intense enthusiasm. James hired an extra hand, bringing instant criticism from Geddes, and made more time to be with her, content to watch as she worked, sometimes reading the books he had always promised himself he would read but had never found time for. It was a time of peace, contentment, discovery and renewal.

Many soft summer afternoons found them in St Andrews. The delicately beautiful woman artist and her tall, striking companion became a familiar sight on the harbour where, for almost a month, she was occupied in painting scenes of the busy little quayside. Then, loving the unique atmosphere of the historical Burgh she moved on to paint the cathedral ruins, St Rule's tower and even St Mary's college with the marvellous holm oak dominating the foreground of her picture. James was frankly amazed by her skill.

'I knew you were talented, but these are outstanding.'

'Anyone could paint a decent picture in a place as lovely as this,' she laughed, secretly delighted by his praise.

'I couldn't.'

By the end of that first summer she had an impressive collection of local scenes. Most were of St Andrews but some were of Anstruther and there was even one of Kilweem, painted from memory.

'Have you ever thought of selling these?' James asked,

looking thoughtfully at his spare room, now crammed with paintings.

'They're not that good,' she retorted. The very idea was preposterous.

'But they are. Look at some of the rubbish the poor tourists are asked to buy. They are nowhere near as atmospheric as these. And you aren't even hanging them. They're lying around. Spoiling.'

'Well, I can't hang any more in here, that's for sure,' she chuckled. 'There's one in the hall, three in the sitting room, two in the bedroom and even one in the toilet.'

'But there are none in Netherdrum House.'

'Netherdrum! Your father would never hang one of my pictures. He'd burn it first. Anyway, he has other, much better pictures than these,' she added thinking of the varied displays on the walls of the big house.

'That is a matter of opinion, isn't it? The appreciation of art is a very subjective thing. And I know my father was impressed by the first two paintings you gave me. He was seriously thinking of buying one for himself, even then.'

'Yes. And that's what started all the trouble,' she countered soberly.

'Yeeees. But perhaps he might appreciate a gift. Something he can't deny liking.'

'This sounds suspiciously like blackmail to me, James,' but she was laughing with him now.

'Would you object very much if I took those two, the ones of Netherdrum House, over to him?'

'Of course not,' she agreed readily enough. 'If you think it might help to win your father over, take them all.'

'It's just a small gift, Father. I know you will like them. And you never know, they might be worth something one day.' James unwrapped the parcel and propped the two small pictures up against the back of a sofa in his father's drawing room.

'If you think a cheap trick like this will make me change

my mind, then think again,' Campbell spluttered, his face already dangerously red.

'Father.' James sighed and opted for at least partial honesty. 'I admit it's a peace offering. I'm tired of the way things are. It's been going on for too long. We need each other, you and I. Wouldn't it be better if we could at least talk to each other civilly again?'

Geddes growled and exhaled a plume of thick, choking cigar smoke in his son's face. 'Pretty pictures won't alter my mind. Take them with you when you go.' But his eyes settled on the paintings.

'No,' James insisted. 'I'll leave them here. They are pictures of this house so they belong here.'

'Do what you like. You always do,' was the ungracious reply.

'I've got work to do.' James made for the door before the relatively peaceful atmosphere could deteriorate. 'Please, Father, think about what I've said. I can't tell you how much it upsets me for us to be at war like this.' It was an unparalleled declaration from a normally reticent man. Despite himself, Geddes was moved by the appeal, but too proud to show it.

'If you've got work to do then go and do it. You're wasting precious time.' But it was said in a tone of voice that was almost pleasant. James hurried away, careful not to let his father glimpse the smile that was lifting his lips.

As soon as James was safely out of the house, Geddes went to the sofa and lifted one of the pictures for a closer look. It was many minutes before he settled it back beside its companion. Maybe, just maybe he could hang them. Not in this room. Somewhere less obvious. They were, after all, very good paintings. Much too good to waste.

Three days later a jubilant James discovered them while he was searching for an account in his father's desk, tastefully adorning the dark green walls of Campbell Geddes's study.

*

The return of winter brought a new dimension to scenes Isobel had already captured under the softer summer light. Encouraged by James the cold, frosty mornings found her busily sketching until her fingers were too numbed to hold the charcoal. James generally went with her on these expeditions, watching from the relative comfort of his unpretentious Ford and producing flasks of milky coffee to help keep her warm. Once or twice he had even tried his own hand at sketching but, frustrated by his complete inability to capture anything like the right image, he soon gave up. His admiration for Isobel's effortless, sensitive work was all the greater.

One morning, early in January, he watched enthralled as she depicted the magic of a light snowfall over the cathedral ruins in St Andrews. After an hour, frozen to the core, he went for a short walk to restore his flagging circulation. By the time he got back Isobel was surrounded by a small crowd. Their scarlet gowns immediately identified them as students. They watched in reverent silence. One young man in particular seemed captivated.

James hovered on the edge of the group until she was finished, a proud smile softening features which could, like his father's, seem severe. When she moved to tidy her things the crowd closed in.

'This is absolutely the best thing I have ever seen,' the young man enthused. 'Would you consider selling it to me? I haven't a lot of money but I could give you a deposit if you could keep it for me until I can pay the full price.'

She faced him, openly amazed. 'You want to buy it?'

'Well, yes. How much do you want for it?'

'I hadn't even thought about selling it. I paint for pleasure. It's a hobby.' She glanced at James who merely smiled encouragingly and took an obvious step back, leaving her to deal with this on her own.

'But I'm serious. I would very much like to have this. You see, it's my last year here. I have loved St Andrews and this will remind me of it for the rest of my life.'

She looked hard at him for a moment, still not quite sure that he wasn't poking fun at her, but then she broke into a slow, warm smile that illuminated her whole face. 'That is the nicest thing you could possibly have said. I have never actually sold a painting but you can have this.' She removed the painting carefully from its stand and thrust it into the surprised young man's arms.

'Thank you,' he grinned hugely. 'What do I owe you?'

'Nothing,' she shook her head making the shiny hair float softly about her head.

'I can't possibly accept this for nothing.' Now he seemed embarrassed.

'Of course you can,' she teased him. 'It's enough to know that it'll be appreciated. I don't want anything for it. Honestly.'

'Thank you. Thank you.' He beamed and displayed the picture to his cheering friends. When he turned to face her again she had collected her things together and, arm linked through James's, was already walking away over the snow.

'You see? I told you your work was good. Now you'll be besieged by handsome young men every time you come here, all begging for a free reminder of their university days. Mind you,' he chuckled, 'I'm not at all sure that he didn't want you at least as much as he wanted that picture. He couldn't take his eyes off you.'

Delighted, excited, her warm laugh rang through the crisp air, floating back to the student who was gazing after her with longing in his eyes.

But once they were back in his car James fell into thoughtful silence. Isobel watched him with the familiar surge of love, content to wait until he chose to tell her what was on his mind. But eventually she could restrain herself no longer. 'What are you thinking about?' she asked, shaking his arm gently.

'Nothing much,' he answered evasively. 'Just an idea I've had.'

'What?' she demanded. 'Come on. Tell me.'

'No,' he grinned at her. 'Not yet.'

'James . . .'

'No!' It was final and in the tone of voice she knew better than to argue with. 'You'll just have to wait and see.'

She made a pouting face, pretending to be hurt at the sharp way he had spoken, then impulsively leaned across and kissed his cheek. 'I love you, James Dryburgh,' she whispered.

A week later James found an opportunity to spend a day in Edinburgh. Telling Isobel only that he had business to attend to, he set out early one morning with a large bundle on the back seat of his car. When he returned, early in the evening, he seemed ebullient.

Isobel contained herself until after they had eaten their meal before tackling him.

'You're as excited as a schoolboy, James,' she teased.

'You'll never guess why,' he beamed, shoving back his wayward hair.

'No. I'll never guess. You might have been to the moon and back for all I know. So why don't you just tell me what you've been up to.'

'I've been to Edinburgh.'

'On business. I know that!'

'Yes. Your business.'

'My business?'

'I've been to see a man about a painting.' His eyes twinkled.

'James! Stop playing games and tell me what this is all about.'

'Three paintings, actually.' He couldn't resist teasing her for a little longer.

'Three paintings?' Now she was beginning to suspect.

'Your paintings.'

'And?' Now she was almost as excited as he was.

'And he said they were very nice.'

172

'Nice! Is that all?' Her heart thudded to her stomach.

'So nice that he has agreed to show them.'

'Show them? Who to?' she asked, not understanding at first. Then, 'Do you mean in a gallery?'

'Well, not on the Waverly steps,' he laughed. The steps were the traditional place for aspiring young artists to display their work, set up for any passerby to look at. 'In the Ross gallery. On Frederick Street.'

'I've never heard of it,' she admitted.

'It is one of the most prestigious galleries in Scotland. Farquhar Stirling, who owns it, is an old friend of my mother's. If he thinks they are good enough to show then you can be certain they'll sell.'

'But I'm just an amateur, James. People will laugh at them.' Suddenly she was full of doubt and angry with him for doing this without telling her. 'I wish you'd asked me about this first . . .' she began.

'It's a good job I didn't,' he interrupted her. 'Look at the way you're reacting now? Even after I've told you that a professional art dealer thinks you have a great deal of talent, you still don't want to believe me. Do you think I would be cruel enough to lie to you about this?'

'No. Of course not. But it's just a hobby, James. No-one will want to buy the stuff I paint.'

'That student did,' he retorted.

'That was different,' she snapped. 'He probably knew nothing about art. He just saw a picture he liked.'

James roared with unexpected laughter. 'Oh, Isobel. Why do you think most people buy paintings?'

She glared at him, concentrating on keeping her expression sullen, determined not to let him win her round to his point of view. Not even to herself would she admit that the idea of exposing her work to public view frightened her, almost as though he had asked her to put herself on display.

But James, who knew her better than she knew, even now, was sensitive enough to realise something of her apprehension. 'Isobel, I'm not trying to force you into doing something you don't want to do. But I really believe you could be successful. All you have to do is let the gallery have half a dozen of your favourite paintings. Trust me. Just this once. If it doesn't work out, well, you'll have lost nothing. If that happens, and I'm sure it won't, then I promise I'll never mention trying to sell your work again. But remember, Farquhar Stirling knows what he's talking about and he would never agree to show your work if he thought it wouldn't sell. And most artists would give five years of their life for the chance to show their work in his gallery.'

Looking at the eager intensity in his deep, brown eyes, Isobel saw a reflection of his faith in her, knew she couldn't let him down.

'Alright,' she conceded. 'What do I have to do?'

He breathed out his relief loudly. 'Not much really. He'll show them for a month, over Easter. There'll be some tourists in the city by then so it's a very good time.'

'I can just send them to him?' she asked hopefully.

'No,' he laughed. 'He wants to meet you, of course. But we can do that when we deliver the paintings. He'll take six. All we have to do is have them decently framed.'

Isobel was quite disproportionately excited by the prospect of visiting Edinburgh. Despite having lived in Strathannan all her life, she had never been to the Scottish capital. Although James had taught her to drive, the thought of making the ferry crossing had been enough to stop her attempting the journey on her own.

At North Queensferry they watched as the small ferry manoeuvred its way to the ramp and Isobel held her breath when James drove his immaculate Ford onto the cramped deck. But, once in open channel, she stared in awe at the cantilevered magnificence of the famous railway bridge. From such close proximity it seemed huge and oppressive. Although she had often seen the bridge from the shore, until now she had never truly appreciated the grandeur of the enormous structure.

The choppy crossing was soon accomplished and they were in South Queensferry, driving under the bridge itself and on their way to Edinburgh.

Knowing this was her first visit, James had planned a brief tour before their two-thirty appointment at the gallery. He began with the New Town area of the gracious city, taking Isobel past the Georgian elegance of Charlotte Street and into St Andrew Square. Isobel listened to his knowledgeable commentary in silence, captivated by the beauty which surrounded her. Then he took her into Princes Street for a glimpse of the smoke-blackened Scott monument before turning past the Scottish Academy, on the Mound, and into the High Street and the Old Town. Here he parked his car and insisted on taking her onto the castle esplanade.

The view was breathtaking. She looked out over the city and north, across the Forth and beyond, feeling she could stay there, buffeted by the wind, forever.

Watching her unashamed enjoyment of the wonderful old city James, who had spent most of his life there, felt he was seeing it with fresh appreciation and loved her all the more for that new gift.

At last he prised her away and drove quickly past the dark buildings of the Royal Mile so she could see Holyrood House and Arthur's Seat. Then he took her the full length of Princes Street, laughing at her excitement as they passed shops, larger than any she had ever been in, and finally escorted her into the Caledonian Hotel for lunch, taking their seats just as the one o'clock cannon fired from the castle, making Isobel jump.

The enjoyment of the morning had banished the apprehension she had been feeling at the prospect of meeting Farquhar Stirling, the gallery proprietor. But her first sight of him inspired wonder rather than awe.

Exquisitely dressed in cream slacks, black and white checked sleeveless pullover and canary yellow shirt with an exuberantly bright pink cravat round his plump throat,

Farquhar clapped his pudgy hands when he saw them and advanced, talking loudly.

'My Dears,' he gushed, offering a soft, well-manicured hand first to James and then to Isobel. 'I am so very glad to see you. Do come and sit down.' Like a fussy mother hen he shooed them towards a pair of white sofas, set back to back in the centre of the spacious room. 'As you can see I am absolutely overwhelmed with clients.' He patted his thinning fair hair and posed elegantly on the arm of a couch.

Isobel glanced round and counted no more than half a dozen people, then realised there were more in a second room at the top of an ornate metal staircase.

The walls were filled with pictures, all discreetly labelled with the title, the artist's name and the asking price. While Farquhar chattered on to James, blatantly dropping names, Isobel drifted quietly round the lower room. Some of the paintings were country scenes, such as she might paint but in more obvious colours. Others were harsh, even childish, city views, while still more were abstract representations which she didn't always understand, even when she used the titles for clues. When she read the price tags she was shocked.

'Well, my sweet, what do you think? Isn't this simply the best work you have ever seen?' Farquhar materialised at her side and placed a proprietorial hand under her arm. She resisted the urge to shake it off.

'I like some of them,' she replied with typical honesty. 'But others I don't understand.'

'Oh, but there is a message in each one if you have the sensitivity to see it,' he twittered, following her gaze to a particularly lurid blur of colour in a garishly overstated frame. 'But perhaps that one is for the true connoisseur.' Seeing the scepticism written so plainly on her face he rushed on defensively. 'That is by one of my most successful artists. He is in great demand. Great demand!' With quick, feminine steps he was beside the painting, delicately wiping imaginary dust from the gilt frame.

'But what is it supposed to be?' she persisted, genuinely interested.

He stared at her. 'It is a different thing to different people. The artist has given us clues. It is up to us to interpret them.' He brought such acid authority to this outrageous statement that she didn't dare to challenge him.

'These are wonderful.' She pointed to a set of delicately coloured scenes giving soft, hazy impressions of the city. Each one was priced at more than one hundred pounds.

'Yes. They are by a very experienced artist. She sells very few, preferring to produce work of only the very highest calibre. Of course, she insists that I handle her sales.'

'Perhaps you would like to look at Miss McLean's paintings now,' James interrupted, not trusting himself to be able to maintain a straight face for much longer.

'Yes. If you insist. Come along then. Show me what little gems you've brought for me.'

They followed him through the shop to a bare room, furnished only with a large easel.

'Keep an eye on things out there will you, lovey,' Farquhar sang out to a younger man, dressed all in white, who smiled sweetly at them as he passed. James had a troublesome fit of coughing.

'Right,' Farquhar seemed not to notice. 'Let's put them on the stand.'

Unwrapping her precious bundle slowly, reluctant to expose her work to professional criticism, Isobel placed the first one, a summer view of one of the colleges in St Andrews. Farquhar stood back, chin on hand, while he considered it. Then, 'Next,' he ordered.

Now she produced a poignant view of Kilweem harbour, empty of boats, the old, ex-fishermen, discarded crates and littered lobster pots all hinting at the imminent death of an industry. She followed that with a distant view of St Rule's tower, again in St Andrews, mist creeping in from the sea to give it a cold, ghostly appearance.

Then she showed him her own favourite, a view across

177

Loch Leven to the crumbling castle where Mary, Queen of Scots, had been imprisoned. Farquhar remained disconcertingly motionless while she replaced it with a delicate play of light and shade in the woods behind Netherdrum House and, lastly, with a picture of the lighthouse at Elie, caught in the last minutes before a storm, the sky behind navy blue and threatening. Looking at it was enough to remind her of the tension in the air that afternoon. She had only narrowly managed to capture the effect she wanted when the storm had broken with deafening claps of thunder and vicious forks of lightning. Beside her Farquhar shivered and she reached to take the picture down, her heart thudding despondently into her stomach.

'Leave it!' The irritation was loud in his voice. Confused she glanced at James, who shook his head and grinned wickedly.

'I thought you didn't like it,' she said.

'Whatever gave you that idea?' Farquhar's eyes were still fixed on the easel.

'You shivered.'

'Perhaps I am cold,' was the acerbic reply.

Dismayed she waited while he continued to examine the picture. At last he looked at her again.

'Never disturb me when I am considering a picture. It destroys the aura. I like to let it envelop me. I have to feel a painting; taste it; breathe it.' He accompanied the extravagant words with equally exaggerated hand gestures. 'And this,' he pointed at the storm scene, 'is a phenomenon. I felt I was there, at the very heart of the storm. I could feel it building. That, my dear, is why I shivered. Not because I did not like it but because it was consuming me.'

Embarrassed by his effusiveness she flushed slightly. 'Is that the only one you like?' she asked, still finding it hard to believe that anyone could be so enthusiastic about her work.

'My, you are a funny little thing, aren't you?' He turned his most patronising smile on her.

She heard James's grunt of anger but she needed no

support from him in this. 'No, Mr Stirling. I am not a funny little thing. I am just a woman wondering when you are going to stop playing silly games and tell me whether you like my work well enough to show it in your gallery. You like that one but what about the rest?' she demanded.

One eyebrow raised itself quizzically, but there was a new look of respect in his pale eyes. 'Oh dear. I haven't upset you, have I? You'll have to learn to take no notice of me and my funny little ways.'

'Do you like them? Will you show them?' she persisted

'Of course I do,' he soothed. 'I have alrady agreed to show the ones dear James brought to me. And these are just as good. I shall show them all! They really are quite exceptional. They have a unique, almost mystical quality about them which I have never found before.'

'Good! Well, if you will get the agreement ready, Miss McLean will sign it for you. Then we must be on our way.' Now James spoke up, his natural authority immediately dominating the situation.

'Yes, yes of course.' Farquhar's manner sharpened noticeably when he was dealing with James.

'Agreement?' Isobel asked.

'Yes. It's quite normal. Don't worry about it, my dear,' Farquhar smiled his satisfaction. 'I think perhaps fifty pounds is about right for these. I shall take thirty-three per cent commission on every sale.'

'I see.'

'If they sell well there is no reason why our price should not be a little higher next time.'

Isobel waited nervously for her paintings to go on show, hardly daring to believe that anyone might actually want to pay so much money for one. She need not have worried. By the end of the first day one had already been reserved. Another two went on the second day. By lunchtime on the second Saturday, Farquhar was on the phone, begging for more. Hurriedly selecting another half dozen she agreed to have them delivered the following week.

'This time,' Farquhar promised, 'we'll get seventy pounds each.'

Now she threw herself into her art with even greater passion, sometimes alone, often with James as a silent but much appreciated companion. When, infrequently, he had to go to Edinburgh on business, she felt lost, incomplete. But even then she was seldom truly alone. Lizzie was often to be found in the farm cottage. Twi, now with three youngsters and a fourth already on the way, had successfully overcome her distaste for her sister's unmarried state and contrived to spend at least one afternoon a week at Netherdrum. Soft-hearted Robbie had been quite unable to maintain any animosity towards his beautiful sister-in-law and, although family pressure prevented him from inviting Isobel to his own home, he no longer raised any objection to his wife's frequent trips to see her sister. He had even been there himself when James invited all of Isobel's family for Christmas dinner. With typical intransigence William and Maggie, and Malcolm, had refused to come, but Hugh and Twi with their families had ensured that Isobel had enjoyed one of the happiest Christmases of her life.

The year which had started so badly ended very sweetly indeed.

TWELVE

*I*t was during the following autumn that Isobel suddenly found that she had no interest in painting. Disturbingly she could find no inspiration in the soft, green countryside and seemed to lack the energy to seek out new places of interest. To her horror the strange fits which had decreased and almost disappeared over the last two years abruptly recurred. There were several occasions when she fell into the dreaded, trance-like state to glimpse people and places she didn't recognise and awoke to the certain knowledge that she had witnessed some future event.

Worse still, she was assailed by persistent nausea, to the point where she started to believe she must be ill. Every morning became a battle as she fought debilitating sickness. Food disgusted her, the very smell of cooking turned her green. Seriously concerned, despite her stubborn denials that anything was wrong, James called the doctor and arranged for Lizzie to be with Isobel when he called.

He had no difficulty in reaching his diagnosis. Still remarkably naive, even at twenty-six, Isobel was surprised and then embarrassed by the personal nature of some of the questions he thought it necessary to ask. When he had gone she sat on in the bedroom, too stunned to move until Lizzie, who had been unable to get a single helpful word out of the doctor, poked her head round the door.

'Well? What did he say? Is there a prescription?'

'No prescription.' Isobel shook her head, causing the long blonde hair to ripple on her shoulders.

'What then? Does he know what's making you so sick?'

'I'm pregnant.'

For once in her life Lizzie was speechless.

'What a little innocent that doctor must think I am. I should have guessed.'

'And I've seen my sisters pregnant often enough to have known,' Lizzie laughed. 'Congratulations! It'll be wonderful having a bairn around here. It'll certainly liven old Mrs McLachlan up,' she giggled wickedly.

James, once he was over the shock, was delighted. 'I thought we would never have children. After all the time we've been together and nothing happened. This is marvellous, Isobel!' He grabbed her and twirled her round delightedly.

'I never even thought about children,' she laughed back at him, immensely relieved by his reaction.

'But you do want them?' he asked, sobering instantly.

'Yes. Of course I do. It's all I need to make my life perfect.' She smiled and looked down at her perfectly flat stomach, wondering at the miracle hidden there.

'But it does mean we will have to sort ourselves out,' James said in the gravelly tone of voice that brooked no argument. 'My son or daughter will not be born a bastard,' he said flatly, the harsh word making her flinch. 'I respect, even admire your reasons for not wanting to marry me before. I know we both hoped for Father's approval. But now there is another person to consider. And maybe, just maybe, this baby will be the thing to get through Father's pride. You know,' he said, drawing her against him and wrapping his arms around her. 'I know he really wants to make peace with us, but he's just too stubborn to back down.'

She nodded doubtfully. Campbell Geddes still refused to acknowledge her existence. Her private fear was that he would never accept her, or her child, and that James would be very deeply hurt.

'But not only for the sake of the child, Isobel. Or because of Father. But because I love you. I'm proud of you and I

want you to be my wife more than anything in the world.'
He kissed her fiercely, underlining his words with proof of
his desire.

Four weeks later, in Cupar Register Office, Isobel became
Mrs James Dryburgh. It was a short, private ceremony with
only Hugh and May, Twi and Robbie, and Lizzie as
witnesses. Her father and William, as well as Campbell
Geddes, had been invited but, as James had rightly predicted,
failed to arrive.

They exchanged their vows quietly then turned to accept
the congratulations of their guests. Isobel was suddenly
aware that James had frozen at her side. Without warning
his light grip on her hand tightened painfully. She glanced
at him puzzled, then following his gaze, she saw Campbell
Geddes standing just inside the door, having obviously
witnessed the short ceremony. For a moment the two men
stared at each other, neither making any move. Then, almost
curtly Geddes nodded, first at James and then, more briefly,
at Isobel. Tugging gently at Isobel's cold hand James led her
to where his father still waited. The expression on his face
was not encouraging.

'I'm glad you came Father. The day would have been
spoiled without you,' James said, generously.

'You are my son. It was my duty,' Geddes replied gruffly.
'I'll not stay.' He turned towards the door but then, hesitating for a second, turned back to his son and offered his
hand. 'I wish you good luck,' he mumbled. 'Both of you,'
his gaze settled briefly on Isobel. Impetuously she reached
up and planted a soft kiss on the red, but unexpectedly cool,
cheek. 'Thank you, Sir,' she whispered.

Geddes grunted and pulled away sharply. He was out of
the door before James could invite him back to the cottage
for the small meal which Lizzie and Isobel had prepared.

It was little enough, thought Isobel, staring after her

father-in-law, but it was a start, a wonderful start to their married life.

Shona Louise Dryburgh was born in the full promise of a glorious summer, early in the morning of the first day of June, 1953.

She was a strong, contented child who captivated her mother's heart. Holding her daughter in her arms Isobel ran a light finger through the downy hair on the sleepy head and vowed that this child would have the happy, secure childhood that fate had denied her.

James fell in love with Shona the second he saw her. 'I secretly hoped we would have a daughter,' he confessed, cradling her happily.

Isobel recovered from the birth with amazing speed. Within two days she was up and about, already starting on a new painting, the baby sleeping placidly in the crib at her side.

'I missed painting while I was pregnant,' she explained to her amused husband. 'I feel as though I have to make up for lost time.'

When she wasn't painting she took her daughter for long, slow walks, revelling in her health and in the warm, summer sun. The hedgerows around the estate were loaded with raspberries, so common in the region. Several times Isobel wheeled the high pram through the gates and gathered the fruit while the baby slept, often wandering three or four miles and smiling when she recalled that this was the reality of that strange vision which had felled her so dramatically on her very first visit to Netherdrum.

Secure in the unstinting love of her adoring parents, Shona thrived. There was no doubt that she was beautiful but hers was a dark, celtic beauty, the opposite of her mother's. The very dark hair was obviously from her father and James proudly insisted that the huge, grey eyes and creamy skin were exactly like his own mother's had been.

Isobel watched her daughter grow strong with pride in her heart. No gift could have been more precious. After the horrors of her own youth it was as if nature was trying to redress the balance with this child. Even the tiny, sickle-shaped mark on Shona's shoulder could do nothing to mar Isobel's pleasure. After that first glance she simply closed her mind to its existence. From the security of her blissfully happy marriage Isobel could believe that it wasn't the mark and its rare gift which had been the cause of all her previous unhappiness. That had been in the people around her. If no-one ever knew about Shona's strange inheritance then she could never be subjected to the same torments.

Shona's secret was safe with her mother.

THIRTEEN

James and his father were sharing a late afternoon drink, a new habit which Campbell Geddes had encouraged to develop slowly over the months since James's marriage. The atmosphere between the two men was still strained and Isobel's name was rarely mentioned, but James sensed that his father longed to see his granddaughter and hoped the day was not far away when the family would be united. He was fully prepared to be patient, getting a shameful feeling from the acknowledgement that every day his father delayed was the old man's loss and just reward for his hostile attitude.

His wandering thoughts were shattered by the shrilling of the phone. Campbell nodded at him and James, being closest, picked it up.

'It's Fiona. For you,' he said, offering his father the receiver with a grimace.

There was a brief and increasingly agitated conversation with Fiona. Slamming the phone down angrily, Campbell Geddes strode back to the fireplace and turned his back on the room, his shoulders sagging and his head bowed.

James resisted the urge to go to his father and place a hand on his shoulders, knowing full well that such a move would be angrily rebuffed. But, as he watched, he was painfully aware that his father was an old man. It was a striking revelation. James had never thought of his father's mortality before. Campbell Geddes had always been an indomitable personality; a man who flatly refused to be bested; a man with the strength of character to withstand any onslaught; a man far removed from the elderly, stooped figure whose very attitude seemed to be crying defeat. James wondered how and when the change had happened but ruefully admitted that he had been so absorbed in his own affairs that he had paid little heed to his father's failing constitution.

'My God!' Geddes slammed his hands on the mantelpiece, instantly dismissing all impression of vulnerability and rounded on James, fury blazing from eyes which were still alarmingly keen. 'When will Alisdair learn?'

'What's he done now?' James sighed, resigned to his half-brother's almost annual requests for financial help which always had this effect on their father.

'This time he has surpassed himself,' Geddes spluttered, pouring himself a tumbler full of malt and drinking half of it in one short, unappreciative gulp. 'Apparently he has run up a huge gambling debt in some nightclub or other in London. London!' he snorted in disgust. 'Of course he can't pay. He has been given a warning and must pay the money by the first of the month.'

Alarmed now by the way his father was panting for breath, James tried to calm him down. 'It isn't the first time. Alisdair must be quite used to people demanding their money from him by now.'

'You don't understand! This lot mean business. Their warning was delivered in a back alley. Alisdair is presently in hospital with a broken shoulder and cracked ribs.'

The expletive which exploded from James's lips was one which Isobel had never heard him use. 'I suppose he expected you to get him out of it?'

'That is why Fiona phoned.' Campbell sank into a chair and drained his glass. James saw how his hands shook.

'Perhaps you shouldn't be too quick to pull him out of it. It's high time Alisdair learned his lesson.'

'James. Alisdair is my son. Wastrel though he undoubtedly is I cannot sit back and allow him to be injured through some debt. Nor can I risk the family name.'

'So you'll pay them off?'

'I don't think I have a choice.' There was unique resignation in his voice. 'But this will be the very last time. You have to make him understand that, James. I will never do this again. He has had all he is going to get out of me. And this time I mean it.'

James gasped. '*I* have got to make him understand?'

'I want you to go to London. Take the money and take care of this debt yourself. Then bring Alisdair back here. I want to talk to him.'

Campbell got to his feet and made a visible effort to straighten his back, but the tiredness and strain were still etched on his face.

'Father, I have no authority over Alisdair. He will resent me interfering. He won't listen to me.' The last thing James wanted was to get involved in this.

'You will have my money, James, and you will have my authority. Alisdair will have to listen to you.'

'No, Father. I won't do this.' Their eyes met in a clash of wills; neither looked away.

'You will, James. You must,' said Campbell, lowering his eyes at last. 'I'm tired, James,' he admitted gruffly. 'I'm too old to deal with this kind of thing.' Then his voice changed and he was strong and domineering again. 'Good God! I've given you a home and a good living and never asked anything in return. When I do ask you say no. Aren't I entitled to your support, James?'

James watched warily, knowing he was being manipulated. Any sympathy he had been feeling dissolved and was replaced by resentment at the undeserving place Alisdair still held in their father's affections. After all, he thought bitterly, he had been the one who had dropped everything and come to his father's aid here at Netherdrum when Alisdair had turned his back on his responsibilities as elder son. And for what? They all knew that when Alisdair finally came into his inheritance there would no longer be a place for him and his family at Netherdrum. And on the one occasion when he had desperately wanted his father's understanding it had been refused, was still being withheld.

'Don't you owe me your support, James?' Geddes repeated.

'No more than Isobel and I are entitled to *your* support, Father,' he said quietly, crossing the room to face his father. 'If I do this for you then I will expect you to make my wife and child welcome in this house.'

'Are you threatening me?' The old man bellowed, his face turning puce with rage.

'Call it what you like,' retorted James with icy control. 'If you want my help, then that's the price you must pay for it.'

The older man turned away and stared down into the crackling flames. Finally he muttered over his shoulder, 'All right. If you leave tomorrow, I'll have the money ready for you in the morning.'

Having made his bargain, Geddes abided by its terms. So, on the first night of James's return from London, bringing a subdued Alisdair and a resentful Fiona with him, both he and Isobel were invited to dine at Netherdrum House.

Ruthlessly correct in his observation of the social niceties, Campbell greeted her with a cold peck on the cheek but pointedly avoided looking at her. At his sleeping grand-daughter, set to rest in her pram under Mrs McLachlan's watchful eye in the kitchen, he cast one dismissive glance, muttered, 'Pity you couldn't have bred a boy,' in a tone so low that only Isobel heard it, and then turned away. From that point on he appeared to be deaf and dumb where she was concerned.

Now, seated at the table, Fiona directly opposite and Alisdair on her right-hand side, with James between Fiona and his father who was at the top of the table, she wanted nothing more than to run away to the cosy familiarity of her own sparsely furnished sitting room. Never had she felt so uncomfortable, so out of place. Miserably she toyed with her food, half frightened to eat for fear of making some terrible gaffe which would embarrass James and was forced to wait until Fiona began to eat to be sure she chose the correct knife and fork from the three sets in front of her. Nor could she enjoy the wine which tasted bitter to her untrained palate. To add to her discomfort the meal was served by Lizzie, her best friend. In vain Isobel tried to catch her eye, longing for some spark of encouragement but, well warned by Mrs McLachlan and keenly aware of her own lowly place, Lizzie kept her eyes firmly downcast.

Isobel knew that in comparison to the glittering Fiona she appeared shabby and ill-groomed. She had drawn her hair back for the occasion, eager to make a sophisticated impression, but already wispy strands were escaping to cling to a face made damp by the oppressive heat of the room and her own overstretched nerves. The plain blue, new look dress with the tightly fitting bodice and flared skirt no longer seemed the wonderful example of fashionable good taste she had felt it to be when she had selected it with such care in Kirkcaldy that very afternoon. And to her lasting horror she saw that perspiration was already making dark, obvious marks under her armpits. Her ordeal was made no easier by the need to keep her arms jammed against her side in the hope that no-one would notice.

The meal itself was taken in icy, nerve-twitching silence. More than once Isobel glanced up to find herself under unpleasantly close scrutiny from Fiona's black, bird-like eyes.

But there was more than her relationship with the Geddes family at stake here. The conversation she had overheard, almost two years ago now, sprung immediately to mind as, sitting silently in Geddes's sitting room with Fiona after dinner, every word of a heated argument filtered through from the adjoining dining room.

'By selling those shares you may well have ruined me! What faith can the other shareholders have in a company when the chairman's own son sells out? Caulay's need only another three per cent and they will have outright control. If that happens Geddes and Sons will cease to exist. All I have worked for will be lost because I was fool enough to think you had some sense of responsibility.' Campbell Geddes's voice was loud enough to carry over the Forth itself. 'I needed the money,' Alisdair's voice was unusually defensive.

'But you should never have sold those shares. Why didn't you come to me sooner? If you had told me, honestly, how serious the situation was, I would have helped you. If only to safeguard the future of the firm. But no, you took the coward's way out . . . the easy way.'

'They were my shares. I simply took care of the problem myself.'

'But you didn't, did you Alisdair?' This time it was James's voice, heavy with contempt. 'You still needed Father to bail you out.'

'You don't understand,' Alisdair said, making a visible effort to control his temper. 'The money from those shares, my shares, would have more than covered the original debt. It was the interest. In the end I had to pay more then three times what I really owed.'

'You stupid bastard,' Geddes hissed. 'We all know that gambling is your real downfall. Private gaming clubs, crooked money-lenders . . . My God! I am ashamed, Alisdair. Ashamed that you, my son, could be so utterly irresponsible and so damned selfish. Didn't you stop to think what this would do to the business?'

'I had no choice,' Alisdair could never explain that the business had gone in exactly the way he had planned it would.

'Choice!' Geddes exploded. 'No-one forced you into that club.'

'I paid for it, Father. I ended up in hospital.'

'Then I hope you've learned something. By God . . . If I was a younger man I'd thrash you myself.'

Both listening women looked up nervously as a chair scraped noisily over the wood.

'Sit down, Father. At least let's try to behave like civilised people.' Again it was James who spoke, his voice strong with authority.

There was a long, long silence until Alisdair broke it, sounding suitably penitent. 'I'm truly sorry, Father. It won't happen again. If you could just let me have something to see me through the next month or so. I know of a wonderful business opportunity. It is guaranteed . . .'

'*NO!*' Campbell roared. 'Where in hell do you think I can lay my hands on all this money you keep demanding? If you need funds then come and work for it. At the factory, while there still is one. I'll make sure you have a decent position.'

'The factory? You seriously expect me to work in a factory? To mix with the sort of people you have working there?'

'Earning your own living is nothing to be ashamed of,' Campbell retorted, thumping his fist on the table so hard that the glasses rattled. 'Look at me! I came from nothing. Nothing! To all this. Through honest, hard work. Work you think you're too good to do. Well, you can be sure of one thing, Alisdair. You will get nothing further from me.'

Alisdair's low, controlled laugh seemed to linger on the air. When he spoke it was with chilling calmness. 'But I'll get it all one day, Father. You can't go on forever. And then all this will be mine.'

There was a long, shocked silence while Alisdair finished his drink and sat back to survey his family with an unpleasantly self-satisfied smile.

'You bastard,' James whispered.

'If I had any doubts about you, you have just resolved them for me, Alisdair,' Campbell was on his feet again but white-faced now and grimly controlled. 'You have only yourself to blame. I will *not* leave Netherdrum to you so that you can gamble it all away within six months. Until you can prove that you are capable of supporting yourself, everything I own will pass to James, and to his children after him. If, after two years, you can show me that you are earning an honest living, that you are not in debt, that you have a little money saved, then, and only then will I reconsider. The house and the factory, if there *is* still a

192

factory after what you have done, could still be yours. The farm and the land will go to James, whatever happens. And nothing will make me change my mind about that.'

'James!' Now Alisdair was on his feet, his carefully preserved composure gone, leaving him white with rage. 'But I am the eldest.'

'You may be the elder but you have shown no interest in me, this estate or the business, other than calculating how much you can wring out of me. James has been everything a son should be. He has shouldered his responsibilities, your responsibilities, and brought the farm into profit. He is not ashamed to work hard and he looks after his money properly. He has never asked me for anything. He will get what he has rightfully earned, Alisdair, and there is nothing on this earth that you can do about that.'

Alisdair turned to face his younger brother with a look of pure hatred. 'Do not,' he hissed, 'be so sure about that.'

In the sitting room, rigid with tension, both women jumped as the dining room door slammed behind Alisdair, then Fiona rose calmly to follow her husband. Isobel sat on alone, distressed by what she had been forced to overhear, disturbed by the threat she had heard in Alisdair's last words. Suddenly the door burst open and James burst into the room. But instead of the anger she expected to see on his face there was stark fear.

'Quickly, Isobel. Father's collapsed.'

He ran back to the dining room where she found him bent over Campbell.

The elderly man was grey-faced and sweating, breathing with difficulty and obviously in pain. One hand clutched frantically at his heaving chest.

'I think he's had a heart attack,' James whispered, as ashen-faced as his father.

Isobel quickly loosened her father-in-law's collar. 'Phone for the doctor, James.'

'Damn it! Stop fussing. Get away from me and let me get some air,' was the quieter than normal but surprisingly strong retort as Campbell struggled to sit up. But his strength had left him and he subsided into a lying position, still gasping for breath. 'Just overheated,' he gasped.

'Yes,' Isobel agreed. 'I felt the same during the meal. I'm sure you'll be alright in a minute. Just let me undo your shirt.' Deftly she unbuttoned his shirt for five or six inches before he succeeded in pushing her away. Then she looked up at James and mouthed silently, 'The doctor.' He nodded and hurried to the phone.

Mrs McLachlan, alerted by James, bustled into the room and between them the two women managed to get Campbell propped up against the wall where his breathing seemed easier. But now the urge to resist had left him and he was frighteningly placid, his eyes closed as if he wanted only to sleep.

The twenty minutes until the doctor arrived seemed never-ending. Banned from the room while he made his examination, Isobel and Mrs McLachlan waited tensely until they heard sounds of movement. They emerged from the kitchen in time to see Campbell being supported to his bedroom. It was a full hour before the doctor left and James was able to talk to Isobel.

'It was a mild heart attack,' he said grimly. 'He refuses to go into hospital but the doctor's given him something to make him sleep. He's been lucky this time. He should be alright if he rests for a month or so. But we will have to make sure he never has to face a scene like tonight's again.'

The doctor's prognosis was right. Campbell recovered with determined speed, stubbornly refusing to admit to anything other than having eaten something which hadn't agreed with him. Isobel spent her days at the big house helping Mrs McLachlan to nurse an increasingly uncooperative and truculent patient, receiving no sign of appreciation from him for her efforts.

Geddes accepted tea, newspapers and even her steadying arm, with no word of thanks and spoke only to complain that his tea was too cold, too weak, or to accuse her of trying to worm her way into his favour. She bore it all with stoic silence, biting back the angry retorts which were so often on her lips, knowing that to cause more unpleasantness could only further endanger the old man and upset James.

But within a month the crisis had passed. Campbell no longer needed their attentions and was intent upon returning to the factory for at least two days a week. James agreed with Isobel that this would do him less harm than to be frustratingly penned up at Netherdrum. Gratefully they escaped to the blissful peace of their cottage and resumed their family life.

FOURTEEN

It had been many months since Isobel had fallen prey to one of her extraordinary attacks, almost as if the happiness she had found with James and Shona had settled her mind. The vision she experienced one afternoon in late summer was all the more disturbing for that.

She was reading in the small garden behind the cottage when she slipped into the dreaded, trance-like state and was forced to watch as Alisdair Geddes drove a large estate car at breakneck speed through the familiar Strathannan countryside. Her heart sank but she consoled herself with the thought that the inevitable visit might be months, or even years, away.

But it was only the next day when James announced, 'Alisdair has just phoned Father to tell him he has a job. Father thinks he has finally seen the wisdom of earning a steady living. It looks as if Father's threat to leave everything to me has finally scared some sense into him. According to Father he has accepted that I'm to get the farm . . . mind you,' he added frowning, 'I can't trust him quite as easily as Father seems able to. Still, he did apologise for the things he said that evening. Not before time, either.'

'He didn't even come to see your father when he was ill!' Isobel blurted out, unable to ignore the tight feeling of misgiving that any mention of Alisdair brought to her.

'He says he thought it would only make Father worse if he did. I must say he's got a point there.'

'I suppose so,' she agreed grudgingly, unable to see any shade of good in Alisdair's character.

'Alisdair is very anxious to repair the damage. He is very keen to get back on speaking terms with the rest of the family.'

'Very keen to keep a hold on his inheritance,' Isobel sniffed.

'What other reason would there be?' James had the grace to smile wryly at her. 'He has suggested a weekend away together. To talk. Father won't go, he's still not as well as he likes to pretend he is, but he is very anxious for me to go.'

Isobel's heart lurched so violently that she almost fainted. The sudden, absolute conviction that there was some hidden menace in Alisdair's suggestion drained the colour from her cheeks.

'Do you think you could stand a weekend with Fiona?' he went on, oblivious to her fear.

'If I must,' she said. 'If you really think it will help.' Then, more generously, telling herself that this irrational fear was the result of her own prejudice, 'A weekend is not a lifetime and I daresay Fiona is as keen to make amends as Alisdair is. Though I still think they're both motivated by money, and not by any sense of loyalty to the family.'

She was rapidly proved right. Far from wanting to restore friendly relations, Fiona did her utmost to make things worse by flatly refusing to socialise with Isobel. In the end Alisdair came to Netherdrum alone, intending to stay for only one night before taking James to visit mutual friends in Ballater for the weekend. It did not escape Isobel that she was not included in the invitation.

To her it was obvious that this was a charade. The exaggerated concern for his father's health, the pretended interest in the business, his false affection for James were all transparently insincere. Why couldn't James and Campbell see Alisdair for the scheming hypocrite he really was? Surely they knew that this was all an act. But, when she mentioned her misgivings to James, he laughed. When she persisted he accused her of bitterness, then challenged her to give Alisdair

197

another chance, for Campbell's sake. After that she kept silent.

The next day James was up and about early. By the time Isobel dressed Shona and came downstairs his things were packed and he was ready to leave. James kissed her and tossed his chuckling daughter high into the air before kissing her, too. Alisdair, waiting by his car, studiously ignored them both.

'I'll be back on Wednesday,' James said. 'The season's just opened. It's years since I did any serious shooting. I must admit I'm looking forward to it.' He turned to pick up a piece of equipment. In reeling horror Isobel realised there were three guns in the mass of gear.

'You're going shooting?' she gasped, struggling to overcome the panic rising from her stomach, a response to the flooding memory of the appalling vision she had experienced on the very first occasion she had met Alisdair.

'Didn't you realise?' James laughed. 'Don't worry. There are at least twelve of us in the party. We can't possibly get lost on the moors.'

'I wish you wouldn't go, James,' she blurted out. 'I hate shooting. It's such a waste . . .'

'It's a good job you aren't coming then, isn't it,' he cut her short, sounding faintly impatient.

'Please, James. I'm asking you not to go,' she dragged on his sleeve. 'You don't understand. I once had a dream . . .' Sensing her mother's agitation Shona set up an unhappy wail, drowning out her words.

'For goodness sake, Isobel! You're frightening Shona. Be sensible, please. Surely you can cope on your own for one weekend.' He shook her off with unusual anger and she knew she had embarrassed him.

'Really Isobel. You cannot expect James to stay here with you all the time. He deserves a little relaxation, wouldn't you say?' hissed Alisdair when he was certain James was out of earshot. 'After all, what fun does he have stuck here with a common little fishergirl and a screaming brat?'

Leaving her feeling as if he had slapped her face he ran nimbly to the car. From behind he looked so like James that she wanted to run after him, hit him, tell him he had no right to look like that, to scream at him, to scream at James . . .

It was too late. The car pulled away, the fear drumming in her heart drowning out the sound of its engine. James's arm protruded through the open window, waving until they disappeared from sight, but it was more than she could do to wave back. It was an omission she would regret for the rest of her life.

She couldn't eat, couldn't sleep. Even staying in the same place for more than a minute seemed a physical impossibility.

'Whatever's wrong?' demanded Lizzie, puzzled by Isobel's uncharacteristic waspishness.

'Nothing,' Isobel snapped. 'I simply don't likes James being with Alisdair. I don't trust him.'

'James can more than take care of himself,' was Lizzie's half-scornful reply.

Catching her mother's mood, Shona too was fretful, and was only comforted when allowed to crawl into the welcoming nest of her mother's lap.

At night Isobel's mind was full of that terrible vision. The faces of the two men had never been clear but now, as she lay tossing in the heat of the late August night, imagination fitted James's face to the body of the victim and Alisdair's tanned hands to the trigger of the gun.

Every day dragged. Each ring of the phone brought Isobel's nerves to breaking point, sent her heart pounding until she thought it would kill her. But at last it was Tuesday evening. He would be home tomorrow. There would be no more shooting now. Surely he was safe.

Sheer exhaustion forced her eyes closed as dawn broke. The shrill ring of the phone brought her instantly to her senses before eight o'clock. Her mouth dry, her chest tight with fear she rushed to answer it. It was Mrs McLachlan. In a strangely cracked voice she said that Mr Geddes had been taken ill and asked Isobel to come to Netherdrum House at once.

'Thank God . . . Thank God . . . Thank God,' Isobel whispered as she replaced the receiver. Relief flooded through her, taking her strength with it. She collapsed onto the stairs and put her face in her shaking hands. Seconds later, making a great effort to pull herself together she was back on her feet, the relief partly replaced by guilt at her selfish reaction to what would be, to James, very bad news.

Rushing upstairs she dragged on the clothes she had discarded last night, fumbling with the hairbrush as she tried to tidy her hair. In her hurry she stuck a finger through a nylon but pulled the spoiled stocking onto her leg regardless. Then, grabbing the still-sleeping Shona from her cot, she bundled her into the pram and ran the short distance to Netherdrum House.

Mrs McLachlan opened the front door before she could knock. The woman was obviously in a state of shock and her voice rasped as she spoke.

'In there, lass.' Gently she took the pram from Isobel's cold hands and nodded towards the dining room.

'Come in, Isobel,' Campbell Geddes came toward her as she entered the room. And she knew.

'Mrs McLachlan told me you were ill,' she said as he took her hands and led her further into the room. She heard her own voice as though it belonged to someone else. A detached part of her marvelled at how composed she sounded.

'There are two gentlemen here, lass. From the police.' His voice was slow, muffled sounding. 'This, gentlemen, is my daughter-in-law. Mrs James Dryburgh.' Grim-faced and bowed, Campbell Geddes stayed by her side as if to offer support. Now Isobel knew the very worst had happened.

'How can I help you?' she asked the two officers, knowing

what she was about to hear yet still feeling strangely apart from it all.

She could not know the effect she was having on the two men. Her unexpected youthfulness, the absolute pallor of her skin, the pink lips, the spun gold of the flowing hair, loose around her shoulders, gave her an enchanted, breath-takingly beautiful and poignantly tragic appearance. They both stared.

Campbell, too, was seeing her properly for the first time. His diseased heart gave a warning twinge as he suddenly appreciated how devastating this would be for her.

'Well?' she demanded, sounding imperious, filled with dread.

The taller of the two men stepped forward. 'Mrs Dry-burgh, I am Inspector John Mathieson of the Fife Constabulary. This is Constable Bell. I am deeply sorry to have to bring you such tragic news,' he hesitated, watching her carefully, trying to gauge her reaction. She didn't flinch. 'Perhaps you had better sit down,' he suggested, raising a hand, meaning to guide her to a seat. Something in her manner stopped him.

'Please go on, Inspector.'

'Your husband, James Dryburgh . . . I am afraid there has been an accident.'

Some part of her mind screamed. Her face barely moved. 'An accident,' she repeated dully.

'It appears he was on the moors with his brother. Although we do not yet have the full report, it seems your husband stumbled and fell on his gun, causing it to go off. He was killed instantly.'

Isobel saw Alisdair call out to James. Saw James turn. Saw the look of shock on his face when he recognised Alisdair's intention. Saw him fall.

'Are you alright, my dear?' Campbell asked, still reeling from his own shock.

She didn't hear but stood, staring into the blind distance, reliving every painful second of James's death.

'Are you certain it was an accident?' she asked at last.

'As sure as we can be, under the circumstances. There will of course be an inquest.'

'There were no witnesses?'

'Your husband and his brother . . .'

'Half-brother,' she corrected, harshly.

'Ah . . . half-brother. They were alone. Not far from the house, yesterday evening.'

'The other guests?'

'All inside the house.'

'Is there any possibility that my husband may have been shot by someone else?'

She felt Campbell's shocked withdrawal, felt him sway slightly.

Mathieson stared at her. 'The only other person present was Alisdair Geddes. Are you suggesting that he could have shot his own brother?'

'Yes, Inspector. That is exactly what I am suggesting.'

'Is there any reason for him to want to do that?'

Campbell groaned and sank into a chair where he panted breathlessly 'Oh God . . . Oh no . . . not that . . .'

'Money, Inspector,' she retorted, knowing that this was hopeless, that Campbell Geddes would never allow his son to come under suspicion, that Alisdair's guilt could never be proved. She went on nevertheless. 'My father-in-law recently told Alisdair that he intended to revise his will in my husband's favour. I believe that Alisdair was determined to prevent that happening.' Her voice was low and flat, devoid of emotion, but her hands shook with the huge effort of control.

'It is a matter for the local police,' Mathieson said curtly. To him it was obvious that this strange, cold woman was eaten with jealousy. 'I will keep you informed.'

When the police had left Isobel remained, standing motionless, unaware of anything beyond her own grief.

It was Mrs McLachlan returning to the room who jarred

her out of her trance. 'Mr Geddes!' she screamed, rushing to her striken employer's side.

Isobel jarred back to the present and saw her father-in-law's ashen face, his blue lips and heaving chest. Instantly she was on her knees at his side, sending Mrs McLachlan to call the doctor.

'Mr Geddes,' she whispered. 'Please, open your eyes.' The flaccid, grey cheeks trembled and the watery eyes opened. 'Oh, lass. What have you done?' he asked, his voice little more than a breathy whisper.

She bowed her head, not in sorrow as he thought but to offer a rare, desperate prayer for him. She needed him and all his hostile strength if she was to survive this.

His weak eyes focused on her more clearly. The harsh features softened and a liver-spotted hand sought one of her cold ones. 'May God forgive me,' he croaked, 'but I believe you were speaking the truth.' The depth of despair and pain in his voice temporarily overwhelmed her own grief. She raised her eyes to meet his and clasped his hand more firmly. 'I'm so sorry,' she whispered. 'I spoke without thinking.'

'I know, lass.' He struggled for breath, gasped in pain and closed his eyes for a moment.

'Try not to talk. The doctor will be here soon.' She was desperately frightened now, could feel the life ebbing away from him, like a cold tide drawing the warmth from the room with it.

'There'll be all the time in the world for rest,' he said, angrily resisting his weakness with his last glimmer of vitality. 'I know I've not been good to you. I was wrong. Any fool can see how happy you made James. And for that I'm grateful. But you're not to worry. I'll see you and the little lass get the farm and enough to get by on. It's only right . . .'

The hand in hers went limp as he drifted into unconsciousness.

Isobel hunched at his side, unable to move, willing him to breathe on, trying to force her mind into his, wanting to tell him that she would care for him; that she and her daughter needed him; that he still had a family to live for.

He didn't hear her. Stubborn to the end he kept his eyes and ears closed and died minutes before the doctor arrived.

Mrs McLachlan found them slumped together, Isobel seeming as lifeless as Campbell Geddes, her head on his shoulder, seeking the support he had been too late in offering; support he had been too proud to give until it was too late.

FIFTEEN

The weeks passed in a daze. Netherdrum was unwelcoming, empty, yet too full of memories. Immersed in grief and numbed to anything beyond her own pain, Isobel appeared to have lost the will to live and drifted through her days aimlessly, as fragile and indeterminate as a wraith.

'You have got to eat, Isobel. For Shona's sake. You can't afford to be ill now.' Lizzie bullied her gently, offering a tray of her favourite foods.

Isobel eyed it without appetite. 'I don't think I can eat anything,' she said, tears filling the huge blue eyes for the tenth time that day. Lizzie sighed, knowing that there was nothing she could say to ease her friend's sorrow. After a minute she tiptoed from the room.

She returned with Shona toddling beside her. The child, who had been carefully shielded from Isobel's distressed condition, stared at her mother's tears in mixed fear and astonishment. Then the need for reassurance overcoming all else she ran to Isobel, her little arms upraised. 'Mammy,' she pleaded, wanting to be lifted up.

Isobel shook her head and turned away. The child broke into heartbroken sobs. Lizzie stood motionless by the door, making no attempt to console her.

Slowly Isobel turned back to her daughter. Her tear-stained face lightened for an instant and then, appalled to understand how cruel she was being, she swiftly bent and folded the child into her arms, holding her so tightly that Shona struggled to break free. Smiling softly for the first time in weeks, Isobel set her gently back on her feet and planted a soft kiss on the tumble of dark curls.

'You're right,' she said, looking at Lizzie. 'I am being selfish. I've got Shona to think about. James would be disgusted if he could see me now.' It was the first time she had been able to say his name without choking on tears. 'I've got to sort myself out. Make some sort of plans for the future.' Lizzie came from the door and knelt on the floor by her friend, holding her hands. 'It's the thought of being on my own that frightens me most, Lizzie,' she confessed.

'You don't have to be on your own,' Lizzie said hesitantly. 'Now that Mr Geddes is dead, Mrs McLachlan doesn't need me. I could stay with you, if you like.'

Isobel's eyes brightened visibly. 'Could you?' she asked. 'Would you? Please?'

Tears in her own eyes, Lizzie hugged her friend. 'For as long as you want me to,' she said. 'Together we'll manage. Somehow. I was so frightened I would have to go and find another job somewhere and I would miss you and Shona so much.'

'Lizzie!' If there had been any tears left Isobel would have wept again then. 'You can stay with us forever, if that's what you want.'

It was almost as if a light curtain was drawing over the past, easing the pain, releasing her mind and giving a purpose to her life again.

The inquest was held a full eight weeks after James's death. The verdict was death by misadventure, as Isobel had known it would be. The funeral was a mere forty-eight hours later. All she could ever recall of it was the composed expression on Alisdair Geddes's face, and the surge of hate for him which overshadowed even her grief for James.

Afterwards she was summoned to Campbell Geddes's study for the reading of the wills. Apart from her and the rather austere lawyer, Alisdair and Fiona were the only people present. They did not acknowledge her.

'On the whole the will is perfectly straightforward,' droned the elderly lawyer. 'Campbell Geddes has left his estate, in its entirety, to his only surviving son, Alisdair Geddes.'

Isobel waited, conscious of Alisdair's sigh of relief and his ill-concealed smirk of mirth. When she glanced at Fiona the open victory glinting in the cold, haughty face sent her stomach to her throat.

'Is there any provision for my daughter?' she asked, afraid to hear the answer. 'Mr Geddes's granddaughter?'

'Mrs Dryburgh. Mr Geddes's whole estate, all his property, has been left to his son, Alisdair. Had your husband survived his father, then the terms of the will would have been slightly different, but, in the event . . .' He left the rest unsaid, looking at her with something dangerously close to pity in his eyes.

'There must be some mistake,' she exclaimed. 'Mr Geddes intended the farm to go to James. Before he died he said he would leave something for Shona.'

'There is no provision for her,' the solicitor repeated gently.

'It seems that Father knew you for the little gold-digger you really are.' Fiona's voice was like an iced dagger.

Furiously Isobel rose to her feet, turned her back pointedly on Alisdair and his wife and faced the solicitor. 'I am convinced there must be another will. He was so determined that Shona should have a secure future.'

'I am sorry, Mrs Dryburgh. Perhaps that was Mr Geddes's intention. But the fact is, no other will was drawn up. If it was his intention to make provision for you and your daughter then, presumably, he felt no urgency. That may be unfortunate but, in law, Alisdair Geddes is the rightful inheritor.'

'Please understand,' Isobel insisted. 'I want nothing for myself. But it is only right that Shona should be provided for.'

'Perhaps my father doubted that he was, in fact, Shona's grandfather,' Alisdair's voice was a malicious whisper.

The lawyer blanched, coughed and fiddled nervously with his papers. 'I don't think this is the time . . .'

'How dare you!' Isobel flew to face Alisdair, anger blazing from eyes which flashed like icebergs. 'She is your own half-niece. An innocent child. Your brother loved her dearly. How could you even suggest . . .'

'Please, Mrs Dryburgh. You are upset. It is an emotional time for you all.' The solicitor prised himself from his chair and eased her gently away from Alisdair. 'I am truly sorry but the will is valid.'

'I see. Then there is nothing more I wish to hear.' Summoning as much dignity as she could, Isobel left the room, painfully aware of Fiona's loud aside as she went.

'I can assure you,' she was saying to the uncomfortable solicitor, 'Mr Geddes had no intention of leaving anything to that woman. She trapped his son into marriage with a child which may not even be his and then tried to turn Father against us. Thank goodness he wasn't as easily duped as we all feared he might be.'

Two days later, having had time to fully assimilate what the solicitor had said, Isobel phoned him. To her dismay he politely but very firmly refused to discuss Campbell Geddes's affairs with her, explaining that Alisdair Geddes was now his client and he could not also represent her. He did, however, recommend a colleague with a practice in Cupar. Isobel made an appointment and visited him the following day.

'I want to know if there would be any point in challenging the will,' she asked, after explaining the circumstances.

His reaction was immediate. 'You are, of course, entitled to do so. But I must warn you that such cases are seldom successful. Even those that are take many years to resolve. The cost of such a case would be enormous. In the absence of any new will you are almost certain to lose. You run the very real risk of ending up with nothing.'

'Which is precisely what we have now.'

'I understood you to say that you have an income in your own right? You are a well-regarded artist I believe?'

'I have been lucky. My works sells well,' she admitted readily.

'That is what I was referring to. If you pursue this case and lose you could find yourself with a legal bill which would absorb all you have.' He adjusted the gold-rimmed spectacles on his nose and peered at her over the top of them. 'You have my deepest sympathy, Mrs Dryburgh, but my advice to you is not to persist. Even though I do not doubt that Campbell Geddes did intend to alter his will to make some kind of allowance for his grandchild and you.'

'I don't want anything for myself,' she interrupted. 'But my husband had nothing of his own. Even the cottage belongs to the estate. It was always understood that the farm would come to him, and then to our children. If James had outlived his father by even one day I wouldn't be here now, my daughter's future would have been safe. No matter what that will says, this is not what James or his father intended.'

'I am sure that Mr Geddes fully intended to make some arrangement for you both,' the lawyer soothed. 'But his premature demise came before he actually did anything about it. It is an all-too-common occurrence.'

'Nevertheless,' she persisted, her face hardening into stubborn lines, 'I cannot allow things to remain as they are. I appreciate your advice but I owe it to my daughter, my husband, and to Mr Geddes to fight for what is right.'

And she would fight. By the time she left the solicitor's office her mind was made up. Even if she had to work night and day to meet the legal bill, she would make sure that Shona had the future that James would have wanted for her.

Less than a week later Isobel got a letter from Alisdair's solicitor. When she read it she felt as if her world had finally collapsed. In cold, formal terms she was informed that the

Netherdrum estate was to be sold. She was instructed to remove herself from the farm cottage within twenty-one days. The demand for rent which accompanied the letter was outrageous.

Now the burden of supporting Shona and Lizzie fell squarely on her shoulders, forcing her to take urgent stock of her situation. Apart from the two hundred pounds that James had left, she had nothing of any material value from her marriage. But she did have a modest, although already decreasing, sum in her bank account, as well as some unsold paintings. Perhaps, if she could produce and sell a picture every month, she would be able to support them, even if it was on a very modest scale. Two or three a month might produce the means to contest the will. Burning with purpose she wrote a letter to Farquhar Stirling, outlining her plans.

Her most urgent task was to find them a home. Leaving Shona in Lizzie's competent care she went back to the solicitor in Cupar He had several pleasant houses for sale, but none of them fell within her slender means.

He also knew of two cottages which were for rent. But her rising hopes were rapidly dashed by the attitude of the landlords who were unwilling to give their tenancies to an attractive young widow with such flimsy means of support.

Isobel repeated the exercise in St Andrews and found the same reception there, and again in Kirkcaldy and Leven. It was increasingly obvious that unless she could provide references and a male guarantor for her rent, she had no chance of finding anywhere decent to live.

Time was running out. Crushingly aware of her new responsibilities she visited her bank manager who, after some considerable persuasion, agreed to provide her with a reference. The other, she knew, would come from Farquhar Stirling. But she couldn't expect either of them to act as her guarantor. The only people she could possibly approach about that were her own family. Neither Robbie and Twi nor Hugh and May should be asked to add to their own burdens in this way, but her father was another matter. She had long suspected that he must have a small nest egg somewhere. Concerned only with her daughter's welfare she buried her pride and went to Kilweem.

The door of the old house, newly painted and spruce, was opened by Maggie. There was an awkward moment when she all-too-clearly debated with herself whether or not to allow her sister-in-law into the house. Her envious eyes gawped at the fitted suit, neat shoes and soft gloves, bought for the funerals, which gave such a misleading impression of affluence. To her insensitive mind, Isobel's highly nervous manner seemed haughty, and she knew her husband loathed his sister. To invite Isobel in could well provoke the sort of violent reaction she lived in permanent dread of. But curiosity won and Isobel was ushered inside.

The house bore no resemblance to the poor cottage which had been her childhood home. The furnishings were reasonably modern and the decoration, though grubby, was contemporary. Only Malcolm's old chair remained to remind her of the past.

'I came to see my father,' Isobel explained. 'When will he be in?'

'In about an hour,' was the brusque reply.

'Oh . . . well, I'll have a walk round the village and come back later.'

'No . . . don't go.' Maggie stopped her awkwardly. 'Would you like to see round the house? You'll hardly recognise it now we've had it all done up.' Her avaricious mind was working as quickly as it could. Wasn't this woman rich? Perhaps there was something to be gained by being friendly.

'Yes. I'd like that.' It would certainly be preferable to braving the village where she was certain to meet someone she knew.

Maggie led the way up narrow, dusty stairs. Isobel soon saw that she had not been exaggerating. Bright new linoleum covered the floor boards and a bathroom had been added. Maggie showed her round proudly, not at all shamed by the chaos which reigned in every room. Downstairs the kitchen had been separated from the living area and the old bed recess was hidden behind cupboard-style doors. The effect was quite ruined by pieces of errant bedding which hung off the bed and prevented the doors from closing properly.

'Father still insists on sleeping in here,' Maggie laughed as she shoved aside a pile of newspapers to make room for Isobel on the settee. 'And I'm right sorry to hear about your husband,' she added, very much as an afterthought.

'Thank you.' Desperate to keep away from that painful subject Isobel said, 'The house is lovely. Not at all how I remember it.'

Maggie preened, delighted at the undeserved compliment. 'Of course, there's still a lot to be done. If we had the cash. But, with the kids and all it's not easy. Aye, it's not easy at all. Father paid for most of this. What a time Willy had getting him to part with his money . . . And if it hadn't been for Hugh I don't know how we'd get by. Aye, your brother did us a right good turn there. We could use some more help like that from the family.' It was completely without subtlety but Isobel didn't seem to notice.

'Yes,' she agreed. 'Hugh was always generous.' She already knew that when Hugh's father-in-law died, Hugh and May had been left with his boat and a mobile fishmonger's round. Unable to operate both on his own, Hugh had kept the boat and passed the van on to his brother and father.

'Some weeks the van doesn't take enough money to cover the cost of food for us all,' Maggie complained. 'And I don't know how we'll get through the winter if business doesn't pick up soon.'

Before she could add to her list of hardships they were disturbed by the harsh sound of a car engine outside. Maggie leapt to her feet. 'That'll be the men,' she confided nervously. Dressed in long, filthied white aprons and reeking of fish, William and Malcolm strode in. Isobel was shocked by the similarities in the two men. William grew more like his father with every passing year.

'Hello, Father. William,' Isobel said softly.

They stopped and gazed at her in stupefied silence.

'Well, and what the hell brings you here?' William was the first to recover his wits.

'Aye. What do you want?' There was no pleasure in Malcolm's voice.

'Hush Father. Sit down and shut up,' William shoved the older man into a chair and muttered something into his ear. Malcolm nodded.

'I came to see Father,' Isobel couldn't repress a shudder when she faced her brother.

'Well,' he said, radiating false geniality. 'Sit down and take some tea with us.'

'No, thanks,' she answered, still standing.

'And how are you, then?' William continued in the same uncharacteristically pleasant tone. 'We were right sorry to hear about your man.'

'Thank you.' She seemed to be saying that a lot these days.

'Aye. Well. That's the way it goes. But, what with the old man dying and all you'll be nicely set. At least you don't have to worry about money. Not like us. Things are not going well. Not well at all.'

'In fact James left me nothing,' she explained her circumstances briefly, conscious of the transformation in her brother's expression which gradually hardened into something much more familiar.

'He must have left you something!' William expostulated, challenging her to deny it.

'Nothing. Not even the house. It all went to his brother, Alisdair. That's why I'm here.'

'So I was right!' Malcolm exclaimed triumphantly. 'You do want something. You'd never come back here unless you were wanting something. Well, you've come to the wrong place.'

Stung by the injustice of the remark Isobel answered more

bitterly than she intended. 'I would have come long ago if I thought I would have been welcome. You have a beautiful granddaughter you've never even seen.'

'I've plenty grandwains already. And why should I make you welcome? After all the shame you brought on us? You don't belong here. You're not one of us. You don't even talk like a good Kilweem lassie. You never did. You sound more like the bloody English. And that bairn of yours'll be just the same. Thinking she's better than the rest of us. Just like you always did.' Hatred gleamed from Malcolm's bloodshot eyes.

Isobel shivered.

'What do you want then? Out with it and then we can all get on with our lives.' William was as hostile as his father.

Behind them the front door clicked. 'I'll just away and fetch the bairns from the school,' gabbled Maggie and escaped before the argument could drag her into it.

'Well?' Malcolm demanded.

'I need to rent a house for myself. And Shona and Lizzie. Netherdrum is being sold,' she explained. 'But I can't get anywhere unless I have someone to act as guarantor for the rent. I wondered . . .'

'You wondered,' William sneered. 'Why should we do anything for you? All the time you were queening it up there with your husband's rich family you never thought about us. And now you expect us to help you? Forget it, Hen.'

'You were invited,' she retorted angrily. 'More than once. I would have been so happy if you had come to see me. But you were always too proud. You didn't even come to my wedding.'

'You were living in sin with that man,' Malcolm bellowed. 'And he wouldn't have married you if you hadn't been carrying his bairn. You surely don't think I would step into a house where my own daughter was living like a common prostitute?'

It was useless. Coldly she turned her back on him and

opened the door, refusing to defend her actions to this bitter old man.

'Aye. And don't come back,' William flung at her as she left.

Somehow she managed to drive her car away from the house and along the coast to Sauchar, hoping to find Hugh at home.

'Isobel!' he cried when he opened the door. 'How are you, Hen?' A pair of soft blue eyes seemed to read her soul.

'Not bad,' was all she could say.

'Come away inside,' he led her into a small, comfortable house where three pairs of eyes regarded her solemnly, wondering why their gentle aunt Isobel looked so sad.

'What's wrong with you three. Are you not going to say hello to your auntie?' Hugh chided them gently.

They chorused their greetings obediently.

'Isobel! This is a grand surprise.' May emerged from her kitchen, smiling her welcome. 'Are you alright?' she asked, concerned by her sister-in-law's pallor.

'I . . . I,' Isobel stammered, still feeling shaken. 'To tell the truth I've just been to see Father and William. They weren't exactly pleased to see me.'

'No wonder you look so tired.' Hugh steered her to a chair. 'What took you there? You must know you'll never make those two change their minds about you. A more stubborn pair you'll never meet.'

'I know that now,' she smiled wanly.

'Well, lass, you'd better tell me what's wrong,' Hugh stationed himself on the arm of her chair.

'Hugh's right, Isobel. Maybe we can help,' May offered kindly.

Their unconditional sympathy nearly destroyed her composure. With a great effort she swallowed the threatening tears. Without James to protect her she knew that life would be full of difficulties. She would never cope if she dissolved into useless tears at every small setback. Forcing herself to appear calm and composed she repeated her story.

'But I will act as guarantor. It's not as if I'm taking any risks, is it? But you should have come to me first.'

'You've got your own family to think about, Hugh. And I hoped . . .' She left the rest unsaid, knowing her hopes of a reconciliation with her father had been nothing more than desperate self-deception.

'And,' Hugh went on. 'I think I might know of a wee house which would interest you.'

'Where?' Isobel gasped.

'You remember Geordie Keir – he was with you and Twi at the school?' Isobel nodded. 'Well, he's got a job in the pits, at Craigie. And a house through there, too. His old house is lying empty. Has been for weeks. They say old Harry Haldane can't get rid of it.'

'Do you think he might rent it to me?'

'I can't speak for him. He's an awkward old devil at the best of times. But it's worth a try.'

'When?' she demanded, some of the colour returning to her cheeks.

'As soon as we've drunk our tea I'll run you down to look at the house. It's not to everyone's taste, though,' he warned.

Half an hour later they were heading west along the coast towards Ainstrie, a small village tucked into a bay in the coast. Hugh drove down the main street, then left along a narrow side road running parallel with the sea. A variety of houses, some old, others new, lined one side while the beach blew through the dilapidated fencing on the other, as though trying to reclaim the land for itself.

At the very end, where the road gradually petered out until it was nothing more than a sandy track, stood a two-storey grey stone house, separated from its nearest neighbours by a hundred yards of low dunes. To Isobel it seemed that the house stood on the beach itself. As soon as Hugh stopped the car she got out and ran towards it.

'I told you it wasn't much,' Hugh panted as he ran to catch up with her. 'We can see through the windows I think.'

They rubbed salt and sand from the grimy panes and peered into the dark interior. But there wasn't much to see and, in any case, Isobel wasn't interested in the inside. It was the outside, the proximity to the sea, which had made her fall in love with the place.

She faced the estuary, letting the sharp edge of the wind buffet her skin, feeling exhilarated, her ears thrilling to the commanding sound of the waves.

'The sea,' she yelled at Hugh over the loud pounding. 'It sounds so good. I have forgotten how wonderful it can make me feel. Netherdrum is beautiful,' she confided to her brother, 'but I have missed the sound and smell of the sea.'

'That's because you grew up with it,' he said, understanding at once. 'It's the same for me.'

For a while, brother and sister stood in easy silence, content just to gaze at the North Sea.

'We'd better be getting home,' Hugh said, moving back to his car reluctantly. 'May'll have dinner ready.'

'When can I see this Mr Haldane?' Isobel asked, keen to get the house settled.

'As soon as we've eaten,' he laughed back at her enthusiasm. 'I'll take you there myself. He lives in Kilweem.'

Hary Haldane turned out to be an acne-scarred little man with a nicotine-stained moustache and a deep mistrust of all women. Isobel despised him on sight.

'Aye,' he agreed. 'The house has been empty for a couple of weeks.'

'Months,' corrected Hugh.

Haldane glanced at him. 'I'll rent it no bother. I'm thinking about advertising it in the *Sunday Post* as a holiday cottage. Lots of folks are taking their holidays around here now.'

'But I would like to rent it from you, Mr Haldane,' Isobel insisted.

'I know you would, Mrs Dryburgh. But I only rent to families,' he said smugly.

'I have a family. A young daughter and a woman who helps me look after her while I work.'

'Very nice. But I mean a normal family. With a wage-earner.'

'I can afford to pay a reasonable rent,' she said, bristling. 'I have funds of my own and I earn a respectable living from my paintings. I am even prepared to offer you six months' rent in advance. In cash.'

Haldane brightened visibly. 'Well . . . I suppose I might let you . . .'

'When can I move in?' she demanded, pressing her advantage.

'Just a wee minute,' he cautioned her. 'I never said you could have it. I need time to think about it. Come back in a couple of weeks. If I haven't let it by then, you can have it.'

'*No.*' This time Isobel wasn't to be intimidated. 'I have to have a decision from you now, Mr Haldane. Otherwise I shall take a cottage I have been offered in Cupar '

Haldane frowned but the promise of six months' rent in advance was too much to resist. 'Alright. But on a long lease. And those six months in advance by noon tomorrow.'

'I'll pay you now,' Isobel produced a modest bundle of notes, withdrawn from her account for precisely this purpose, counted out the exact amount and handed it to him. 'Perhaps you would give me a receipt,' she suggested, meeting his popping eyes calmly.

'Aye.' He grabbed her money as if he was frightened it might dissolve into the atmosphere. 'And another thing. I know who you really are. When you were a lassie you were just wee, queer Isobel McLean and I recall what they used to call you. So I'm warning you, if there's any funny business I'll put you out.'

'There will be no funny business, Mr Haldane,' she snapped. 'My God,' she whispered to herself. 'Will they never forget?'

SIXTEEN

Certain that James would have applauded her actions, Isobel helped herself to the furniture from the farm cottage. Hugh willingly transported it in the back of his ancient van. Within a week Isobel, Shona and Lizzie were installed in their new home. As soon as the place was clean and tidy Isobel started work, knowing she simply couldn't afford to relax. Setting up her easel in the bedroom she painted furiously, producing wild, undisciplined pictures of the sea which had nothing of the gentle quality she had captured so easily in earlier, happier days.

Farquhar, whose profits had shown a gratifying upturn since his discovery of Isobel, was more than willing to show anything she produced, but even so it would be more than a month before she got any return from her work. Already the balance in her bank account was shrinking at an alarming rate and desperately needed to be bolstered if they were to live with any degree of security. But, more than that, Isobel was driven by the knowledge that her only hope of winning for Shona what James and his father had surely intended to be hers, was by earning sufficient money to take the case before the courts. As she worked, rising early and painting on until the light failed, it was as if James was with her, encouraging her, giving her the will and determination to succeed.

But sales were agonisingly slow. The new, angry edge to her work lacked the immediate appeal of the tender, wistful pictures she had produced with such ease when James was alive. The money seeping into her account barely covered their living expenses and she was forced to draw on her dwindling savings with depressing regularity.

In vain she struggled to reproduce the softer, more romantic style but it continued to elude her. In desperation she faced the prospect of finding a conventional job with a regular income, but that would signal the end of her hopes for Shona. Stubbornly she closed her mind to the ravaged state of her finances, closed her ears to Lizzie's warnings about unpaid bills, and determined to work until she could no longer afford the paints.

Privately Lizzie worried that her friend had broken under the strain. Isobel's eyes were hollow with fatigue, she was thin to the point of emaciation. And still she worked like a creature possessed, driven by the unshakeable belief, a belief that had its roots not in rationality or logic, but in the profound, supernatural core of her gift for seeing the future, that the way to their salvation, to Shona's birthright, was through her paintings.

Isobel was out, miles away on the beach, collecting pencil sketches, when Farquhar arrived unexpectedly at the grey, windswept house. He left his shiny, immaculate and hugely conspicuous Daimler parked on the narrow beach road and rapped imperiously on their weathered door.

Lizzie was reduced to rare speechlessness by the affected vision on her doorstep, then had to suppress the urgent need to giggle at his high-pitched, womanish voice.

'I am looking for Isobel Dryburgh. I was told that this was the right house but . . .' he cast disbelieving, critical eyes over the shabby exterior.

'No mistake,' she choked. 'But she's not in.'

'Then where is she?' he demanded, reaching down to flick sand from his white patent shoes.

'She'll be away sketching somewhere. On the beach likely.'

'In that case you had better fetch her. Tell her that Farquhar Stirling is here and wishes to speak with her most urgently.'

Lizzie hesitated, playing with the idea of telling this effeminate and vastly overdressed man to look for Isobel himself, but knowing how important he was to her friend's career she thought better of it. 'I suppose I could,' she allowed.

'Yes, indeed you could. In the meantime I will come in and wait.' He pushed past her and smoothed imaginary wrinkles from his cream suit. In the small, neat but poorly furnished sitting room he perched on the very edge of a chair and waited.

'So you see, my dear, this could be the answer to all your problems.' Farquhar's pale eyes slid over the shabby furniture as if that should be the most pressing problem in Isobel's life.

Sitting opposite him, Isobel had paled and her hands shook, but her mind was working furiously.

'But nothing's certain, is it,' she said at last. 'Just because I have a show, doesn't mean my work will sell.'

'I don't think you need concern yourself with that.' He dismissed her reservations with a fluttering wave of a perfectly manicured, chubby hand. 'The Americans are greedy for new artists. If there had been any serious doubts about your ability to sell there I wouldn't have been approached with this offer. And remember, it is the American tourists who have been buying your work, so you already know your style appeals to them.'

'But America . . . it's so far away. And so expensive,' she added doubtfully. And such a wonderful opportunity, but she kept that thought to herself. Instead, she raised her head and faced him squarely. 'Don't think I don't appreciate what a wonderful opportunity this could be, Farquhar. But you must be able to see for yourself that I can't afford the fare to New York. Why can't you just ship my paintings over there and wait to see if they sell?'

He sighed extravagantly. 'You really don't understand the first thing about the art world, do you my dear?'

Isobel flared instantly. 'Don't patronise me, Farquhar! Of course I understand. But do you understand my position? I can't go to Edinburgh, let alone New York! I can barely afford to feed us from week to week.'

'Alright. Alright. I apologise.' He patted her hand placatingly and only succeeded in antagonising her further. She snatched it away angrily.

'Calm down, Isobel and listen to me. I *am* aware of your circumstances, though I admit I hadn't realised quite how dire they are. But, honestly, this is an opportunity you simply cannot afford to miss.' He raised his voice over her persistent protests. 'Without you there, at the opening, you cannot hope for success. In fact I am certain that the offer will be withdrawn if you do not go.'

'It's impossible, Farquhar.'

'Nothing, my dear, is impossible.'

'This is,' she insisted.

'This showing, and the sales it will generate, but more especially the publicity you receive, will establish you as a serious artist. You will never lack for money again. I guarantee it. Your career will be launched on a far greater scale than you could ever hope to achieve by simply selling a couple of paintings a month through me. After this show those same two paintings will fetch ten times as much as they would in Edinburgh.'

'Farquhar,' she snapped in mixed disappointment and anger. 'I know all that but it doesn't change the fact that I haven't got the money to go.'

'Yes you do,' he insisted, a sweet, self-satisfied smile making his face more effeminate than ever.

'I have less then thirty pounds in the bank,' she admitted bluntly.

'Plus two hundred from recent sales, the cheque for which is in my pocket,' he said, producing a monogrammed, calfskin wallet. 'That should be enough to keep this house going while you are away.'

She chuckled with glee. 'More than enough. Thank goodness. But still not enough to take me to America.'

'You will go to America, Isobel, because I will advance you the money to cover your expenses. You may repay me from the sales of your paintings,' he offered, revealing the well-hidden, generous side to his nature. 'But don't go thinking I've gone soft in my old age. I wouldn't even consider doing this if I wasn't sure you are going to be a huge success. Remember, I stand to gain a great deal of commission on this.'

When the liner docked in New York, Isobel's heart was thumping painfully. She stood at the rail looking out over the rather bleak, mist-shrouded docks and wanted to scream in sheer excitement. This was, she knew, the opportunity of a lifetime, her one chance to become internationally known and respected. The chance to secure Shona's future. In little more than twenty-four hours from now the art critics of New York would view a selection of her work and her career would take its first step towards true success. It was almost too good to be true.

The hotel Farquhar had booked for her was modest, at her insistence. Isobel stood in her room and donned the long, floaty dress in pastel shades which she had chosen specially for the event, coiled her smooth hair into the nape of her neck and looked critically at her pale, slim reflection, seeing nothing of the breathtaking beauty which stared back from solemn eyes.

Gradually over the past day the flying excitement had evaporated to leave sickening nerves. She was painfully aware that success was by no means a forgone conclusion. Not for the first time she wished her strange gift could be summoned at will, to give her some hint of what the night might bring. But that had never been possible. Everything;

her future security, Shona's birthright, even their continued residence in the little beach house could depend on the outcome of this evening. It seemed too much to rest on a mere five hours.

In the hour before the gallery opened her nervousness increased to the point where she was physically sick. Surrounded by brash Americans and Farquhar, who seemed completely at ease with these loud-mouthed, opinionated people, she felt insignificant, incapable of sustaining even the briefest conversation with people who gushed and flattered with embarrassing insincerity. What was worse, she knew they couldn't understand her accent.

'Here, lovey. Drink this and relax.' Isobel sipped the glass of cool champagne Farquhar pressed into her hands and followed it too rapidly with a second.

The evening passed in a haze of half-remembered faces, strident voices and copious amounts of that ice cool champagne. But, before the night was over she was gratified and not a little suprised to see discreet sold stickers appearing by several of her later pictures. Why then, when she eventually fell into bed, her head reeling, did she feel so apprehensive?

The following morning she and Farquhar had a brunch appointment with a columnist from the *Times*. Slightly hungover, Isobel did not relish the prospect but, expecting to be able to talk about her art, her inspiration, the soft Strathannan countryside, felt she could probably cope with this encounter better than she had dealt with last night's opening.

But it was not a happy occasion. The heavily made-up, aggressive woman journalist had researched her subject with exhaustive thoroughness. Armed with a sheaf of notes which apparently charted Isobel's life from birth onwards, she displayed a total lack of interest in the paintings and a dogged determination to expose all the more painful events from Isobel's past. This, she insisted, was what the American public wanted.

'So,' she persisted after Isobel had repeatedly refused to be drawn on the subject of her strange power to foresee future events. 'They called you a witch? Why don't you explain exactly what you can do? For example, do you know how much you will make from this show? Or maybe you could tell me something about myself?' She waited, looking expectantly at Isobel, red lips parted avidly, pencil poised.

'Don't be ridiculous,' Isobel snapped, tired, headachy and thoroughly irritated.

'Mrs Dryburgh has the gift of second sight,' interrupted Farquhar hastily. 'It is not something she can control, but she has been privileged to see snatches of the future.'

'Give me an example,' the woman demanded, edging to the very brink of her chair.

'No,' retorted Isobel. 'I thought we were going to talk about my pictures.'

'The American picture-buying public is interested in *you*, Isobel. It is your background, your past, this witch thing that will bring them out to buy.'

Isobel failed to repress a shudder.

'Mrs Dryburgh is extremely fatigued after her journey and the excitement of last night,' said Farquhar. 'Why don't you allow me to answer for you, my dear?'

'Really Isobel!' Farquhar tut-tutted his annoyance for at least the third time in fifteen minutes. 'That woman was quite right, you know. Your unique background will help to make you a personality over here. If you want this to be a success you simply must co-operate.'

'I will not rake up my past for breakfast time entertainment,' she shot back at him. 'I am doing my best to forget all that. I am here to sell my paintings, Farquhar, not provide cheap fodder for chat show hosts and bad-mannered journalists.'

Farquhar spared a sideways glance at her angry face and decided to let the subject rest. 'It'll all look better after a relaxing weekend, lovey,' he murmured.

They were in a hired, chauffeur-driven car on their way

out to Long Island where they had been invited to spend the weekend as guests of a business associate of Farquhar's.

Isobel relaxed fractionally and smiled guiltily at the ageing homosexual who had proved to be such a staunch friend. 'You're probably right,' she offered, squeezing his plump hand. 'I'm just tired. I'm overreacting I expect.'

But, as the weekend progressed, she felt worse not better. Overwhelmed by the lavish reception party in her honour which greeted them at the luxurious Long Island house, intensely humiliated by the article which appeared in the papers, exposing all the more unpleasant aspects of her past, making her the object of open curiosity for her host and the other guests, and stung to the core by the biting reviews from critics who had expressed nothing but praise to her face, Isobel yearned for the peace of Strathannan and the company of her daughter.

'I think I'll go home,' she suggested despondently to Farquhar as they returned to New York three dreadful days later.

'Go home!' He was horrified. 'But the Boston gallery is showing your work from tomorrow.'

'They won't like me any better there than they have here.'

'Don't let the critics get to you, dear Isobel. They make their living writing wicked words. Your paintings are selling marvellously and that is what matters.'

'I sold six. Hardly something to be proud of. And they certainly won't go on selling now that everyone has had the opportunity to read what the professionals think. "Soulless, immature, childish, contrived."' She recited the words which had stung so much.

'Ignore it. I did warn you not to read the reviews.' He smiled, perfectly content with the way things were going, already looking forward to Boston.

Beside him Isobel was rigidly silent, but her eyes strayed repeatedly to her handbag where her return ticket was safely lodged, while the seed of an idea grew and flourished in her churning mind. She already knew there was a ship leaving for Southampton tomorrow. Perhaps she could exchange her own ticket for one on the earlier sailing. The more she thought about it the more attractive her germinating idea seemed.

Pleading tiredness, Isobel excused herself from the dinner planned for that night. In her room she made two phone calls, then repacked her things, humming contentedly to herself. That done she collected the keys to her hired car from the receptionist and, lingering only long enough to leave a scribbled note for Farquhar, hurried out of the hotel, her mind already back in the tranquility of Strathannan.

She was in no particular hurry. There was no need to board the ship until early the next morning but she did need to get away from Farquhar who would, she knew, try to talk her into staying.

She drove nervously at first, awed by the density of the traffic but then, as her confidence increased, with almost careless abandon, until, at last, the urban sprawl thinned. Aimlessly now, relishing her own company, relieved to be free of the ceaseless noise and demands of others, she wandered for miles. It was after midnight on a rain-soaked night before she finally started back towards the city and the ship which would take her back to England, then Strathannan and her daughter.

The rhythmic swish of the windscreen wipers and the blurred glare of the lights were hypnotic. Her faint, comfortable tiredness gave way to sudden exhaustion. Knowing she could easily afford an hour or two of rest she looked for somewhere to stop.

She was still driving when she felt the unexpected warning signs which told her one of her attacks was imminent.

Desperately she searched for a safe place to pull off the road, braking sharply and praying she could stop before the inevitable insensibility overtook her.

Teeming, wild, disconnected images were already invading her mind. Frantically she gripped the wheel, concentrated her slipping mind on the roadside lights and tried to force her consciousness back to reality. But it was too late. She was already back at Netherdrum. Beautiful, warm Netherdrum, well tended and serene. The hum of the car's engine became the busy sound of summer insects, the drum of the rain gently softened to a summer breeze through the trees. And there was Shona, a young adult now, walking through the grounds, a young child running at her heels; then Twi, bedridden and in appalling pain. Shona again, much younger this time, crying alone in the corner of a partly furnished room; back to Netherdrum, neglected and overgrown and Shona looking at the little cottage where she and James had lived, dilapidated now and ramshackle, with such a sad, lost expression that Isobel felt tears prick the back of her own hallucinating eyes. Then, rapidly overlaying the chaotically changing images, the overpowering smell of antiseptic and a fleeting, puzzling glimpse of a vacant-eyed, faded woman. A woman she should know. Isobel grappled with her revolving mind, searching for recognition, and finally broke under the horror of the truth.

It had been the most violent, most intense experience she had ever known, sapping everything from her, leaving no room for rational thought, or her own safety.

And then there was nothing but the deep, beckoning, friendly blackness of release.

By the time Farquhar read her note they had already fished her car from the depths of the Hudson. Her body had been washed away by the currents in the river. Immeasurably saddened he started the grim return journey to Scotland to break the news personally to her family.

News of the tragedy preceded him by several days. The consensus of opinion in the British press was that, depressed by the death of her husband and the unfavourable reaction of the New York critics to her work, Isobel had committed suicide.

Numbed by grief, Lizzie refused to believe it. Even Farquhar who had been with her so recently thought it was hardly credible. But the evidence was undeniable.

In Edinburgh, Alisdair Geddes read the reports with unconcealed relief. For him, Isobel's death was a welcome twist of fate, removing all threat to his inheritance. With uncharacteristic generosity it was he who offered to travel to America to identify the waterlogged body which was eventually washed up in New York Bay.

PART TWO

Shona

SEVENTEEN

Twi McArdle took her tea into her front room and collapsed into her favourite overstuffed and shabby armchair with a sigh of relief. The life of a farm hand's wife was one of hard, unremitting and frequently unrewarded labour. Adding the burden of four growing youngsters and an overworked, perpetually tired husband made it almost intolerable at times.

Life was appreciably harder here at Blackwell's farm than it had been while Robbie had worked for Waddle. But the kindly farmer had retired two years ago. The new tenant had brought his own labourers with him. Robbie had been fortunate to find another job and was in no position to complain, even though Blackwell demanded inhuman hours from his hands. And at least this house was bigger. With four boisterous children they needed every inch of space in their old, cold, three-bedroomed house.

Even in her blackest moments, Twi knew that her life was considerably better than that of either of her sisters-in-law. Hugh earned even less than Robbie and at least she was free of the constant fear of the North Sea which haunted May, Hugh's wife. Nor, thank God, did Robbie drink his wages away as William had done ever since Father's death.

The dogs, two fiercely protective border collies, set up a yapping, snarling clamour in the back yard, announcing the arrival of her brothers and their wives. Robbie, too, would be home at any minute and then they were all in for a hard evening as they battled over what was to become of the orphaned five-year-old Shona.

A tear welled in one eye but Twi sniffed and brushed it

233

away. She, like everyone else, had been devastated by Isobel's shocking death. But the time for sentimentality was past. Tonight Twi would do her Christian best to settle Shona's future, but she had the welfare of her own family to consider before that of her unfortunate niece.

'I'm telling you, there's no way I'm having her What use is another lassie to me? Another mouth to feed, that's all.' William roared belligerently, his face beetroot-red and beaded with sweat.

'I thought we were talking about offering the bairn a home, not seeing what use she could be,' snapped Twi, refusing to be intimidated by her brother's foul temper.

'If you're all so keen to play good samaritans, you can have her.' His face drew level with hers, almost choking her on a gust of sour beer. She turned away in disgust.

'That's enough, Willy. Nobody said you had to have her. We need to talk it out. Calmly. We'll get nowhere screaming and yelling at each other.' Hugh guided his snarling brother back to a chair and grimaced at Twi.

William glowered back from beneath wild, shaggy eyebrows and a shock of red hair, but it was far from easy to provoke Hugh who remained calm and reasonable in the face of the ugliest displays of temper.

It was obvious that these three were closely related. Physically they were as close as they had been as children, marked by the same startling, wiry red hair and strong build. William, the eldest, was a hulking bear of a man. At six-foot-four his body was cumbersome, his face flaccid and his movements lumbering. Blessed with little intelligence and hampered by an increasing inability to see any point of view other than his own, he was a humourless, irascible, uncouth man and, Twi suspected glancing at his silent, dowdy wife, a violent one.

Hugh was a milder replica of his brother. Despite his height and equally solid build his manner had none of the menace of William's. His eyes held the permanent glint of humour, an impression strengthened by the crow's feet crinkling round his eyes and the ready lift of his mobile mouth.

Beside her brothers Twi, with the lined face and careworn expression of a woman who worked too hard and too long, seemed insubstantial. The ready tongue, strident voice and the urge to organise anyone or anything which strayed into her orbit soon dispelled that impression. She was thirty-one years old and looked forty-five.

'Well I don't know what's to be done with her,' William muttered when they had all calmed down a little.

'Me neither, but I do know we have to do something,' Hugh encouraged them gently.

'Aye, you're right enough there, Hugh. Something will have to be done. And quickly.' Robbie was desperately sorry for his little niece but couldn't afford to add her to his own overly large family.

'What do you mean by that?' William challenged, always quick to take offence.

Robbie sighed. 'Just what I said. The lassie needs our help.'

'Not from me she doesn't,' William spat the words out.

'Willy, please be reasonable,' Twi begged.

'Reasonable!' he yelled. 'Do you think it's reasonable for any of us to feed and clothe her when her own family turned their backs on her? Old Geddes was the richest man for miles around. There's not enough money for my own family as it is.'

'It's the same for all of us,' interjected Hugh, only too uncomfortably aware of the lack of space in his own compact home.

'Robbie and Twi have more room than any of us,' William said slyly.

'We've no more room for another bairn than you have,' Twi retorted.

'We all know there's no easy way out of this,' interrupted

Hugh hastily, trying to forestall a full-blown row. 'It's going to be hard for any of us to take the lassie in. But when all is said and done, she is family.'

'Aye, family, and that's what counts.' Calming down rapidly, Twi did her best to support Hugh's efforts to work them towards a solution. 'What do you suggest, Hugh?'

'I think the only fair thing is for each of us to take her for a few months at a time. That way we can all share the load and Shona will get to be with her family. Where she belongs.'

'What about clothes and shoes? Bairns are not cheap to keep dressed these days.' William sought and found objections. 'I won't have her needing new shoes every time it's our turn to have her.'

'Och, surely that's not a problem?' May, Hugh's wife, spoke for the first time. 'Between Twi's two lassies, your own three and our three we'll manage to keep her dressed in what they've outgrown. And I'm sure we'll be able to squeeze her in with our lassies to sleep.'

'Aye, we'll manage somehow,' Hugh sounded relieved. 'So, that's it settled. It's just a case of deciding who's going to have her first.'

'Not me. You can have her. She knows you better.'

'Trust you to land someone else with it,' Robbie glowered at his brother-in-law.

'I don't mind her coming to us first,' Twi offered generously. 'But I don't think it'll work. Don't forget the bairn's just about to start school. If we all have her for a few months at a time she'll be in and out of different schools all the time. We can't have that. She needs to be able to settle down and make friends.'

'Aye, that's true enough.' Hugh glanced at his wife who merely smiled, content to let him make the decision. 'If we had her through the week she could go to school with our Betty. Then William and Maggie could have her for the weekends and you and Robbie could take her here on the farm for the holidays.'

'That means you'll be having her longer than William and Maggie,' Robbie pointed out.

'Not really,' said May. 'She'll be at school all day.'

'It doesn't matter about that,' said Hugh. 'So long as we get her settled. We'll take her Monday morning to Friday night. After school on Friday she can go to our Willy's. Holidays she'll be up here with you, Twi.' He rubbed his hands together in satisfaction. 'Do we all agree then?'

'I suppose so. If that's the best you can come up with,' William conceded with extremely bad grace.

'But if she needs anything special we'll all chip in,' insisted Robbie, necessarily concerned with his own strained finances.

'Agreed,' Hugh said quickly.

'Well, school starts in three weeks. We may as well fetch her up here tomorrow and leave Lizzie to tidy up. She's anxious to get back to her parents,' said Twi turning to Hugh. 'I'll bring her down to you on the last day of the holidays, if that's alright.'

'Aye, Hen,' he smiled. 'That'll be fine.'

EIGHTEEN

The dark-haired child huddled dejectedly among the dunes and gazed out over the North Sea. It was grey with angry white flecks whipped up by threatening rain. It matched her mood.

She shivered and hunched even further inside her thin coat, knowing with the instinctive sensitivity which was her own legacy that today would mark the start of something bleak and unhappy.

'Shona! Shona! Where are you?' She heard Lizzie's anxious voice, distorted by the rising wind. 'Shona, I know you're there somewhere. Get in here. Now! I won't call you again.'

Recognising the familiar signs of incipient anger, Shona scrambled to her feet and brushed the sand from her bare legs. Lizzie was scanning the beach from the back door. Reluctantly Shona trailed home.

Today she was leaving the little grey house, right on the edge of the beach, where she woke up each morning and knew what sort of day it was simply by listening to the sea; where the sound of the waves crashing on the shoreline lulled her to sleep every night; where no matter what else happened the sea was always there, loud, strong and reassuring.

The house was already empty. In her mother's room the bed was stripped of its covers, the mattress rolled back, the pictures taken down, the brushes, combs and hairpins packed away. Even the sun had gone. Shona wondered if it had deserted her forever. Like her mother.

Lizzie had packed all her things, too. Shona watched, awed by the astounding sight of Lizzie's tears. But when she put her baby-soft arms round the woman's neck, offering what little comfort she could, she was roughly rejected. Rubbing her eyes, Lizzie firmly detached the clinging arms and shooed the child away to play in the dunes.

Now, grim-faced and swollen-eyed, she dragged an old comb painfully through Shona's softly curling, almost black hair, trying to restore some order after the whipping the wind had given it.

'I've already made you tidy once,' she scolded, wiping the young face with a sour-smelling rag. 'Now, away and sit on the stair. Your Auntie Twi'll be here any minute.'

Two bags held everything in the world that was hers. Clothes and shoes, a hairbrush and a variety of sewn and knitted dolls. Her pencils and paper were in a separate, brown paper bag from the greengrocers, carefully emptied of potato dust so that her precious paper would stay clean.

Shona dragged herself and her bags to the cold stone stairs to wait.

The sharp clack of Lizzie's heels echoed in the empty rooms overhead, making Shona feel more miserable than ever. Rummaging in her bag she found Dolly, the one her mother had made for her, then leaned her heavy head against the unyielding wall and stuck her thumb in her mouth as a gesture of defiance. If Lizzie saw that she would jerk her hand away and rap her knuckles with the hardest thing she could find.

Shona dozed, then jerked upright when Lizzie thumped down the stairs, a bundle under one arm, and opened the front door. Aunt Twi and her oldest cousin, ten-year-old Alex, a great big boy who never smiled – at least never at her – stood on the doorstep.

'Well, are you all ready then?' Twi demanded sharply, tired out and made even more irritable than usual by the bus ride and long walk out to the house.

Lizzie sniffed and glared at Shona. 'Remember your manners,' she snapped.

'Hello, Auntie Twi,' Shona complied sullenly, wondering what they would do if she simply refused to move.

'Come on then. There's no point in hanging around.' Twi held out a rough hand, but still Shona made no move. 'Get a move on, Hen. Give Alex they bags.'

Alex grabbed the bags and, when his mother's back was turned, grabbed his small cousin, too, and hitched her roughly to her feet. 'Hurry up,' he hissed.

'Before you go, Mrs McArdle . . .' Lizzie offered a paper-wrapped parcel.

'What's this? I don't think we can carry anything else, Hen,' said Twi, thinking of the shopping she still had to do.

'It's two of Isobel's paintings,' Lizzie explained.

'What would I do with paintings?' Twi laughed scornfully. 'You keep them, Hen.'

'No, you don't understand. They might be worth something. You could use them to buy clothes for the wain. Or keep them for her when she's older. They'll be all she has of her mother.'

'Worth something? I thought she sold them all. If these are still here it must be because they weren't good enough to sell.' Twi was well aware that Isobel's financial situation had been desperate before she went to America. Her money had gone, her jewellery had been sold and so, too, as far as she had known, were the paintings.

'Isobel never knew I had these. They used to be in the study at Netherdrum House. Mr Geddes hung them there himself. They were his favourites. I took them when Alisdair got the house. Mr Geddes wouldn't have wanted him to have them. I've hidden them in my room ever since. For emergencies.'

'Maybe you should keep them, Hen. I know you didn't get paid towards the end.'

'No. That wouldn't be right. I'll be alright, but the wee lassie has nothing. They're for her.'

Lizzie thrust the bundle into Twi's hands and closed the door before she could change her mind.

240

Twi looked at the incongruous bundle for a moment, then grabbed Shona's hand and marched her smartly down the sand-blown road.

By the time they got back to the farm it was raining. Persistent misty drizzle soaked through every layer of clothing. Shona's little legs shook with fatigue from the long climb up the hill to the cottage but she was determined to keep up with her aunt and cousin.

Her concentration on each plodding footstep was so intense that she didn't hear the dogs until it was too late. Two black and white border collies raced out and threw themselves enthusiastically at her. Two pairs of muddy paws descended on her shoulders and Shona thumped down into the muddiest puddle in the whole of Strathannan. Delighted with such an easy victory the dogs bounded over her, licking her face and nuzzling her ears. She let them, sensing with her extraordinary perception that they wouldn't harm her.

Twi groaned and looked pointedly at her son.

'For goodness sake! What are you sitting there for?' demanded Alex. This was typical of a girl. He supposed he would have to drag her back to her feet. Dumping his parcels on the doorstep he ran back his face set in faithful imitation of his father's when there was trouble brewing. But really he wanted to laugh. Every time his small cousin tried to get up the dogs sent her sprawling back into the puddle. She looked so pathetic.

Shona saw him coming, knew what he must think and wanted to drown in the murky water; wished the dogs would eat her, that she and her shame could just disappear forever. But nothing was that easy. So, jutting her small jaw out she waited, expecting the worst. But to her amazement he didn't say anything at all horrible, just stood there looking at her with a faintly puzzled expression on his face. Then, offering a huge hand he yanked her to her feet and yelled at the dogs to get away.

'Well,' he said at last. 'You've made a good start. The

dogs like you and they're not daft when it comes to people. They always know a good 'un.' He smiled now, revealing impishly uneven teeth. 'Are you okay?'

She nodded, staring with huge, solemn grey eyes, not knowing what to make of this transformation. And then she smiled at him, her mud-splattered cheeks dimpling, the smoky grey eyes glowing with trust.

In that moment Alexander McArdle was captivated.

Leaving Alex to wash the worst of the mud from his cousin, Twi sought the privacy of her bedroom. Closing the door carefully she sat on the bed and unwrapped the parcel.

The pictures were typical of Isobel's early work, soft and muted with a quality of mystery about them. Three years ago she had heard that Isobel's earliest paintings were fetching three hundred pounds each. She couldn't understand why and she certainly wouldn't want these dismal things hanging on her walls.

Twi sighed, imagining the wonders she might work with that sort of money. More than a whole year's wages! All the things which would make life easier could be bought from the proceeds of these two eerie watercolours. She gazed at them for a moment longer then, very deliberately, rewrapped the parcel and tied the string in a complicated knot, as if it might protect them.

Across the bottom of her wardrobe there was a huge, deep drawer. She pulled it right out and shoved the parcel through into the space at the back, out of temptation's way. Better, she thought, to try and forget these pictures existed until Shona was old enough to take possession of them for herself.

'Katrina! Mary!' Twi hurried back to the kitchen followed by two tall, thin girls of nine and seven who stared at their young cousin in hostile silence. 'Say Hello to Shona,' their mother instructed.

'Hello,' sighed Mary and 'Hello' growled Katrina.

'I've got to get the dinner on the go, so you two take her to your room and get her settled in.'

The older girl, Katrina, ignored Shona and rushed to her mother's side, saying in a stage whisper, 'Why do *we* have to have her? There's no room for her here.'

'There's plenty of room.' Twi's flat tone made it clear that she was heartily sick of the whole subject.

'No there's not,' Mary added her weight to the argument. 'We'll be all squashed.'

'Too bad.' Twi rounded on her daughters furiously. 'What sort of welome is this for the poor wee lassie? Her Mammy's just died and she's all alone in the world. The least you two can do is be kind to her.'

Doubt clouded Katrina's face. 'Come on then,' she offered dully. 'I'll show you where to put your things.'

Shona dragged her bags to a small bedroom at the back of the house. It was neatly but sparsely furnished with an old double bed, a plain wooden chair and an old-fashioned wardrobe.

'Put your bag down and get your things away. Mammy gets right cross if you leave things lying about.' Mary, a plain, sullen-faced girl, eyed Shona's bags with interest and a greedy glint in her eye. 'What have you got there, anyway?'

Shona squatted on the bare floorboards and obligingly tipped the contents of the first bag all over the floor.

'That's not much,' Mary sniffed.

Shona emptied the second bag on top of the first.

'You've not even got as much as me,' seven-year-old Mary turned away in disgust.

'Come on, put your things away.' As the eldest, Katrina knew she would be the one who got the blame if the room got messy.

Shona's two jumpers, two skirts, three vests and half a dozen pairs of knickers were quicky disposed of. The dolls were tossed unceremoniously into the depths of the wardrobe.

'What have you got there?' Katrina prised the small fingers from the brown paper bag.

Shona clutched it closer to her. Mary was instantly alerted.

'Give it to me,' she ordered.

Shona shook her head stubbornly.

'Give it to me!' Mary repeated, pouncing on the bag and tearing it. Shona grabbed in vain at the falling pencils. Everyone knew that if you let your pencils fall they were ruined. All the leads broke and you could never sharpen them properly again.

The two older girls watched in open-mouthed delight as about twenty-five pencils, in colours they had never even imagined, clattered to the floor. Then they were on their knees scrambling for possession of them. 'Can I have my pencils back, please?' Shona asked.

The other two looked at her. 'What else have you got in there?' Katrina had realised that the bag still held something.

'My drawing book. Can I have my pencils back, please?'

Mary tugged violently at the edge of the book until it slipped from the younger child's grip.

'It's new,' pleaded Shona. 'My Mammy gave it to me.'

'It's new,' Katrina mocked, thumbing through the snowy pages with grubby hands.

'Please can I have them back,' Shona demanded loudly. These were her most treasured possessions. Mammy had told her there could be no more when these were finished and she had saved them carefully ever since last Christmas.

'Give the lassie her things,' Alex ordered from the doorway, his younger brother, Jamie, like a shadow at his heels.

'Who says?' Mary challenged.

'I do.' He stepped forward, threatening her.

'Get out of here, Alex,' Katrina roared, shoving him back into the hall.

'Don't shove me!' he yelled, retaliating with a hefty push of his own.

'Mammy! Mammy! Alex is hitting me,' Mary screamed with all the power of her young lungs.

But instead of Twi it was Robbie who arrived at the bedroom door. 'What's all this about,' he demanded.

'Nothing,' replied Alex, defensively.

'He hit me, Daddy,' accused Katrina. 'For nothing.'

'You shoved me first.'

'Did not.'

'Did so.'

'Stop it! *Now*!' Robbie's furious roar silenced them immediately.

'Now. Why were you fighting?'

'It was her.' Mary pointed at the astounded Shona.

'Her?' exploded Alex. 'It was n . . .'

'Enough!' Robbie grabbed his son's arm and propelled him through the door. 'You two laddies get back to your own room and leave the lassies alone in future,' he ordered. Turning back to Shona he smiled and asked, 'And what were you doing, Miss?'

Shona adored her gentle uncle Robbie but she had never seen him so angry before, and certainly not with her. All she could do was cross her legs and hope she wouldn't wet herself. She always needed to go when she was scared.

'I asked you a question, Hen,' Robbie prompted gently. 'It's polite to answer. Now, tell me what it was all about.'

Shona could only shake her head, her huge, grey eyes wide with fear.

Robbie sighed. 'My, you're a strange wee thing,' he said, ruffling her hair affectionately. Then he glared at his own two daughters who were nudging each other and giggling. 'You two shouldn't be arguing with her already. Give the lassie a chance to settle in.'

'She wouldn't let us see her pencils,' Mary said spitefully. 'She's got loads and loads of pencils and she wouldn't even let us see them. Look!' She pointed to the scattered crayons and sketchpad.

Robbie grinned. 'I see,' he said, pulling Shona gently towards him. 'They are very nice pencils, aren't they?'

245

Shona nodded. 'Can I have them back please, Uncle Robbie?'

'See! I told you! She'll not even let us look at her stuff but we have to share everything with her. It's not fair.' Mary pouted.

'You can all use the pencils,' Robbie decided. 'And the book. I'll divide it up and you can each have the same number of pages.' With that he began ripping pages from her precious book. 'There,' he said, handing them a sheaf of paper each. 'That's about equal. Now play with it nicely. No more arguing.' And he left them to it, certain he had dealt with it as fairly as possible.

As soon as he was out of the room the two older girls swooped on the crayons, dividing them into three unequal heaps.

'Here,' Katrina handed the smallest bundle to Shona.

Shona looked. A black, a dark green, a purple, a brown and the muddy yellow which was so ugly she had never used it. 'Thank you,' she said.

'Mammy! Mammy!' Mary rushed from the room, her voice shrill with glee. 'Shona's wet her knickers.'

In those first few days the wide eyes lost their brightness and the rosy, healthy cheeks paled. The dimple, which could only be seen when she smiled, never appeared.

Then, just as she was starting to get used to them all, had finally managed to find a way to sleep in the overcrowded bed, she was told to repack all her things because tomorrow she was going to stay with Uncle Hugh and Auntie May. And the day after that she was starting school.

'Take your clothes off, Hen. There's a braw, hot bath waiting for you. I'll wash your hair and you'll be braw and clean for your Auntie May,' Twi said cheerfully. Shona stood meekly and allowed her grimy clothes to be dragged over her head.

'Good lassie. Now, run away to the bathroom before you get cold.'

Shona scampered over the cold floor and clambered into the yellowing tub. The water was delicious. Hot and deep. She wallowed in the sheer luxury of it, offering no resistance when Twi sluiced her hair and soaped it into a high lather, letting some of the foam leak into her eyes, making them sting and burn. Shona never made a fuss or misbehaved if she could help it, remembering all too clearly what Mary had whispered to her on her very first night here. If she was a nuisance, if they didn't like her, if she ate too much, she would be sent where all the girls nobody wants are sent. Down a huge, dark hole in the ground to dig out coal with her bare hands. Mary had even showed her pictures of the men with black faces and lamps on their heads who made sure the little girls never escaped. Shona shuddered when she thought about it.

'Stand up and let me rinse your hair.' Twi tipped a basin of warm water over the lovely, dark curls and smiled as drops glistened on the thick, curling lashes and dripped off the dainty nose. And that skin! A real Celtic child. Twi deftly bundled the damp, squeaky-clean hair on top of Shona's head.

'Out you get and I'll dry you off.' She rubbed the damp skin briskly before Shona could feel the cold. 'Turn round so I can do your back, Hen.'

But the towel fell limply from her hands as she stared at the small, crescent-shaped mark, high on the child's shoulder. It was unmistakable. Twi trembled with revulsion and grabbed the edge of the bath for support.

Trying not to shiver Shona looked round timidly. Her small heart fell almost to the floor. Auntie Twi was looking at her with such a strange expression on her face, and the fear and horror which emanated from her were a physical reality to the hypersensitive child. Shona knew she had done something very bad. Very, very quietly she tiptoed back to the bedroom and struggled into her fresh clothes, ignoring

247

the water dripping down her back. Then she sat on the floor, right in the corner, cuddling Dolly as closely as she could screwing her eyes tight shut so she wouldn't cry. No-one liked people who cried. She had heard Uncle Robbie telling Mary that lots of times.

Shona had never been anywhere on her own before. Auntie Twi lifted her onto the bus, paid the conductor and asked him to set her down at Sauchar. Then she stepped back onto the pavement. Shona wanted to jump off the bus but knew that would only make Auntie Twi even more angry with her. Instead she slipped into a window seat and watched Auntie Twi for as long as possible, but Twi made her way back up the hill without even looking back to wave.

Shona's tummy felt funny, as if she was going to be sick. She couldn't do that, either, so she concentrated on what was going on around her. People got off the bus, others got on. The conductor was so busy with the funny ticket machine which hung round his neck that she was sure he would forget to tell her where to get off. As he hurried past her she opened her mouth to ask if she should get off yet, but by the time she had plucked up the courage to speak he was already at the back of the long vehicle.

Now they were in a town. Shona didn't recognise it. All the houses looked the same, new and light grey. More people got on and a huge, fat woman wedged herself into the seat next to her. Shona knew the conductor wouldn't tell her where to get off now. He wouldn't even be able to see her. And now she needed to 'go'.

'Here you are, Hen. This is your stop,' the conductor called. The enormous woman grunted and dragged herself off the seat to allow Shona to scramble down the aisle.

'Don't forget your bags.' The conductor laughed when she couldn't carry them all and finally lifted her down onto the pavement and deposited them at her feet. 'Stay here, lass. Someone's coming to fetch you,' he called as the bus pulled away.

Auntie Twi hadn't said anything about anyone coming to fetch her. What if she was supposed to go straight to Uncle Hugh's house? But she didn't know the way on her own. And she needed to 'go' worse than ever.

She stood restlessly, wondering what to do. Five long minutes passed and still there was no sign of anyone coming to collect her. She would just have to start looking for Uncle Hugh's house on her own. Clutching her bags untidily she stepped decisively to the edge of the pavement.

'Hello there, Shona.' A firm hand descended onto her shoulder just in time to stop her walking out into the traffic. A man with bright red hair and a kind, smiling face crouched down so that his face was on a level with hers. 'Come on then, lass,' he chuckled. 'Yer Auntie May has made a special tea for us tonight so we had better hurry home.' He took her bags effortlessly in one hand and held her arm with the other. 'Careful how you cross the road,' he warned as he steered her through the traffic.

Within minutes they arrived at a white, harled house, facing onto a narrow, setted street. Hugh opened the door and called, 'May! We're home.'

May, a cheerful, neat, brown-haired woman bustled from the kitchen, drying her hands on her apron. 'So you're here! Come along in Shona. Don't be shy.' She took a cold little hand and drew the hesitant child into the room before helping her to take her coat off. 'There, that's better. My goodness, what lovely hair you have,' May said, fingering the dark curls lightly. 'I wish I had hair as pretty as this.'

Shona almost smiled.

'Now, come away up the stairs and see the lassies. They're all excited about you coming here.' Hugh led her to a bright, sunny room which was filled with little girls. All smiling.

'This is Karen and Pamela's bed,' he nodded towards a bunk bed where his two oldest daughters beamed down on their cousin. And this,' he went on, pointing to a three-quarter-sized bed, 'is where you and Betty will sleep.'

Suddenly she was surrounded by the three laughing girls who helped her to unpack her scanty possessions.

'These are braw dolls,' said Pamela, only seven years old and the shyest of the three.

Shona paled and, remembering what had happened to her paper and pencils, shoved them all into the surprised child's arms.

'Oh no, Hen.' Hugh rescued the dolls and handed them back to her. 'These are yours. You don't have to give them away.' Puzzled by the look of blank amazement which crossed her face he added. 'You can let the girls play with them, but they'll always be yours.'

'You can play with our things, too,' offered Betty, taking her cousin's hand and leading her to a cupboard full of toys.

'Thank you,' Shona said, and now there was a smile on her pretty mouth.

'And tomorrow,' said Hugh, 'you and Betty are starting the school.'

School was wonderful. Shona followed every word the teacher said, letting her vivid imagination transport her to the strange, exciting worlds of the stories which were read every afternoon. With the quiet, composed determination she had inherited from her father, she made up her mind to learn to read those stories for herself. By the end of the first week she already recognised half the letters in the alphabet.

On Friday there was another shock for her.

'Are you remembering that you're going to your Auntie Maggie and Uncle William's tonight?' May asked. 'I'll collect you from the school and take you there.'

Shona nodded, her face suddenly wearing the blank, traumatised stare that May had seen when Hugh first brought the child home.

'Don't worry, Hen,' she reassured her. 'I know you've

never met any of them before but you've five cousins there so you'll have plenty of company. And your Auntie Maggie's kind.' But she certainly couldn't say the same about William.

It was a short bus ride to Kilweem and, because May went with her, Shona was able to enjoy it.

'This is Kilweem, Hen,' said May after only fifteen minutes. 'Watch where we get off. Next week you'll have to come on your own.'

It was simple. The bus clattered down a wide road, past a tall cross with steps leading up to it and then stopped by an old grey building with a clock on top. This, May told her, was the tollbooth. Shona would easily remember that.

Hand in hand they walked down a steep, setted street. At the bottom Shona could see the top of a boat and suddenly they were on the quayside itself. Dropping May's hand she ran to the very edge of the cobbles to peer down into the lapping water.

'Careful, Shona. Never go so near the edge. It's dangerous. You might slip and we don't want you falling in.' May pulled her back gently. 'This is where your Aunt Maggie and Uncle William live. Your Mammy lived here too when she was a wee girl, and your Uncle Hugh and Auntie Twi.'

Shona thought the small harbour was wonderful. She would like staying here, so long as her Uncle William's house wasn't the dirty looking one with the broken window.

But May led her straight to it and knocked sharply on the peeling door. It was opened by a thin, unkempt woman with a cigarette hanging from her mouth. Shona thought she looked very old.

'So, you're here then?' said Maggie, hardly bothering to glance at her unfortunate niece. 'I suppose you'd better come in.' Shona followed May inside. Even at her tender age she knew that this house was very untidy indeed. Every seat and flat surface was home for discarded clothing, old papers, abandoned toys or unwashed plates. The mantelpiece was littered with letters, cigarette packets, empty beer bottles and reels of thread. A cigarette burned unheeded in an ashtray and the whole place had a stale, musty smell.

The two women smiled half-heartedly at one another while May tried to keep her eyes from straying too obviously over the scene of domestic neglect which faced her.

'Sorry about the mess. The kids never think about clearing anything away.' Maggie blamed her own slovenliness on her children.

The tension was relieved by the sound of many feet clattering on the stairs, announcing the arrival of Shona's remaining five cousins, children she had never before met.

'It's her,' yelled the first one, a tall, pasty-faced girl. Two more very untidy girls and two grubby boys crowded into the room after her.

'Are you gonna stay with us?' demanded a runny-nosed girl who was even smaller than Shona.

Shona nodded.

'She'll be here every weekend. How often do I have to tell you?' Magie screeched. 'And you had better be nice to her.'

'We will,' laughed the biggest girl, grabbing Shona's hand. 'Come on, I'll show you where you're sleeping and then we'll away out to play.'

Shona was hauled up some dark, bare stairs to a room that held one double bed, a single bed and a small canvas camp bed in the narrow gap between them.

'Yours is the wee bed,' the smallest girl said unnecesarily.

'Dump your things and let's get out.' The oldest girl flung Shona's bags in the general direction of the bed and pushed her back down the stairs.

They sat on the cold doorstep, playing jacks and squabbling among themselves. After an hour Shona knew the oldest girl was Dot, and was eight years old. The plump, funny one who grinned at her all the time but never spoke was called Janice. Dot whispered that Janice 'wasn't right' and they all had to take turns looking after her. The youngest one, who stuck her tongue out every time Shona looked at her, was called Mhari. Although she was smaller than Shona she was already six years old. Their brothers, ten-year-old Alan and nine-year-old Malcolm sat with the girls while they pumped Shona with questions. How old was she? What school did she go to? What toys did she have? What had happened to her Mammy and Daddy?

It was dark and cold before they went in. Shona quietly copied the others who distributed themselves over the messy floor while Maggie impatiently thrust a jammy piece of bread into each outstretched hand. Shona looked doubtfully at her own grubby fingers but when all her cousins accepted their suppers without first bothering to wash their hands, she did the same.

Before she had time to eat it, the front door crashed open. Silence fell abruptly and the tension was palpable. Stuffing the remains of their sandwiches into their mouths the children rose and made for the stairs.

'Come on,' Dot hissed urgently in Shona's ear. 'That's our Dad. We'd better away to our beds.'

'Where's my dinner?' The loud grating voice fixed Shona to the spot for a second too long. A huge hand clamped itself onto her upper arm and she was dragged painfully into the centre of the room.

'So, you're here, are you?' The coarse voice slurred.

She hung her head, terrified of the monster she had glimpsed coming through the door.

The hand tightened on her arm. 'What's up with you?' he growled.

Shona plucked up all her courage and looked up into the face of the biggest, ugliest man she had ever seen. A shiver of fear ran through her. His red hair reminded her of Uncle Hugh but the face underneath was dangerously red and angry.

'Let her be, Willy. She's a quiet wee thing,' Maggie whispered.

'So, you're a quiet wee thing, are you?' he snarled. 'Well, if you know what's good for you you'll keep it that way.

And stay away from me.' He dropped his hand from her arm and gave her a shove which made her stumble backwards.

She sat where she landed, too frightened to move.

'Did you not hear me?' he roared in a voice so loud it made her head ring. 'I told you to get out of my sight.'

Shona remained firmly anchored to the floor.

She heard the howl of fury, saw his face contort but still couldn't make her legs work.

'I'll teach you to do as you're told, you wee bitch,' he bawled, dragging her towards him again.

Shona found herself lifted into the air and tucked under his arm. Her whole body jolted as he threw himself into a chair and dumped her, face down, across his thighs. Stunned, terrified, she hardly noticed when he tore her knickers down to her ankles. The spade-like hand descended with a resounding thwack on the delicate flesh of her backside, leaving raised, white weals.

Pain shocked her into life. She screamed and thrashed wildly but ineffectively. He held her easily with the other hand. Three times he hit her, three times she flinched, twice she screamed. The third time she bit her lips and stayed silent, tensed and waiting for the fourth blow. It never came. Instead, incredibly, he stroked the bruised flesh gently, running calloused fingers over the reddened skin. Instinctively she hated it, even more than the beating, and screwed her eyes together, clenched her muscles and flinched as the huge, harsh finger strayed between her thighs and into the place she hadn't known existed. Then he pushed her away.

'Do what you're told in future or you'll be getting plenty of that,' he said, bringing terrible, yellow eyes close to hers. 'And don't tell anyone about this or I'll thrash you so hard you won't sit down for a month.'

Shona stepped back, wide eyes fixed on her brutal uncle with wounded, confused intensity and stoically refused to cry. Slowly she bent and pulled her knickers back over her bruised flesh.

'Away to bed, Hen,' muttered Maggie, giving her a hard shove in the right direction.

William sank back into his chair and spat into the fire. 'Where's my tea?' he repeated.

Maggie hurried from the kitchen with a steaming plate.

'What the hell is this muck?'

'Tripe,' she whispered, already backing away. 'And onions. An' there's tatties there, too.'

'I can't eat this,' he roared, smashing the plate onto the mucky hearth. 'Get me something decent. A pie or something.'

'I've no money.'

'No money?' He closed on her. 'I gave you money last week.'

'Ten days ago. And only what was left after you'd drunk the most of your wages,' she defended herself, still backing away.

Even upstairs the silent children heard the animal-like sound from deep in his throat and the harder, sharper noise of an open-handed slap and two more, duller thuds. Then silence.

Shona stood just inside the bedroom door and shivered. Her cousins cowered in their beds. Making as little noise as possible she crept into the truckle bed and pulled the thin covers over her head.

NINETEEN

By the time she was fifteen Shona was extraordinarily beautiful. Her hair fell in waves of inky silk framing flawless skin and intense, smoky eyes. Her figure had ripened and softened and the angular child-ishness had been replaced by the promise of incipient womanhood in budding breasts and shapely hips. In line with most of her contemporaries she wore her skirts short, used huge amounts of black eyeliner and worshipped the Beatles. At Sauchar, she and Betty spent many dreamy hours reading teenage magazines and listening to records on the new automatic player Hugh had bought for them.

Her character, too, had matured. The frightened child had long ago ceased to exist. In her place was an independent, ambitious young woman in whom the sensitivity inherited from her mother was tempered by inner strength and sharp, analytical intelligence. The driving force of her life was the absolute determination to pull herself above her present beggarly status.

Denied the security of a real home, Shona had long ago learned to rely on her own resources and depend on no-one. Countless weekends in the cheerless Kilweem household had hardened her. Like her five cousins she bore William's frequent punishments with silent, simmering resentment. Only the knowledge, constantly reiterated by William and Maggie, that she should be grateful for their mean hospital-ity, and the realisation that there was nowhere else for her to spend her weekends, kept her there. She counted the months until she could escape.

Aware of her maturing figure, like any other fifteen-year-old girl, Shona enjoyed the attentions of the local boys. But, when she felt William's eyes boring into her and travelling appraisingly over her body, she burned with shame.

Too many times recently she had had to flinch away when he tried to touch her, always making it seem like an accident when his hands brushed against her breasts. Once he had come up behind her and ground his pelvis into her buttocks. The hard feel of him, his animal-like smell, had sickened her.

Not knowing how to deal with him, Shona finally confided in May. Her normally understanding aunt flushed crimson and retorted that Shona had better read fewer books and get into the fresh air more often. Shona never spoke about William's unwelcome attentions to anyone else.

The Kilweem house was less crowded these days. Her cousins, Alan and Malcolm, had been united in their hatred of their father and had fled as soon as they had left school. Though she had liked the boys and missed them both, their departure had one distinct advantage. Shona found herself sharing their room with Janice. It suited her perfectly. She was genuinely fond of the retarded seventeen-year-old and spent many hours amusing her, but the real benefits of this new arrangement came in the evenings when Janice wanted nothing more than to spend her free time in front of the newly acquired television set. The bedroom was left free as a treasured private retreat for Shona, the only place where she could be on her own.

Then came the night when she was woken by a strange noise.

She sighed. This was the one drawback to sharing with Janice. The girl was such a noisy sleeper, tossing and turning all night long. Tonight she seemed even more restless than usual. The whole bed was shaking with the violence of her movements and she was making queer little grunting sounds.

Shona turned slightly and peered at the other bed, but her eyes were unused to the dark and she could see very little.

Gradually, as her eyes grew accustomed to the poor light,

Shona made out a vague lump on the other bed. She stared, wondering how Janice could seem so huge, then, with a feeling of stampeding nightmare, realised there was someone else on the bed with her. That someone else was William.

For a moment Shona thought he was beating Janice but, as she watched in mixed fear and revulsion, she saw that Janice was actually clinging to him, that her plump arms were entwined round his neck, pulling him to her. From where she lay Shona could hear her uncle's fast, heavy breathing.

Savagely he shoved Janice away and knelt above her, laughing as she begged him with small, whimpering sounds to come back to her. The muted light from the window silhoutted the swollen penis which jutted out in front of him before he thrust himself viciously back into his daughter.

Her innocence brutally destroyed, Shona lay rigid with shock as the unnatural pair heaved their way to satisfaction. That achieved, William hauled himself upright and stood at the end of the bed, hoisting his pyjamas up, hiding his softened member from his niece's hypnotised gaze.

He had seemed to be completely unaware of her, but now he turned and stared directly at her, as if challenging her. She jerked her eyes closed and held her breath until she heard his ponderous footsteps on the stairs.

Janice was already soundly asleep.

William's bloodshot eyes followed his niece as she helped herself to tea and cornflakes. Shona watched Janice, hardly able to believe that she could look so ordinary, so unconcerned. Untidy, dark head bowed she was completely absorbed in a children's comic.

Shona risked a look at William. The shock when she met his eyes, his ghastly, insinuating smile, the conspiratorial wink, made her feel sick. Brushing her untouched breakfast aside she dashed out of the house and spent the rest of the blustery October day in the shelter of the dunes, trying to work out what she should do. The whole thing terrified her but, recalling May's scandalised reaction when she tried to tell her aunt about William's attacks on her own body, Shona felt there was no-one she could confide in.

Then, shortly before Christmas, Janice disappeared. She simply wasn't there one Friday night. When Shona asked Maggie where she was her aunt flushed, then paled, and eventually stammered out that Janice had gone into a home.

'A home?' Shona echoed. 'But why?'

'It's none of your business. The lassie's gone away and that's all anyone needs to know about it,' was the savage retort.

Later Dot whispered, 'You'd best say no more about our Janice.'

Shona rounded on her cousin. 'But why was she sent away, Dot? And where is she? Can we go and visit her? Why didn't anyone tell me? I didn't even have a chance to say goodbye.'

Dot threw an apprehensive glance at the kitchen door. 'If I tell you, you've to promise not to tell anyone else,' she whispered.

'I promise.'

'You'd better not,' Mhari, the youngest daughter and the only one of the five from Kilweem that Shona didn't get on with, spoke up. 'She's not one of the family. Daddy'll kill you if he finds out you've told her.'

Dot sent her a withering look. At eighteen and soon to be married she was considerably braver than her younger sister.

'Just in case anyone asks you about our Janice, I'll tell you. But it's a secret, mind.'

'I won't say anything.'

'Our Janice has gone to Dundee. To a home for unmarried mothers.'

Shona blanched. 'Oh . . .'

'Daddy insisted she went. He didn't want her staying here where everyone could see she was expecting.' Dot sighed. 'Poor Janice. She doesn't even know who did it. Some rotten lad took advantage of her. What sort of person would do that? They all know she's not right.'

'Poor Janice,' echoed Shona. 'What will happen? Will she come home afterwards?' She already knew the answer. Even in 1968 the Calvinistic attitudes of the staunchly Presbyterian community would see Janice's condition as the worst possible disgrace.

'Daddy says no. He called her a slut. But it wasn't her fault.' Dot's mouth trembled with emotion. 'Even Mammy doesn't want her back. It's not fair. I tell you, Shona, I'll be glad to be married and away out of it.' Dot's pale eyes glittered with tears, a rarity in this household where the rough was accepted as easily as the smooth.

Close to tears herself, feeling more than a little sick, Shona could only nod and turn away.

Gradually her sickness and pity for Janice congealed into cold, hard anger. And from that anger came self-disgust. Disgust at the sorry creature who had allowed herself to be so intimidated by someone as depraved as William obviously was. It was too late now to help Janice who was probably better off in the home, but Shona was determined that William wouldn't have her for his next victim.

She was in the kitchen, washing dishes, when the door behind her opened. Even without turning round she knew it was William. Steeling herself for the encounter she carried on with her task until his thick, calloused hands crept round from behind and onto one breast. Very slowly she turned to face him, hate blazing from her. The expression in her eyes, ice cold like the winter sea, made him falter and the hand loosened for a second.

'If you,' she said, her voice clear, level and infinitely threatening, 'ever touch me again I will make sure you regret it.'

The slack face, red and beaded with sweat, stared back, gaping in amazement at the transformed creature in front of him. But then his mouth lifted in a confident, stupid leer.

'Och aye?' he sneered. 'And what could a poor wee thing like you do to a man like me?'

The hand made its way back to her breast. She stopped it angrily.

'If I was to tell the police where you used to smack me when I was little, where you used to put your fingers. If I was to tell them how you like to touch me. If I told them what I saw you doing to Janice . . . you would end up in prison.' Her eyes never left his face.

'Nobody would believe you,' he hissed, but she could see doubt in his bloodshot eyes.

'I think they would,' she insisted softly. 'And I'm sure I could persuade Janice to tell them what her daddy used to do to her. She hasn't got the guile to lie.'

'Never.'

'Well, touch me again and we'll find out, won't we?' She turned her back on him leaving him confused, frustrated and, above all, angry.

'I'll get even with you, you wee bitch,' he hissed before slamming out of the house.

A week after her confrontation with William she caught the bus up to the farm for Christmas with Twi and Robbie. As usual Jamie, their youngest son, was at the bus stop to meet her. At sixteen he towered over her.

'Mam says to hurry up. She's baking and you're to give a hand.' Jamie's voice was suddenly deep and gruff. He grimaced self-consciously, then grinned as they started up the hill. 'Alex is coming home tonight,' he called over his shoulder, striding ahead with her bags.

Shona had to run to match her lanky cousin's stride. By the time she reached the cottage she was out of breath and flushed a becoming pink.

The kitchen was fragrant with baking. Twi greeted her cheerfully enough and even Mary and Katrina seemed infected with the general spirit of goodwill. At nineteen and seventeen both girls had regular boyfriends and better things to concern themselves with than a continuing feud with their reticent cousin.

'Pour yourself a cup of tea and give us a hand with these sausage rolls,' Twi instructed.

Shona set to with a will, glad to be able to make herself useful.

'There are already three dozen of the things here, Mam. Surely that's enough.' Katrina surveyed the littered kitchen tiredly.

'Another dozen'll not go wrong. You never know who might arrive at this time of the year.' Twi rolled out the last batch of pastry, pushed it over to Mary and collapsed wearily into a chair.

'Good Lord! I've never seen so much food in all my life.' The sound of Alex's voice brought her instantly to her feet again, her face shining with joy.

Of Twi and Robbie's four children, Alex was acknowledged as the clever one and was at Glasgow University, studying to be a vet. Money was short so he spent weekends and most of his holidays working and seldom came home. Shona missed him. Of all her cousins he was the only one she could really talk to. His cheerful, easy-going company had made holidays at the farm something to look forward to. In the general excitement she couldn't even see him, didn't get her first glimpse of him until he had hugged and kissed everyone else. He stood just inside the door, beaming with delight at the uproarious welcome.

It was as if she was seeing him for the very first time. He had changed, broadened, hardened. His chin was dark with stubble and his hair was longer, more unruly, than it had been a year ago, falling carelessly to his forehead, almost touching his shoulders. He was talking animatedly to Jamie and she caught the glint of white teeth, saw the slightly crooked one which gave his smile the impish quality she remembered from childhood. But Alexander McArdle was no longer a child. At twenty he was a man.

Suddenly aware of her he looked straight at her, the clear blue eyes seeming to draw hers like magnets. But something had changed. Gone were the easy relationships of a year ago and she felt stiff and awkward. He, too, seemed affected. His bright smile faded and he stared at her as if something about her shocked him. It was a difficult moment, saved by Jamie who laughed, 'Are you two not talking then?'

Then Alex was in front of her, but instead of grabbing her, hugging her, kissing her, as he had his sisters, he took her hands and smiled down into her eyes. 'Hello, Shona,' he whispered.

Shona controlled the impulse to kiss him, as she would have done in the past, and merely smiled back, swallowing her disappointment. How she wished he had treated her like the others, as if she really was part of his family. Instead he had made her feel even more different and apart.

'Are you not going to introduce me?' a silvery voice asked.

'Aye! Sorry . . . this is Shona Dryburgh, my . . . my . . . my cousin,' he faltered unusually. 'Shona, this is Louisa. My fiancée. She's spending Christmas and New Year with us.'

'Fiancée . . .?' No-one had bothered to tell her he was engaged. Somehow she managed to smile at the bubbly, attractive blonde in the incredibly short, geometrically patterned, black and white dress who had slipped a proprietorial hand through Alex's arm.

Christmas Day, with the ritual of opening presents and the cooking of a huge meal, passed in a blur of frenzied activity.

At night there was whisky, beer and sherry and they all played silly games until they were simply too tired for more. Shona noticed that Louisa never left Alex's side unless nature demanded it.

'I'm for bed,' Jamie yawned, stumbled to his feet and set a trend.

At the door, waving a sprig of mistletoe, Alex waited, grinning mischievously. He caught his mother and sisters and pecked them lightly on their cheeks before demanding similar payment from Shona.

'One kiss and you can pass,' he announced lightly, but his grip on her hand was like iron and his eyes were dark with emotion.

Frightened, excited by the sudden, dangerous tension between them, Shona snapped: 'Stop messing about, Alex. If you want to kiss someone, kiss Louisa.' She managed to laugh but it sounded hard and mean.

But Louisa had been captured by Katrina's boyfriend under a similar sprig of mistletoe and, for the first time that day, wasn't paying the slightest attention to Alex.

'Just one,' Alex insisted, holding her firmly round the waist and drawing her to him.

Her senses seemed centred on his eyes, his hands. All thoughts of resistance melted and she turned her face up to his. His lips were warm, soft and demanding. They lingered together for seconds longer than they should have done. It was she who finally moved away, still feeling the firm pressure of his lips on hers. He released her reluctantly.

'Goodnight, Alex,' she whispered, hearing the tremor in her own voice.

She lay awake for hours. When Louisa crept into the room, much later, Shona pretended she was sleeping.

The real highspot of the festive season was Hogmanay. The McArdles brought in the New Year with traditional Scottish enthusiasm. Just before midnight Alex, the only truly dark-haired male there, was sent to shiver on the doorstep, a piece of coal in one hand, a bottle of whisky in the other, ready to play his allotted role as first-footer. Precisely on the hour he knocked at the door and was let in, supposedly bringing good luck for the new year with him. Glasses were charged and 1969 was toasted, allowing the real celebration to get under way.

Minutes later the McArdles were joined by their only

close neighbours, also bearing bottles of whisky. The glasses were refilled. Already several people were flushed and garrulous.

By one o'clock they were all making their noisy way towards the cluster of houses at the bottom of the hill, bottles in hand. Katrina's boyfriend was already so drunk that he staggered and rolled his way down the steep lane, singing loudly.

Inside the next house a party was in full swing. The McArdles were welcomed enthusiastically. 1969 was toasted for perhaps the sixth time in an hour.

Now there was dancing, to Scottish country music. Shona found herself doing some sort of waltz with Jamie and then with Robbie who steered her round the room, treading on her feet and giggling helplessly at his own ineptitude.

By three o'clock they had reassembled in yet another house, but now the music was slow, the dancing a perpetual shuffle, and half the celebrants were asleep where they sat. Shona suddenly realised that her head had drooped towards her chest. She straightened with a jerk and whispered to Twi that she was going home.

'Wait. I'll walk with you.' She heard footsteps behind her as Alex ran to catch up.

'It's alright. It's not that far.' She kept on walking, wondering why she had to sound so sharp with him when she had spent the whole evening wishing he would notice her.

'I'm going home anyway, so unless you really can't stand my company I might as well walk with you,' he teased.

'Where's Louisa?'

'Still having the time of her life. This is her first Scottish new year. She can't believe it. She'll come back with Mum and Dad, later.'

The cottage was cold and dark, the living room strewn with empty glasses and half-eaten food, and heavy with the smells of stale beer and cigarettes. The fire was no more than a faint orange glow.

'Might as well keep the fire alive.' Alex threw more coal onto the embers. 'Come and warm up a bit before you go to bed. Tell me what you've been doing. It's ages since we've really talked.'

He gave her no chance to get away but led her to the fire which was already crackling hopefully. They sat on the rug, holding their hands out to the heat, the room behind them dark, the whole house silent and alive with barely contained anticipation.

She felt his arm slide round her shoulders and tried to move away.

'I think I'd better go to bed.' But there was little conviction in her voice.

'No. Not yet.' It was an order. His arm stayed solidly where it was.

Shona had to suppress the strong urge to move closer, to snuggle into the temptingly warm and broad chest. His other hand was stroking her hair, slipping to her neck, pulling her closer, so close she could feel him breathing.

Again she did nothing to resist him, understanding that this was something she had always wanted. For long minutes they stayed joined while his tongue explored her mouth, tempting her, inviting her.

At last she pulled away. 'We shouldn't be doing this, Alex.'

'Why not?' he asked, pulling her back to him, smothering her protests with his mouth, then burying his face in her neck, murmuring her name.

'What about Louisa?' she asked softly.

But he was kissing her again, more roughly, more urgently, his hands tentatively at her breasts, gently exploring. And she was responding, as if she no longer had control of her actions. Feelings she had never suspected gripped her and she surrendered to them willingly, aware only of his tongue, his hands, the hardness of his strong, young body.

The door behind them clicked open, the light flashed on. They sprang apart like guilty infants. Shona raised her hot face and brilliant eyes to look into a ring of shocked and disapproving faces. The magic vanished leaving her feeling empty, cheap and ashamed.

'So that's why you were in such a hurry to come home,' Louisa accused, bitterly.

'Shona! How could you? Get up this minute.' Twi's outraged voice was shrill and brittle.

Shona scrambled to her feet, tugging at her dishevelled blouse.

'I'm sorry, Shona,' Alex said, looking more angry than embarrassed.

'You should be ashamed, Alex. Taking advantage of the lassie when she's had a drink or two too many.' Robbie sounded less than sober and slightly amused.

'I've only had the one drink, Uncle Robbie,' Shona insisted.

'How could you, Alex? With your own cousin. And Louisa in the house. It's obvious you've had far too much to drink or this would never have happened.' Twi chastised her son and absolved him in one long breath before turning back to Shona.

'As for you. What do you think you were doing? Is this how you say thanks for all we've done for you? Well, I'm telling you, I'll not have that sort of behaviour in this house. Is that clear?'

'We were only kissing, Aunt Twi,' Shona answered hotly.

'Kissing!' Louisa screeched. 'So that's why your blouse is hanging off.'

'You know Alex is engaged,' Twi yelled.

Shona's reply was drowned under a barrage of abuse as Mary, Katrina and Louisa all shouted at her.

'Not any more I'm not,' Alex's deep, controlled voice silenced them all.

'What?' Louisa whispered, her face draining of all colour.

'I'm sorry.' He looked genuinely distressed. 'I was going to leave it till after the holidays. I didn't want to ruin

Christmas for you, but . . .' His voice was drowned out by her loud, abandoned sobs.

'You've ruined everything, Alexander McArdle. Everything. I hate you,' she wailed.

'I hope you're proud of yourself, Shona,' said Twi bitterly. 'Imagine . . . in front of the fire in my own living room. You're as bad as your mother was.'

'My mother! What do you mean?' Shona stormed. 'Don't you dare say bad things about her. And Alex and I . . . we didn't do anything.'

'Bloody hell . . .' Robbie sighed his exasperation. 'That's enough! All of you! Let's not say things we might regret in the morning. Away to your beds. It'll all look different in the morning.'

Katrina put her arm round Louisa's shoulders. 'Dad's right. Leave it until tomorrow.'

'*No!*' Louisa pulled away and walked over to face Alex. 'You can't leave me now, Alex,' she pleaded, tears streaming down her face.

'I'm sorry,' he repeated. 'I didn't mean it to happen like this.'

'But I'm going to have a baby.'

The room seemed to freeze. Shona felt the blood drain from her face and a lump of despair settled like ice in her stomach.

'My God . . .' Robbie gasped and stared from Louisa to his son, who sank into a chair and dropped his face into his hands. 'You stupid pair of . . .'

'Bed. Now. Everyone.' Twi recovered quickly. 'We'll sort this out in the morning, when we're all sober and able to think straight.' She turned to Louisa. 'Don't worry, Hen. We'll make sure he stands by you.'

Darting one triumphant look at Shona, Louisa allowed herself to be led off to bed. Alex, white-faced and shocked, leapt to his feet and shoved his way roughly past his parents. They all heard his door slam. The others filed out in silence.

Unable to face the bedroom, where she suspected Louisa

268

would be sobbing her heart out to a sympathetic Mary and Katrina, Shona curled up on the uncomfortable sofa and tried to sleep.

Perhaps because of the emotions awakened by Alex she dreamed she was in bed, being fondled by strong hands. She moved sensuously, imagining Alex, wanting Alex. So vivid were the sensations that she opened her eyes, fully expecting to find him there with her. Instead, towering over her, breathing noxious fumes into her face, was William McLean. She felt the cruel weight of him as he pinned her to the bed, his knee immobilising her legs. She screamed but no sound came. All her struggling failed to dislodge him. He had exposed himself, was pushing at her, forcing . . . forcing . . .

She screamed and shot bolt upright, and found herself still on the sofa. The dying embers of the fire threw weird, red and orange flickering patterns on the walls and ceiling.

It had been a dream. But so vivid, so terrible. A warning perhaps. Her whole body trembled with the violence of the shivering fit which attacked her.

When everyone finally got up the next morning the atmosphere did nothing to restore her. Louisa continued to sob pitifully while Twi's attitude, if anything, was even harder than the night before.

'Thanks to you we've had no sleep,' she accused Shona and then went on to make it perfectly plain that she blamed her for the whole incident. Then she added that she no longer trusted Shona to be in the same house as Alex, who had temporarily been dispatched on some spurious errand. To Shona's intense mortification, Twi insisted on taking her back to Hugh and May's where she angrily explained the exaggerated details to her bemused brother and sister-in-law.

'Well, you've certainly stirred things up,' Hugh said, but not without a twinkle in his eye.

'Uncle Hugh, it wasn't as bad as Auntie Twi's making out. To hear the way they're carrying on you'd think we'd been caught . . . you know . . .' she ended lamely.

'Oh aye, I know,' Hugh laughed. 'And it sounds to me as if everyone overreacted. Try not to worry, Hen. There's never been a Hogmanay yet without an upset of some sort or another. It'll all blow over. By now Alex has likely apologised to Louisa and been forgiven. After all,' he added, a warning note to his voice. 'There's a bairn on the way.'

Shona's face was the colour of putty, and just as expressionless, as she realised there could be no future for her and Alex now.

TWENTY

Shona was quite unable to concentrate. The classroom was too hot, too stuffy and the teacher's voice droned on and on, seeming to echo endlessly inside her aching head. The print on her textbook blurred and swam out of focus. She sighed and rubbed her gritty eyes. Higher exams were looming and she couldn't afford to miss any of the work if she was to achieve the grades needed to take up her provisional place at university in Edinburgh, and a life of her own.

Shona had been increasingly unsettled of late. Especially at the farm where Twi's attitude made her feel like an interloper. Her aunt invented one flimsy excuse after another to keep her niece away from the cottage, even though Alex was now safely married to Louisa and the father of a toddling daughter.

The situation was exacerbated because Twi felt that Shona should be out to work and paying her own way.

The same problem presented itself at Kilweem where her only cousin still at home was the spiteful Mhari. Like all the others she was working, and loudly and repeatedly resented having to donate a large portion of her wages to the household budget while Shona still contributed nothing. Her increasingly hostile manner was encouraged by William and Maggie. But at least William no longer molested Shona. In fact he seemed at pains to avoid her. But she still sensed the menace from him, as if he was only barely containing himself.

At Sauchar May and Hugh actively encouraged her to stay at school. Nothing was ever said in that generous

271

household to give the impression that she was resented. But, because Pamela, Karen and Betty all had jobs, even here Shona couldn't quite repress a feeling of guilt as she watched them all go out, a full hour before she needed to leave for school.

However, education was her route to an independent life and she stubbornly refused to be deflected from her ambition. She would get her university place and then she would be on her way up in the world.

The bell rang, signalling the end of lessons. Shona escaped gratefully into the fresh air, hoping the sea breeze would clear her aching head.

By the time she got home it was still splitting. May took one look at her chalky face and packed her off to bed.

In the morning she felt a little better but still had the crushing sense of impending disaster and acute depression which had dogged her for the past fortnight. Instead of passing it was actually intensifying, as if building towards some dire climax. Shona tried everything she could think of but no matter what she did or where she went she couldn't shake the oppressive feeling.

All through her exams it persisted. But Shona wasn't going to throw away her future without a fight. Swallowing aspirins like sweets to deaden the persistent headaches she applied herself with grim ferocity. When she finally laid her pen down, satisfied that she had done her best, she fully expected to start feeling better. Exam nerves was the only logical explanation for her highly nervous condition. Now they were over she would surely recover. She was even a little ashamed of having allowed herself to get into such a state.

But that night she was so tense she couldn't sleep. When she did finally drift off she jerked awake again within minutes, her heart pounding in unexplained terror. Now she had to accept that this was far more than a simple case of the jitters. Something, she knew, without understanding why she knew, was going to happen.

All next day she was on edge, her mouth dry with dread. Whatever it was, was going to happen soon. By evening the feeling was so intense that she was reluctant to go to bed, fully believing that what she was experiencing was the intimation of her own death. Instead of settling down to sleep she read, terrified of what might happen if she allowed herself to drift off. Around her her cousins slept peacefully. Their rhythmic breathing seemed to envelop her. She fought the hypnotic effect but, inevitably, her eyes closed, her head nodded and her book slipped to the floor.

At three o'clock her sleep was as peaceful as any child's. Only very gradually did she become restless. Her eyelids fluttered and her head moved on the pillow. Minutes later she groaned softly, a fine film of sweat beaded her face and her hands clutched spasmodically at the covers. Then she was crying out, thrashing and twisting as if trying to escape whatever was invading her dreams. Finally she screamed.

When she opened her eyes the first thing she saw was Betty's frightened face and she knew she'd screamed aloud. She stared back at her cousin, her face like chalk, her body shaking, her mind consumed by unidentified horror, her body burning with remembered heat.

'What's wrong?' May ran into the room.

'It's Shona, Mum. I think she had a bad dream.' By now everyone was awake.

'Is that all?' Karen asked, still more than half asleep. 'Make yourself a drink and you'll feel better.' Satisfied that no major calamity had befallen her cousin she went straight back to sleep.

'You two go back to sleep and all,' May ordered. 'Shona and I'll have a cup of tea.'

May threw a housecoat round the trembling girl's shoulders and led the way to the kitchen where she busied herself at the stove, not yet probing the cause of her niece's distress.

Shona sipped her tea, hardly tasting it. 'Go back to bed, Auntie May. I'm alright. It was just a bad dream.' She shivered, but still unaccountably hot, slipped the housecoat from her shoulders.

'Are you too hot?' May asked, wondering if she was running a temperature.

'A bit,' Shona admitted. 'But I'm not ill or anything. It was just the dream . . .' She shivered again. The details were lost but the sense of impending disaster was stronger than ever.

May looked more closely at Shona and placed a cool hand on her forehead. It was icy cold. The girl was grey with shock and shouldn't be left alone yet. 'I'll sit with you for a wee while. When your Uncle Hugh's at sea I never really sleep. I know it's silly after all these years but I can't get used to sleeping in that big bed all on my own.'

Shona shivered convulsively and dropped the cup. May did a hasty mopping up job and stationed herself purposefully in front of her niece. 'Can you not tell me what's bothering you, Hen? You've not been yourself for weeks.'

Shona turned her head away but not before May had seen that, most unusually, the great grey eyes were flooded with tears.

Shona shook her head. 'I don't know what's wrong. It's just a horrible feeling. I've had it for ages. As if something awful's going to happen. Perhaps it's to do with the exams . . . I've been working so hard. I'm probably just tired.'

May watched her thoughtfully. 'Aye, that's likely it,' she agreed. 'You'll feel better when you know the results. But try not to worry. I'm sure you've passed. Don't fret, you'll get your place at Edinburgh.'

'I hope so. And I can't think of anything else that could be causing this.' Shona clasped her cold hands round the hot cup and made a determined effort to pull herself together. 'I'm certain it's the exams and it'll not help to stay up all night feeling sorry for myself. I'm going back to bed. You do the same, Auntie May, before you get cold. I'm alright now. Really.'

The bed was still warm and she slipped back between the

sheets longing for easy, restful sleep. But still her heart pounded with unnamed terror. The oppressive feeling of imminent tragedy almost suffocated her.

She was called from class the next day. The Rector, a severe, unsmiling man, told her that her uncle's boat had been lost the previous night after an explosion and fire. There were no survivors. As he spoke, the previous night's dream returned with dreadful clarity. Shona gasped with the agonizing horror of it. And then she fainted.

Shona entered a nightmare world from which it was impossible to escape. She had loved her good-humoured, warm-natured uncle like a father. Her pain was made all the greater because of the unacceptable knowledge that something abnormal inside her, something she had had glimpses of in the past, had foreseen his death.

Her days were long and black. The house was filled with weeping people; her own heart was breaking; the girls seemed dazed. May was devastated. In a week she aged fifteen years. She was diminished, fragile, old. Shona was relieved when the memorial service was over and she could return to school for the last few days of term. She was empty, drained and had nothing left to offer May in the way of comfort.

The depleted family did its sad best to organise their lives without Hugh as their guiding strength, but they all knew it could never be the same again.

Long before her father's death, Karen, the oldest daughter, had become engaged to a local boy. The grieving shadow of a woman which was all that was left of May persuaded her to go ahead with the wedding on the early July date she had planned for, but on a much reduced scale. When Pamela quietly admitted that she, too, wanted to get married, in August, May actually appeared relieved.

Shona was puzzled. May adored her daughters and had dreaded losing them. But it soon became obvious that

Hugh's death was having repercussions that no-one had foreseen.

Choosing an evening when there were only the two of them in the house, May explained to Shona. 'Hugh never had any insurance. Not on himself and not on the boat. I've no money, Hen. Just the social security and that doesn't go far.'

'I'll get a job,' Shona offered immediately.

'No, Hen. Thanks all the same, but that's not what I want. And it's not what Hugh would have wanted. He had his heart set on you going to university.'

'That can wait. I'll work for a couple of years first. Lots of people do that these days.'

'No. It really is for the best if you go to Edinburgh, like you planned. Then at least I won't have to worry about you.' Shona sensed there was more to come and waited patiently.

'Now that Karen and Pamela are getting wed and you're off to Edinburgh, there's only me and Betty left, and she'll be married before too long, you mark my words. This house is too much on the money I get. And it's not the same. Not without Hugh.' She paused, sniffed gently and rubbed at her eyes. Her next words shocked Shona deeply.

'I've decided to go and live with my mother. In Kilweem. She's getting on and she needs looking after. To be honest I could use the company. I can't stand being on my own,' she confided, tears filling her eyes again. 'But you know my mother's house. It's just wee. Just the one bedroom. You'll all be welcome to come and visit for a night or two but you can see, can't you, that we couldn't all live there?'

'Of course I do,' Shona choked, patting her aunt's hand.

'I'm going as soon as I can, Shona. It's better that way. I know you don't like William but I've had a wee word with Twi and Robbie and they say you can spend your time with them until you go to Edinburgh.' She shifted uneasily. 'I don't want you to think I'm leaving you to fend for yourself, lass. I'll always be there if you want someone to talk to. You do understand, Hen, don't you?'

Shona had always thought of the cosy, Sauchar house as her real home. Now it was being torn from her in the cruellest way, but for her aunt's sake she forced a smile.

'Don't worry about me, Auntie May. You know I can take care of myself. And I think you're doing the wisest thing.' But, when she tried to withdraw her hand, she discovered her aunt was holding it with an astonishingly strong grip.

'That dream, Shona . . . that bad feeling you had. It was Hugh, wasn't it? You sensed he was going to die, didn't you? You see things, just like your mother did, don't you?' May's voice was harsh and accusing and there was a strange look in her watery eyes.

Shona found she couldn't answer. Nor did May seem to expect her to. With a barely disguised grunt of disgust she dropped Shona's hand and turned away. Appalled, Shona realised she had seen fear and revulsion on her aunt's face.

Left with no other choice, Shona presented herself at the farm cottage only to find that Twi was less than enthusiastic about the arrangement.

'I'm not feeling very great, Shona. I could do without an extra body about the house. I was hoping for some peace and quiet.'

'The lassie'll not be in the way, Twi. She'll be a help to you,' Robbie soothed.

'It's no help I'm needing. It's quietness,' his wife retorted acidly. 'In any case, she's no business hanging around here all summer. She needs to get herself a job.'

'I will. I'll start looking this afternoon,' Shona promised. 'That way I can at least pay towards my keep.'

'No, lass . . .' Robbie began.

'Aye!' Twi cut him short. 'That would help. But I'm not

fit to go running around after you, mind. You'll still need to pull your weight around the house.'

'I always do, Auntie Twi,' Shona said quietly, stung by her aunt's hostility.

'And it might be best if you go to William and Maggie's for the weekends. That'll give your Auntie Twi a wee break,' Robbie suggested apologetically.

'Yes, Uncle Robbie. Thank you.' Every cell in Shona's body revolted at the humiliation of it all. She longed for October and her university place, with the room in a student hostel which went with it.

Within a day she found herself a job in a café catering for the increasing numbers of tourists visiting the quaint coastal villages. The hours were long but, anxious to spend as much time as possible away from her reluctant hosts, Shona volunteered to work a seven-day week. Even then, by the time she paid a generous portion of her wages to Twi and a smaller but still significant amount to the avaricious William and Maggie, there was very little left to spare.

The job lasted until the end of September. Then, at last, there was only one more week before she could escape to Edinburgh and a new life.

Her last days in Strathannan were spent in a kind of limbo. The empty days loomed drearily before her. Trying to keep out of the ailing and bad-tempered Twi's way, she spent two hours on the beach at Ainstrie, gazing at the house where she, her mother and Lizzie had lived, wondering at the smallness of it, its shabbiness.

Then, feeling extraordinarily restless, she wandered back through the village and, on impulse, jumped onto the St Andrews bus. Forty minutes later she was walking down a narrow lane. Despite never having been there since she was a baby she knew precisely where she was going, almost as if something was guiding her there.

The gates were closed, chained and padlocked and the paint on the once impressive pillars had flaked off, leaving discoloured patches on the stone. When she looked carefully she could just make out the letters of Netherdrum.

From the bottom of the curving drive only the side of the house was visible. It beckoned to her, pulling her towards it and she found herself edging round the pillars, through a rickety pedestrian gate which grated when she forced it back. Then she was walking up the drive itself.

The mellow old house looked lost and uncared for. The boarded windows gave the whole place a blank, characterless feel. The overgrown gardens yelled neglect.

Very slowly she circled the house, passing ruined sheds, dilapidated stables and crumbling walls with the growing feeling that the house was trying to tell her something, that it had brought her here for a purpose, but she didn't know what. How marvellous this could all look, she thought. It was a house which deserved to be loved, to belong to someone who would care for it properly. The way she would. Oh, how she would love this wonderful old house!

Now she found herself in a small, walled garden. For a fraction of a second her vision wavered and then cleared again, revealing the garden as it had once been, splendid with masses of flowers, fragrant with the scents of summer and sleepy with the buzz of insects. She blinked and stared again at the tangled reality in front of her and wondered what disaster had reduced such a magnificent house to this sorry mess.

Creeping sadness darkened her day. Anxious to get away from the source of this depression, she hurried from the garden and wandered through the woodland at the back of the house and across a pretty stream until she found herself facing a small, derelict cottage. The shock made her heart leap and her legs weaken. This, she knew, was the reason she had been brought here.

The building was ramshackle and decaying, with flaking paint and broken windows but she was absolutely, frighteningly certain that this had been her parents' home.

Cautiously she touched the front door. It swung open as

if to welcome her. But inside there was nothing. Even the sink was missing. All the rooms bore similar signs of degeneration, except the largest one. There she found a rickety table and a chair. Heedless of the dust and grime Shona perched on the table and ran her hands idly through the accumulation of dirt and dust. Something caught her eye. Impatiently she rubbed at the dust and blew it clear. The surface which was revealed was stained with faded rings and blobs of pale colour, like those which might have been left by watery jars. Her heart bubbled with excitement. She had been right. Her mother had painted here. She closed her eyes and tried to imagine her at work in this very room.

Something hazy shimmered deep in her mind, the merest glimpse of a young woman at an easel, a wonderful, deep echo of contentment. And then it was gone. No amount of concentration could bring it back.

Feeling oddly disappointed, as if she had missed something vital, Shona re-emerged into the sunlight and made her way back to the gates. So preoccupied was she that she almost walked past the elderly but upright woman standing just inside the gates.

'Can I help you?' a strong voice demanded.

Shona jumped guiltily. 'No. Thank you. I was just leaving.'

'This is private property,' the old lady rebuked her sternly.

Shona smiled, transforming her face and winning a cautious smile in return. 'I didn't think. I'm sorry. I assumed there was no-one here, it all looks so neglected. But I didn't touch anything. I just walked around, seeing if I could remember anything.'

'Remember anything? Why should you remember anything?' The old woman was peering closely at the strikingly lovely young woman who gave such a strong impression of dignified composure, as if she had every right to be there.

'I used to live here. When I was a small child. I've never been back since. I hoped I might find something to jog my memory.'

'And did you?' There was more interest than suspicion in the ageing eyes now.

'No. Not really.' Shona smiled again and started to walk on.

'Just a minute,' the elderly woman called after her. 'Tell me who you are. Perhaps I'll remember you. I've been here since I was just a young lassie.'

Shona spun round. 'That long? Then you must have known my mother. Isobel Dryburgh.'

'Isobel Dryburgh!' exclaimed the woman. 'So that explains it,' she murmured, realising how very like James this young woman was. 'Then you must be the baby. Now, what was the name?' She frowned as if trying to recall details which had long ago receded to the back of her mind. 'I've got it! Sheila. That's right, isn't it? You and your mother and Lizzie all went off to live in Ainstrie when James and old Mr Geddes died.' She looked at Shona and challenged. 'That is right, isn't it?'

Shona chuckled, understanding that the old woman was testing her.

'My name is Shona.'

The elderly lady nodded in satisfaction. 'So it is.' The watery blue eyes twinkled. 'Imagine you coming here after all these years. Look, there's a seat. Sit down and talk to me for a while. Tell me what brought you here.'

Shona's arm was taken in a surprisingly firm grip and she was led to a broken bench.

'Here, this will hold us, I hope.'

'You remember my mother?' Shona asked, thirsty for information to supplement the little her aunts and uncles had told her about her family. How strange it was that she should be so suddenly consumed with curiosity about her long-dead mother. In truth she had the most shadowy memories of her. Those details she did know were the bits and pieces gleaned from family conversations. She had the lasting impression of a tragic but beautiful woman with a great talent for painting. Only rarely had her mother's other

281

gift been mentioned, almost always as if it was something to be ashamed of. It had been Hugh who had finally explained it and the great unhappiness it had caused Isobel, to the twelve-year-old Shona. As the years passed and she began to suspect traces of that same gift, weaker but still apparent in her own character, some inner instinct warned her that this was something to be kept very much to herself. Now she wondered if it was this mysterious link with her mother which had brought her here. But for what purpose?

'I was housekeeper here,' the old woman was saying. 'In old Mr Geddes's time. I recall when your mother and James got married.' The lined face crumpled into a nostalgic smile. 'She'll remember me. Tell her you met Eleanor McLachlan.'

'My mother died in a car accident when I was five. Nineteen fifty-eight.'

'Now I recall hearing something – I am sorry, lass.' Mrs McLachlan looked genuinely sad. 'Such a waste. She was a lovely woman. So happy. So gentle. Artistic . . .' she seemed lost in her memories. Shona deliberately brought her back to the present.

'You've been here all those years?' she asked.

'On and off. I live in the village now. When old Mr Geddes died and Alisdair inherited he tried to sell this place. I was told to move out, like your mother. But something must have gone wrong for the estate was never sold. Better if it had been, really. Then it might have been properly looked after. It would break Mr Geddes's heart if he could see it now. He loved the place. Alisdair and his wife lived here for a couple of years, then they rented it to some Arab businessman. But it's been empty for more than three years now. I'm paid to check on it, that's all. It gives me something to do. Makes me get out of my chair and walk a mile or so each day,' she chuckled.

'So it still belongs to Alisdair?'

'Oh aye.' Mrs McLachlan eyed her in surprise. 'I thought you would know that, being his niece.'

'We've never met. After all, he's a lot older than me and

from what little I've been told, he and my mother didn't get on all that well.'

'No, and I can understand why.' Without being specific, Mrs McLachlan managed to convey her low opinion of Alisdair Geddes.

'He doesn't come here himself?' Shona asked, curious about this relative she had never met.

'No. He lives in Edinburgh. Place called Strachan House.'

'Strachan House? It sounds grand.'

'I don't know. He bought it when he sold the factory. Didn't you know that, either?'

'No,' Shona admitted wryly. 'I've never had any contact with any of my father's family. After my mother died I lived with her relatives. They told me what they could about her, but very little about my father.'

'That's a pity, lass, for your father was one of the nicest people ever to grace this earth. As far as I know there was only Mr Geddes himself, Alisdair and your father left of that family, and you, of course. Maybe you should contact him?'

'Maybe,' Shona said dubiously. 'But if he and my mother didn't get on, I shouldn't think he'd want to meet me.'

'That was twenty years ago. People change. You've got nothing to lose. Here, if you've got a pen in that bag I'll write down his address for you.'

'Thanks,' Shona rummaged for a scrap of paper and a pencil. 'Perhaps you're right,' she said, scanning the meaningless address. 'I'll think about contacting him.' She seemed lost in thought for a moment, then sighed regretfully and got to her feet. 'I wish I could stay and talk some more. I know there's such a lot you could tell me about my parents, but I've got a bus to catch.'

'Well be sure and come back. And the next time, knock on my door first and I'll show you round the main house. I'm at number two. On the main street.'

'Thank you, Mrs McLachlan. I'd really like to do that. But at least I found the cottage today. Thanks again for talking to me.'

'It was a pleasure. Not many folks have the time to spare for an old woman these days. Just you be sure and look me up next time you're here.'

'I'll do that,' Shona promised. Then she picked her way over the damp grass, sparing one last look at Netherdrum House. Her abiding impression was that the old house was waiting, patiently, silently waiting. As she walked through the sagging gates she had the illogical feeling that it was waiting for her.

Back at the farm she found Twi in bed, wrestling with another bout of the debilitating pain and bleeding which assailed her every month.

'The doctor says I'm to go back into hospital until they can see what's causing it,' she said, dread written all over her face.

'You probably need some minor treatment and then you'll be as right as rain,' Shona offered in a vain attempt to cheer her aunt up.

'I don't think so. The doctor thinks there might be something there. A growth . . .'

'Well, the sooner you get it seen to the better, Auntie Twi. You can't go on like this.'

Shona had been shocked to realise just how poorly her aunt was. Twi was like a bent, old woman. In a matter of three months her weight had dropped from a sturdy thirteen stone to a fragile nine. Shona needed none of her extranormal perception to know that her Aunt's complaint was serious.

'So,' Twi steered the conversation away from her own precarious health. 'You met old Mrs McLachlan? I remember her well. She was a kind-hearted soul. She must be eighty if she's a day.'

'She lives in the village. Still keeps an eye on the big house. She remembered my mother and even invited me to go and visit her again. I might do that one day . . . She also suggested I try to contact Alisdair.'

'Alisdair! He and your mother hated one another.'

'They weren't friends, that's certain. But, like Mrs McLachlan said, people change. And he is my only relative on my father's side.'

'It's up to you,' Twi sniffed her disapproval. 'Though why you would want to go searching him out is beyond me. He never took the slightest interest in you and you've family enough without going looking for strangers. Mind you, he'll be worth a bit. Maybe you could persuade him to let you have some of what your grandfather should have left you. If he had done that in the first place we'd have all been a lot better off.' Twi was too tired to bother to disguise the bitterness in her voice.

'That isn't why I want to see him, Aunt Twi.'

'More fool you,' Twi snorted.

Holding back her anger Shona sought safer ground. 'I found the cottage where my parents used to live. And a table all covered in paint marks. My mother must have used it. I do wish I'd seen some of her work. I've heard she was very good.'

For a moment she thought Twi had suffered some sort of seizure. The woman's face contorted grossly, then flushed crimson.

'I had forgotten,' she gasped. 'My God! How could I have forgotten?'

'Forgotten what, Auntie Twi?'

'The pictures! I've got two of them. Your mother's paintings. And I had forgotten all about them. They must be worth a small fortune.'

'Can I see them?' Shona asked excitedly. 'Where are they?'

'Lizzie gave them to me the day I brought you up here from Ainstrie. All wrapped up in brown paper they were. She said they were for you.'

'They're mine?' Shona could hardly believe this.

'Aye, they're yours. But don't get all steamed up about them. If I remember right they were awful, dreary things. They can't have been any good or your mother would have sold them. She was near penniless when she died.'

'Where are they, Auntie Twi?' she repeated.

'The wardrobe. The bottom drawer.' Twi pointed.

Shona hauled out the huge, stiff drawer and rooted among the best table linen stored there. 'There's nothing here.'

'Not *in* the drawer,' Twi snapped. 'Behind it. Under it. I hid them.'

Eventually the drawer crashed to the floor. Shona scrabbled in the dusty recess at the back. There, in exactly the same place that Twi had hidden it all those years before, was the parcel.

Still facing the wardrobe Shona loosened the string, fumbling impatiently with the huge knot, and hauled off the paper. For a moment she was stunned. The beauty of the pictures overwhelmed her. The delicacy of the colours, the sad quality of the scenes, brought a sudden, painful lump to her throat. For many minutes she simply stared at them. As she looked at a view of Netherdrum House it seemed to her that the paint shimmered and moved, that she could hear the wind in the trees, smell the flowers, see the movement of the clouds.

'Shona! Shona! Will you wake up and bring them over here this instant.' Twi's angry voice brought her back to the present.

'Sorry, Auntie Twi.' She gathered the paintings and took them to her aunt.

'Well,' said Twi, shaking her greying head. 'I still can't understand why anyone would pay good money on these dismal things. They're not very realistic, are they? They're eerie. Weird. Like Isobel.' Twi had forgotten the gentle, generous side to her sister. All she recalled now was the unhappy girl whose strange gift had set her apart from her peers.

'I don't think my mother was weird, Auntie Twi. Just

different. And these paintings are beautiful.' Shona defended her dead mother hotly.

'Och, you would say that. After all, you're just as bad as she was.' Shona started to deny it but knew it was pointless.

'Don't look so outraged,' Twi said sourly. 'It's there alright, even though you're careful to hide it. You've even got the mark. I saw it when you were a wee bairn. That's why I wouldn't have you getting mixed up with our Alex. I saw the way he looked at you! He would have ditched Louisa for you. Thought he was in love with you! But I wasn't having that. I wasn't having any grandwains with any strange marks on them, turning out to be fey, like you and your mother.' Exhausted by the release of this long-held venom, she fell back against her pillows and closed her eyes.

Shona winced and turned away, frightened by the sudden anger of this sick and embittered woman. 'What shall I do with these?' she asked, tonelessly.

'I don't care. They're yours. Take them with you. Maybe you'll get something for them.'

'You should keep one,' Shona offered, keenly aware of the debt she owed her aunts and uncles. 'After all, you kept me all this time.'

'Aye, so we did. But I don't want one, Shona. Isobel never had any lasting happiness and I don't want anything of hers that might pass that curse on to me or mine. No,' she shoved them away. 'You take the bloody things. I don't want them.'

Knowing she would never return to the farm to live, Shona packed all her things and, first thing on Saturday morning took herself to Kilweem for what was to be her last weekend with William and Maggie.

Much to her relief, Mhari was visiting friends in Dundee. Her aunt and uncle, as usual, planned to spend the evening at the Lobster. Shona enjoyed a rare evening of privacy and was in bed long before they came home.

Their drunken progress along the quayside was audible minutes before they clattered their way into the house. William's slurred voice was enough to waken anyone who had hoped for an early night. Then came the sounds of two people getting ready for bed, heavy footsteps on the stairs, the clanking flush of the toilet cistern and Maggie's loud, bad-tempered rebuttal of William's advances with the hard instruction to 'git tae sleep'.

At last there was silence. Minutes later, fitful snoring filtered up from the bed closet William had insisted on using since his father's death. Shona plumped up her lumpy pillow and closed her eyes.

The heat of foul breath on her face woke her. She came to her senses suddenly, feeling the bed give under William's weight as he clambered on top of her. Her eyes jerked open and she found herself staring into yellow, bloodshot eyes, felt herself suffocating in his rancid breath. In the diffused light filtering through the window his flabby, lined face was contorted with something she recognised as lust. She screamed and squirmed violently. Then everything dissolved into alternating pulses of inky blackness and sharp, painful brilliance as he silenced her with his fist. Even while her head still reeled she registered red fear and revulsion as he clawed at his pyjama bottoms, shoving them down to reveal waxy, white flesh and the rearing, purple organ which he was already thrusting at her.

Desperately she tossed herself to the side but, pinioned by his enormous weight, she simply couldn't get away from him. He held her easily with one hand then, when another hoarse scream escaped her bruised mouth, threw a pillow over her face and held it there. Frantically, panicking, she lunged from side to side, always gripped by her uncle's massive body. The more she struggled the harder it was to breathe. In the end she subsided into panting, heavy silence, desperately trying to draw air through the heavy pillow, her senses swimming as she hovered on the edge of consciousness.

Her battle to breathe made his assault easy. Coarse hands ripped away her brief panties and hauled her nightdress up. Sharp teeth fastened painfully on her nipples but her yell of pain and outrage was muffled by the pillow. Sickened, head spinning from lack of oxygen, she could do nothing to protect herself when the hot proddings in her most tender region warned her that he was going to violate her. Every ounce of strength went into one last heave as she again attempted to throw him off. But it was useless. She heard the lewd laugh, the obscene words he panted into her ear and realised that he was relishing the struggle, that every movement she made excited him more.

He held her as easily as if she was a newborn infant. The thrust, when it came, was brutal, savage, as if he deliberately wanted to tear and injure her. Every muscle in her body clenched in self-defence. Grunting, he drew back and forced himself into her again. Hot metal rasped inside her. On and on he went until she thought her ribs must break.

Suddenly he stiffened, jerked and collapsed heavily on top of her. She lay, unmoving, exhausted, semi-conscious, half suffocated, her body limp, open and vulnerable as he finally lifted the pillow from her face. Coarse and cruel he looked down on her, a hard leer on the fleshy mouth. Very slowly he stroked her breasts, running dirty fingers down into the mass of bruised and swollen flesh between her legs. His fetid breath made her stomach churn.

'That's to pay me back for all I've done for you. Keeping you all these years without a single word of thanks.'

'*No!*' It was all she could say.

He sneered. 'If you say one word to anyone, I won't deny it. I'm smarter than that. I'll say you asked for it, begged for it. I'll make sure everyone knows what a wee slut you are. You couldn't prove any different. It'll be your word against mine.' Spittle flecked his lips. Shona's stomach heaved uncontrollably. He moved back just in time to avoid the eruption, pausing only to hitch his trousers round his waist before hurrying out of the room. Behind him she retched again and again onto the floor beside her bed.

She heard the door close behind him but still she vomited, heaving as if she might purge the whole thing from her body until, bleeding and sore she sank back against the pillow and closed her eyes.

She never knew how long she lay there before she found the will to fling herself from the bloodstained dampness of the bed. In the bathroom she filled the sink and sluiced herself with cold water, rubbing at herself with coarse soap, gasping as it stung the raw flesh.

Moving with a purpose now, seeming unnaturally calm, she stuffed her things back into her bag, carefully keeping her ashen face away from the bed and crept downstairs.

William's irregular snoring met her when she emerged into the living room, causing devastating, unexpected anger to explode inside her. One glance at William's ugly form was enough to make her control it, knowing she would be helpless against him. Closing the living room door carefully behind her she tiptoed into the kitchen. But as she struggled to unlock the back door, the sound of the living room door opening again made her spin round. She expected to see William but there, facing her with absolute and implacable contempt, was Maggie. The older woman met Shona's swollen eyes steadily, a sneer turning down the corners of her mouth.

'Creeping away like the wee whore you really are,' she accused. 'I know what you've been up to. I've watched him all these years, lusting after you. And you showing yourself to him, letting him touch you.'

Shona stared, still traumatised, unable to say a single word in her own defence.

'I saw him go into your room. I heard the noises you were making.' Now there was something else in Maggie's face, as if she was relishing the memory. Shona's stomach heaved its warning again as Maggie stalked across the kitchen and threw the door wide open. 'And don't·come back,' she spat at Shona's back.

It was barely half past five on a Sunday morning. Shona made her way past the harbour and scrambled heedlessly over the rocks on the point. She arrived at the foot of the Butts with her mind blank. Ahead of her stretched the fine golden sands with the dunes rising gently behind her. Like an automaton she dragged her aching limbs along the beach. For more than a mile she walked, letting the breeze knife through her, welcoming the chill, willing her body to turn to ice. Her lips turned blue, her limbs became numb but still she walked.

The wind whipped through the sand and whistled in the dunes. To her dazed mind it was as if it was speaking to her, as though she had been here before. 'Witch girl. Witch girl. Witch girl.' The voices carried on the breeze. She started to run, knowing they were running with her. Panting, panicking she tore along the sand.

At last she stumbled and fell. The sharp prick of a broken shell embedding itself in her palm shocked her back to awareness. Like someone emerging from a dream she looked around her in the still calm of the deserted beach, disturbed by not a single hint of wind.

She picked herself up, gazed round as if seeing where she was for the first time then, head erect, stride purposeful, she headed for the shelter of the dunes. There, in a small, sandy basin, she curled up, like an animal, and was instantly asleep.

She woke hours later. For long seconds she thought she must still be asleep but when she stretched her legs the soreness between them brought instant recall.

Shivering she burrowed in her bag and, still sheltered by the dunes, changed her crumpled clothing and brushed the worst of the sand from her legs, striving to make herself appear normal for the journey she would now make to Edinburgh. Satisfied she set off along the beach, her face set and hard.

Every step she took divorced her from the past. She knew

there was only one way she could survive this and that was to close her mind to it, to refuse to let it ruin her life. Today was to have been the beginning of a new life for her, her first day of freedom. Nothing, she determined, had changed. Today she would cut the unhappy ropes which, of necessity, had bound her to Strathannan. Today she would take her rightful place at university and start to build a future. She could not, would not, allow William's brutal attack to wreck everything she had worked so hard for.

TWENTY-ONE

Shona's hard-earned university career lasted less than two months. While her fellow undergraduates were still adjusting, making friends, studying and generally revelling in life she was already making plans to leave.

Even in the supposedly liberated days of 1971, the university authorities were less than enthusiastic about the prospect of allowing a pregnant eighteen-year-old to continue with her course. Gently but firmly she was told to suspend her studies for a year and given the names and addresses of several welfare agencies.

She had known. Within forty-eight hours of the attack she had sensed the new life within her. And hated it. Already the weight of impending responsibility dragged at her, responsibility which would not end with the safe delivery of a healthy child.

William had won. With that last, callous act he had ruined her life. There was no hope of ever returning to read for her degree now.

Shona took silent, grim stock of her situation and forced herself to confront reality. She was going to have a baby, a baby she didn't want, could never love, and it was her responsibility. And her responsibility alone. An abortion was out of the question. Not religious by inclination Shona knew she could not deliberately end this life, knew she would never be able to forgive herself if she murdered this child, but she doubted her ability to cope alone and there was no-one to whom she could turn for help. William and Maggie were out of the question; May was caring for her invalid mother and still trying to come to terms with Hugh's death, and to add to Robbie's burdens now while Twi fought cancer was unthinkable. So, she would just have to deal with this on her own. And the one thing she couldn't afford was self-pity. It was up to her and to her alone to get through this. With a breaking heart and cold, granite-like determination, she set about securing a future for herself and the child.

Her first priority was to find herself a job. Fortunately, so close to Christmas, there was no shortage of work in the Scottish capital. Without any difficulty she found a place as a sales assistant with Darlings, a large fashion store towards the end of Princes Street. It kept her on her aching feet all day and paid just sufficient to cover the rent on her bed-sit in York Place.

The room was tiny and sparsely furnished. A creaking, sagging double bed dominated it, leaving barely enough room for a couple of old chairs and a shabby settee. A square of worn carpet covered the worst of the holes in the ancient linoleum. The claustrophobic, depressing effect was not lessened by the view from the grimy, first floor window which looked out over the noxious, noisy spread of the bus station in St Andrew Square.

The grubby, mildewed bathroom and inadequate cooking facilities were shared but her room had the saving grace of a single electric ring and kettle. With great ingenuity she contrived to do most of her cooking with them.

Her only source of heat was a double-barred electric fire to which, in the freezing days of December, she was forced to resort more and more often, watching in horror as the prepayment meter gobbled her precious tenpenny pieces at an alarming rate.

Christmas and New Year were the most miserable of her entire life.

Careful dressing and good fortune had made her condition barely discernible but, by March, her swelling body was unmistakable. The child was moving now, kicking and turning as if to remind her that it was there, that even her own body was no longer her own. Shona hated it, resented it more with each new discomfort. The bitter realisation that she would have a permanent, living reminder of William's attack obliterated all feelings of tenderness she might otherwise have had for a child. She began to think carefully about placing the child for adoption.

Inevitably she had to give up her job. With no way of supporting herself there was no alternative but to apply for state help.

Forced to the utmost economy she scoured the second-hand shops and jumble sales for essential clothes and baby items, rushing home with her purchases to scrub, disinfect and scrub them again.

Tired, lonely and depressed she cried easily, slept too much and felt she had sunk to the very bottom of humanity, then consoled herself that, logically, things could only improve.

How the days dragged. June passed incredibly slowly, making way for an unusually hot July. Every movement drained her. The baby was already overdue. It was another two weeks, before, at two o'clock in the morning, a sudden flood of moisture down her legs and the first gentle contractions told her that the child was finally on its way.

Twelve hours later, with a last, supreme effort, Shona's daughter made her damp entry into the world. Shona peered tiredly at the flailing bundle and felt nothing, not even relief that there was no sign of red hair detectable on the moist, almost bald head.

The baby was handed to her, still damp and unwashed. Shona took her unwillingly then, shaking her head wordlessly, handed her back to the disapproving midwife.

The rest of the day slipped by in fitful sleep. Shona was only dimly aware of the activity surrounding her, irritated by the intermittent cries of the babies, disturbed by the other mothers when all she wanted to do was sleep her life away. When a nurse asked if she wanted to feed her newborn daughter she shook her head and turned on her side, refusing even to look into the crib.

The next day was the same.

Some time during the second night she was disturbed by a soft, mewling sound. She struggled to turn her sore body and realised, with an angry shock, that the baby had been left at her bedside. The strengthening cries left her in no doubt that the infant was hungry. Shona lay down and turned her back again, determined to ignore it. A nurse would have to take it back to the nursery before it upset everyone else in the ward.

But no-one came.

And still the baby cried.

Somewhere further down the ward another child whimpered but stopped almost immediately when its mother picked it up. Still Shona's baby hiccoughed its distress, its little, wavering cries tightening her heart. Shona buried her head in her pillow and found her own eyes were wet. Abruptly she sat up and wiped away her tears. If the nurse wouldn't come and take the baby away she would take it back to the nursery herself.

She struggled out of bed but couldn't avoid looking in the crib. Tiny fists flailed the air, the eyes seemed to look straight at her and the minute body heaved with sobs. Shona was appalled by her own cruelty. The baby's helplessness was obvious, its distress so apparent that even her injured heart was moved, sending her to her daughter with tears of remorse and pain in her eyes.

Gingerly she lifted the baby from the crib but needed no nurse to show her what to do then. With an audible sigh, eyes screwed together in satisfaction, the child started to suck. Shona sat in awed silence, tears coursing down her cheeks, stroking the infant's downy head as love, frightening in its force, overwhelmed her.

Out of sight, behind the ward doors, the worried frown disappeared from the night sister's face and she and the duty nurse exchanged relieved smiles.

Over the next seven days Shona experienced a range of emotions she had never known before. Love for this tiny, totally dependent being dominated everything. Determination to cherish her, to provide for her, to make certain she didn't suffer as a result of her unhappy conception, and the novelty of having another human being so close to her, reduced everything which had gone before to insignificance.

Back in the bed-sit the reality of coping with a young baby alone, in such inadequate conditions, took its toll. Shona lost weight, her creamy skin became sallow and the eyes, huge and shadowed, seemed to dominate a face of infinite sadness.

Ailsa's demands were ceaseless. If she cried in the night the neighbours above, below and at the front, all complained. Shona slept lightly, alert for the first whisper, terrified that some complaint might reach the landlord and she would lose even this cheerless home.

Money was Shona's never-ending, overwhelming problem. The strictest, most careful budgeting failed to stretch her allowance to cover everything they needed. Ailsa was always spotlessly clean and well fed but Shona frequently went without to provide for her daughter. As the months passed and Ailsa grew, needing bigger clothes and toys to amuse and stimulate her, Shona's small wardrobe disintegrated until her only pair of shoes was almost unwearable.

More than once she took her mother's paintings from the small suitcase hidden under the bed, unwrapped them tenderly and gazed at them, fighting the temptation to see them. But, it was as if this one link with her dead mother spoke to her. Shona knew, with a certainty so intense it frightened her, that she must never sell these paintings, that to do so would be a betrayal. Somehow those two pictures were a symbol of hope, without them there would be none. Always she put them away again, wrapping them lovingly, never yielding to temptation.

Just when the situation seemed irredeemable, when she was starting to believe that she might, after all, be forced to part with her only reminder of her mother, when winter and its dearer heating bills was on the doorstep, Shona had her first piece of good fortune. The friendly social worker she had turned to in desperation found a free place for Ailsa in a council-run crêche, and then recommended a child-minder who would collect the baby and look after her until early evening, so freeing Shona to find a full-time job.

Much as she loathed the idea of passing Ailsa's care to strangers, Shona was realistic enough to acknowledge that this was the only possible way forward. Immediately she found a job back at Darlings for the pre-Christmas period but, not content to remain there on a permanent basis, she also applied for several more promising posts. To her delight she was invited for interviews for almost all of them.

Her delight was short-lived. Even in interviews which were going well she soon learned to recognise the tight disapproval which greeted her when, responding honestly to direct questions, she revealed Ailsa's existence. Despite her assurances that she had made adequate arrangements for her daughter's care, she didn't get a single job offer. Another round of applications produced three more interviews. This time she was very careful to promote the impression of an ambitious single woman with no ties. She was successful at all three and finally accepted a post with the small Edinburgh advertising agency of Ross Innes. The salary was generous and the work promised to be challenging. She would start with them in the new year. For the first time since her frantic flight from Strathannan the future looked bright.

*I*t was the type of cold, wet, miserable February evening which discourages loitering. Shona finished work just before six and left her west end office with her umbrella already raised. She picked her way through the rush hour crowds, anxious only to get home to Ailsa. When a hand descended from nowhere and fastened itself securely on her arm, she knocked it aside in fright and started to run.

'Wait, Shona. It's only me,' Alex panted as he struggled to keep up with her.

'Alex?' she gasped, lowering her umbrella for a better look at him. It was him alright. Older, more mature and with the absolute power to reduce her to quivering incoherence.

'I didn't mean to startle you,' he offered by way of apology.

'I need to talk to you. Can we get a drink or something?' he asked, raindrops sparkling on his eyebrows.

She hesitated, thinking of Ailsa's minder who was expecting her in fifteen minutes.

'It's important, Shona.'

'Okay. But I need to make a phone call first.'

'Make it from the pub,' he decided, hurrying her into Rose Street, taking charge quite naturally, as he had done so often in the past.

She made her call, then watched Alex while he bought the drinks. How attractive he was. Tall, dark but appealingly unkempt with his long, slightly dishevelled hair and casual clothes which proclaimed a healthy lack of vanity. She knew

Alex wasn't afflicted by the brash, swollen egos which spoiled so many good-looking young men. He was at ease with himself, content to be what he appeared to be, never feeling the need to impress or pretend.

But there was something different about him tonight, something not quite right. The impish, crooked smile she remembered so well was missing. From the first moment she had sensed he was troubled. Now, looking closely at his face which wore no trace of lightness, and his deep blue eyes which were shadowed with worry, she was certain of it.

'What is it, Alex?' she asked as soon as they were seated.

'Bad news, I'm afraid. It's taken me all day to find you, Shona. Why didn't you let us know where you were?' he demanded.

She flushed and felt unequal to a detailed explanation. She settled for a half truth instead. 'I didn't think . . . I mean no-one ever visits or anything. There was no point.'

'Then how the hell are we supposed to contact you? I only managed to find you because the university told me you were working at Darlings and the girl you used to work with there told me where you are working now.'

'For goodness sake, Alex! Will you tell me why you're here?' She already had her suspicions and the sadness which darkened his face confirmed her worst fears. 'It's Aunt Twi, isn't it?'

'Mum died yesterday morning.' His voice was gruff with grief.

'Oh, Alex. I'm sorry.' Her own voice cracked as she spoke.

'The funeral is on Friday. I'd like you to be there.'

'Of course I'll come. And thanks for coming to tell me.'

'To tell you the truth, I was glad of the excuse to get out of the house. People calling in every half hour, wanting to know all the gory details; telling me what a wonderful mother she was.' He shrugged expressively. 'I couldn't take much more of it.'

'What about Uncle Robbie?'

'He's alright. He'd had time to get used to the idea that Mum was dying. She was so bad at the end that I think it was a relief when she finally went. Anway, Katrina and Mary are there with their families. And Jamie. The place is overflowing with people.'

They lapsed into sad silence until he suddenly leapt to his feet. 'I'd better be going. They'll be wondering where I've got to. You will be there on Friday. Dad especially asked for you to be there.'

'Of course I will.'

'Thanks, Shona.' He kissed her lightly on the lips, lingering fractionally longer than fraternal affection demanded, before hurrying away.

Twi was buried in Kilweem churchyard. Shona timed her arrival so that she could slip inside the small church just as the service began, so avoiding her relatives.

Afterwards they clustered at the graveside, shivering in the stiff sea breeze. Shona fought tears and gently rocked Ailsa's pushchair hoping her daughter would stay asleep until the service was over. Even though she stood at the back of the small gathering she could not be unaware of the speculative glances aimed at her and the sleeping child. She kept her gaze resolutely to the front, looking at no-one.

While the other mourners dispersed, Shona hung back in the shelter of the church porch, trying to avoid having to talk to anyone, to have to explain. She was on the point of leaving when she sensed someone very close behind her. So close that she felt the animal-like draught of breath on her neck.

'I would have thought you'd have had the decency to keep away from here.'

She whirled round and came face to face with William. Behind him Maggie waited, her expression so hostile that Shona shivered.

'I came to say goodbye to Auntie Twi,' she said, turning her back on him again.

'She wouldn't have wanted you here with your wee bastard,' William hissed. 'Be grateful she didn't see how you ended up. I always knew you'd come to a bad end.'

His words triggered the dormant anger in her mind. The grief was temporarily banished. The full terror of that night, the cruel way he had defiled her, hit her like a physical blow. This time there was no shame, no humiliation in the memory, only rage. The harrowing experiences of the past year had toughened her and it was a more confident young woman who faced her uncle now. A person determined to defend both herself and her innocent daughter.

'This is your daughter,' she said, her voice absolutely steady, and got some satisfaction from the way his slack mouth drooped open. 'That's right. Your daughter,' she went on loudly, confident there was no-one left in the churchyard to overhear.

'*No!*' was Maggie's outraged denial.

'Yes,' Shona retorted. 'Take a good look, William, and marvel at how something so wonderful can be the result of a monster like you raping his own niece.'

'That was no rape,' he spluttered. 'And I warned you to say nothing about it.'

'I have told no-one.' She stared at him coldly. 'I was too ashamed to admit what you did to me.'

'You didn't complain at the time,' he sneered, gaining confidence with every word. 'You never stopped me. There's no such thing as rape. Any woman can stop it if she really wants to. You must have wanted it or you would have stopped me.'

'My God!' she breathed. 'Only someone as evil as you could believe that. How could I stop you? You're three times my size and you had a pillow over my face, suffocating me. I was barely conscious. You raped me and you know it.'

'Bitch!' He raised his hand but she stepped back out of reach.

'You dare!' She threatened him so imperiously that he lowered his hand and contented himself with snarling obscenities at her.

Now she only wanted to get away from him. She turned the pushchair quickly. And ran it right over Alex's feet as he emerged from the church. The appalled expression on his face told her he had heard every word. For a moment their eyes locked.

'No . . . oh no,' she whispered and before he could stop her she dodged round him and tore out of the churchyard.

Too stunned to move Alex watched her go, then faced his uncle.

'You bastard,' he growled, anger exploding redly in his brain. William's fist took him off guard, catching him hard under the ribs, leaving him doubled up in agony while his aunt and uncle made their escape.

For once in his life William thought more quickly than anyone else. While Shona waited dismally for the train back to Edinburgh, knowing Alex must despise her, William and Maggie were already satisfying the curiosity of the assembled relatives who had been openly discussing the parentage of Shona's baby.

Well aware that Alex would soon follow them with his own version of events, they determined their strategy on the way to the cottage and wasted no time in telling their tale.

'You'd hardly credit it,' fumed Maggie, exhibiting a latent talent for dramatics. 'After all we done for her.' A tear was persuaded to slide down her withered cheek, an event so rare as to be remarkable in its own right, lending credibility to her story. Her audience was all her own. 'What would make a young lassie say such a terrible thing?' she declared.

It was inevitable that someone had to ask. It was Robbie's

eldest daughter, Katrina, who said, 'What did she say, Auntie Maggie?'

'No, Maggie. Don't say anything,' simpered William. 'The poor lassie can't be right in the head. It wouldn't be fair to tell folk what she's saying.'

'You can tell us. We're family. We'll not pass it on,' lied Mary, eyes popping.

'Well, I suppose we really should tell you. But only so you know what sort of lassie your cousin's turned out to be,' said Maggie, self-righteously.

'She was always stuck up,' Mary commented maliciously. 'A right wee troublemaker she was.'

'Troublemaker! Aye, she's that right enough,' William added with a thin veneer of outraged dignity.

'It's what she's saying about your Uncle William,' Maggie confided. 'Och, it's hard for me even to tell you about it.' Then, 'It's about the bairn,' she whispered conspiratorially.

'Aye . . .? Go on, go on,' they encourged her avidly.

'Well, we didn't know about the bairn until today. What a shock that was! When I asked her about it, trying to be friendly you understand,' they all nodded dutifully, 'she said . . .' She waited again, going for maximum impact.

'What? What did she say?' demanded Mhari, wide eyes looking from one to the other of her parents in amazement.

'She tried to get money out of us. Threatened to put it about that William's the father of the bairn if we don't give her something. Behind with her rent she is . . . Blackmail! That's what it was,' Maggie finished with a flourish, and waited until the gasps had died away. 'I mean . . . the very idea! If only she had told us she was in trouble we'd have helped her all we could. But she never once came to see us after she went to Edinburgh. Not once. She must have got herself into trouble at that fancy university and now, when the man's left her, she can't cope so she comes here making trouble for us. After all we did for her when she was a bairn. You'd think she'd be grateful . . . Mind you, she's never been the same with us since William told her she was wasting her time going to university. Aye, and he was right there,' she ended smugly.

'But why would she do a thing like that?' Robbie's sad voice startled them all. 'I always thought Shona was a good lassie, and truthful. Are you sure you understood her properly?'

'Of course I did. And she said it in front of Alex. He'll tell you himself when he comes in,' declared William.

'Alex? Aye, where is he?' Robbie asked, missing him for the first time.

'He went back to the church to pay the minister,' Jamie supplied the answer.

'So that's what he was doing there!' William exclaimed. 'Well, it's a wee bitty awkward, Robbie. He only heard the end of the conversation. He got it all wrong and thought I really was the bairn's father. He wouldn't listen when I tried to explain. You should have heard the name he called me.'

'Aye, there was no need for him to fly off the handle like that,' added Maggie.

'So where is he,' persisted Robbie. 'And where's Shona?'

'She ran away,' William said.

'And Alex?'

'I gave him a thumping, Robbie. I couldn't let him think I'd father a bairn on my own niece. Just the one thump, mind, and not hard. Enough to wind him and calm him down a bit, that's all. And he would have thumped me if I hadn't got to him first.'

Robbie gawped, unable to accept what he was hearing but too benumbed by grief to want to argue now.

'I'm sorry, Robbie, but the laddie's old enough to know better. It had to be done,' preached William.

When Alex came home, half a hour later, the damage had all been done. Shona had been judged and found guilty. Nothing he could say could change their verdict.

*

A couple of days later Shona came out of work to be confronted by Alex for the second time in a week. She spotted him as she emerged from the front door and stopped dead, wondering whether she could possibly run back inside the building.

It was as if he read her mind. 'You are not going to run away from me a second time,' he said, taking her arm firmly. 'I want to talk to you.'

'Not now. I have to collect Ailsa from her minder.' How glad she was to have a valid excuse.

He stopped and faced her squarely. 'What about tonight?'

'No. It's too late to get a sitter.'

'You can't avoid this, Shona. What about tomorrow, then? If not I'll come to your place and we'll talk there.'

'*No!*' She couldn't stand for him to see her mean home. 'I'll arrange something for tomorrow night.'

'I'll call for you, about eight.'

'Okay,' she turned to go.

'Then you had better give me your address, hadn't you?' There wasn't the slightest hint of humour in his hard, blue eyes.

Shona dreaded and longed for eight o'clock. He despised her. What man wouldn't. But even with that knowledge she yearned to see him again.

She took more care with her appearance than usual, wishing she could afford to splash out on a new dress. But even so the effect was not too displeasing. The mirror reflected a slim, attractive girl in a fashionably shortened black skirt and vivid blue blouse. Shona smiled when she remembered how awful that same blouse had looked six months ago, draining the colour from a face which was too thin and drawn with strain, hair which was lifeless and dull. And she had been too tired and depressed to care what she looked like. But now her startling colouring rose even above the blue blouse, a testimony to the contentment she found with her daughter, the satisfaction she got from her job and a new anticipation of what life might hold for her. The contrast between her shining, very dark hair and the creamy, flawless skin would draw admiring glances wherever she went.

He was a couple of minutes early. She wouldn't ask him in so, with time to kill, they walked from the flat to the restaurant in the high street, their attempts at conversation falling under the weight of the mightier issues between them.

Striving to pass the meal pleasantly he told her he was now a fully qualified vet, working for a small practice in Peebles. Unwilling to give him any lead into her own life she listened attentively but added very little to the conversation. In the end he resorted to talking about the family. May's mother, he said, had died. May herself had gone to live with Pamela and her husband in Glasgow.

'As for William and Maggie,' he added, introducing their names carefully, noting the faint uncomfortable flush which spread over Shona's cheeks, 'I don't know how you put up with them for so long. And that Mhari is every bit as sour-faced as her mother.'

She couldn't answer but kept her eyes firmly on her coffee cup. He watched her in silence for a few seconds before pressing on, determined to get this whole unhappy business out into the open.

'I guess you had a pretty rough time as a child, didn't you? Shuffling around from one house to the other. I didn't think anything of it at the time, but you must have felt like a leper. Especially after that New Year . . . Remember?' He smiled at last and it was still the boyish grin she loved.

She couldn't help smiling back at him. 'Of course I do! After the way everyone reacted how could I forget? Such a fuss. But your mother only did what she thought was right. And,' she added softly, 'my childhood wasn't that bad. I was happy enough with Hugh and May and your parents never made me feel I wasn't wanted. Not while I was a child, anyway.'

'Don't think too badly of Mother,' he said sadly. 'She told me . . . just before she died . . . about why she didn't want us to get involved. That stupid mark thing.' He looked uncomfortable.

'It's not stupid, Alex. Aunt Twi was right in a way. I have inherited something from my mother . . . something strange. But it's not as strong in me as it was in her. It's nothing to be frightened of.' There was a plea for understanding in her eyes.

'I know that, Shona! I've known you all your life, remember?'

She dropped her eyes and fiddled with her knife. 'I had bigger problems than that to contend with.' She knew there was no way round the subject. They might as well attack it now.

'William?' he asked gently, taking her cue, noticing how tightly her fists were clenched. 'He is the baby's father?'

'Ailsa,' she shot at him defiantly. 'My daughter's name is Ailsa.'

'Ailsa. She's William's?'

Her hands trembled but her eyes were challenging and her mouth firm when she looked back at him. 'No. She's mine. But William fathered her.'

'Can you talk about it? Would it help?'

'He raped me.' It was blunt, hard and uncompromising.

He held her eyes evenly and she saw no flicker of shock, or anything other than genuine sympathy in his face.

'Tell me, Shona,' he whispered intensely, and she realised that she wanted this chance; that his understanding, his support was the most important thing in her life.

'It started when I was a kid. Whenever I did anything wrong, anything at all, he put me across his knee, smacked me . . . put his fingers in . . . inside me.' Her head spun with the effort of control while her stomach revolted under the richness of food inside it. 'Then, when I started to grow up,' she blushed now. 'He would touch me, brush against me, as if it was an accident. That's why I hated going there so much. But I never really thought he'd do anything.' She ignored the profanity which escaped Alex and went on. 'That night they'd been out, drinking. It was my last weekend before I went to university. Mhari was away and I was on my own upstairs. I was asleep. I woke up with him already on top of me.' She shuddered.

'It's okay. You don't have to tell me this if you don't want to.'

'Yes I do,' she shot back at him. 'That's why you're here, isn't it? To see if I was telling the truth?'

'I came to see if I could help.'

She might not have heard. 'He forced me. Put a pillow over my head and almost suffocated me. There was nothing I could do.'

Alex looked away to hide the pain in his eyes.

'Look at me, for God's sake! What chance did I have against him? I don't even weigh eight stone.' Suddenly aware that her voice had risen and several people were frowning in her direction, she went on more quietly. 'I spent the rest of the night on Kilweem beach and caught the train to Edinburgh the next day. I started my course but had to leave at Christmas because of the baby.'

'I'm sorry.' He knew how hopelessly inadequate that was.

'Don't be!' she snapped. 'I don't want pity, Alex. I'll never forgive William, or Maggie because she knew what was happening, but I was the winner in the end. I have the most wonderful little daughter in the whole world.' Tears glittered in her eyes as she spoke. 'I just try to forget who her father is.'

'It's okay, Shona,' he whispered, catching her hand. 'I'm on your side. You should know that. But why didn't you tell me? I could have helped.' He made no attempt to hide the tears in his own eyes.

It was too much. 'Oh, Alex . . .' she shook her head,

valiantly trying to control her emotions. 'I didn't tell anyone. I just wanted to hide away . . .'

He let her sip at her coffee and regain some of her composure before he spoke again. 'I didn't bring you here to upset you. Oh, I admit I was shocked when I heard what you said to William, but I never doubted you. Not for a second.' He smiled at her and won a glimmering softening of the huge, grey eyes in response. 'I wanted to make sure you were alright. To see if there is anything I can do to help.'

'Thanks. There's nothing. We manage.'

The worn appearance of her shoes and the bright blouse, resurrected from childhood, had not escaped his notice. For minutes he said nothing, but the anger inside him churned until he had to speak again.

'I still think you should have told someone. Me, Dad . . . Auntie May. We could have made it easier for you.'

'William would have denied it. It would only have made things worse. No-one would have believed me.'

'You're wrong! If you had said something then, as soon as . . . when it happened. Of course we would have believed you. And a doctor could have proved you'd been raped. William could have gone to prison.'

'My God, Alex! Do you know what you're saying? Dragging it all through the courts . . . No, I couldn't have done that.'

'Alright. But you should have told someone. My father, you know he's fond of you. Or Auntie May. They would have helped.'

'Are you sure?' She laughed but it was a bitter, disbelieving sound.

'They all know William, know what an animal he is. If only you'd told someone at the time. Of course they would have believed you.'

'Don't you understand? No-one wants to believe someone in their own family is capable of something like that.'

Something inside him seemed to snap. 'How can you

sound so bloody pious?' he stormed. 'Why did you accept it so easily?'

'Don't yell at me, Alex,' she retorted furiously. 'You don't understand the first thing about what I've been through. There's been nothing easy about it. William almost ruined my life. I've had to teach myself to make the best of it. If I let myself get bitter I'm finishing the job for him. I'll destroy everything and make Ailsa unhappy, too. I'll never forgive, or forget, but I have had to accept it. There is no alternative.'

He stared at her, incredulity plain on his strong features. 'But that's not enough. You deserve better than that.'

'I don't want to talk about it any more,' she glared at him but he was watching her with such a strange, intense expression that she flushed and looked away.

Several minutes passed in silence. Shona's colour faded to her normal, peach-tinted cream and Alex's breathing slowed.

'I'm sorry, Shona,' he offered at last. 'I really didn't mean to upset you. You must hate me for being so insensitive. I only wanted you to see that you're not alone. You'll always have me.' His hand strayed to her cheek but then he seemed to check himself and stood up abruptly. She could still feel the place where his fingers had brushed her skin.

Outside the cool air calmed her, seeming to take the remaining tension between them with it.

They made their way down Cockburn Street and onto the Mound, not touching but achingly aware of one another.

'Thank you for telling me,' he said when they reached her front door. 'It can't have been easy raking it all up again. And I really would like to help. What can I do? Anything – just ask.'

'There's nothing. But thanks, anyway.'

'Just say the word and I'll do it – anything,' he offered again, moving forward so that her back was towards the door. His hand tangled in her hair, then slipped to caress her neck. The tension between them was suddenly dangerous.

Shona felt that some part of her might explode, knew that this situation was fraught with danger. But when his face came to hers she only wanted to feel the warmth of his lips on hers again, to taste him, to touch him.

He was gentle at first, but sensing the urgency of her response, parted her lips and explored with his tongue. For long minutes they clung together. Only the greatest effort of will allowed her to break away.

'Alex, we shouldn't be doing this,' she begged.

'Why not?' he demanded, holding her face steady while he crushed his lips to hers, kissing her until she was breathless.

'No,' she yelled. 'Stop it, Alex!' She squirmed away and struggled to turn her key in the lock.

'Shona,' he groaned and pulled her roughly round, gathered her into his strong arms and held her so tightly she could feel the hammering of his heart. His kiss was the hardest, most demanding, most arousing thing she had ever known. Her body ached and all her strength was needed to push him away.

'No, Alex. I want you but it's wrong. You know it is.'

'Shona! You don't understand,' he shouted as she slipped through the door.

'I do. Just stay away Alex. Stay away.' She slammed the door shut and clicked on the safety latch, ignoring the pounding from the other side. Eventually he gave up and she heard his footsteps clattering down the stairs.

She leaned against the door, trembling. Alex had rekindled feelings she had managed to ignore for years. But this was her own fault. She should never have agreed to meet him; their chemistry was far too potent. As it was she had stopped things just in time. No matter what she felt for Alexander McArdle, he was not for her. He had a wife and daughter of his own.

TWENTY-THREE

Strachan House on the outskirts of Edinburgh, at Fairmilehead, was the rather grand name for a large, detached, pre-war house in a once select road containing about a dozen similar buildings. It was not at all what Shona had expected. An old, grey stone house, rather austere and cold in appearance with large, blank windows and a featureless, forbidding aspect. Shona stood half-way down the short drive, wondering if her reception here was going to be as chilling as the house itself seemed to be suggesting.

Since Ailsa's birth she had become increasingly curious about her father's half-brother. The more her sense of isolation increased, the more her thoughts turned to Alisdair, hoping desperately that in him she might discover the family she longed for.

But, despite this strong desire to meet Alisdair, she had the insistent feeling that to try and do so today would be a grave mistake. Intuition warned her to go home, back to her little daughter and forget Alisdair Geddes, at least temporarily. Understanding very well that this heightened instinct was part of her own peculiar gift, she knew better than to ignore it. Sadly she accepted that any meeting with her uncle should be postponed. She would, she decided, phone, or perhaps write, and suggest they meet.

Relieved to have made her decision she turned to leave and walked straight into a tall, thick-set, middle-aged man, a large dog cruelly restrained on a short leash beside him.

'What do you think you are doing?' he asked in the plummiest of accents.

She found herself looking into a puffy, bad-tempered face, a face which must once have been quite handsome, she thought. Dark hair with thick streaks of grey accentuated the sallowness of his skin. He towered over her.

'Nothing,' she stammered, unprepared for such hostility.

'Nothing? Sneaking round in my drive . . . nothing! What were you up to?' A steel-fingered hand fastened itself round her upper arm. The dog growled menacingly, only to be silenced by a vicious jerk on its lead.

'Please,' Shona protested. 'Don't do that.'

'Unless you tell me what you were doing I shall call the police.'

She could see he meant it. 'I came here to see someone.'

'Who?'

'Alisdair Geddes.'

'And what would *you* want to see *me* about? Are you trying to sell something?'

'You are Alisdair Geddes?' she asked, horrified.

'Of course,' he inclined his head as if he was Royalty.

'My name is Shona Dryburgh,' she blurted out, giving way to rash impulse.

'Dryburgh?' he repeated, his voice losing some of its arrogant tone. 'Are you suggesting you are some kind of relative?' Now he eyed her speculatively.

'I am your niece.'

'I don't understand,' he said flatly, releasing her.

'I am the daughter of your brother, James and his wife, Isobel.'

'Half-brother,' he corrected her tersely. 'And even if that is true, it doesn't give you the right to trespass.'

She gasped at his coldness. 'I wasn't trespassing. I simply wondered whether I should knock at your door and introduce myself.' She was already walking away from him.

'Where are you going?'

Again she stopped and answered when she should have walked out of his life.

'Home. I can see there's no point in us trying to get to

314

know one another.' Her voice had all the haughty control of his.

'Assuming you are who you say you are, what do you want from me?'

'Nothing,' she snapped. 'But you are my uncle. As far as I know you are my only relative on my father's side. I wanted to meet you. Is that so strange?'

'But why?' he persisted. 'You've never bothered before. You do want something, don't you?' His eyes travelled pointedly over her and she was uncomfortably aware of her shabby jacket and scuffed shoes.

'No! I'm sorry I came. Just forget you ever saw me. I won't be back.'

But Alisdair had suddenly seen the opportunity to turn this to his advantage. 'I apologise, my dear,' he said, a smile transforming his face. 'But you can't be too careful these days. And it was rather a shock, meeting you like this. To be honest,' he lied, 'I had forgotten I even had a half-niece. Look, come inside. Let's talk. Please.'

He turned and waited for her to join him then, yanking at the dog's lead, strode up the short drive. Rashly ignoring her instinct to get as far away from him as possible, she hurried to keep up.

From close up the house had an even more depressing look. The woodwork was long overdue for repainting and the masonry was badly eroded. Damp patches extended from the lower windows to the neglected soil beneath. He ushered her through the old-fashioned front door with its cracked glass and stained fittings and she found herself in a long, gloomy hall. It was cold, damp and musty smelling. Moving ahead of her he threw a door open and led her into what was obviously a library. One wall was lined from floor to ceiling with books, but many of the bindings were decayed and in urgent need of renovation. The shelves themselves wore a thick coat of dust and the windows were grimy, completely excluding the bright sun. The furniture was sparse and very old.

'Sit down,' he offered, hauling a dull curtain farther back in an effort to admit more light. 'Now, start again. Tell me all about yourself.'

This was more encouraging. Shona sat uncomfortably on a hard-backed chair while he stationed himself directly in front of her, watching her with close interest. She took a deep breath, kept one eye on the dog who was now glowering at her from under a huge desk and began.

'I am Shona Dryburgh. The daughter of James and Isobel Dryburgh. I am sure you must remember me as a child.'

He nodded. 'Of course. But to be honest I wouldn't have recognised you. From what I recall you don't resemble your mother. She was fair-haired.'

'Then perhaps I am like my father. Like my grandfather?' She searched for some likeness between herself and this supercilious, vaguely threatening man. Not the eyes; perhaps the mouth, the nose . . . 'I don't remember my father very clearly and I have never even seen a picture of my grandfather. Your father.'

'His portrait is behind you. Satisfy your curiosity if you like.'

She swivelled in her chair, then got to her feet and stood close to the picture. A thirty-year-old Campbell Geddes, his dark hair combed severely back from a hawklike face; his still, unnatural stance giving him the appearance of a stern, formidable man, stared out at her with eyes from which all hint of the determination, energy and personality which had distinguished him in real life had been extinguished by a talentless artist.

Shona frowned. She could find nothing to cheer her in this dead picture. The man who stared woodenly over the room had an air of Victorian grimness about him and she could readily believe that he would have found it entirely possible to leave her and her mother without any means of support.

The day was ruined. Sadly she turned back to face her uncle.

'I can assure you it's a fair likeness,' he said. 'In fact, your father bore a very close resemblance to him.'

'Do you have any pictures of my father?'

'No.' He seemed to wait for her to go on.

'I understand that you and my mother didn't like one another,' she said, watching for his reaction, feeling as though she was playing some deadly game of cat and mouse.

'Yes,' he smiled at her. 'I must say I'm relieved you know about that. It might have been very awkward otherwise. But it was my brother and I who didn't get on. We had nothing in common. He was jealous of my inheritance. Upset because father preferred me to him. But, that was all a very long time ago. It can do no good to rake it all up again. Perhaps you and I will do better?' He smiled again, but she had the feeling that it was false. Certainly the smile did not reach his eyes which remained cold and, to her suspicious mind, calculating.

'I hope so,' she conceded with little conviction.

'So, tell me more,' he invited.

She hesitated, knowing already that she would never like this strange man. Despite his smile and the plausible, understandable reason for his initial hostility, she had the very strong feeling that his antipathy towards her was, if anything, stronger than her instinctive dislike of him. But perhaps she was being over sensitive. After all there was no reason for him to dislike her and it did look as if he was making an effort to be friendly.

'What do you want to know,' she asked, striving to sound enthusiastic.

'Let me see . . . What do you do for a living?'

'I work here in Edinburgh, for an advertising agency. I'm a junior accounts executive.'

'I'm impressed. Those sort of jobs pay well, don't they?'

'Not at my level and I have a small daughter to support.'

'You're not married?'

'No.'

'I see.' His eyebrows lifted in distaste. 'Do you still live in Strathannan?'

'I have a bed-sit in York Place.'

'Really? I have a friend who lives there. What number do you live at? You might know her.'

'Forty-six A. What's your friend's name?' She was relieved to have found some common ground.

'Rosemary. But it's Moray Place, not York Place. And you couldn't possibly know her. She's not your type.'

Shona flushed, wondering why the spiteful little exchange had made her feel so uncomfortable.

'Your mother was an artist,' he went on casually. 'Do you paint too?'

'No. I don't have her talent.'

'She was very good indeed. Two of her paintings are on display in the academy. Lent by the Hutchesons. They have a huge collection. Worth a fortune.'

'I've seen them,' she retorted sharply, sensing something wrong with this line of conversation. 'Do you live here?'

'Yes. Do you have any of your mother's work?'

She ignored his question. 'What about your family? Do you and your wife have any children?'

The question seemed to unsettle him. 'Not that it's any of your business but my wife and I divorced ten years ago. There were no children.'

'I'm sorry.'

'I suppose you must be quite comfortably off,' he said abruptly. 'All those paintings must be worth a great deal of money.'

'Not to my mother,' she snapped. 'She was almost destitute when she died.'

'Rubbish!' he contradicted her sharply. 'They were selling very well for a long time before she died. She even had a show in the States.'

'Oh, they sold. But not for the vast sums they fetch nowadays. She was never a wealthy woman.'

'But she must have left you something. Even just one of

her paintings is worth a great deal of money these days. And what about sketches? Or paintings she thought weren't good enough to sell?'

Suddenly it was vitally important that he never found out about those two paintings she still had hidden under her bed. 'There was nothing. Absolutely nothing.' She crossed to the door, anxious to leave.

'Just one more thing before you go,' he hissed, all pretence at friendliness gone. 'I know there were two of your mother's paintings at Netherdrum. They disappeared when my father died. And they have never been traced. Your father gave them to my father so they are legally part of his estate and should have come to me. I believe your mother took them. If she gave them to you I suggest you return them to me. Otherwise I shall take the necessary steps to get them back.'

She felt the blood drain from her face and certainly couldn't trust her voice to deny the accusation. Instead she held her head high and managed to convey the impression that the suggestion was beneath contempt.

With all the calm dignity of a born aristocrat she walked slowly back through the depressing house and down the short, scruffy drive without a backward glance. Something told her that at one of those big, featureless windows, Alisdair Geddes was watching her and she had no desire to catch even the briefest glimpse of him.

TWENTY-FOUR

*L*ife in a one roomed bed-sit with an active toddler was an impossibility. Apart from the practical difficulties of heaving the heavy pushchair up and down the stairs and fending off complaints from neighbours who constantly groused about the noise Ailsa made, the buiding was damp, dark and depressing. For Ailsa's sake Shona longed for a more pleasant environment where her daughter could mix with other children, make friends and have the freedom and space to run and play naturally.

Moving was out of the question. Her present salary simply would not stretch to a higher rent. Her only hope was to win the promotion she was working so hard for. The promotion which was already twelve months overdue. Shona was acutely aware of the discrimination she was subjected to simply because she was an unmarried, working mother and was angrily conscious of the fact that she had to work twice as hard, be twice as conscientious and get twice the results of her male colleagues before anyone would take her career aspirations seriously. In fact, driven by anger and determined ambition she eclipsed her male colleagues and the advancement she so richly deserved could not be long delayed.

In the meantime she made the best of the bed-sit and doggedly saved up for the many small items she knew she would need for the new flat she dreamed of. Weeks of diligent self denial bought a set of crockery, new pillows and a second-hand, black and white TV which provided company in the long winter eventings when Ailsa was asleep.

From time to time she unwrapped her mother's two

pictures. The temptation to sell them was as strong as ever but so was the feeling that to sell them would be a betrayal. The deep conviction that these paintings were some sort of talisman for her future ensured that she would never willingly part with them. And now there was the added fear that they weren't even hers to sell.

Two weeks before Christmas Shona finally got the news she had been hoping for. Her promotion had been approved. The rise up the seniority ladder brought an appreciable rise in salary with it.

She left the office that night humming happily to herself. Not only did she have her promotion but her Christmas bonus was safely in her purse. Fifty pounds would buy Ailsa enough presents to make sure she had a wonderful Christmas as well as completing the set of cutlery for the new flat she could now start to hunt for. Throwing caution to the wind Shona gleefully made her purchases on the way home.

By the time she collected Ailsa she was exhausted but happy. The child was tired, hungry and fretful. Shona carried her, and her parcels up the stairs but on the small, half landing below their room, she stopped suddenly, halted by an overpowering sense that something was wrong. Cautiously, quietly, with a feeling of impending disaster, she crept up the remaining stairs. A few steps from the top she saw that her door was already open. She shoved it warily and it swung back, revealing a scene of complete devastation. Everything that was movable had been tossed into the centre of the floor. Mattresses had been ripped from the bed and cot, every drawer was hanging open and each cupboard emptied. Shona stared, unable to move as she surveyed the ruins of her small home.

Ailsa started to howl. 'It's okay. It's okay,' Shona whispered into her hair. 'I'll soon put it right.'

Carefully she picked her way through the debris of her

hard-won possessions. Why would anyone think she could have anything worth stealing? The answer was on the mirror, crudely daubed with left-over emulsion paint.

'You were warned,' was the message. A signature would have been superfluous. Even as she read the words she knew who had done this, and what had been taken.

Dumping Ailsa unceremoniously into her high chair, setting her off into frantic screams, Shona plunged through her scattered things until she located the suitcase. It was empty, the lock torn off. Her precious, invaluable paintings were gone.

Voices and footsteps on the stairs jolted her. She flew to the door and slammed it shut as her startled neighbours arrived on the landing. No-one must know what had happened here. Certainly the police couldn't be called. What could she tell them? That her own uncle had broken in and taken pictures which were legally his? Pictures she had denied having.

Slowly, desolately she set about cleaning up, throwing out the shards of her new dinner set, the television, the paint-stained bed linen and pillows, everything she had saved so hard to buy. But she didn't allow one single tear to dampen her eyes.

Shona changed the locks on her front door and added strong bolts but still didn't feel secure. The very thought that Alisdair knew where she lived unnerved her. As soon as the holiday was over she started the search for a new home.

It wasn't easy. Most landlords wouldn't begin to consider a single girl with a toddling child. It was a month before she found anything that was even remotely suitable.

It was a flat, at Morningside, with a separate bedroom and its own bathroom and cooking facilities. The furnishings were minimal and the whole place urgently needed a fresh coat of paint. The rent was much higher than she had planned to pay.

She took it. At the top of a four-storey tenement type building it was still far from ideal for a growing child, and the neighbours complained about the constant patter of Ailsa's active footsteps, but it was a considerable improvement over the York Place bed-sit.

The continuing need to pay a childminder, the higher rent and Ailsa's constant need for new clothing strained Shona's modest budget to the very limit. More than once she faced a long trek home because she couldn't afford the bus fare.

But gradually, as she gained experience and her flair and absolute determination to succeed were rewarded by more promotions, she found she could afford to save a little. By the time Ailsa was five and ready for school Shona was actively searching for a small flat to buy.

Persuading a building society to lend to an unmarried mother was quite another thing. Her interviews with a succession of self-important managers, all male, left her seething with indignation and the indisputable knowledge that, even in 1977, a woman in her position was considered to be a bad risk. Indignation matured into cold rage. As she pointed out to the unfortunate manager of the society where she had carefully deposited her savings, she had weathered the most difficult period of her life without falling into debt. Her salary was the equivalent of a man of the same age and she was in a reasonably secure job. What more, she demanded, did they want? He was reduced to a string of stammered excuses before her display of cold, assertive anger. Less than a week later she had written confirmation of the availability of a mortgage.

Four months later she and Ailsa moved into a spacious, two-bedroomed ground floor flat in Stockbridge. It even had a small garden.

She struggled to furnish it but carpets were out of the question. Several times Shona woke in the night in a sweat of fear when she contemplated the twenty-five-year commitment she had made, knowing that every single penny of her salary was more than accounted for. Against that, the botanical gardens were opposite, Ailsa's new school was only round the corner and she had friendly, kind-hearted neighbours, one of whom willingly volunteered to take Ailsa to school with her own daughter and collect her again afterwards. The benefits more than outweighed the financial penalties.

As she watched the roses bloom in her daughter's cheeks from hours of fresh air in the park, when she heard her playing so happily with the other children, Shona knew she had done the right thing. Ailsa would have the happy, carefree childhood that she herself had been denied.

Mother and daughter settled into an unremarkable but contented routine. Only rarely did Shona permit herself to contemplate how different her life might have been. An occasional longing to escape from the city and return to the pleasant Strathannan countryside, and the strange compulsion to visit Netherdrum again, were firmly rejected as impossibilities.

The more frequent, wayward speculation about Alex was equally sternly and much more sadly denied. As were the advances from colleagues and her growing circle of friends who were attracted by the graceful, quiet dignity of the dark-haired young woman who was so protective of her private life. But Shona's experiences with men had all been painful. Too painful to risk more injury. She hid behind her rôle of devoted mother, avoiding all entanglements with the opposite sex.

In truth, the continuing struggle to raise her daughter single-handed and to meet her ever-increasing commitments consumed all her energy. Sometimes she despaired of ever having really nice clothes or decent furniture. But so long as Ailsa was healthy, happy and well cared for, nothing else mattered.

TWENTY-FIVE

*I*n Kilweem much had changed. The three boats which graced the harbour brought in little in the way of fish. Few local people earned a living from the sea. But the whole area now attracted a respectable number of tourists, and most of them found their way to Kilweem's attractive quayside.

The cluttered harbour with its decaying lobster pots, characteristic, pantiled houses with their distinctive crow-stepped gables and the quaint, cobbled wynds featured on picture postcards and an infinite number of amateur photographs. However, the area was seriously marred by a narrow-fronted house facing directly onto the quayside and contrasting horribly with its neat neighbours.

This particular house was a disgrace to the whole village. There was almost no paint left on the front door and the unprotected wood was decaying publicly. The window-frames were no better and downstairs, in a position of prominence which made it an unavoidable eyesore, a piece of stained plywood had covered a broken pane for the best part of two years. The remaining, filthy windows were partially covered by holey curtains which defied gravity by clinging to sadly sagging wires.

Maggie and William McLean were impervious to it all. Even if they had cared about the abiding impression their sorry dwelling made on all those who saw it, they would have been unable to put it right.

William was unemployed and unemployable. At fifty-four, hugely overweight, irascible, truculent and foul-mouthed, he spent most of his time planted squarely either in the bar of the Lobster or, when that mean establishment was closed, firmly fixed in front of the television with half a dozen cans of McEwans to hand.

Maggie, who had never been afflicted with pride, either in herself or in her home, generally joined him. Scraping by, as they did, as long-term patrons of the welfare state, they had very little money left for the finer things of life – certainly not new curtains or paint – by the time they had made their regular excursions to the off-licence.

Having been raised to accept this way of life as the norm, Mhari, their one remaining home-based offspring, was little better than her parents. At twenty-four she too was unemployed, or at least, her earnings were not of the type to be easily disclosed on the average tax return. But, unlike her parents, there were things she yearned for. The occasional new outfit, make-up and the odd trip to town were among them. It was no secret, nor did it appear to cause her parents any shame, that she supplemented her state benefit by resorting to what is generally known as the world's oldest profession. This accounted for her regular visits to Dundee where she would stay for a day or two and return, bone tired, but with a purse full of bank notes. One local lad who had paid the going rate for Mhari's dubious favours had returned from the clinic, acidly commenting that money was not all that Mhari brought home from Dundee. His furious confrontation with her in the public bar of the Lobster had kept the neighbourhood gossips fully fuelled for more than a week.

Even William's brother-in-law, Robbie McArdle, was reluctant to meet William on home ground, but the two frequently spent an inebriated evening together in the Lobster before Robbie made his perilous way back to the cottage on his old push bike.

It was during one of these evenings that the seeds were sown for a plot which was to cause Robbie lasting anguish.

The two men, Maggie and Mhari were at their usual table, several empty glasses already lined up in front of them. William obviously had something on his mind and persistently fingered a piece of paper in his jacket pocket. Three or four times it seemed that he was about to speak, but each time he thought better of it and drank another pint of beer instead. Eventually the liberal amounts of heavy loosened his tongue.

'Got a funny thing in the post this morning,' he announced to the bar in general.

'Oh?' Robbie wasn't really interested. In fact he wasn't interested in anything William had to say and only came here with him because the cottage got so lonely at night.

'Aye. Right queer. From a sol . . . sl . . . Solllllliisssssssitor.'

'What was it then?' Robbie asked, listening now.

'It was something about they trying to trace Shona Dryburgh. They're asking me because I'm her uncle. They want to know if I can give them her address.'

'Wonder what they want with Shona?' Robbie mused aloud.

'No idea. It doesn't matter, anyway. I don't know where the hell she is. And I don't care. Not after what she said about me.' William had repeated his tale of Shona's perfidy so often that he had come to believe in it himself, especially after a few fast pints.

'Let me see that.' Maggie, a dull gleam in her eyes, grabbed the paper from her spouse's filthy hands and read the letter through, stumbling over some of the longer words. 'Well, well,' she exploded. 'Of all the undeserving wee cows!'

'Eh? What's the matter with you?' William demanded belligerently.

'Can you not read, you stupid git?' she hissed inelegantly. 'It says, "in connection with the estate of the late Alisdair Geddes."'

'So what?' asked William, gulping down the last of his beer and looking pointedly at Robbie for a refill.

'He's dead you mean?' Robbie was quicker on the uptake.

'Aye,' she sighed. 'He's dead.'

'Shame,' said Robbie morosely. 'And him a young man and all. He couldn't have been much older than me. Funny thing, the older you get, the more dead people you know.' He collected the glasses and swayed over to the bar.

'God give me strength,' snarled Maggie, glaring at her sodden husband. 'Can you not see it yet?'

'Stop your nonsense, woman. If you've got something to say, then say it. If not, then shut yer gob,' barked her husband.

'Alisdair was Shona's uncle, right?' sighed Maggie.

'Aye,' they chorused.

'Think about it! If he's dead and some firm of solicitors wants to find Shona about his estate, then he must have left her something. Stands to reason.'

Six bloodshot eyes peered at her over the top of three pint glasses.

'My God! You could be right!' grinned Robbie, happy for someone else's good fortune.

'It's not fair,' continued Maggie. 'After all we did for her when she was a bairn. The way she treated Willy here afterwards. And does she ever come to visit? Do we get so much as a Christmas card? No, of course we don't. And now she's going to inherit something from that Alisdair. What has she ever done to deserve good luck like that? And look at us, worked all our days for nothing! It's not fair.'

The silence was broken only by slurping gulps as they finished off their beer.

'I wonder what she's getting?' ventured Mhari. 'Whatever it is she should share it with us.'

'Aye,' agreed her mother. 'Where is this lawyer?'

William examined the letter closely. 'London,' he said at last.

'Write back and tell them we don't know where she is. Serve her right if she doesn't get a thing,' Maggie said spitefully.

328

'I'm not writing any letter to no solicitor,' whined William. 'You know I'm no good at letters.'

'Well I'm not doing it. You do it, Mhari.' Maggie placed the responsibility on her semi-literate daughter.

'I'm not writing but if you give me the money I'll phone the morrow. Tell them no-one knows where she is.'

After William and Maggie had delved into their pockets and produced enough ten pences to cover the cost of the call there was just enough money left for another round.

'I want to speak to Mr Robertson. Please.' Snug in the call box, Mhari affected her poshest voice.

'Who's calling?'

'It's about the letter he wrote to Miss Dryburgh,' she offered helpfully.

There was a click and then silence, another click and a deep, male voice.

'Miss Dryburgh! We have had such difficulty tracing you.'

Something made the denial wither on Mhari's tongue. Instead she said, 'Look, I'm in a call box and I've only got one more ten pence. You'd better call me back.'

'Eh . . . yes . . . of course,' he stammered. 'Give me the number.'

She did, then replaced the receiver and waited, pocketing the rest of the coins with a satisfied smile. A couple of minutes later the phone rang. She picked it up and spoke before he could.

'Mr Robertson?'

'Yes.'

'Right. What was it you wanted, then?'

'Well, I daresay you are aware that your uncle, Alisdair Geddes, died tragically some three months ago.' He paused, waiting in vain for her to express her regret.

'Go on.'

'There is the matter of his estate.'

329

'What about it?'

'I really cannot discuss it over the phone, Miss Dryburgh. I would be much happier if you would come to my office.'

'Your office is in London. I'm not going all that way unless I ken . . . know it's going to be worth my while.'

For a second Robertson was speechless. The thick, almost unintelligible accent and aggressive manner were not at all what he had expected from the Geddes family. 'Very well,' he agreed. 'I cannot give you the details, of course, but I can assure you that it will be very much to your benefit to come to this office.'

'You what?'

He coughed. 'You stand to inherit a considerable sum.'

'Money you mean?'

'Yes.'

'Oh. Aye . . .'

'When may I expect you?' he asked. 'Would next Monday be suitable? Eleven shall we say?'

'Aye,' she chuckled. 'Eleven's fine by me.'

'Very well. You will, of course, need your birth certificate as proof of identity.'

'Oh . . . right.'

Mhari ran the short distance home. By the time she had repeated the conversation to her parents they were goggle-eyed.

'So, she is getting something,' Maggie said.

'Aye. And a fair wee bit by the sounds of it,' her husband agreed.

'He thought I was her,' Mhari said tentatively. 'You know, it would be dead easy for me to go on pretending I was her. After all, who's going to tell him any different?'

William's addled brain finally understood what his daughter was suggesting. 'But you'd have to prove you were her.'

'The birth certificate,' Mhari said, dully. 'And we haven't got that.'

'No,' Maggie chortled gleefully. 'But Twi had it. I'm sure she did.'

'Surely it'll not still be at the farm. Shona'll have taken it with her,' said Mhari pessimistically.

'Maybe not, Hen. Maybe not,' smiled Maggie.

That night they all presented themselves at Robbie's front door. When they explained, he was staggered by the effrontery of the proposal.

'You can't be serious. It'd never work.'

'Of course it would work, Uncle Robbie. But only if you've got the birth certificate.'

Robbie disappeared and returned minutes later with an old shoe box full of papers. They had to contain their impatience while he sifted slowly and methodically through them.

'Twi always kept things like that in here. If we've still got it it'll be here somewhere,' he muttered. 'Mine . . . Mary's . . . Katrina's . . . Jamie's . . . Alex's. Aye! here it is!' He held the yellowing document aloft.

Mhari reached up and snatched it from his hands.

'I still don't like this,' Robbie said. But half an hour later the other three had persuaded him that not only was it possible but entirely within their moral rights.

'If no-one claims that money it'll go to the government. It's better we have it. They'll never find Shona. She doesn't want anyone to know where she is. Nothing can go wrong,' Mhari insisted.

'Aye. We all know that. But where are we going to find the fare for Mhari to go to London?' asked William.

'Not just me, Father. I'm not doing this on my own. You lot are coming with me.'

'We can't do that!' objected William.

'Oh aye we can,' Maggie added her support, already planning how she might spend her share of the money. New shoes, maybe, and a colour TV. 'If we're all sitting in that solicitor's office calling her Shona, he'll have to believe that's who he's talking to.'

'I can't afford to go to London,' Robbie said, trying to extricate himself before it was too late.

'You leave that to me, Uncle Robbie,' Mhari said confidently. 'Just you lot make sure you're all clean and smart. We can't go to London looking like we live in a pigsty.'

Lady Luck smiled on Mhari in the form of one Royal Navy frigate and a nuclear submarine which, coincidentally, docked at Rosyth the very next day. Astutely transferring her business to Dunfermline from her more usual Dundee, she was more than adequately rewarded. In two, long, hard-working nights and equally tedious days she made enough money to take them all to London and back in some style.

Sunday found them on a south-bound train, first class of course. They spent the night in a smart hotel, a unique experience for them all, hotel staff included. On Monday morning at precisely ten minutes past eleven, they presented themselves at the offices of Robertson, Ferrars, Greene and Robertson, Solicitors.

Safely enthroned behind his leather-topped desk, Timothy Robertson rose with one hand outstretched.

'Miss Dryburgh,' he enthused. 'Please, sit down.' His eyes bulged at her ludicrously high heels, skin tight, imitation leather skirt, white fun fur and huge, very cheap, dangly earrings which compromised Mhari's very best outfit. His smile became even more rigid as he surveyed the motley collection of people trailing in behind her.

'And . . . Er . . . Perhaps you could introduce me to your . . . friends, Miss Dryburgh, while my secretary finds us some more chairs.'

'Oh aye. This is my mother . . .' she corrected herself just in time. 'My mother's brother, William McLean and his wife, Margaret. And this,' she indicated Robbie who was shuffling uncomfortably at the back of the room, 'is my Uncle Robert. My mother's brother-in-law.'

'Ah. Yes. I see.' Indeed he did see that these people were not what he had expected them to be.

The huge, shambling, red-headed man had the build of a

redundant sumo wrestler and considerably less charm while his scrawny, miserable-looking wife appeared to have been assembled from jumble sale rejects. Only the brother-in-law was anything near presentable, though even his suit was badly fitting and ten years out of date.

'I am very pleased to meet you,' Robertson said, deliberately choosing not to shake hands.

'Right. What's all this about?' William demanded, not that Robertson understood a word of the rapid Scots dialect.

'Shall I explain why I have asked you to come here?' he asked hopefully.

'Please do,' invited Mhari, acting her heart out.

'As I said, your uncle died three months ago. Unfortunately he was intestate . . .'

'Eh? . . .' gaped William.

'It means he couldn't . . . you know . . . do it, you ignorant lump,' Maggie whispered in her husband's filthy ear, then turned to Robertson. 'Can you not speak the Queen's English?' she asked.

'He left no will,' explained a scarlet Robertson. 'We have examined the family and there is no-one else with any claim on the estate. You, Miss Dryburgh, are the sole survivor. As you know, Alisdair Geddes had no living brothers or sisters. And no children. So that leaves you,' he beamed.

'What does it leave her?' Maggie asked, unable to contain her rapidly growing greed.

'In a word, everything.'

'Everything?' Mhari breathed.

'The Netherdrum Estate, a house in Edinburgh, a small London flat, a portfolio of shares, somewhat depleted. Everything that was his.'

'Bloody hell,' swore William. 'Am I hearing this right? You're telling me that . . .'

'I'm sorry, Mr McLean. You will have to speak more slowly. It is some time since I heard your charming accent. Please bear with me if I have some difficulty in understanding you.'

'I said,' roared William as if the man was congenitally deaf, 'that my lassie here's worth a wee fortune.'

'Your lassie, Mr McLean?' the solicitor frowned.

'Oh aye,' interrupted Maggie. 'We think of her as ours. She's been with us since she was a wee bairn. She's just like one of our own.'

'I see,' he said when he had finally managed to translate the words. 'But I understood that Miss Dryburgh was brought up by a Mr Hugh McLean?'

'I was,' ad-libbed Mhari. 'And with Uncle Robbie here.'

The solicitor paled and wished Alisdair Geddes had chosen some other legal practiner to be his representative. 'Could you please explain?' he suggested.

Mhari repeated the story she had known all her life. 'When Grandfather died everything went to Alisdair. Mammy got nothing. She moved away from Netherdrum into a wee house at Ainstrie.'

'Your father died just a few days before your grandfather, I believe? In a shooting accident?'

'Aye, right unexpected it was,' agreed Mhari.

'And your mother?'

'Mammy was killed in a car accident when I was five.' Well-rehearsed, Mhari repeated her tale flawlessly. 'We were right poor.'

'Poor?' repeated Robertson. 'But your mother was famous. She was an artist.'

'She wasn't famous then. Her pictures sell for a lot more now than they did when she was alive.'

'I see,' he sat back in his chair, intrigued.

'Well,' she went on. 'My mother had two brothers; Hugh who died, and Uncle William here. And a twin sister who was Uncle Robbie's wife. They all looked after me.'

'The truth is,' interrupted Maggie. 'We all loved Shona but none of us could afford to keep her all the time. We'd no spare money in they days. She spent the holidays with Robbie, weekends with us and weekdays with Hugh.'

'And Hugh is . . .?'

'Dead,' repeated William impatiently.

Behind him Robbie fidgeted uncomfortably.

'I see,' said the lawyer again. 'It is a very unusual way to raise a child.' And certainly accounted for the rather common young woman with her bleached hair and layered make-up who faced him. She wouldn't, he thought idly, be out of place soliciting on a street corner.

'It was the best we could do for her,' said Maggie defensively.

'I'm sure it was,' Robertson soothed.

'And I was dead happy,' said Mhari, just in case there was any doubt.

'And now?' asked Robertson.

'I'm still dead happy,' said Mhari, frowning.

'Where do you live now, Miss Dryburgh?' Robertson could feel an ominous dull thud building behind his eyes.

'Oh . . . I still stay in Kilweem with Auntie Maggie and Uncle Willy,' she almost suppressed a giggle.

'Well, that's all very clear,' Robertson assured them, anxious only to get rid of them. 'So, if you have the birth certificate?'

She handed it over.

'That seems to be in order. Of course, I will need the sworn statement of two people who have known you, to confirm you are who you claim to be. It's just a formality.'

She gawped, silenced by this unexpected stumbling block.

'What about Robbie and me?' asked Maggie. 'We're not blood relatives and nobody knows her better than we do.'

'Well . . .' He seemed to consider it.

'Now see here you!' bellowed William, leaning over the desk and engulfing Robertson in his hung-over, morning breath. 'We're not coming all the way down here again. It's too much money. It would be easier for you to sort it all out now.'

Robertson covered his nose with a hand. 'Yes,' he agreed

desperately. 'Perhaps that would be best. Come back at two and I will have the necessary forms ready for you to sign.'

It was almost too easy. Several months later a jubilant Mhari received the proceeds from the sale of Alisdair's London flat, to add to the money raised from the sale of his shares and the liquidation of some small business assets. It was more money than she had ever seen. Even after it had been divided among the four of them, she had much more than she could ever expect to earn in years of weekend visits to Dundee.

William and Maggie set about disposing of their share with uninhibited glee. Having small imaginations their ambition stretched no further than their own limited horizons. But they did embark on a gloriously abandoned rehabilitation of their run-down house.

Determined to show her critical neighbours a thing or two about who could afford what in Kilweem, Maggie insisted on installing expensive leaded windows, with a front door to match. Under the ground floor windows, neat window boxes might have lent the place a picturesque feel, if anyone had actually taken the trouble to plant them with flowers. As it was they acted as convenient litter bins, a repository for cigarette packets and old beer cans, mostly dumped there by William himself. Fortunately this minor eyesore was generally hidden from view by William's spanking new Ford Capri which was more or less permanently parked outside.

Then, of course, there were the many intemperate evenings at the Lobster where William discovered that his standing had hit an all time high with the landlord.

Mhari splashed out on a new wardrobe and some sophisticated hi-fi equipment which she never discovered how to operate. Then she took herself and a friend off to Benidorm where they enjoyed a sort of buswoman's holiday, easily recouping the cost of the package tour. When she came home she, too, bought herself a new car.

Robbie watched this unrestrained spending with horror, devoutly wishing that he had never allowed himself to become involved in the first place. The way the other three were carrying on would make anyone suspicious, but it was far too late to back out now.

By the time the solicitor raised the question of inheritance tax, the cash was almost gone and between them, Mhari, William and Maggie were considering selling off some of their remaining illegal assets. They embarked on a greedy inspection of the two other properties.

Strachan was first on their list. They were intensely disappointed. All three had expected something much grander than the large but rather ordinary family house in an inconvenient outpost of Edinburgh. Since Alisdair's death the house had been boarded up, giving an unpleasant impression of neglect. The modest gardens had been allowed to ramble into ruin and Strachan House looked nothing more than the unattractive liability it had become. Their collective eyes did light up, however, at the sight of a cupboardful of silver and crystal and the few paintings on the walls and in the attic which might be worth something. Without much discussion they decided that the depressing house itself should be sold. Netherdrum was a different matter. Although the grounds were overgrown to the point where a JCB would be needed to clear a path through at some places, the old house itself was sound. The furniture had been protected by dust sheets and was still in excellent condition. Even their untutored and largely unappreciative minds could comprehend the value of some of the pieces. Maggie wandered from room to room with an expression of awe on her face. Living in a place like this, refurnished of course with some modern stuff from one of the high street stores, she would really be someone.

The caretaker, an ancient woman with the appearance and manner of a bad-tempered stork, positively radiated disapproval. She led them back into the gleaming entrance hall and waited, her hands folded primly in front of her, watching them, for all the world, thought Mhari, as if she didn't trust them. She glanced up and caught the old woman's eyes on her yet again. A scowl crossed her features, but then she thought better of it and substituted the haughty expression she felt was more fitted to her assumed station in life.

'You don't remember me then?' Mrs McLachlan asked, squinting at Mhari.

'Should I?'

'I was housekeeper here in old Mr Geddes's day. I remember your mother very clearly.'

'I was just a wee bairn then. I don't recall a thing about the place.' Mhari hoped this would bring an end to that uncomfortable line of conversation.

'You've never been back here since?'

'*No!*' screamed Mhari, flushing an angry red. Surely this old hag worked for her now? Well, she would see about that.

'That's strange,' Mrs McLachlan persisted. 'I was sure you had been here, looking for the place where your mother used to paint.'

Mhari grunted and turned away, but Mrs McLachlan's old eyes followed her with peculiar intensity.

'We can't live at Netherdrum. It's too close to home. Someone would be bound to find out. What would we do then?' Mhari dismissed her mother's suggestion out of hand.

'Nobody would think anything of it. We've already told everyone that we've had a big win on the pools,' insisted Maggie, still seeing herself as lady of the manor. 'It's natural that we'd use our money to buy a bigger house.'

'Not that big!' Mhari was nervous. To live in a house like Netherdrum was beyond her wildest dreams. 'What if Shona comes back?'

'She'll not come back. If she was going to she'd have come before this. She's likely married with half a dozen wains by now. Anyways, she'll be too ashamed to show her face around here again. And no-one knows where she is. Even that solicitor couldn't find her. No, we're safe enough now.' Maggie was superbly confident.

'Netherdrum is too big.' Mhari was still cautious.

'It's only a big farmhouse, really. And what's the point of us living in this hovel when Netherdrum is lying empty?' Her mother was persistent.

'Let's think about it later, after Strachan House is sold and we know how much we get for it.' And she went back to puzzling over the arrangements to transfer Strachan's contents to Netherdrum.

TWENTY-SIX

Alexander McArdle was a fiercely independent young man with an absorbing and vastly satisfying career. The most intelligent of Twi and Robbie's brood, he had slogged his way through his veterinary degree with incredible determination, supplementing his meagre grant with a variety of part-time jobs and existing below the poverty line for a gruelling six years. He emerged qualified and triumphant, with a failed marriage behind him, resolutely ignoring his mother's pleas for him to return to the family home.

His time at university had given him a taste for freedom. Having once escaped the claustrophobic demands of his family he had no intention of being trapped again. Within a month of graduating he had a junior post with a veterinary practice in Peebles. Four years later, by dint of some extremely hard work and considerable skill, he bought himself into the partnership.

Consequently, Alex rarely returned to Strathannan more than once or twice a year, usually to keep his father company over New Year. But, last New Year he had been on call at the practice, so it had been several months since his last visit home. Usually glad to see his eldest son, of whom he was very proud, Robbie's welcome this time was a strange mixture of enthusiasm and resentment.

'So, you've decided to pay your old man a call then, have you? I thought you'd forgotten where I live.' He saw the irritation flash across his son's face and regretted the hard words instantly. Trying to make amends he grinned and said, 'I'm glad to see you, son. Come away into the sitting

340

room and have a drink.' He steered Alex into the house and settled him in one of the comfortable old chairs. 'What will you have?' he asked, throwing open the doors to the wall cupboard.

'What have you got?' Alex asked carelessly, expecting the usual half dozen cans of export and a bottle of Bells, and still fighting the guilt his father's first words had stirred in him. He knew he should come here more often than he did.

'Everything,' declared Robbie. 'Bells, 'fiddich, vodka, rum, gin . . .'

'Gin?' laughed Alex. 'You hate gin.' At last he turned round and was visibly shaken by the massed bottles. 'Are you planning a party? You've enough bottles in there to set yourself up in competition with the Lobster.'

'Aye . . . well,' muttered Robbie. 'What else have I got to spend my money on since your mother died? And I like to keep something in, in case the family drop by.'

Some of that family dropped by that very night, in the form of William and Maggie, who sensed Robbie's remorse at his own involvement in their crime and took great care to keep a warning eye on him. Their unheralded arrival tonight was especially unwelcome.

For Alex their appearance unearthed some emotional memories of Shona. He couldn't bring himself to even look at William. With nothing more than a hostile look in Maggie's direction he settled himself down in the most remote chair and prepared to sit the evening out in silence, rejecting his instinct to retire to the nearest pub, because he knew that would upset his father.

The conversation between Robbie and his self-invited guests was stilted and strained at first but, helped along by copious amounts of alcohol, it soon became rambling and disjointed. Alex watched his father, aunt and uncle deteriorate into varying stages of inebriation and heartily wished he was back in his cosy Peebles flat. His head started to nod.

He was saved from fast sleep by the arrival of Mhari, come to drive her parents home. With her bleached blonde hair, indecently tight skirt and a jumper which was more suggestive than blatant nudity, she was everything he remembered her to be.

'You're looking well,' he lied unenthusiastically, yawning and preparing to close his eyes again.

Mhari wasn't having that. She perched on the arm of his chair, one thigh resting on his right arm. 'Thanks,' she beamed at him. 'I like to buy good clothes. None of that cheap catalogue stuff for me.'

He watched, amazed by her dexterity as she extracted a cigarette from her packet and lit it with an expensive lighter. If his nails were that long he would undoubtedly inflict a horrible injury on himself. Aware that she expected him to talk to her while she waited for her parents to finish their drinks he went on. 'You look as if you're doing very nicely for yourself.' Mhari's precise occupation had always been something of a mystery.

'Oh aye,' she agreed. 'Very nicely. I've just bought myself a brand new Escort. It's braw.'

'They're nice cars,' he said, suppressing a yawn. 'Where are you working now then?'

'Working?' She looked at him as if he should be certified. 'Nowhere.'

'Oh! I just assumed . . .'

Almost too late she saw her error. 'Oh, I see what you mean,' she laughed. 'Mother, Father,' she demanded their sodden attention. 'I was just telling Alex here about my new car,' she said in the tones a teacher might use to a class of retarded five-year-olds.

'Oh aye,' slurred William.

'And,' she went on. 'I'm not sure if you've told him about our wee bit of good luck. I'm sure he's wondering how come I've got a new car and youse've had the house all done up when none of us is working.'

Mental dawning sent its visible light over William's mottled features.

'Oh aye. Aye,' he said on a loud belch.

Maggie, too far gone inside her vodka bottle to care, merely grinned.

'Do you mind if I tell him about our pools win?' she asked, resisting the urge to wink at Robbie who was squirming with discomfort.

'No, Hen. You tell him,' William beamed, proud to have such a clever daughter.

Grinning from ear to ear she turned back to Alex who, wide awake now, had watched the pantomime in complete bemusement.

'They don't like everyone to know,' she confided.

'You won the pools?' he asked incredulously.

'Aye,' she confirmed. 'A real big win it was, too. And we gave your daddy something, to help him along.'

'I see . . .' So that explained the well-stocked cupboard.

Behind them Robbie stared at his feet and then shuffled out to the toilet to hide his guilty face.

Quickly bored with his visit home, especially since Robbie was still working on the farm from seven in the morning until past seven at night, and with far too much energy to spend his day quietly at the cottage, Alex took advantge of the good weather to revisit some of his childhood haunts.

The day before he was due to return to Peebles found him in St Andrews. On the way back he avoided the new roads and meandered along the familiar country lanes.

About five miles from home he came upon the imposing pillars of Netherdrum. Even from the road it was obvious that the estate was in a sorry condition. On impulse he drew his car into the verge and went to have a closer look.

Alex could vaguely recall the house from when he had visited there with his mother. The details escaped him now, but he could still remember playing in the rambling grounds. The gardens had been well kept in those days and an adventurous challenge for an energetic seven-year-old.

Nostalgia tempted him to investigate further. He slipped through a gap where a pedestrian gate had long ago deserted its post and ambled towards the house. It appeared to be in surprisingly good shape. The downstairs windows still had curtains at them and the pale, sunlit stone looked warm and inviting, despite the chaos of the surrounding grounds. He walked on, meaning to go down to the farm which he remembered quite clearly, sure now that Netherdrum House itself was deserted. But suddenly the solid wooden door opened and an elderly lady came swiftly towards him.

'If it's Miss Dryburgh you're wanting, she's not moving in until next month.' Despite her age she gave the distinct impression of great vitality.

He turned his most disarming smile on her. 'I'm afraid I'm just being nosy,' he admitted candidly. 'I assumed the place was empty.'

'It is private property.'

'I know. I apologise.' He still smiled, the crooked front tooth giving an otherwise-too-handsome face an impish, boyish look.

Mrs McLachlan fell obligingly under his spell. 'There's not a lot to see these days. The place is like a jungle. Such a shame.' It was conversational.

'The house itself looks alright,' he said, warming to her.

'Och, it's fine. Solid. Well built.' There was a touch of pride in her voice now.

'Do you live here?' he asked, wondering if she was some elderly relative of Campbell Geddes's.

'Oh no,' she chuckled. 'But I used to be the housekeeper here. I'm too old for that now but I still walk up every day to make sure everything's alright. I have done for years.'

Then he recalled her first words. 'What did you mean about Miss Dryburgh? About her not being here yet?'

'Miss Dryburgh is selling her other house in Edinburgh, and moving here. But not until next moth.'

'What happened to Alisdair Geddes?' Alisdair's name had

been notorious when he was a child. They all knew that Alisdair had been responsible for forcing Isobel and Shona out of their home.

'He died. Over a year ago now. That young lassie inherited. She was here just the other day. Funny thing,' she mused. 'I didn't recognise her and I've usually such a good memory for faces.'

'What do you mean?' Alex asked, assuming this Miss Dryburgh was Alisdair's daughter.

'Well, she was here once before. Trying to find the farm cottage where she had lived as a baby. She was such a nice young thing. Not at all like she is now with the bleached hair and make-up. I'd never have recognised her. Never in a thousand years.'

'Who are you talking about?' Alex demanded sharply.

'That lassie,' she snapped, irritated both by her failing memory and his manner. 'Oh be damned!' she exclaimed in exasperation. 'I can't recall her name . . . James's lassie. What was she called . . .?'

'Shona,' Alex supplied.

'Shona! That's it,' the lined face lit up. 'But how did you know that? And why are you asking all these questions, young man?'

'Shona Dryburgh is my cousin.'

'Oh my.' Her dismay was obvious. 'And after what I've just said about her.'

'That's alright. I'm as puzzled as you are. The girl you described doesn't sound like the Shona I know. But I haven't seen her for a long time. I had no idea she had inherited this place.'

'Why don't you come back next month?' she suggested. 'Your cousin will be here after the tenth. And I had better be on my way. I've to organise some of the village women to come in and give the place a thorough cleaning.' She started off down the drive.

'Thanks for talking to me. Can I give you a lift to the village?'

'Oh no,' she laughed. 'I need the exercise. It's what keeps me going.'

'Okay,' he chuckled back at her, liking her immensely. 'By the way, my name is Alex McArdle. I used to visit my aunt Isobel here when I was a child.'

'I hope you don't expect me to remember your name, young man. But I rarely forget a face. If you're ever in the village come and see me. Number two. Right on the main street. I asked your cousin to come, but she never did.' She shook her head and laughed suddenly. 'Where are my manners? I am Eleanor McLachlan.' With that she waved her hand briefly and continued on her spritely way.

'You mean Shona's never been back to see you?' Alex asked Robbie later that night. 'That's funny. I'd have thought she'd have wanted to tell you about Netherdrum.'

Robbie grunted. He was conscientiously glued to the television and didn't seem at all interested. Alex sighed. There were times when he thought he would never understand people. What a good thing he had decided to become a vet and not a doctor.

His visit to Netherdrum and a certain curiosity about the apparent change in his cousin pulled her to the forefront of his mind for the first time in five years. He sensed a puzzle here and puzzles were made to be solved. He would have to drive through Edinburgh on his way back to Peebles. He would, he decided, see if she still worked at the same place and, if so, ask her to have lunch with him.

To his delight the telephonist at Ross Innes put him straight through to her office.

'Alex?' She made no attempt to hide her pleasure.

'I hope you don't mind me calling, Shona, but I am going to be in Edinburgh today and I suddenly realised that it has been too long since we last met.' It was a lie, but he could hardly tell her the truth.

346

She laughed, a lovely bubbly sound that made his heart beat faster. 'It has been ages, hasn't it. How are you, Alex?'

'Fine. Just fine,' he said. 'Are you free for lunch? Maybe we could have something to eat together?'

'Oh Alex . . . I've got a lunch appointment with a client. I can't possibly cancel.'

'Oh.' His voice was flat with disappointment. He was amazed at how quickly he had responded, just to the sound of her voice. 'Tonight then?' he persisted, doggedly.

'I thought you were only here for the day. Won't Louisa be expecting you tonight?'

On the other end of the line there was a long, deep silence. The silence, she thought, of guilt.

'Thanks all the same, Alex, but I don't think so.'

'Is that what you thought?' he exploded at last. 'Last time we met, is that why you wouldn't have anything to do with me?'

'What . . .?'

'Louisa. Is she why you wouldn't get involved with me?'

'Well . . . yes. I don't have affairs with married men, Alex.'

'Louisa and I separated about a year before Mum died. She's remarried now. Lives in Kent. I never see her, or the baby . . .' She heard the note of regret in his voice. 'I thought you knew.'

'Oh no,' she whispered softly. 'I'm sorry, Alex.'

'So,' he repeated. 'Will you have dinner with me tonight?'

'I think I'd better. Then at least I can apologise to your face.'

They ate in a small restaurant off Frederick Street. Encouraged by him she told him all the small details of her life. She spoke about herself, but her attention was all for him. The devastating magic was still there. She had known it the minute she saw him again. The impish smile, untamed hair, strong body and intense eyes all seemed comfortingly familiar but enticingly exciting.

He listened, increasingly intrigued because she didn't mention Netherdrum. He certainly couldn't raise the subject himself. After all, it would hardly be tactful to admit that he had deliberately sought her out after hearing about her inheritance. If she knew that he would never be able to convince her that it was her he was interested in and not the money. And it was her he was interested in. He had known that from the first second. The wonderful, creamy skin, the soft, dark hair and the luminous grey eyes had captivated his heart all over again. He admired her independent spirit, her fierce pride in her daughter. He longed to touch her, taste her. But this time he would go very slowly. He wasn't going to risk losing her again. Already he recognised that he wanted to share his life with her.

Later he took her home. Inevitably she asked him in for coffee. The modest proportions of her flat surprised him, as did the clean but old and worn furniture. On this evidence no–one would guess that she was a substantial heiress. And she still hadn't mentioned it.

'I still can't believe that I was stupid enough to assume you knew I was divorced,' he admitted, sitting on the lumpy sofa with one arm tentatively round her shoulders.

Already she was breathing fast, fear and longing so hopelessly mixed inside her that she didn't know whether to ask him to leave or simply melt. When he kissed her the doubt in her mind dissolved like candyfloss. His tongue was strange, exciting, yet familiar as it probed her mouth. His hands at her breasts were gentle, caressing, adoring, demanding as they teased her nipples to hard points of arousal. She was lost in him, burning where he touched her, clinging to him, needing him. But, when his hands strayed to the top of her thighs she stiffened, then panicked and rolled away. Horrified she sat up, then turned away in shame.

'I'm sorry, Alex . . . I didn't mean to do that. I . . . It's just . . .' But she couldn't tell him that she had never had a relationship with a man, that her only real experience had been one which still made her feel sick to think about. 'I need time,' she pleaded. 'This is all moving too fast for me.'

His arms slipped round her again, easing her back to him, soothing her. 'It's all right,' he reassured her. 'We've got all the time in the world. There's no need to rush into anything. I'm just too impatient. I can't help it. I want you so much.'

The blind panic receded as he kissed her again.

'I can wait,' he whispered. 'Until you are ready. I won't ever try to force you into something you don't want. It has to be right for both of us.'

How she loved him! But how could this have happened so quickly? Or perhaps she had always felt like this about him. 'I've never been with anyone,' she admitted, almost ashamed of this lack of experience. 'Only that one time . . . you know.' The memory made her go hot, then cold.

He was appalled by his own lack of sensitivity. 'God! You must think I'm as bad as him.'

'No, Alex. How could you ever be like him? I'll be alright. It's not your fault. Just be patient with me.'

'It's okay.' Again he kissed her, then simply held her to him, content to have her in his arms.

'I have to be in the surgery tomorrow,' he said later. 'I really should be getting on my way.'

She nodded silently, hating to let him go.

'I'll have some free time at the weekend. I'll give you a ring when I know which day I have free. Maybe we could have dinner again?'

'Yes please,' she said softly.

'You could come down to Peebles if you like. It's lovely down there and it's not a long drive.'

'I haven't got a car,' she laughed at the idea. 'I can't afford one. I don't have a lot of money to spare.' It was a plain statement of fact, not a plea for sympathy.

'Well, with any luck that situation won't last forever,' he

said, referring to the inheritance which had been pushed out of his mind for at least two hours.

'I think it might,' she answered sombrely. 'I heard last week that Ross Innes have been taken over by a London firm. It looks as if I might lose my job unless I'm prepared to move south. I can't afford to do that, even if I did want to take Ailsa to live in London – which I don't.'

'You'll find another job,' he said, perplexed, then added another hint. 'Surely money won't be a problem for you?'

She frowned, uncertain of what he meant. 'I've got a mortgage on this place and even on my salary, I'm struggling. As far as another job's concerned, there are very few advertising agencies in Edinburgh, and none of them are looking for staff. You know how bad the unemployment is round here. And I'm not even qualified for anything. I didn't take a degree. I can't type. All I can hope for is a job as a clerk or something.' She shrugged dismissively unwilling to burden him with her worries so soon in their relationship, but he saw the shadow of worry which clouded her magnificent grey eyes.

'I'm sorry. I didn't realise. It must be hard raising a child on your own.'

'Only financially. Sometimes I wish I could have spent more time with her when she was little. But don't go feeling sorry for us. We manage just fine.' Her head was up and there was a familiar, defiant set to her mouth.

He chuckled. 'No, somehow you don't inspire pity, Shona. I get the impression you could cope with just about anything.' It was meant as a compliment and she accepted it as such.

When she went to bed that night her last thoughts, before she drifted into happy, relaxed sleep, were of Alex.

Alex's drive home included a deliberate detour into Fairmilehead, past Strachan House. He saw enough to realise that it was even more run down than Netherdrum House. A notice by the gates announced the forthcoming auction sale with the name and address of the solicitors handling the transaction.

The rest of the drive back to Peebles gave Alex the opportunity to think things through again. What a strange day it had turned out to be! More successful than he dared to hope but leaving him more intrigued and mystified than ever. Unless Shona was an extremely cool and incredibly accomplished actress – and a talented liar – it was obvious that she had no idea of what she was supposed to have inherited. But there was still the possibility that Mrs McLachlan had been mistaken and it was some other relative of Alisdair Geddes's who had been to Netherdrum. The more Alex thought about it, the more likely this explanation seemed. After all, Eleanor McLachlan was an old lady and it was entirely possible that she had confused the names. She had told him herself that Netherdrum's new mistress had blonde hair. Shona's luxurious, almost black hair could never be mistaken for blonde. It certainly looked as though the old lady was confused. It was a great pity, though, because Shona was clearly in need of some financial help. He smiled to himself. If things progressed the way he hoped they would, then he would be able to offer her that help himself.

But, as Alex slipped off to sleep that night he was aware of a deep niggle of uncertainty. The insistent feeling of something not quite right.

That niggle of doubt dogged him all week. Never a man to turn away from a challenge, by the time he went back to Edinburgh the next weekend, Alex was itching to solve the mystery of this mysterious Shona Dryburgh.

'Have you heard about Alisdair Geddes,' he asked conversationally as he sat in Shona's little flat on Saturday afternoon.

'What about him?' she snapped.

Something stopped him from blurting out the truth. 'Good God, Shona, it sounds as if you hate the man.'

She flushed, then laughed at herself, 'Oh, you might as well know. I went to see him. When Ailsa was a baby. I had some crazy idea . . . You know . . . a tender reunion with a long-lost relative. All that sort of rubbish.' She shuddered expressively. 'I found him alright. But he was horrible. Arrogant and cold. Threatening, really. He made it perfectly clear that he thought I was only there to see what I could get out of him. But that wasn't it at all. I simply wanted to meet him.'

'That was years ago.'

'I know. But I wouldn't want to meet him again.'

'So you haven't heard?'

'Heard what?' she asked, alerted by his restless manner.

'Alisdair Geddes died. About two years ago now I think. A car accident.'

She frowned, paled slightly then said. 'I didn't know. Poor man. I didn't like him but I never wished him any harm.'

'Did he have any children, or any brothers or sisters?' Alex probed, sitting forward keenly.

'No. He was divorced and there were no children. He told me that himself. My father was his only brother.'

'What about your grandfather, old Mr Geddes. Did he have any brothers or sisters?'

'Not that I know of. But I'm not really sure. I never knew much about him. Why?'

'I was wondering who inherited from Alisdair. They would get Netherdrum wouldn't they?'

'I suppose so. Unless he sold it off. I went there once, just before I left Strathannan. It was empty then so it could very well have been sold.'

'But you don't know who could have inherited from Alisdair?'

'I expect there's a cousin somewhere.' She frowned at him suspecting a deeper motive than idle curiosity. 'Why all the interest, Alex? It doesn't affect me anymore.'

'Are you sure? For all you know, *you* might be the next heir.' He said it with deceptive levity.

'Alex . . .!' she laughed. 'Don't be ridiculous. Now, where shall we go?' To Alex's absolute amazement she dismissed the whole idea and seemed to forget it on the spot.

'The zoo. The zoo,' pleaded Ailsa, taking hold of Alex's hand and demanding her fair share of his attention. It was already clear that she had taken a great liking to him.

'Okay,' he chuckled down at her. 'You win. It's as good a place as any. If you can stand the smell.' He grimaced, pulling a ridiculous face and the little girl giggled helplessly.

Instead of returning to Peebles that night Alex made a phone call to the practice and arranged for a few days leave. Then he booked into a modest hotel in Edinburgh, intent on getting to the bottom of this mystery, with or without Shona's co-operation.

In the morning he made some enquiries of his own, aiming to build up a range of evidence which she would be unable to ignore. It was the work of minutes to discover from the Edinburgh lawyers handling the sale of Strachan House, that it was being done on the instruction of the present owner – Miss Shona Dryburgh.

'Is that the Shona Dryburgh who owns Netherdrum House?' he asked the young receptionist, exerting all his considerable charm.

'Yes,' came the dimpling reply.

'Alisdair Geddes's niece?'

But she either couldn't or wouldn't give him that information.

Now Alex was faced with a real dilemma. Not for one minute did he doubt that Shona herself had known nothing of Alisdair's death before he had told her about it yesterday. Even then she had dismissed the possibility that she could have inherited anything as ridiculous. But what should he do now? If he told her what he knew he might be raising her hopes for nothing. On the other hand she was entitled to know. He even suspected that she might resent the fact that he hadn't been completely honest with her from the beginning, and she would certainly be hurt if she realised that he had wondered if she was deliberately concealing her inheritance from him. Never one to shy away from a problem, it didn't take him long to make up his mind.

When Shona came home from work that night she found him waiting outside her front door. Instead of her usual, cheery grin, all he got was a very half-hearted smile. Even Ailsa found a very subdued welcome.

'What's wrong, Mummy?' she asked, keenly attuned to her mother's moods.

'Nothing, Darling. I'm just in a bad temper because I had a rotten day at work.' She hugged her daughter. 'Go and play with your friends. They're all waiting for you.'

'Will you be alright?' Ailsa asked with adult concern.

'Of course I will. And Alex is here to cheer me up.'

Ailsa beamed. 'I wish Alex was here all the time,' she said before running off to join her playmates.

'I'll second that,' Alex murmured, tipping Shona's chin up and claiming a long, sweet kiss.

She sighed and raised her face for a repeat. 'I'm glad you're here, Alex. You are exactly what I need.'

'Hard day?' he asked, wondering whether to break his news now or wait until she was rested.

'You could say that. Any day when you get the sack is a little hard to take.'

'Oh no. So soon?'

'I've got three months. I suppose I should be grateful for that much.'

'I've brought some wine. Let's open it and talk.'

'Okay.' She smiled and produced glasses. 'That's the best suggestion I've heard all day.' She raised her glass wryly. 'Here's to full employment.'

'Here's to solving a mystery,' he countered.

'Ah . . . All right, Alex. I know you're up to something. What are you doing here tonight? I thought you were supposed to be back at work?'

'Something more important came up,' he said cryptically, drawing her close to him. 'First, before I tell you what this is all about, please, don't worry about your job. I love you, Shona. I think I always have. I'll take care of you and Ailsa, whatever happens.' He put his finger to her lips and silenced her gently. 'But, I'm not going to ask you to marry me yet. There is something we have to sort out first. After all, I don't want you to think I'm a fortune hunter.'

'What are you talking about, Alex? Has this got something to do with all those questions about Alisdair? You can't seriously think I might have inherited something?' Despite the bad news she had found herself mulling over Alex's words all day.

'I am absolutely serious.'

'I don't know what to say,' she admitted, fifteen minutes later. 'I simply cannot believe that I could inherit anything through Alisdair. There must be a cousin of the same name.'

'Possible. But highly unlikely.'

'But who on earth would pretend to be me? Surely they don't just let anyone walk in and claim to be someone else.'

'I don't know. But the question is, what do you do now?'

'*We* have got to find out who this other Shona Dryburgh is.' Infected by his intensity she had accepted this as a challenge, a challenge they would share.

'Yes,' Alex agreed enthusiastically. 'And we can't waste time. Strachan is up for sale and unless we do something fast it will be too late to stop it.' He was pacing the room, impatient to do something positive.

'I think,' she said thoughtfully, 'that we should speak to Mrs McLachlan again. Just in case she made a mistake with the name. Could we stay with your father for a couple of days? I know he doesn't think much of me but I've always had a soft spot for him. He was kind to me when I was a kid. I'd really like to see him again.'

'He'll be pleased to bits. I think he's very lonely without Mum. And anyway, I want to tell him about us.'

But Robbie was anything but pleased. Under different circumstances his shock might have been comical. His eyes grew round and actually looked in danger of popping out, his mouth sagged open and he flushed to the roots of his thinning hair.

Alex rushed Shona and Ailsa to their room and rushed back to have words with his father. But Robbie looked so upset that Alex swallowed the angry comment which was already on his lips and said, 'Shona's very upset, Dad. She's fond of you, you know.'

'Aye. Well. Maybe it's seeing her again, and that bairn. You know she tried to say it was William's.' Guilt-stricken, Robbie resorted to the most obvious reason for his nervousness.

'I know what William said! And I also know the truth. And so do you.' Alex faced his father passionately. 'Shona was never a liar. And you know what William's capable of, Dad.'

Privately Robbie knew his brother-in-law to be capable of anything. 'Aye,' he conceded unhappily. 'I've often wondered what really happened.'

'That's all I wanted to hear,' Alex assured him. 'Now, just give Shona a chance, please Dad. For me. I love her very, very much.'

'I think we should tell you why we're really here, Dad,' Alex said to his father after dinner.

'Yes, Uncle Robbie. Maybe you can help,' added Shona, unaware of the panic rising in Robbie's chest. Sweat beaded on his forehead as he listened to them and he started to tremble.

'No,' he yelled when they had finished. 'Youse two are living in a dream world. Folk like us don't get to inherit places like that.'

356

'They do if their grandfather owned it,' Alex insisted.

'You're being stupid. Both of you. Away back to Edinburgh and forget about it. You're just wasting your time and I don't want to hear no more about it.' He stumbled to his feet. 'I'm away for a drink.'

'I'm sure she said number two,' Alex drove a reluctant Shona along the main street of Brighead and finally stopped outside a compact house with a highly polished door knocker and freshly scrubbed doorstep.

After Robbie's unexpected outburst, Shona had reverted to the view that this was too improbable to be true. Alex nagged, raged and pleaded with her, accusing her of being defeatist, weak and finally, of allowing William to beat her. Stung by that last comment, Shona had stormed to his car and waited furiously for him to drive her to Brighead where Mrs McLachlan, she was sure, would finally put an end to all this.

Shona knocked and from within the house came the cheerful call, 'I'm coming. I'm coming.'

For a moment Eleanor McLachlan stared at them in puzzlement, but then she beamed and took Alex's hand. 'This is a wonderful surprise. Come along in, both of you, and the wee lassie, too.'

They followed her into a quaintly old-fashioned sitting room that felt immediately comfortable. 'Sit yourselves down and I'll get the kettle on.'

They did as they were told but Alex's disappointment was written all over his handsome face. He had hoped that Mrs McLachlan would recognise Shona immediately, but so far she had hardly even looked at her.

'I told you she wouldn't know me,' Shona whispered. He glared at her.

'I warned you I wasn't very good at recalling names, young man, but I never forget a face so I'm glad you've called. I get so few visitors these days. In fact I hardly see a soul since they told me not to go back to Netherdrum.' She sniffed. 'It seems I'm no longer wanted up there.'

As she handed Shona her cup she stopped, peered at her face for a moment, then gasped. 'Well, and I was only thinking about you the other day. Aye, I thought I was right. I didn't think anyone could change that much.'

'You do remember me then, Mrs McLachlan?' Shona couldn't miss Alex's victorious grin, nor could she resist smiling back at him.

'Of course I do. I recall you telling me you'd been looking at the farm cottage where your mother and father lived.'

'Yes! We sat on a rickety old bench and talked until I had to go and catch my bus.'

'I remember asking you to visit me,' the old lady admonished.

'That's right,' agreed Shona. 'But I've never been back to Strathannan, until now.'

'This is not the lady you spoke to me about; the lady who is moving into Netherdrum?'

'Oh no! That was a girl with blonde hair. Lots of it. All frizzed out as if it hadn't seen a brush through it for weeks. And fingernails two inches long.'

'Are you quite certain that she was calling herself Shona Dryburgh?' Alex prodded.

'Quite certain. She is James Dryburgh's daughter. I remember her telling me that. But she doesn't look at all like him. Or her mother. Isobel was such a dainty little thing. Not at all like this Shona.' She looked at her guests sharply, waited a moment, and when neither of them seemed inclined to say anything more she snapped. 'Well? Are you going to tell me what's going on? I may be old but I am not senile yet.'

'No,' grinned Alex. 'I never for one moment thought you were.' He told her as much as he could. The old lady listened attentively, then turned to Shona.

'And what are you going to do now?'

'I'm going to find out just exactly who this other Shona Dryburgh is,' was the determined reply.

'Well, good luck and just remember, if you need my help I'll do all I can,' she offered. 'I can't say I was very taken with the other Miss Dryburgh. Or her mother and father. Ill-mannered and coarse the whole lot of them, and there is no excuse for bad manners.'

'What were they like?' Alex asked. 'Could you describe them.'

Her answer, accurately supplied from her excellent memory and made easier by the marked characteristics of the three people involved, reduced Alex to speechlessness. Over Mrs McLachlan's head his eyes met Shona's in mutual horror.

'Well!' he exclaimed as soon as they were back in his car. 'That certainly explains a lot. But what the hell do we do now?'

Shona sighed and rubbed a hand over her aching head, and when she spoke her voice had shock in it. 'Alex, I'm sorry for the way I behaved earlier. But it all seemed so far-fetched. It still does.'

'Even now?' he demanded, making no move towards her, determined to push her forwards. 'Are you still going to sit back and let William and Maggie win? Let them help themselves to what you know is yours? Is that what you want? Are you going to be a victim all your life?' It was deliberately cruel and he hated himself for saying it.

The effect was electrifying. She rounded on him, anger blazing from her eyes, her whole body quivering with fury. 'Of course not,' she yelled. 'I am going to see a solicitor as soon as we get back.' There was steel in her voice now. 'I will never allow William to deprive Ailsa of what should, one day, be hers.'

'Good!' Now he smiled and leaned over to kiss her. She jerked her head away angrily.

'Don't! Not after the things you said.'

'Shona, I'm sorry. I know I hurt you. Deliberately. But

359

you were ready to walk away from it. I couldn't let you do that. I had to make you fight back. Don't you see,' he pleaded.

'I've been fighting all my life.' It was a rare display of self-pity. 'If it had been anyone but William . . .'

'I know. Of course I understand that.' This time she didn't resist when he pulled her into his arms. 'But it's different now, Shona. You're not on your own. You've got me to help you. If you want me to.'

'You know I do,' she whispered. As his mouth found hers, he tasted the warm salt of her tears. Silently he held her until she had stopped crying. Then, very gently he dried her eyes.

'Thanks,' she said, her voice soft and hoarse.

'Let's go home and get this sorted out once and for all.'

'Yes,' she agreed, eagerly now. 'But it's too late to do anything today. Maybe we should go back to the farm and tell your father what's going on. We can go back to Edinburgh and see a solicitor first thing in the morning.'

'Alright,' he nodded and started the car. A terrifying thought had struck him and Robbie's nervous manner was making more sense by the minute. He prayed his father wasn't involved in this but he certainly wanted to make sure before they took things any further. 'So long as we get to the bottom of this, one way or the other.'

It was the other, and much sooner than either of them expected. When they arrived back at the farm Robbie was nowhere to be found. They put Ailsa to bed and waited all evening in growing impatience. At last, at eleven o'clock, a car drew up and three figures tumbled out. Robbie, still sober and William and Maggie, both extremely drunk, filed into the sitting room bringing an ugly, threatening atmosphere with them. William strode directly across the room to face Shona, his whole manner one of barely suppressed violence.

360

'What the hell are you doing here?' he snarled. 'Back to cause more trouble are you?'

Shona faced him squarely, absolute contempt clear in her pale face. She didn't bother to answer him.

'We met at the Lobster,' explained Robbie who had, in fact, dashed panic-stricken to Kilweem.

'We want none of your stories,' whined Maggie. 'You nearly ruined my Willy's good name the last time you came here.'

'Let's not start all that again,' pleaded Robbie, who could sense a fight developing. 'It's not important now,' he added significantly.

'Wee bitch!' spat William.

Alex growled and inserted himself between Shona and his uncle, hatred blazing from his eyes. William raised a feeling of such deep loathing in him that it was physical, making his stomach ache and his pulse race.

'William never had a good name, so how could it be ruined by anyone?' he asked, refusing to be cowed.

William was too drunk to back down now. 'You shouldn't let her into your house, Robbie. The wee cow said I raped her. No man can be expected to forgive that.'

'You did rape me,' Shona accused coldly.

'That's a bloody lie!' William shot forward, his wife loudly at his side.

'She's nothing more than a cheap little whore,' she screeched.

Shona was chillingly controlled. She ignored her aunt. 'You raped me, William McLean. Just like you raped your own daughter. When Janice got pregnant you packed her off to a home. What a pity for you that I wasn't so easily disposed of.'

William bellowed his fury, grabbed a glass, smashed the lip of it and lunged at her in a paroxysm of rage. It took the combined efforts of Robbie and Alex to restrain him. Robbie's face was white with shock. Maggie collapsed into ugly, drunken tears.

William thrashed and heaved violently. It was all they could do to hold him. 'I warned you never to speak about it,' he yelled at Shona. 'I'll deny it. You'll never prove it.'

Shona never took her eyes off his bloated, puffy face. Her own expression mirrored all the hate and revulsion she felt for him but her voice was perfectly controlled. 'I don't want to prove it. I have no desire to live through that again. Nor do I ever want my daughter to discover what an animal her father is.'

He relaxed visibly. Alex and Robbie felt the heavy body sway slightly as the tension fell from it. A loose grin contorted the fleshy mouth. 'Aye, well,' he slobbered. 'Youse two just away back to Edinburgh and we'll forget about all this.'

Robbie looked from Alex to Shona, his face a mask of regret. 'I'm sorry, lass,' he said. 'I should never have doubted you.'

Shona didn't hear him. Her concentration on William was absolute. 'Oh no,' she said with such authority that they all looked at her. 'You can't get rid of me that simply. I mean to see you go to prison.'

The slack, drunken grin faded.

'I can prove that Mhari is impersonating me and that you and Maggie are helping her to do it.'

William became terrifyingly still. Even his breathing seemed to have stopped. His eyes narrowed and with an animalistic roar building from his throat into a furious, deafening climax he surged forward. Alex and Robbie were brushed aside as if they were insects. With astounding agility for such an immense man he turned and kneed Robbie in the groin. Then, even before he had hit the floor, doubled over in pain, William landed a huge punch on the point of Alex's jaw. Alex merely looked surprised, spat out a tooth and collapsed silently at his father's side.

'Now I'm going to fix you, you wee bitch,' William growled.

Cornered at the back of the room, Shona realised she was

trapped. The façade of cool anger slipped as her eyes travelled desperately over the inert form of Alex and to Robbie, still writhing in agony, and back to the hulking brute who was closing on her.

As if in slow motion she saw him take another tumbler, smash the top off against a chair and hold the splintered, jagged edge out towards her.

She stared as if mesmerised, then screamed. At the last possible moment she dodged to the side. The glass, and William's right hand, sped past her face. His unbalanced body swayed for an instant before crashing into hers, taking her to the ground beneath it.

Winded, he struggled to recover his drunken senses. Then he was straddling her, breathing fetid fumes over her, leering as he brought the broken glass to within inches of her face.

Shona hardly breathed. His weight was crushing her. She felt sick. Her head spun. Very slowly, with malicious, cruel deliberation, he moved the glass back until the sharded edge was a full foot from her eyes. Even more slowly he brought it back towards her.

'I'll make you so's no man will ever want to look at your ugly face again,' he snarled.

She closed her eyes, waiting for the pain. The jagged glass was so close she could feel it brushing her skin. She held her breath.

But instead of coming straight at her cheek, the glass slid to the side, grazing her jaw. William slewed sideways. Shona opened her eyes to see Maggie, Robbie's heavy poker in her hands, standing over her, her face a frozen portrait of horror.

Already blood was pooling on the side of William's face. Still immobilised by his weight, Shona shuddered and tried to haul herself clear. An ashen-faced Robbie slipped his hands under her armpits and dragged her to her feet.

'Are you alright?' he asked in a shaky voice.

'Better than you are I think,' she answered in a barely audible whisper.

By now Alex was scrambling into a sitting position. His horrified eyes searched for Shona and cleared in relief when she gave him a brave smile of reassurance.

'Your face!' he got unsteadily to his feet and touched gentle fingers to her cheek. They came away smeared with blood.

'It's only a scratch,' Robbie said.

The clatter of the falling poker redirected their attention. Maggie fell to her knees beside the silent, unmoving bulk of her husband. Her hand probed the bloodied mass of his skull, then she recoiled and screamed.

Alex rushed to his uncle's side. When Shona tried to follow she found herself restrained by Robbie who already suspected the worst.

In vain Alex searched for a pulse then, overcoming natural revulsion, turned William over and attempted mouth to mouth resuscitation. To the other three, watching help-lessly, the minutes seemed like hours.

After ten minutes Robbie knelt at his son's side and gently pulled him away.

'That's enough, son. It's too late. He's dead.'

Alex straightened slowly. 'I think we had better call the police,' he said.

TWENTY-SEVEN

The complicated, tangled mess of manslaughter and fraud took more than a year to resolve and there was no way to prevent the whole, sorry story from coming out in court. Fortunately for Shona, who was heavily pregnant at the time, the trial was held in camera. The more unpleasant details, so ruthlessly exposed in court, were at least never available for public consumption.

In the end and much to Shona's relief, Robbie, who was ill with shame and remorse, was released on probation. Having been quite unable to spend a single penny of his illegal windfall he had returned it all. The court accepted that he had merely found himself enmeshed in a chain of events and had lacked the courage to back out before it was too late. He was branded a weak and foolish man, but that was all.

Maggie, too, was treated with surprising leniency when it was learned exactly what she had suffered at William's violent hands over the years. Hers was a suspended sentence. She returned to Kilweem a chastened woman. Her real punishment was the contempt of the whole village.

Mhari was not so lucky. Her unrepentant and belligerent attitude in court, where she consistently denied her involvement, earned her a prison sentence. In the end it was Her Majesty's Inspectors of Taxes – who had finally noticed a glaring discrepancy in their records of one Shona Dryburgh, living and working and paying tax through the PAYE system in Edinburgh, who also appeared to be living in Strathannan after inheriting a vast sum from a dead uncle –

who finally provided the evidence which convicted her. They were helped by an inspiring Eleanor McLachlan and an embarrassed Timothy Robertson, at whose incompetent feet the blame was finally laid.

For Shona the whole thing was a nightmare. If it hadn't been for the unconditional support of her husband she doubted she would have come through with her sanity intact.

Now it was over, all she wanted to do was settle down with her family, Alex, Ailsa and baby James, and live a normal, happy life.

But fate hadn't finished with her yet.

Far from finding the peace she craved, she experienced a return of the dreadful, increasing restlessness which had preceded Hugh's death. Mercifully, this time there was no accompanying sense of doom, but the feeling of something unfinished, of something urgently trying to push its way into her consciousness was inescapable.

Increasingly her nights were disturbed by strange, violent dreams, of which she could remember nothing on waking. Night after night she woke pale and sweating, knowing that her dream had revealed something of the utmost importance, but totally unable to recall what it was.

Seriously worried Alex called the doctor, but the sleeping pills he prescribed merely made her sense of frustration deeper and did nothing to relieve the dreams.

Only gradually, over a period of eight weeks, did she begin to recall disjointed fragments on waking. Each night brought another piece of the jigsaw until, instead of dreading the night, she began to yearn for it and the completion of the picture.

Repeatedly she saw the same small, ageing woman. A woman she didn't recognise, whose face was thin and blank, frighteningly blank.

Night after night Shona saw this woman, standing by a barred window, staring unblinkingly out, the face never losing the dull, vacant look. Then came the night when the woman turned and shuffled aimlessly to a chair, only to sit limply, the same empty expression taking all character from her face.

A few nights later Shona woke to remember her moving from her chair to take her place with others at a table, all with the same unnervingly vacuous look, and chew her way through a meal. Finally she saw the woman sliding into bed, in what looked like a small hospital ward, and fall into a deep sleep, as easy and untroubled as a child's.

Night after night this scene was repeated. Shona waited for more but it was as if there was nothing else. Repetition made her as familiar with the woman's features as she was with her own. But who was she and why was she intruding on Shona's life in this way?

Shona had been visited by this strange dream for so long that it had become strangely comforting. When it suddenly stopped she woke in the morning with a cold, empty feeling in the pit of her stomach and a sense of dread in her heart. She knew there must be a message in the dream but feared she had missed it.

Alex was inclined to dismiss it as a peculiar reaction to the stressful events of the past year. Unwilling to make a fuss, Shona agreed, but still, deep in her mind, she knew that in some way the dreams had been important. The dream never returned, but a day seldom passed when she didn't think about it.

Her days were full. Now that she was Alisdair's acknowledged heir there were many things to be attended to. Netherdrum itself was the most pressing. Both the house and the grounds had deteriorated alarmingly and the house itself needed some subtle modernisation to make it comfortable. The only way they could afford the renovation work was to proceed with the sale of Strachan House which Mhari had so nearly achieved.

Preparing for this sale, deciding what should be kept and what should be disposed of, was a massive undertaking. Alisdair had not been a methodical man. Private papers were merely shoved into boxes then stored in Strachan's dirty attic. Betting slips, unopened bank statements, solicitor's letters and insurance policies were all jumbled together in a confusion of crumpled paper.

Defeated by the enormity of sifting through them, Shona simply concentrated on clearing out the bulk of old and broken furniture, transferring the papers to three huge suitcases and leaving them in the Netherdrum attics, meaning to go through them as soon as she had time.

A totally unexpected letter from a firm of solicitors who had acted for Alisdair sent her to hunt desperately through them.

Sitting on the dusty floor of the Netherdrum attic, she and Alex prepared to search out the documents they needed. Reaching into her pocket Shona withdrew the letter which had sent them there and read it through for the hundredth time.

'We are,' it read, 'writing to you as the legal heir and only living relative of Mr Alisdair Geddes, who was our client. Mr Geddes had responsibility for the medical and residential accounts for a Miss Margaret Smith, a patient at the Stanley Hope Sanatorium in New Jersey, Conneticut, USA. Until now Miss Smith's accounts have been met through a trust fund set up by our client, but this is almost exhausted. Further monies must be paid into the fund in order to meet Miss Smith's expenses for the coming year. Please contact us urgently with your instructions.'

Shona had never heard of Miss Smith, but that, Alex pointed out reasonably, was only to be expected. He thought she was probably an ex-girlfriend. Whoever she was, Shona was driven to find out more about her.

The solicitors proved a disappointment. They, it seemed, were not directly involved but were acting in response to a letter from yet another legal firm, based in New York, with whom Alisdair had dealt directly on the matter. Shona was more and more intrigued. And if this poor woman was in a sanatorium she was obviously ill and in need of help. After her own experiences of hardship she was not inclined to abandon the woman to state charity without first discovering a lot more about her. She even played with the idea of going to America to see for herself. But first she wanted to see if there was anything in Alisdair's private papers which might explain the puzzle.

After hours of fruitless search through thousands of unrelated papers, Alex finally whistled and said, 'I've got it.'

'What?' Shona dropped the wad of bills she was wading through and leapt to his side.

'In my opinion,' Alex quoted from the letter he was holding, 'the patient known as Miss Smith is unlikely to recover significantly. She is unable to care for herself and the probability of her leading an independent life is remote. My advice to you is to make arrangements for her long-term care. Signed Maurice Hinkleman. MD.'

'So the poor woman *is* ill,' Shona said thoughtfully. 'I don't see how we can do anything other than meet her costs. After all, it's not her fault that Alisdair died,' she sighed, obviously uncertain.

'You don't even know who she is! And those bills might be crippling,' Alex warned her. 'Look, why don't you go over there and find out some more about her before you make a commitment.' Alex was far from ungenerous by nature but common sense made him cautious in this case.

'Yes . . . I suppose that would be the most sensible thing to do. But only if you come with me.'

'As if I'd let you out of my sight for more than a day,' he laughed, pulling her towards him. Miss Smith and Alisdair were forgotten in the joy and energy of the next hour.

'So you see, Miss Smith has been with us for twenty years now.' Maurice Hinkleman, Junior Chairman and chief medical officer of the Stanley Hope Sanatorium peered at Alex over the top of horn-rimmed glasses.

'But you don't know how she came to be here?' persisted Shona.

'Twenty years is a long time, Mrs McArdle. There is no-one on the staff who was here then. Sadly my father, who arranged for her admission, died five years ago. As I have already said, the record indicates that she was involved in some sort of road accident. After a long period of hospital-isation she came to us to be cared for until . . .' He left the rest unsaid. 'She is, of course, perfectly well, but a little vague. She has no memory of the accident or of anything that went before it. Her mental age is that of a ten-year-old child. But she is quite content with us.'

'Does no-one visit her? Has she no relations, or friends?' Shona asked, moved almost to tears by this sad woman's plight.

'No. Sadly there are no living relatives. No-one has ever visited her.'

'Not even Mr Geddes?' Alex asked, astounded.

'No-one, Mr McArdle. Miss Smith appears to be quite alone in this world and, unless you feel able to undertake to meet her expenses, then I am afraid I will have to find her alternative accommodation. It is something she would find very traumatic.'

'That seems a very hard attitude after twenty years, Dr Hinkleman,' Shona said quietly.

'It is a commercial necessity, Mrs McArdle. We are not a charitable foundation.'

'No, and neither am I,' she retorted.

'Well,' interrupted Alex, sharing his wife's dislike of this officious litle man. 'Perhaps we could meet Miss Smith before we make a decision, but you must understand that she is no relation to my wife or, as far as we know, to Alisdair Geddes. Before your solicitor contacted us we had no idea of her existence.'

They followed the doctor through wide, sunny but anti-septically white corridors, ending at a stout metal door with strong locks at top and bottom. When he stepped aside to usher them through they felt as if they were in a prison ward. Patients, both male and female, sat or stood, some in groups, others alone. There was a pervasive smell of disinfectant and a background noise of soft music.

Shona hovered uncertainly just inside the door. The skin all over her body prickled, her heart was hammering and, again, she had the intense feeling of something critical about to happen.

She glanced at Alex who smiled reassuringly and squeezed her hand in support. Still grasping his warm, strong hand she looked more closely at the inmates. Some were playing cards, looking quite normal and relaxed. One middle-aged woman sat knitting in a chair by a barred window. When she saw Shona looking at her she smiled briefly, then turned away. Shona smiled back and allowed her gaze to travel on. But, before she had focused on anything else she gave an audible gasp and swivelled back towards the knitting woman. Her eyes settled not on the patient but on the window behind her. It was the same as or at least very similar to, the one which had featured so strongly in the repetitive dream. With the certain sense of premonition came a feeling of sudden faintness. The blood had drained from her face, beaded with cold sweat.

'Are you alright?' Alex whispered urgently, trying to steer her towards an empty chair.

She nodded her head, impatient with her own weakness. 'Yes,' she hissed back at him, sounding more bad-tempered than she had wanted to.

Understanding more of what she felt than she realised, Alex caught hold of her hand and held it firmly before hurrying to catch up with Hinkleman.

'Miss Smith is in the reading room,' the doctor was saying, seemingly unaware of Shona's extreme nervousness. He led them on, past a man of about thirty who lay curled on the floor in a foetal position, sucking his thumb.

Past a head-high partition, Shona was drawn immediately to the window. In front of it, as she had known she would be, stood the woman. Even before she turned in response to Hinkleman's snapped command, Shona knew her face. But nothing, not even the dream, could have prepared her for the shock of recognition.

The last time she had seen this woman Shona had been four years old. She carried no physical image in her mind to make this instant recognition credible, only half-remembered snatches, dismembered moments from her past. But there was absolutely no doubt in her mind that this sad creature was her mother.

For the first time in her life Shona fell to the floor in a sudden, dead faint.

The woman looked down at the collapsed figure with absolute disinterest, then turned back to the window.

'I must know how she came to be in that sanatorium.' Shona confronted the lawyer who had acted for Alisdair Geddes. 'All these years . . . on her own . . . in a place like that . . .' her voice cracked and trailed away.

Alex, his hand grasping hers, went on. 'All these years we have believed that my aunt was dead. Killed in a road accident. My God, Alisdair Geddes even came here to identify the body. How on earth could this have happened?' There was barely controlled anger in his voice. Even now he could hardly believe the enormity of it.

The lawyer nodded, his face professionally inscrutable. 'Indeed a body was found. Less than a week after the accident. Mr Geddes, as you know, came from Britain to identify the body as that of Isobel Dryburgh – his sister-in-law. Of course, after so long in the river, identification was not easy, or pleasant. It is quite possible that he was genuinely mistaken. From what you say he was not very well acquainted with your mother, Mrs McArdle?'

'Even if that is true, as soon as he saw my mother, your Miss Smith, he must have realised he'd identified the wrong body,' challenged Shona. 'I don't undertstand . . . Why

372

would he go on pretending that my mother was dead? Why pay to keep her locked up all these years?'

'As Mr Geddes himself is now dead, we may never know,' said the lawyer. 'But, from what you tell me, and this is pure speculation of course, it seems he thought he had good reason to do so. After all, your mother had made it clear she intended to challenge his father's will in the courts. Had she done so, and been successful, he would have lost a great deal.'

'But who was the woman who died. The woman who Alisdair Geddes identified as Isobel Dryburgh?' asked Alex.

'The real Miss Smith,' replied the lawyer without hesitation. 'A woman without a family, a drug addict with a history of suicide attempts. We will never know the precise truth but it is certain that your mother's car left the road and entered the river at some speed. It was assumed she had been killed. Now it is obvious that she was thrown clear, although she suffered a massive head injury. She wandered for some time before finally collapsing and being taken to hospital. Her memory was gone, she had no idea who she was and no-one came forward to identify her. The story made the papers at about the same time as the body of the real Miss Smith was washed up in the bay, close to the site of your mother's accident. I assume, and the police assume, that Alisdair Geddes saw his chance and grabbed it. He identified Miss Smith as your mother and then made discreet arrangements for your mother's care under the dead woman's name, so removing any threat to his inheritance.' The careful mask of indifference slipped just a little. 'In all my years as a lawyer I have never come across anything quite like this.'

'But there is nothing to stop me taking my mother home?' Shona asked.

'No. As soon as the legal formalities are complete there is no reason why she should not return to Scotland. I believe the doctors even hope there may be some small improvement in her condition when she is in familiar surroundings.

Though, after so many years, you must not hope for any dramatic change.'

Shona was already on her feet, impatient to start making the arrangements.

Three weeks later, Isobel Dryburgh returned to Strathannan for the first time in more than twenty years. She had accepted the change in her life without visible reaction, allowing herself to be organised like a small child, saying nothing more than please and thank you, regarding everything and everybody with the same blank stare.

The journey from Heathrow to Turnhouse was accomplished in silence. Isobel gazed placidly through the windows while Shona agitatedly twisted her hands in her lap, wondering what the trauma of returning to Netherdrum might do to this poor woman.

With her hair newly styled and wearing the smart clothes Shona had chosen for her, Isobel was undeniably lovely. Her figure was fuller but still shapely, the complexion, unmarred by worry for the past twenty years, was amazingly clear and unlined, her carriage was straight and elegant, her blonde hair remained fine and glossy. She was still a remarkably attractive and youthful woman. With pain in her heart Shona noticed how people looked twice at her mother, with admiration in their faces. Until they saw the eyes. They were so blue and clear, and so very, very blank that it was unnerving. Too often the admiring glances turned to pity.

At last they were at Netherdrum. Watching her mother closely, Shona was heartbroken to see not the slightest flicker of recognition in the serene face as they drove past the mellow old house.

'Be patient. You have to give her time to adjust to this.' Alex, caring and gentle as ever, helped Isobel from the car and won the soft, half-smile that came for any small act of kindness.

'This is home, Mother. Come with me and I'll show you your room.' Shona linked her arm through the older woman's and led the way into the farm cottage which was their temporary home, the very cottage which had been Isobel and James's first and only home. 'Do you remember this house?' she asked.

'No.' The voice was bland, uninterested.

The room prepared for Isobel was decorated in soft peach hues and faced out over the small back garden. 'I'll leave you to rest before dinner,' Shona said, still hoping for some response, some small indication that Isobel knew where she was.

But, 'Thank you,' was all she said as she obediently arranged herself on the pretty bed and closed her eyes, immediately ready to sleep.

'Give her time,' Alex advised again as he brushed a stray tear from Shona's cheek. 'Don't expect too much. You may be disappointed. Enjoy having her with you. Let her know we love her. That's all we can do. Time will do the rest.'

And time was the one thing they had plenty of now.

Isobel's progress over the next eighteen months was slow but definite. Shona could hardly contain her delight as, very gradually, the blank look of incomprehension was replaced by one of warmth, clarity and, above all, interest. Alex had always maintained that the love of a family around her would give Isobel her best chance of recovery, as far as her physical injury would allow. He was convinced that the trauma of being so ill in a foreign country, of never seeing anyone she might have recognised from her past, had exacerbated her condition. And now, much to his delight, he was being proved right.

Isobel's first response was to the children. To begin with, almost as one of them, but gradually taking her rightful place as their grandmother. And Netherdrum House itself and the work being done on the gardens enthralled her. The gardens were her especial delight and were the things which cemented her road to recovery as she planned and planted, working alongside the gardeners to choose the right shrubs, trees and flowers.

Now, after two years, no-one meeting her for the first time would have been able to guess at the horror of her past. All they would see was a gracious, rather reserved and delicately beautiful, middle-aged woman of impeccable manners and sensitive nature.

Only Shona and Alex knew what a thin veneer that recovery was. Only they understood that Isobel knew only what they had told her; that she recalled nothing for herself; that her own past was still shrouded in the clinging fog of amnesia. But still Shona clung to the hope that someday, something would happen to bring their shared past within reach. And even if it didn't, at least they were together.

Alex, who had sold his share in the Peebles veterinary practice, found he had more spare time on his hands than he liked. Never one to be content to observe from the sidelines, he applied himself to overseeing the work at Netherdrum House but was soon made to understand that his well-intentioned advice and constant presence were not appreciated by the builders.

Accepting the rebuff with good-natured resignation, he then spent several days inspecting the old farm buildings and got a mechanic to thoroughly overhaul the various bits of machinery. Shona had felt the enthusiasm building in him and wasn't at all surprised when he announced his intention to rejuvenate the farm. But, for all his energy and determination, Alex wasn't foolish enough to think he could farm successfully on his own. With Robbie's guidance he hired an experienced farm manager and installed him in one of the three empty cottages on the estate. Together they applied themselves to bringing the farm into profit, Alex doing his fair share of the manual labour. He thrived on the work. His body broadened and hardened and his skin toughened while he glowed with health and vitality. Shona too found herself milking cows, mixing animal feed and cleaning the milking equipment, and loving every minute of it. Ailsa and Jamie were delighted to find their mornings heralded by the stomp and low of cattle coming into the yard to be milked.

As soon as he was satisfied that the farm was operating smoothly, Alex left his manager to run it and turned his attention, at last, to his main ambition. The builders had converted the stable block at Netherdrum into a veterinary surgery. Using the proceeds from his share of the Peebles practice, Alex equipped it to a very high standard and hired a young assistant, planning to serve the other farms in the area. In so doing he filled a desperate gap in the community and returned to the career he loved. The energetic, skilful young vet who so clearly loved animals and understood the difficulties of the farmers, and who never complained no matter how late the hour or how bad the weather, was soon both respected and popular.

Shona, who was drawn happily into the many resulting friendships, felt fulfilled in a way she had never thought possible. If anything she loved Alex even more than ever, with a love which was tinged with admiration for the wholehearted way in which he looked for and then overcame challenges, seeming to have the knack of turning everything to success. Thanks to his efforts their future was financially secure.

Her own days were so busy that she went to bed at night exhausted, longing only for the close intimacy of their bed and, later, sleep. But it was the healthy exhaustion of a full and happy life. Caring for her family, still sometimes helping at the farm and becoming increasingly involved with the surgery as well as keeping an eye on the final decoration of Netherdrum House left few spare minutes.

And now, at last, they had moved into Netherdrum, leaving the cottage to their delighted farm manager and his own expanding family. On their first full day there Shona sat on the floor of their comfortably restored sitting room, a blazing fire in the hearth, and carefully unwrapped a brown paper parcel. It revealed two pictures, their condition as good as on the day Campbell Geddes had first hung them in his study, twenty-five years before. Lovingly she placed them on the hooks Alex had fixed and stood back to look at them, silent tears filling her eyes.

They had been discovered only yesterday in the crammed attic. Shona had not seen them since the day Alisdair had stolen them from her.

'At last,' she said to Alex, 'they are back where they belong. Seeing them here I know we will be happy in this house. I always knew there was something very special about these pictures. That, in some way, they were connected to my future!'

'I can still remember your father giving them to your grandfather,' Isobel laughed softly. 'They were a sort of peace offering.' She walked over to examine the pictures more closely. 'Two of my favourites.'

Behind her there was an audible silence until Shona finally whispered, 'You remember? You really remember?'

Isobel laughed, a warm, throaty chuckle. 'Yes. I had so many paintings then. The cottage was overflowing with the darn things. You know,' she turned to her daughter and smiled, 'I really would love to paint again. It is so beautiful here . . .' And then she stopped, aware for the first time of precisely what she had said.

Shona, unable to speak for tears, fell into her mother's arms and felt them go round her as a mother's arms should.

'I really can remember,' Isobel whispered, appalled, elated, saddened and a little frightened by this gentle opening of the gates of memory.

It was many minutes before either woman had regained enough composure to draw apart and dab at their wet eyes. Even Alex stared out of the window, fighting emotions which were threatening to engulf him. They were barely in control of themselves when the door behind them opened and Robbie followed by Ailsa and Jamie, now an active toddler, joined them.

'I can hardly believe I'm going to live here and share this house with you,' stammered Robbie, catching the emotional mood.

Alex grinned affectionately at his father. 'Well, there's plenty of room,' he said lightly. 'And plenty of work to keep us both occupied. But most of all, you know we want you here with us.'

'You know fine what I mean,' retorted Robbie. 'You've been better to me than I deserve. After what I did. Taking your money.'

'But you gave it all back, Uncle Robbie,' Shona laughed, tucking one hand through his arm, the other through her mother's. 'You weren't much of a crook. Hiding it all under the bed like that and never spending a penny of it.'

'I had no need of it. What would I have spent it on? And anyway,' he added ruefully, 'I knew it was wrong, right from the start.'

'You always were a softie,' Shona teased him gently. Then, very firmly she detached herself from them and went to stand with her husband. Alex obligingly slipped an arm round her slender waist and gave her a quick hug.

'Listen to me, Uncle Robbie,' she said, facing him seriously now. 'I want you to promise us something. I don't want you to mention the court case, or the things which led up to it, ever again. Today is a new beginning. For all of us. Let's put the bad things in the past behind us and concentrate on the good things in the future. But most of all, let's enjoy being together.'

She leant forward and planted an impulsive kiss on Robbie's embarrassed cheek, but her eyes settled emotionally on her mother who had watched and listened in fascination, but had now turned to look out of the window, understanding at last what a great many things she still had to learn about those missing years.

As she stood there the voices behind her became distant and indistinct, the focus of her mind blurred, the window shimmered and wavered, as if the glass was distorted. Her head was invaded with kaleidoscopic images as every vision she had ever experienced raced fleetingly through her mind. Her own mother, Thomas, even her younger self pushing Shona's pram, then Alisdair and, finally, her beloved James. She felt herself tremble, knew she had sobbed aloud and felt Shona's reassuring hand on her shoulder. Slowly, though, the teeming images faded, leaving a gently undulating blankness, as if there was nothing else for her to see. Now there was a deep, calming feeling of absolute peace and Isobel knew that this strange gift, which had haunted her throughout her life, had finally left her.

Turning away from the window she allowed Shona to draw her back to the present and into the warm, loving circle of her family and to a future which promised only happiness and contentment.